Swords
of the
Rainbow

Swords of the Rainbow

edited by Eric Garber and Jewelle Gomez

ALYSON PUBLICATIONS
LOS ANGELES

Manufactured in the United States of America.
Printed on acid-free paper.

This is a trade paperback from Alyson Publications Inc.,
P.O. Box 4371, Los Angeles, California 90078.
Distributed in the United Kingdom by Turnaround Distribution,
27 Horsell Road, London N5 1XL, England.

First edition: April 1996

5 4 3 2 1

ISBN 1-55583-266-0

CREDITS
The Tale of Small Sarg by Samuel R. Delany, from *Tales of Nevèrÿon*, copy-
right © 1979, 1988, 1993 by Samuel R. Delany. Published by Wesleyan
University Press/University Press of New England. Used by permission of
the author. The tale's opening epigraph is from *Reading the Cantos: A Study
of Meaning in Ezra Pound* by Noel Stock (Minerva Press, 1966), p. 34.

Library of Congress Cataloging-in-Publication Data

Swords of the Rainbow / edited by Eric Garber and Jewelle Gomez. —
    1st ed.
      p. cm.
    ISBN 1-55583-266-0 (alk. paper)
    1. Fantastic fiction, American. 2. Science fiction, American. 3. Gays'
    writings, American. 4. Lesbians—fiction. 5. Gay men—Fiction.
    I. Garber, Eric. II. Gomez, Jewelle, 1948-   .
    PS648.F3S98   1996
    813'.087608920664—dc20   96-13429
                                                                  CIP

To Jeffrey Sunshine for his devotion to Eric and for his practical assistance. To Diane Sabin, who is my sunshine. And for Eric Garber. If we believe in magic, he'll always be with us.

Contents

The Queer Avenger
Jean Stewart

"Samantha, come here," Don called imperiously. "I need you."

"Yes, dear," Samantha growled. She was sweating, wedged beneath the bottom sixteen-inch-high shelf of a tall bookcase filled with books. One shoulder was scrunched against the wall. Her knees and neck were bent at uncomfortable angles. Every joint in her body seemed to ache from the past half-hour of useless effort. Not only was she on her tenth straight hour of work at the bookstore, the repair she was attempting to make to this empty shelf was turning out to be a total waste of time. Even with the hardened wood putty she had pasted into the screw hole yesterday, the screw still wasn't going in right. The low shelf was wobbling merrily every time she twisted her Phillips-head screwdriver.

"Please excuse Samantha's manners. She stays up most of the night painting," she heard Don explaining in a low voice. "She may be co-owner of the store with me, but like any dedicated artist she tends to be ill-tempered when she's asked to cover an extra shift." With a small sigh, Don finished, "It takes time away from her art, you see."

Who's he talking to? she thought, exasperated. *Not another rock band wanting poster art, please!*

A feminine but firm voice murmured an indecipherable reply. Don followed it up by stating, "Samantha, I must insist that you come out."

"Not now, Don," Samantha groaned. *Honestly! For a best buddy, you're pushing the limits of my patience today!*

"Yes, now!" he said in that short, sharp way that told her he thought a big profit was on the line. Then, as if recalling that he was with a potential customer, he added with elaborate courtesy, "I'd like you to meet someone."

Muttering curses, Samantha began crawling out from under the low bookshelf, her Phillips-head screwdriver clenched in her teeth. Then she noticed the shoes waiting for her by the gay fiction aisle: Don's neat Italian imports and a pair of come-fuck-me pumps attached to deliciously slim ankles. Enthralled, Samantha immediately tried to follow that appealing length of leg with her gaze. With a painful and resonant thump, her forehead banged against the bookshelf above her.

"Ugh!"

The screwdriver popped out of her mouth, rolled across the hardwood floor, and came to rest against one of those gorgeous black high heels.

And then there she was—kneeling gracefully before Samantha, retrieving the screwdriver and peering intently into Samantha's eyes. "Are you all right?"

Rich brown skin the color of cinnamon sticks. Deep brown eyes beneath high, arching eyebrows. Long black hair woven into many thin braids and pulled back from her face with a gray ribbon that matched the color of her expensive business suit. She looked young—early twenties—near Samantha's own age.

In the grip of a series of confounding emotions, Samantha could only rub the bump on her head and stare at the customer. It wasn't just that the woman was incredibly good-looking in that stylish, classic sort of way that proclaimed "career success." And it wasn't the unmistakable self-confidence in that penetratingly direct eye contact. No; it was the sense of recognition that floored Samantha.

She knew this woman. But...*I don't remember ever having met her,* she thought wonderingly. *So how can I know her?*

Extending the Phillips toward Samantha, the woman asked, "Lose something?" There was the ghost of a smile as she said it, but the question was put very seriously, and Samantha felt prodded to respond in kind.

Before she could begin to mull over what else she might have lost, Don remarked querulously, "Are you going to stay under there forever, O'Toole, like a badger in her den? Or are you going to do us the great favor of emerging?"

Solicitously, he gave the lady in the well-tailored gray business suit a hand, and she stood. Clambering out from under the shelf, Samantha could hear him murmuring, "Please forgive her—she's rather reserved." Blushing, Samantha got to her feet, then began brushing the dust bunnies off her khaki pants, her heart beating erratically. Glancing over at them, Samantha noticed that the woman was still subtly inspecting her. Disconcerted, Samantha pocketed her screwdriver and studied the floorboards.

This is unbelievable, Samantha marveled. She knew she was big and long-limbed—an androgynous dyke—but nothing to stop traffic. Even more amazing was receiving this sort of attention when she was clad in simple khakis and a starched white cotton shirt, with her short, shaggy dark hair long overdue for a trim. *And why do I keep getting this feeling that I know her?*

Waving his hand in the general direction of the paintings that were hung all along the front of the bookstore, Don announced, "Samantha, this lady is interested in your work." And he sent her a quick, narrow-eyed little glance that said, *And if you don't behave yourself and get us a sale here, I'll kill you!*

"Oh," Samantha uttered. With a small shrug, she considered the woman before her. "Um. Have...we met?" she couldn't resist asking.

Rolling his eyes quickly up to the heavens, Don looked about ready to throttle her.

"Not in this lifetime," the woman admitted. "My name is Lithben." She paused, watching Samantha. "Lithben Flannery."

Automatically, Samantha reached out to shake hands. As their palms connected, a wall of flames seemed to surround Samantha, eclipsing Lithben, Don, and the store. Stunned, Samantha blinked, and just as suddenly her actual surroundings were back in place. The bookstore hummed with the quiet murmur of Saturday-night shoppers, and Don stood by her side, glowering at her.

"The paintings, Sam," he prompted, obviously annoyed.

Nonplussed, Samantha released the woman's hand and took a step backward. *What happened?*

She cast a furtive look around, then noticed a woman entering the front door, shaking out an umbrella before she folded it closed. Outside, a typical Seattle winter night was unfolding in the form of another gusty wind-and-rainstorm. Samantha decided that the overhead lights must have flickered. *Probably just a power surge through the electric lines,* she surmised.

Turning to Don, Lithben gave a sweet smile and asked, "Would you mind leaving us alone to work things out?"

Don sent a perplexed glance from Lithben to Samantha. "Well, I usually assist Sam with the sale of her art," he began. "She sometimes has difficulty parting with things...."

"She'll manage, I'm sure," Lithben pronounced. Then she smiled expectantly at Samantha.

3

Goddess, she's beautiful, Samantha thought, feeling vaguely over-whelmed but wanting more than anything else to have a few minutes alone with this woman. "Um—okay," Samantha stammered. "Don't worry, Don. I can handle it."

Perturbed, Don murmured, "Right." Then, with a slight and very false smile, he acquiesced. "Very well. I'll be in the office if you need me." Stiffly, he turned and strode down the aisle, heading for the back of the store.

Samantha found herself alone with a woman who was openly appraising her. And she was rapidly discovering her own unexpected reaction to such a prolonged, honestly direct regard; she felt both aroused and vulnerable. Worse, she had no idea what to do. The past few years of commitment to both the store and her painting had left her with little energy or time for romance. After several torrid but emotionally jarring romances in college, she had decided that she was a loner by nature. She had little experience and no notion how to deal with a woman such as this.

Feeling more shy by the second, Samantha broke eye contact. "Which painting are you interested in?" she mumbled. Nervously, she began leading the way to the front of the store.

Following her, Lithben responded, "All of them, actually. I want them all." She burst into soft laughter when Samantha swung around in surprise. "Oh, I saw the prices, all right. And I do mean what I say," Lithben assured her. "I've been searching for paintings like these for a very long time."

They stopped about ten feet before the cashier's counter, both of them gazing upward at the acrylic paintings hanging in clear view. There was a total of eight canvases, each one measuring four feet by three. Eight separate depictions of a warrior dressed in ancient armor, her left hand raising a sword. In each painting, beside the battle-ready warrior stood a woman in robes clutching a tall wooden staff. Using an array of colors and intricate detail, Samantha had rendered the paintings in an incredibly realistic style.

In the first picture, the pair were Egyptians; in the second, Ethiopians. The succession continued across the wall: Vietnamese, Chinese, Persians, Sarmatians, Japanese, and Celts. Within each simple frame, the clothing the pair wore provided a dateline from thousands of years BCE through the first five centuries of the common era. And although the women in the paintings were all different in both facial appearance and costume, there was a common suggestion of attitude that united the exhibit. These women were tough; it was evident in their stances, their faces, and particularly in their eyes.

Samantha couldn't help but wonder if Lithben saw the herstory in this

4

progression of women. Or—like most everyone else—would Lithben assume these characters were the stuff of fantasy, the basis for some sort of action comic book?

Lithben commented quietly, "Very unusual. Where did this idea come from, Samantha?"

For a moment Samantha hesitated, afraid of being mocked. The truth behind these visions often provoked laughter from her friends, so why would a complete stranger believe her? Then she felt the woman touch her arm and turned to gaze into warm brown eyes. "I have these dreams..." she began, then faltered.

"...that seem real," Lithben finished.

Bemused, Samantha nodded. *How did she know?* All at once she felt wary about revealing any more. She turned away, her thoughts falling into a familiar refrain. *What am I doing? I can't sell the paintings, anyway. I never painted this stuff to sell it. Why did I ever let Don convince me to hang them here?*

Moving with extreme care, as if Samantha were a skittish horse ready to bolt, Lithben reached up and placed her smooth cinnamon hand against Samantha's freckled cheek. "What you see at night when you sleep...what you paint..." Lithben whispered. "They're not dreams. They're memories."

What? Is she nuts? Samantha's dark brows came down in a vee, and she pushed that distractingly tender touch from her face. "They're dreams," she retorted, not bothering to keep her voice low. "And that's all."

Overhearing Samantha, a few customers standing in line at the cashier's counter turned around. They eyed the two women curiously.

Lithben reached out, firmly took her arm, and marched Samantha away from the onlookers to the other side of the store. "When you made those paintings and hung them in a public place, you were calling me," she asserted, her voice low and husky.

She was surprisingly powerful for a slender, femme-looking woman, and Samantha found she couldn't wrest herself from the grip on her arm. Even as she tried to bend her knees and plant her worn cowboy boots, she was being swept steadily along into the corner of magazine racks where the monthly buff-boy publications were on display. A young, sturdily built college guy there took one look at Sam's wide hazel eyes and Lithben's determined jaw and sighed with envy.

"Why is it you butch women get all the luck?" he asked Samantha. "I swear, sometimes I wish I was a lesbian!" He winked at Lithben and shouldered by them, leaving them alone.

Samantha felt her face getting hot and knew she was scarlet with embarrassment. "This is ridiculous! Let me go!" she huffed, trying to tug her arm free.

"I will, I promise, but first we have to talk," Lithben insisted.

"Look—no offense meant, but I'm freaking, okay?" Samantha pleaded, trying to peel those slim fingers from around her lower biceps.

"Just hear me out," Lithben whispered. "We only have a few minutes before it starts all over again."

"Dammit!" Samantha yelled. "Let me go!" With all her might she heaved against the restraining hand just as Lithben released her.

Stumbling backward, Samantha collided with the circular rack behind her. Seconds later she was on the floor next to the rack she had knocked over, covered with an assortment of postcards. Grimly, Samantha picked one up and examined it. *Male nudes in provocative poses. Great.* She flicked the card away, mortified.

Just then the front door of the bookstore slammed open. The wind and rain of the storm outside came rushing in, piercing the quiet literary ambience with a long, ominous howl.

Startled, Samantha sat up and turned to see the bulk of a tall, broad-shouldered man filling the doorway. A huge button on the left side of his Mariners jacket read ALLIANCE FOR CHRISTIAN VALUES, and another one on the right side declared, I AM THE THIRTEENTH APOSTLE. He began quoting Paul and shouting that it was the word of Jesus—and instantly Samantha knew that this man was trouble. Delivering a passionate condemnation of everyone currently in the store, his posture rigid and his fists clenched tightly, the man strode forward. Everyone else stood stock still, staring at him.

Listening to that hysterical, madman-in-the-wilderness tone, Samantha prayed that the cashier was hitting the silent police alarm button located near the register. She was not fond of ranting, smugly superior religious types who insisted on barging into gay businesses and making a scene. And this guy was *big*.

He was at least six-foot-four, roughly 230 pounds. Dressed in a loose baseball jacket, T-shirt, and blue jeans, he seemed built like a prizefighter. Swallowing the instant lump of anxiety in her throat, she noticed that he was scrupulously searching the store as he spoke, as if he were looking for one particular person. Finally, he darted a glance Samantha's way. And then he gazed beyond Samantha, focusing sinister eyes on Lithben. With a snarl, he made for her like a hound on a scent.

Time suddenly seemed to shift into slow-motion. The whole scene became a series of stop-action camera shots—the world as Samantha sometimes saw it after she had been painting for hours and hours on end. It was a perception that seemed surreal and outlandish, and it bathed everything in an aura of great significance. She was immersed in a magnificent clarity of mind; she knew— *just knew what to do*—without any clear idea how.

Springing to her feet, she stepped into the apostle's path, physically bumping her solid dyke frame into him and effectively blocking him from reaching Lithben. For an instant, as he snatched Samantha up by the front of her oxford shirt and shouted at her in frustration, stark terror flooded her. He had hard, obsidian eyes, and he was spitting in her face as he hollered passages from Leviticus. She grimaced and turned away, and he began to punctuate his verses by shaking Samantha emphatically. Instinctively, she knew this was not just another bigot who delighted in using the Bible as a weapon. There was something in his eyes—something that seemed hideously evil.

During those few moments in his grip, all Samantha's senses sharpened. She smelled perfume, faint yet distinctive, and it tugged at her mind like some forgotten memory. Out of the corner of her eye, she watched the wide-eyed college guy at the cashier's counter go pale and then hug his buff-boy magazines close to his chest. She could hear herself breathing shallowly and fast. Then the apostle's fist drew back, and her gasps for air involuntarily deepened.

He wouldn't dare, she thought.

His fist shot forward, and Samantha heard a loud bang explode between her ears. Blind with pain, she was suddenly down on the polished hardwood floor. Confounded, she lay there for only a second or two before struggling to her feet.

Standing again, woozy and shocked and then all at once enraged, Samantha fought to clear her head. Like bolts of lighting, a freezing fire of adrenaline streaked through the core of her.

Determinedly, almost single-mindedly, the apostle had stepped around Samantha and taken hold of Lithben's wrist.

"Stop it!" Lithben ordered, her voice strained with both fear and anger.

Ignoring her, unleashing another long litany of Bible verses, the apostle began dragging Lithben toward the front door.

Impulsively Samantha threw her arms around his neck and leaped on his back. With a derisive laugh he snapped forward, tossing her over his shoulder. She landed on her shoulder and rolled. Once more, she shoved herself off of the floor and reeled to her feet.

Lithben exhorted, "Bec! Be careful!"

Bec? Samantha thought, flicking a quick assessing look at the lovely stranger. She pulled her gaze back to he apostle, rasping, "The name's Samantha." *Jeez! Nothing like forgetting my name while I'm taking lumps trying to save you.*

The apostle laughed quietly, eyeing the two women as if he was thoroughly enjoying himself. "She doesn't know you," he whispered to Lithben. "You are alone." Yanking her to him, he began pushing Samantha roughly aside, preparing to muscle his way to the door.

Without conscious thought, Samantha found her fist shooting out, connecting with his throat in a resounding thud. Mouth open, eyes astonished, he let go of Lithben and clutched at his trachea. Then, with a slight wheeze, he collapsed.

Astounded by her success, Samantha cast a befuddled gaze around the bookstore and saw half a dozen people standing about, seemingly frozen in place, watching her intently.

"I could use some help about now," she announced.

No one moved.

Swearing under her breath, she resolved she would finish this herself. She wanted to get a locked door between her and the apostle as soon as possible. As he lay on the floor, hands wound around the base of his neck and straining for air, she carefully edged over to the other side of him and took hold of his jacket. Tugging him by the collar, she pulled him across the hardwood floor, pushed the glass door open with her hip, and dragged the apostle all the way out to the curb.

Letting go of his jacket, she meant to go back inside the store. Instead she lingered there, dazed and breathing hard. All at once Lithben was taking her by the elbow, murmuring something soothing in an incomprehensible foreign language. Once more Samantha smelled that heavenly perfume and felt dizzy with springtime. As Samantha blinked slowly, completely disoriented, Lithben bent over the man, fishing hurriedly in his pants pocket. Clenching something in her hand, she straightened and turned to Samantha.

She's robbing him? Samantha thought wildly, touching tentative fingers to her incredibly sore jaw. Looking into those earnest brown eyes, she instantly knew that she was wrong.

Taking Samantha's left hand, Lithben slipped a battered gold ring onto her little finger. "This is yours," Lithben told her.

Gravely, Samantha asked, "Do you know this guy?" She squinted at Lithben, trying to hold on to lucid thought. The delayed physical impact of the punch and the throw to the floor were overwhelming her now that the adrenaline rush was receding. Though she was focusing resolutely on the task, she was having great trouble standing upright. Suddenly, all Samantha knew was that she thought Lithben was beautiful. At the same time, she suspected that—like the apostle—Lithben might be more than she appeared to be.

Bending near, Lithben whispered, "You know me, don't you, Bec?"

As Samantha blinked at her, perplexed, Lithben moved closer. Rising up on tiptoe, Lithben softly kissed the upper rim of Samantha's ear. Involuntarily Samantha swayed, but Lithben kept her hands on Samantha's arms, steadying her. With a small smile, she finished cryptically, "When the moon is full, Bec." Running her gaze over Samantha as if drinking her in, Lithben stepped away and sighed.

Samantha noticed that the rain had stopped. There was no wind, no cold. And for a Saturday night, Broadway was strangely empty. Not a person passed on the normally crowded sidewalk, not a car was traveling down the dark city street. Samantha, Lithben, and the apostle were by themselves in what was fast becoming a thick, swirling fog.

Feeling very odd, Samantha made her way to the curb edge. Her knees gave out all at once, and she sat down with a thump. Mysteriously, the fog was becoming very thick. She could no longer see the apostle, who had been lying nearby on the sidewalk. She could no longer see Lithben either. Closing her eyes, Samantha felt herself falling sideways. *I'll just rest for a while…*she thought vaguely.

Sometime later she felt rain on her face and looked up. Above the swishing sound of car tires on a wet street, above the background noise of pedestrians shouting about a "gay-bashing," a man's voice was fussing at her.

Don was cradling her in his arms, pressing a cold, damp cloth against her horribly sore jaw. "You're not some sort of Queer Avenger, you know!" he was admonishing.

Later, when the police came to take statements, no one was exactly sure what had happened. Although everyone in the store said that they saw the apostle hit Samantha, they each gave a different description of the man. To the sturdy college guy the apostle looked like his nemesis in junior high school, a mean football player who used to beat him up every day after school: short, stocky, with cold blue eyes. To Don the assailant looked like a raging, jealous ex-boyfriend who had found it essential to be married to a woman while he slept with Don on the side: tall, thin, brown-eyed, with a beaked nose. For the various gay men and lesbians who had come forward during the apostle's tirade, anxious to see what was going on, the man looked like some homophobic archvillain from their own personal pasts. In short, all the physical descriptions ended up directly contradicting one another.

As for Samantha, once she had time to think about it the apostle seemed horribly reminiscent of a particularly nasty redneck neighbor she had once had, seven years earlier, when she lived in northern Virginia.

And the other puzzling aspect of the whole event was that everyone claimed that their feet had felt rooted to the spot once the intruder had grabbed Samantha. At the time, Samantha thought it was an incredibly flimsy excuse for why they had all stood there and let her take on the nutcase by herself; but later on she began to wonder about it.

For one thing, Don—her coinvestor, closest confidant, and spiritual brother—swore that when he had followed Samantha and Lithben out of the store he had been only a moment behind them but had been surrounded by a bustling crowd of Saturday-night pedestrians. Initially, there was no sign of Samantha, Lithben, or the strange man. Shaken, Don alleged that he had dashed about, calling Sam's name, and then a minute later had seen her lying by the curb unconscious. Lithben and the man had gone.

For another thing, the little gold band was on her left pinkie, and it was stuck. No amount of soap or Vaseline would permit that strangely engraved antique to glide over the knuckle and off her finger. Don rolled his eyes every time she talked about Lithben giving it to her—especially if she mentioned that remark, "When the moon is full." He obviously thought Samantha had imagined the bit with the ring while she was passed out, though he humored her by saying that it was a lovely old heirloom and a great story.

Days later, Samantha discovered that the moon had been full that night. In the winter, in Seattle, it was often hard to tell such things. After all, the weather for weeks had consisted of rain in its infinite varieties. She hadn't seen the moon through the camouflage of cloud cover.

Pretty much left at a loss by the whole incident, Samantha went back to painting and working at the bookstore, resuming her daily life as if nothing had happened. However, she found she was constantly scrutinizing women; in the store, on the street, from the window of her apartment near Volunteer Park. She was looking for Lithben, wrestling with an oddly aching yearning. At first she tried to ignore this unlooked-for aftereffect, but that didn't hide the truth. There was no denying that she wanted Lithben. Badly. As time went on, Samantha wanted her with a depth of desire she had not known she could feel.

She began to think she was crazy.

That was when she began to paint her.

A month passed. The first portrait was done and framed, mounted on Samantha's bedroom wall, and a full-length study was nearly finished on her easel. Feeling driven to immerse herself again in brushes and paint, she left work early one night and caught the bus home.

At her stop, a few blocks from the apartment building, she hopped from the lighted bus into the darkness. A few other passengers got off with her, then began dispersing into the night.

As the bus pulled away, Samantha noted how bright her surroundings appeared. With ease, she could see trees and grass across the street in Volunteer Park; a distinct silver-blue glow illuminated the night. Surprised, she turned her face up and gazed into the blazing white of a full moon. Glorious as it was, a shiver of apprehension raced up her spine.

Seconds later she heard a shrill cry, which was abruptly cut off. Spurred to action, making a quick guess about the direction the sound had come from, she ran toward the park.

As she dashed across the street, she turned and backpedaled, hollering to another bus passenger, "Someone's in trouble! Call the cops!"

Then she swung about, charging up the grass embankment. Ahead of her a shadowy shape slipped into the trees. Arms and legs pumping, she followed, plunging into the dark gloom of the urban forest.

Crashing through the brush for what seemed like an eternity, Samantha felt the sting of a hundred small branches as they lashed across her face and neck. Ahead of her she could hear someone else breaking a similar path. Ducking her head against the assault of the undergrowth, she stumbled around a tree, digging in her jeans pocket for the canister of pepper spray she had bought a few weeks back. At least three minutes later, gasping and frantic, she thrust through the last of the brush and loped into a meadow.

Before her in the moonlight, the big man was laughing. He was gripping a small African-American girl by the arm, his hand clenched over her mouth as he watched Samantha approach.

"So you want her too, do you?" he taunted, his voice somehow familiar.

11

Whimpering, the terrified child tried to wriggle free, but he roughly snatched her back tighter against him.

"Let her go!" Samantha raged, palming her spray cylinder, trying to figure out how to get close enough to attack.

"I have won many, many times in the days since the Celts," he sneered. "You are no match for me or mortal men now, Bec."

Bec? Stunned, Samantha really looked at him for the first time.

Hard, cruel black eyes looked out at her from a prizefighter's face. The thirteenth apostle! Her hand clamped around the pepper spray, slippery with sweat, and a voice in her head remarked, *I wish I had my sword.*

Immediately Samantha thought, *What?!* Yet there was no denying the strange, almost fated sense of resilience that was stealing over her even as she wondered, *What is this "days of the Celts" stuff he's talking about? And who the heck is Bec?*

And then she saw the long blade he was drawing from a sheath on his belt. Smoothly he brought it around to touch the bulky wool fisherman's sweater that covered the little girl's chest. "She is mine—all females are mine—to do with as I wish," he hissed, "as long as there is Imbalance."

"What the hell are you talking about?" Samantha demanded impatiently. "She looks all of six years old! Let her go!"

With a lethal smile he professed, "Imbalance of power between the genders leads to a vile energy loose in the world." He rubbed himself against the child, whispering invitingly, "Will you try to stop me? You of this culture which looks the other way, which insulates itself with fat joints, ice-cold beer, evenings of television, and a Christ worship that feeds on hate?" He laughed, shaking his head. "You do not even believe in yourself, so how can you believe in me—let alone battle me?"

He momentarily dropped his cold gaze to the little girl, eyeing her hungrily as she quailed below him, helpless.

Now! Move!

Lunging forward, raising the pepper spray and mashing the release button at the same time, she managed to score a direct hit on his eyes. In reaction, his blade hand came up. With an impulsive, sure knowledge, Samantha knelt low, reached in, and grabbed the little girl's thick fisherman's sweater. The apostle was bellowing, alternately wiping his eyes and slashing wildly with that long, swordlike knife. The first three slashes passed harmlessly overhead as Samantha scooted back, tugging the child to the ground beside her. In a flash, Samantha wrapped the girl in her arms and rolled, tumbling over and over away from where the madman stumbled about, cursing "Bec," cursing the moon, cursing with words Samantha knew and yet didn't know.

And as she at last stilled herself, twenty paces from him, and gathered the child up preparing to run, she observed the fog swirling all around them. The sharp stillness of the night registered, and she warily shot a look toward where she had last seen her foe. In his place stood a tall figure in a hooded monk's robe. And though his face was in shadow, somehow the black eyes shone out at her; eyes filled with deadly rancor. "You dare interrupt my delights," he warned, his voice low and charged with power, "while I hold dominion over your world?"

Aghast, wondering, *Is that the same guy? How did he change his clothes? Why isn't he still blinded by pepper spray?* she stared at the bizarre apparition for a full minute, then flung back angrily, "Why don't you try picking on someone your own size!"

"Such as yourself, Bec?" he intoned. "Do our clashes in the moonlight begin again? It's been...so long." There was a wicked ingratiation to the way he said the words. Then he whispered, "I have missed the taste of your blood."

He took a step closer, and she scrambled to put herself between him and the child. Rising to her knees, she lifted the pepper spray once more, intending to empty the cylinder.

Approaching slowly, seeming almost to glide more than walk, he began to chuckle.

Determined, Samantha pressed the spray release. Nothing happened. Again and again, she uselessly forced her thumb down on the spray button, then looked up at him, dumbfounded, as he continued to glide closer. Meanwhile, the child behind her back was exhorting in a soft, urgent voice, "Call the sword, call the sword!"

Understanding that she meant the long knife the man had held earlier, Samantha searched beyond the monk's robe. Glittering in fading moonlight, the sword was approximately twenty feet away.

"It's your sword," the child was insisting. "Call it!"

"How?" Samantha snapped, throwing the pepper canister angrily at the robe-clad figure moving silently across the grass. "How do you call a—a—" she stopped, watching the canister pass right through the solid-looking form before her. Then the monk began slowly lifting his arms. His sleeves slipped back. Samantha became aware of exposed white bones—not fleshy human hands but skeletal fingers—reaching out for her.

13

In a voice Samantha hardly recognized as her own, she shouted, "Nemen!"

In the space of a breath, the short sword was in her left hand, her painting hand, and she was standing to face the ghostly monk.

In a choking fury, the monk halted his advance. He began to back away, shrieking, "You can't do this! The matriarchies are dead! Imbalance has set me free!"

"Order him gone," the child instructed.

"Go!" Samantha shouted. "In the name of Macha!"

And with a swirl of fog he was gone.

Samantha took a deep breath. *And who or what is Macha?*

Squinting in disbelief, she used the short sword to sweep aside the cloudy, white nothingness in front of her. The fog had become so thick, she couldn't see the border of forest she had run through to get here. She couldn't see the view of the city she knew could be had from this particular hillside in Volunteer Park. And when she swung around, expecting to see the little girl she had rescued, she found instead a slender, dark-skinned woman sitting casually on the dewy grass.

"Lithben," Samantha breathed, amazed.

"Of course," she stated, smiling at Samantha as if very pleased.

"Lithben," Samantha repeated softly, completely at a loss. Distressed, she took a few steps into the fog, trying to see. *Where the heck did that little kid get to?* she worried.

"The child is safe now, thanks to you. Do not fear," Lithben advised. "Put away your sword."

"What are you doing here, Lithben?" Samantha asked, then suddenly fixed a suspicious gaze on the sword she held. *I called a weird name and it appeared in my hand!*

Peering over at Lithben, Samantha studied the clothing she wore, the soft, free fall of her wiry raven hair. She was dressed in jeans and a thick fisherman's sweater. Except for the extreme difference in ages, Lithben seemed for a moment much like that child. Confounded, Samantha considered the possibility, then abruptly dismissed it. *Nah. Can't be.*

After a brief examination, noting that it seemed to be a real sword she carried, and very old, Samantha slipped the blade back into the worn leather scabbard she found on the grass a few feet away. With a welcoming smile, Lithben raised a hand to her. Uncertain, Samantha took it all the same, allowing Lithben to draw her down beside her.

Crossing her legs, Samantha settled herself and fell to examining Lithben. Her memory had not exaggerated the effect this woman had on her: Lithben was easily the most captivating woman Samantha had ever seen. Within seconds of seeing her again, Samantha was longing to touch her, kiss her. She desperately wanted to fall back on the grass, pulling Lithben on top of her. Instead, she twisted the ancient ring on her finger. After the bizarre events she had experienced this night, she felt very far out of her depth. All she could do was stare at the woman.

"That man wasn't real," Samantha contended quietly. "What's going on?"

In the ethereal glow of moonlight forcing its way down through the fog, she saw Lithben's lovely eyes narrow. "It has been rather confusing for you, hasn't it?" Lithben commented.

Not sure of anything anymore, Samantha leaned closer to her. "Are you real?" she demanded. Without waiting for an answer, she darted out a hand and seized Lithben by the wrist.

Instead of attempting to pull away, Lithben rose on her knees and came toward her. Placing her hands on Samantha's shoulders, she pushed and sent her down into the soft, wet grass. Slowly Lithben climbed over her and gently lowered herself. With a shallow gasp, Samantha felt hands easing through her own short dark hair. She felt their legs entwine. Unbelievably, Lithben was pressing into her, murmuring against Samantha's neck, "Is this real enough for you, Bec?"

Samantha's body answered for her, oblivious to the name invoked. Breaking into a long, deep shudder, Samantha gloried in the feel of womanly warmth stretched upon her.

"Do you like this?" Lithben whispered.

Feeling Samantha tighten and tremble, Lithben laughed softly. Those small, warm breaths of air passed over the sensitive area down on Samantha's neck, and she helplessly tensed and trembled again. Desperate to recover some control, she gripped Lithben's hips, trying to still the subtle, sensuous rhythm the woman had begun against her.

Lithben crooned, "Isn't this what you wanted?"

Goddess, yes! Samantha thought, while her stupid mouth gasped, "Wait...too fast...I don't even know you."

Lifting her head, Lithben looked deep into Samantha's eyes, regarding her almost pensively. "You still don't know me?" she asked, then looked hurt enough to cry. "You've managed to win back your ring and your sword, and you still don't know me?"

Frowning at her, Samantha struggled to make sense of what she was saying. *What is she talking about?*

Dipping lower, Lithben lightly kissed her lips, then leaned back. Feeling teased and raw with want, Samantha hesitated, then lifted her head and tried to recapture that enticing mouth. One of Lithben's hands moved into Samantha's hair; with a soft tug, Lithben checked Samantha's small pursuit.

Hovering above her, compelling Samantha to maintain eye contact, Lithben continued the strange interrogation. "You *knew* me in the bookstore, didn't you?" she coaxed. "You were so flustered—shy, as ever—but you knew me within minutes of our meeting. Am I right?"

And as Lithben watched her with those brilliant dark eyes, Samantha understood that, yes, everything Lithben said was true. And somehow, Lithben was still strangely familiar. The feel of her body, the way her hands moved so knowingly through Samantha's hair, making her dazed and eager with desire. Samantha was open, waiting, dangerously vulnerable. And all at once, from the serious way Lithben was surveying her, she knew there was more to this than she was capable of guessing. Samantha suspected that she represented some sort of major challenge to Lithben.

Why? What's at stake here besides getting seduced in the park?

And then Lithben came lower, touching her lips to Samantha's once again. The tip of her tongue slipped between Samantha's lips, and it was as if an electric spark had jumped between them. With a swift intake of breath, Samantha betrayed the jolt she felt. At once Lithben repeated the kiss and made her gasp again. And then Samantha just lost all control, along with any concept of propriety or will to go slow. Her back arched, her hands sought purchase, clasping those hips tighter to her pelvis. And Lithben fell to kissing her with a thoroughness that was devastating. Samantha was hers; her body was telling her so, rising up against Lithben, pleading for more.

Hands opened Samantha's bomber jacket, slid under her shirt, caressing ribs and the sides of breasts. And by now Samantha was being far from passive herself. Her hands were searching all over the woman above her, lingering and circling on every spot that made Lithben tense in response. Breathing as if she were in a race, Lithben was kneeling over her, kissing and stroking, her knee pressing insistently between Samantha's thighs.

Oh, Goddess! She feels so good! Samantha silently proclaimed to the universe at large.

The sensations rushing over her—intense erotic hunger, staggering emotional neediness, wondrous delight in fueling Lithben's passion—these were all familiar, recognizable, as if she had always been with this woman.

As if we've made love a million times...

And then, in the midst of this wild scene in the fog, part of Samantha's mind began to flash with fantastic images. The aroused, hot-blooded woman in her arms was Egyptian—no, Ethiopian—no, Vietnamese. Lithben was a rapidly changing face, a strong and ever-changing womanly physique clad in a variety of costumes. From Chinese to Persian. One instant a proud Sarmatian Amazon, the next a Japanese Samurai, then a red-haired, fair-complected Celt. In a burst of insight, Samantha realized that she was envisioning the robed figure from each of her paintings—the woman who stood beside the warrior, clutching a long staff. *The sorceress...*Samantha discerned, and then froze.

Reading the sudden alarm in Samantha's eyes, Lithben breathed, "It's all right, Bec. I won't hurt you."

"No," Samantha whimpered, grasping the hands that were undoing the metal buttons of her jeans. "This is crazy...."

Only slightly impeded by Samantha's efforts, Lithben sent a hand past the barrier of thin cotton underwear.

"Remember me," Lithben ordered softly.

She was fast, insistent. The fingers skimmed past Samantha's lower belly, over the tuft of hair, into thick moisture. Like a live wire, Samantha jerked; she tried to free herself with one last resistant effort to turn. Denying her any escape, Lithben fell gently on top of her, effectively pinning Samantha to the earth. Those fingers were artfully caressing Samantha's sex, conducting her relentlessly onward. Samantha stiffened, tried to rein in her voracity. Regardless, she was gasping, caught in a towering wave of liquid fire. Samantha felt herself erupting, turning inside out, bucking wantonly into Lithben's hand and the thigh behind it. With deft and certain strokes, Lithben nudged her over the edge, into the abyss. Samantha cried out, lost in rapture.

What happened next, she wasn't sure. Time seemed to alter the moment the orgasm began, and Lithben took complete and tender command of her. Somehow Samantha was sure Lithben was extending the experience, coaxing her beyond any previously experienced physical realm with whispered words in the same unknown-known language. That deliberate, ravishing hand just wouldn't stop. It felt so endless, so bone-boiling good that Samantha abandoned all defenses. She opened completely, surrendered body and mind, gave herself up to the woman steadfastly milking desire from her.

There was a voice in her ear. "Remember who you are, Bec."

A new set of images flickered through Samantha's brain. A warrior, the woman with the sword, dressed in all the costumes she had captured in her paintings. The tumult of vision slowed.

And then she was Bec, a Celt, carrying sword and shield. Lithben was the sorceress who was her lover. In their last incarnation, she and Lithben had been companion warriors, fighting side by side throughout their lives. Startled, Samantha realized she could actually see what each of them had looked like; she could feel the woman she had been then—nearly fifteen centuries ago. She was able to recall clearly holding Lithben close, talking that unusual language Lithben was speaking to her, even now.

They were here together—their ninth incarnation—on their customary mission. They incarnated to defend women and children and stand against the tyranny. But this time they had more than that to do.

In the centuries since their last adventures, strange forces had been unleashed by the ascent of patriarchal societies. The "Imbalance" that the apostle had referred to was the primary power of men and the resulting might of greed. Imbalance was evidenced now in the societal tolerance of rape, and child molestation, and the hidden, secret battering and torture endured by hundreds of thousands. Imbalance was the reckless, wanton consumption of the earth's natural resources, the casual, deliberate poisoning of the land, the water, the air all life needed to survive.

Nine incarnations. And nine was the number of wisdom. This time they were to dispense their knowledge of woman-power and the love of the Goddess. This time they were to recruit a force to enact a change. After centuries of the patriarchies, the Imbalance bordered on wrecking the planet. And so the patriarchies were about to be ended. The matriarchies would reemerge.

Sweating, limp, and defenseless, Samantha opened her eyes and groaned. With one last burst of insight, she stated, "The little girl—it was you. You can shape-shift."

Lithben hugged her. "Oh, Bec. I was waiting for you at the edge of the park. I didn't think he would look for a child."

Feeling so glad to be with her, Samantha cuddled closer, murmuring and feeling gelatinous from the lengthy pleasuring. "Goddess bless us. How could I have forgotten you, Lith? How could I have forgotten this?"

With a sigh, Lithben disclosed, "Dithorba—the one you call the apostle— he caught you last time. He took your power, your ring, your sword. Then he sacrificed you, calling you a witch and burning you in the center of our village." She stopped and gazed down at Samantha, her eyes wet with unshed tears. "You had to bury that old terror deep in order to dare the physical plane again. And in doing so, you buried me too."

Licking her dry lips, Samantha whispered, "I've come back to drive him from power?" Recalling the hooded, faceless monk floating across the grass, raising its skeletal hands, Samantha swallowed with dismay. *How can I fight something like that?*

Caressing her cheek, Lithben stated, "We fight him together, Bec." Smoothly she took Samantha's left hand and held the last finger aloft. "It's my spell on this ring that bonds me to you, so that no magic of his can harm you." With a nod of her head toward the sword a few feet away, Lithben elaborated, "It's my spell on the sword that gives you the ability to wound him on contact, even when he is in his spirit form."

"Then how did I end up being barbecued before the entire village?" Samantha asked, frowning. Agitated, she meant to sit up, but savoring the feel of Lithben's body, she ended up merely rolling Lithben onto her back. Leaning over her, very close to that supple mouth, Samantha whispered, "With all these spells, how did the apostle catch me at all?"

Brown eyes glimmering, Lithben confessed, "He used the priests against us, Bec. They came upon our little cottage, a group of twenty monks on a pilgrimage, stopping at our well and asking for water. I made the great mistake of trusting those men of God." Lithben paused a moment, then revealed, "They stoned me to death while you were working in the fields."

For just a second Samantha's mind blazed with a memory: a broken, bloodied woman's body lying twisted in the mud. With a sharp intake of breath she lurched up, scrambled to her hands and knees, ready to run. Her heart was pounding, her limbs quivering with a wild rage.

Lithben had risen with her and was speaking soothingly in her ear. "Oh, but we still exist, Bec." Swiftly she sank a hand into Samantha's hair and turned Samantha to face her. "See? We are together, just the same." She gave Samantha a swift kiss and pulled her down again. "We are going to bring in the age of womankind and put things right. And there are others—so many others—waiting to help us."

Breathless, Samantha was lying on the dewy grass, her head spinning, allowing herself to relax gradually into Lithben's comforting arms. Remembering Don's jesting remark that crazy night in front of the bookstore, she reflected, *So I am the Queer Avenger, after all.* Mystified, she watched the last of the fog blowing away. The moon sailed into clear view above them.

Her voice low, Lithben urged, "Come home with me, Samantha."

Rallying her wits, Samantha turned to her. "And where is home this time?"

Smiling, Lithben whispered, "I've prepared a small house on East Fourteenth Street."

"Really?" Samantha laughed, reacting with lightheaded relief to hearing one of her favorite areas of the city.

"Yes. Now, c'mon." Jumping up, Lithben quickly retrieved the sword in its leather scabbard. Then, returning, she impatiently tugged Samantha to her feet. "For tonight, the battle is over, and a wealth of karmic credit awaits us."

Linking arms with Samantha, Lithben set off across the grass. With a grin, Samantha mused, *Fifteen centuries later, girl meets girl.*

In the moonlight, the glances that played between them were radiant with delight.

Roses for the Prince
Mark Shepherd

R uadh threw the leather pack over his shoulder, hoping that the amount of damine he had gathered in the hills would satisfy his master, Borras. The old man had been after him to restock their dwindling herb supply for weeks now, but the recent spring downpours had made collection impossible; now, with a clear sky above him and creeks slowly returning to their banks, he was able to make some progress.

He threw back the hood on his tabard, wondering if it was too hot yet to put it back on. Sweat had already formed on his mostly hairless head, and when he ran his hand over it he felt rough fuzz, which told him it was time for another shave. For most of the day he had gathered the herbs skyclad with the tabard folded away in the pack, wearing only his laced boots to protect his feet. Then the mosquitoes had attacked, biting portions of his extremities that had, especially lately, become rather important to him. Running around the forest naked had its advantages in the summer, but not when the bugs were doing their best to make a meal of your exposed skin.

He made his way among the boulders gracing this part of the Galorinn Hills, shuddering as he passed the ancient glyphs the Old Ones had carved into the rock. Borras was a direct descendant of the Old Ones, and his recent teachings had shed some light on the meaning of the diagrams. He stood in the center of a temple fashioned by nature, regarding the symbols with a little more familiarity.

*Arrows for ground, clouds for air, flames for fire, and a running stream for water. The four elements of the universe. Ruled by the one...*he thought, as he listened carefully for what the boulders had to tell him today. Sometimes he heard the echo of a long-ago ritual, the mesmerizing chant of a festival, or simply the crackle of the fire that once burned beneath his feet, smoothing the rock over centuries until it felt like iron. Through the soles of his feet he felt the beat of a drum, and as he focused the beat became louder, stronger. He knew this pattern, the beat of a new year's celebration, when the fields had been harvested and the new mothers were ready to bear children. The ground below him recorded everything. He wondered if the boulders recorded his quiet passing, when he had occasion to pass through here—if in a thousand years a young man would stand in this very spot and know that he had just gathered a pack full of damine, the magic flower of love.

A hawk screaming overhead shook him from his thoughts, reminding him the sun was fading quickly. *I am in the Galorinn Hills, which border the mountains of Vilarus. In those mountains live the creatures of my nightmares!*

Though he had never seen any of the monsters said to inhabit the Vilarus range, he knew the stories well. Though he had never seen them, he knew they existed, for they had taken his mother and father when he was eight years old. Even now, whenever he had strayed too close to the mountains, he heard them screaming as *something* dragged them away into the darkness. Ruadh had lived with the memory for ten years now, and even though he was a man in his eighteenth summer, the loss of his parents tore at his heart now as it did then.

He followed a game trail down from the hills, and when he reached the end of it he saw motion toward the main road. Then came the sound of horses and the clatter of a wagon. Not so unusual a sound, as merchants frequented this road and often stopped at the village of Galorinn after a hard day's travel. But the fair was months away, and the king had just celebrated the birth of a son, the new heir to the throne; but the rush of travelers had come and gone.

When he reached the road, he saw that the travelers were not common merchants. Two soldiers, wearing the uniform of the Myran crown and brandishing the royal banner, came into view. The trees were thick here, but in late afternoon the sun blazed in from the horizon, ducking under the leaves and giving them a bright, humid dusk. Ruadh saw the caravan clearly, and as the carriage rolled into view, his heart skipped a beat. It was no common wagon but a true carriage, with lamps at the four corners and a well-dressed driver on top wearing the Myran livery. He had seen such ornate woodwork only on the royal carriages at the capital—vehicles that would seldom, if ever, be drawn over muddy roads like these.

Behind the carriage were four more mounted soldiers, each staring solemnly ahead. As they passed Ruadh on the road, they didn't even acknowledge him, which came as no surprise. Dressed as he was in a shabby tabard and covered with dirt and insect bites, he probably did not look presentable.

He let none of this bother him as the carriage trundled slowly past. Ruadh wanted to catch a glimpse of whoever was inside. Royalty this far from the capital was a rare sight indeed, and chances were good he would never be this close to the crown again.

Instead of a middle-aged or even elderly man looking through the passenger's window, he saw a young man his own age.

He had long black hair that fell past his shoulders; his skin was fair to the point of looking white. As their eyes met, Ruadh felt himself melting as unfamiliar feelings swept through him. Deep blue eyes bored through him, and the short, delicate nose looked like a child's. In the brief moment they gazed on each other, Ruadh stopped breathing. All he saw was the man's face, but in that instant he knew this was the most beautiful man he had ever seen.

Then the man inside *winked* at him.

Ruadh swallowed hard as he realized the gesture's significance. His confusion, tempered with excitement, turned to desire. Many different interesting scenarios played through his mind, most involving nudity, as he considered ways of gaining an audience with this representative of royalty. The caravan proceeded around a bend and slowly drifted out of sight as he stood there gripping the bag of damine with white knuckles.

This late in the day they must stop in Galorinn, at least for the night, Ruadh thought. He crossed the road and continued down the path to the keep where he and Borras lived, now with added spring in his step. *Didn't Borras have errands for me in town tomorrow?*

The keep had belonged to a count a hundred years before, and for nearly all that time it had remained empty until Borras, as a young man, had claimed it for his own. A tall, fat tower, reaching through a thick grove of oak, stood within a circle of fallen rock wall. In the years Borras had lived here, he had done only a minimum to tame the property; sections of the roof had caved in, and vines grew in abundance inside and outside the walls.

The keep was dark when he arrived, with only a moon to see by. Ruadh walked through a riot of wildflowers and weeds that had grown on the main

23

atrium floor, using his master's snores as a reference point to find his own room. He knew where to walk on the crumbling rock steps. Using the bag of damine as a pillow, he collapsed on top of the thick blanket covering his hay mattress and immediately fell asleep.

The royal stranger haunted his dreams. He woke with a start, thinking the stranger was lying on the mattress beside him. There was only a bare space, but it was warm, as if someone had lain there. He smelled a musky scent, sweat that wasn't his own. Only a tall, narrow wind hole allowed some air and light in, and he wondered if someone or something had just left through it.

His hardness strained against the blanket. Ruadh rolled over. The tip of his cock glistened in the moonlight as it bobbed over his flat stomach. With both hands he satisfied it before drifting back into a dreamless sleep, letting the seed dry where it splattered on his neck and chest.

The arrival of strangers woke him early in the morning, and in the atrium he found his master talking to two men wearing riding clothes. He saw a handshake, gestures of farewell. By the time he reached the bottom of the stairs, the men had mounted their horses and were riding off. He watched their retreating backs, noted the fancy tack. Then he remembered: they were two of the soldiers who had escorted the royal stranger's carriage.

Borras, who stood in his night robe and still looked asleep, held a parchment and small purse in one hand and covered a yawn with the other.

"What is it, master?" Ruadh asked.

"Something I thought would never happen again," he said, sounding very sad. But then, he usually did. His master had a permanent look of worry about him, as if he were constantly embracing a tragic disaster. He handed Ruadh the parchment and the small bag, which felt heavy with coin.

"These are herbs for protection," Ruadh said after a quick glance at the list. "What are we protecting against? Are we in danger?"

Borras shook his head and ambled off toward his room. He was either going back to bed or about to brew a stiff pot of kaffe. "We are safe. Those men, they are in *great* danger."

Without elaboration, Borras shuffled back up the stairs. "Your speedy acquisition of those items would be appreciated. Most of them are out of season; you will have to go in to town for them." He paused and looked down at Ruadh, regarding him with a completely unreadable expression. "Use the gold sparingly."

"Aye," Ruadh said. By the time he was mounted on Borras's brown mare, he smelled freshly brewed kaffe and thick smoke poured out of the keep's chimney.

He's heating the cauldron, Ruadh thought as he rode off. *Which he does only for the most powerful of magic.*

During the ride in to town, his thoughts turned again to his dreams. The brief glimpse of the stranger's face repeated in his mind, each time with a different expression, each a gesture of seduction. Most young men his age felt lust toward their own sex, but this was becoming an obsession. This was a feeling beyond his brief encounters in the public baths—something that went deeper and made his blood run hot.

Before he realized it, he was at the outskirts of Galorinn, plodding down the long, narrow streets, avoiding the worst of the mud. Ahead was the market square, but he would pass shops and a boardinghouse before he would have to dismount and leave his horse tied. The boardinghouse was the finest in town, and as he drew closer to it, he saw the royal carriage parked in front of it.

Most interesting, he thought as he climbed off the mare and tied her to a rail. *I wonder if—*

His eyes wandered upward to the second floor of the house; sitting in the window, gazing directly at him, was the royal stranger.

Ruadh froze in place as their eyes met. This was no fleeting glance, as when the carriage had passed him. He stared for several long moments, studying the stranger's eyes and his mouth, which slowly turned to a smile.

Then someone behind the stranger rudely pulled the blinds shut.

Once the contact was broken, he felt as if his breath had been taken from him. *I must find out who he is, why he is here. Is he a prisoner? Did he commit some crime that no one wants to speak about?*

He remembered his task and turned to the market square. Although there were aisles of vegetables and meats, what he was looking for would be at the herbal shop in one of the older stone structures. He entered the shop, which was, as usual, darkened, forcing him to wait a moment before continuing to the counter.

"I thought I would see your pretty young face," an old woman said from the darkness. "Your master sent you for some special items, did he not?"

His eyes adjusted quickly, but he already knew who she was. Ragallach also practiced the craft and even belonged to the circle Borras had founded, some three decades earlier. Over the years they had remained in close contact, but the rest of the group had gone to other parts of the kingdom.

"He wants to cast protection, but he wouldn't tell me for what or whom," Ruadh said as he spread the list out on the counter. A thick candle beside it threatened to sputter out. "Do you know what's going on?"

Her long gray hair flowed onto the counter, and with a gnarled hand she moved it out of the way. "The gnomes have been telling me things," she said mysteriously, regarding him with her one good eye. Her face was a twisted mass of wrinkled flesh, and her toothless smile even now sent chills down his back. Despite her advanced age she moved with great speed and agility. She poured some wax out of the candle, which gave a brighter light. "Visitors, we've had. Changes, about to happen." She looked at the list. "Protection, I see. Who is this for?"

"Two men. They rode with the carriage out there, in front of the boardinghouse. They came early this morning."

She stared at him, her wrinkled face pinching shut even more, which Ruadh didn't think was possible. "That carriage?" She looked at the list. "Protection? The fools," she spat. "If it's for that visitor, they're wasting their time. Nothing will protect them."

Before Ruadh could ask for elaboration, she was gone to the back, where she kept most of her exotic stock. Some of the herbs on the list, if indeed they were herbs, he had never heard of.

"Who is he?" he called, hoping she heard him. He knew she was hard of hearing, and he also knew this was especially so when it was convenient for her. "The stranger. The royal stranger. He's staying at the boardinghouse, isn't he?"

Ragallach returned, her arms burdened with a dozen paper and linen bags, and dumped her load inelegantly on the counter. "Who?"

"At the boardinghouse," Ruadh replied impatiently. "Who is he? Is he a duke?"

She cackled a drawn-out, dry laugh. "Oh, hardly. He is a prince. Prince Laon."

"A *prince?*" He dropped two gold coins on the table. "But I thought the king had an heir only recently," he said, as he collected the order in his own canvas bag.

"This prince is no heir," she said, then fixed him with that horrible stare again. Ruadh had to look away. "Do not ask any more about him, young magician. He is more powerful than you, Borras, or even *I* shall ever be. He is danger. Stay away from him."

"But—" Ruadh began. This was not the answer he wanted to hear.

"Out with you," Ragallach said harshly. "I'm closing early today." And with a single gesture with that gnarled hand, she shooed him out of her shop.

During the ride back to the keep, Ruadh realized that tonight was not only full moons but full Leia. Borras had planned some sort of celebratory ritual, but now the boy suspected this was going to be postponed.

Something—or someone—is preventing me from seeing the stranger, he thought, frustrated now more than he ever had been. As he passed the boardinghouse, two guards stood before it, turning everyone away. Ruadh was more convinced than ever that there was a royal conspiracy under way, and he decided he was the only one who could—or would—do anything about it.

When Ruadh returned to the keep, Borras was indeed deep in thought. He handed the bag over to the old magician with caution, and Borras took it absently.

"Will you need my help for this ritual?" the boy inquired.

"No, no. Not for this one. The farther you are away from here, the better."

"But the full moons—" Ruadh said. If he could divert the magician's attention to something other than the spell, all the better. If he helped with the spell, he would learn what this nonsense was all about. Now that he was excluded from the proceedings altogether, he didn't want them to happen at all.

"The full moons will wait, as will Leia," Borras snapped. "There is one thing you can do. Bring more firewood." With a wave he dismissed Ruadh.

I'll show you who will wait, Ruadh thought, fighting back anger. He considered disobeying Borras, leaving the keep without fetching the wood, but he knew the consequences would be painful. Borras was again treating him like a child, just because he wasn't a high priest yet. *He forgets I'm eighteen and a man,* Ruadh seethed, on his way to the woodpile.

As he brought the second armload of logs to Borras's workroom, he cast a furtive glance at one of its many bookshelves. This collection of texts was off-limits to Ruadh, for reasons that weren't clear to him. He happened to spot one book in particular, which was labeled simply *Love Spells.* Confident Borras was far away, he took the book and quietly hid it under the mattress in his room.

I'll show him, he thought. Borras returned, declared the woodpile sufficiently stocked, and told Ruadh to leave the keep until sunrise.

"But where am I to go?" he asked, to which Borras said, "Go stay with Ragallach, if you need shelter. But remember, the woods are our home as well. It would be good for you to sleep under the stars."

"I'm off, then," Ruadh replied. He watched the old man enter his work-room and close the door. A heavy bar locked it from inside. After retrieving the book he'd stolen, he grabbed a light backpack, which held flint, candles, and incense along with a variety of herbs. It was a portable spell kit, which he took with him on trips like these. He grabbed the bag of damine for good measure and quietly stole out of the keep.

One of the first lessons in magic Borras had given Ruadh had emphasized that there were certain spells that were forbidden. He didn't specify who for-bade them or what the consequences would be. He had said simply that some spells would hurt the spell caster, particularly an inexperienced one. Love spells fell into this category.

Despite his master's warnings, he felt it necessary to cast a love spell, and since tonight was one of triple fullness, his success was guaranteed.

Orchids, acorns, spring water, damine. These were the things called for in the spell he chose, which, according to its author, was the most powerful in the book. It was also one that should only be cast by masters of the craft, but in his highly aroused state, as evidenced by an awakened cock that led him through the forest like a hound straining against a lead, Ruadh didn't think this restriction applied to him.

"He will be mine," he whispered to the forest. The declaration felt good, correct. "He will be mine, and we will fall in love."

He knew a grove near a fresh spring, with a clear view of the night sky. Picking his way through the forest, he found the orchids and the acorns and carefully put them away in his pack. The moons hadn't risen yet, but he knew they would; Leia glowed blue and full in the sky, her yellow rings cut-ting it like a knife.

Referring to the book, he followed directions for the circle, the symbols, the runes, which he had never used before. He did know the spell originated with the Old Ones and had been used for a long, long time.

Ruadh stood naked in the circle and appealed to the goddess for her help. He chanted the spell, which was in the ancient tongue, and he under-stood little of it. But it was the most powerful spell in the book, and that was enough for him.

On the ground he sprinkled the orchids, the acorns, the spring water, and lastly the damine and waited for something magical to happen. And waited. And waited. And waited a bit longer, contemplating the big blue planet above in her splendid fullness. At some point during the spell, he noticed his erection had withered and his gonads had retreated into his body.

This is not a good sign, he thought as he stared down at his flaccid, sleeping member. Uncertain of his success or failure in creating his magical love trap, he dismissed the elements and thanked the goddess and the planet Leia for their help.

It might be the kind of spell that takes a while to work, he thought, as he considered the spell and what might possibly have gone wrong.

He gathered his things and started back through the forest toward the keep. *Perhaps the old man has fallen asleep by now,* he thought as he threw his tunic back on.

Indeed, whatever Borras had been working on was complete. Again the old man snored loudly from his workroom, and fighting back drowsiness of his own, Ruadh found his room in the keep's darkness.

He knew he should feel elated at this point, after working the magic, but he just wasn't convinced he'd performed the spell correctly. He held the pilfered book in both hands and felt guilty. Secreting it under his mattress, he lay back and stared at the dark ceiling, wondering for the first time if he had just made a horrible mistake.

Ruadh might have slept for a moment, or a candlemark. Whatever the duration, he awoke with a start, convinced that he had heard something outside, just beyond the wind hole.

Scratching, clawing. He sat up suddenly, unable to breathe.

Through the wind hole he saw one of the moons, newly risen. She cast a bright light through the opening, spreading a bar of gray-white on the floor beneath it. Then suddenly a head appeared, silhouetted in moonlight. A scream froze on Ruadh's lips.

With the agility of a mountain lion, the intruder pulled himself up over the sill, making no sound except for the scraping of claws against rock. For several long moments the intruder stood silently in the middle of the room, the moonlight behind him, concealing his face in shadow.

"Who are—" Ruadh began, but his words broke off.

"I'm the one you summoned," the intruder whispered, turning his face toward the moonlight. Long black hair hung past the angelic face, reaching down over a bare chest as white as the moon beyond him. He wore only breeches, Ruadh noted, relaxing some as he realized that indeed, this *was* the royal stranger, the ghost of his dreams, the object of his most recent intimate fantasies.

With his face to the moon, the royal stranger smiled, showing a set of white teeth—and two long fangs, like a wolf's.

Then Ruadh understood. *What have I done?* he thought, knowing he should be terrified of this creature of the night. But the terror would not come; instead it was tempered with a rising need to press his flesh against this stranger's, to feel their seed slide between them.

"I am what you wanted," the stranger said, stepping toward him. "I am what you asked for. Prayed for. You worked powerful magic to bring me here."

The stranger's hands were claws, twisted like bird's feet.

"You are a lobais," Ruadh said, standing, however shakily. "You eat the flesh of humans and walk only at night."

The stranger laughed, a low guttural grunt that sounded like a wolf's. "Only of those I choose," he said. "I am Prince Laon, son of King Myr. The lobais seed is part of our family, and it skips generations with regularity." The prince had moved closer to Ruadh, whose breathing had become shallow. His heart pounded at his temples. "I am to be banished to the Vilarus Mountains. It is a custom with our family, when the lobais reach manhood."

"Laon," Ruadh whispered, and without realizing it had shed his tunic.

The spell, Ruadh thought, fighting a surge of panic. *If I don't break from it, this lobais will make me part of him.* But the will simply would not come. Instead he found his hand wandering over Laon's chest, tracing the hairless nipples with his fingertips, feeling their sudden point as they hardened.

"So you are shaved all over," Laon observed as his own hands wandered down past Ruadh's flat, perspiring belly.

"Our craft tradition," Ruadh said, wondering why they were even talking.

As much as he wanted to pull away and protect his mortality, he simply could not. The spell he'd woven held him tightly in its net, and any attempt to fight it melted into desire for the stranger.

Their mouths met, and Ruadh ran his tongue along the fangs, strangely unalarmed at their length; their bodies met and became one.

"Give it to me," the prince whispered in his ear. Ruadh knew what he wanted. He turned until his back was against Laon's chest, his buttocks pressed against the prince's groin. Laon reached around and with the gnarled claws clutched Ruadh's hardness with one, his chest with the other.

They stood balanced against each other as Laon probed his opening with his cock, found it, and pushed. Ruadh gave himself completely; his breath caught at the first thrust, and Laon put a clawed hand over his mouth. As if by instinct, Ruadh knew what to do. When the thrusts became too painful, he bit into Laon's hand, hard. His blood tasted warm and salty, like thick sweat.

"Yes," Laon whispered. The thrusts fell into a rhythm, and Ruadh felt himself loosening, his buttocks opening, gaping, reaching for the cock the prince impaled him with. Then Laon's warmth poured into him, and the prince gripped Ruadh's cock as if he were strangling it. A stream of seed exploded over the floor. The magician cried into the lobais's claws, which muted his scream. Laon's blood dribbled down his chin as his body spasmed.

Fangs sank into his shoulder. A numbing, aching pain seized his body in complete stillness.

He watched his blood run down his chest, two tiny streams that ended at his waist.

Ruadh knew he would never be human again.

He will be mine, and we will fall in love, Ruadh thought as the edge of a dream faded from his sleep. Then he remembered, and when he woke he felt the fever upon him. His right shoulder was crusted over with scabs, and his entire side was paralyzed with ache. He knew what he had done, that he had ignored his master's warnings. And in that moment of clarity he had no regrets whatsoever.

Laon held him close, curling his body around Ruadh's, protecting him. The sun was just beginning to rise, but even the dawn light was painful, and he looked away.

"The fever will pass, little one," Laon said. "I will show you how to protect yourself from the sun, how to feed. We will find others of our kind, deep in the mountains, far away from humans."

"My master..." Ruadh blurted out; then he saw the still form on the floor. Borras lay on his back, clutching a dagger in one hand. His mouth was frozen in a scream. Something had ripped his throat out.

"He was going to kill us both," Laon said simply. "I had no choice."

Ruadh felt strangely unmoved at the sight of his dead master; he knew that what Laon said was true.

"We can stay here until the fevers pass," Laon continued. "Then we can seek out our clan in the mountains."

31

Something seemed wrong, out of place. Then Ruadh knew what it was. "The guards. The ones who brought you. They hired my master to work magic for them."

"They did, did they?" Laon replied, sounding faintly amused.

"They'll find us," Ruadh said and struggled to sit up. Laon gently pulled him back to his side.

"No, they will not find us," Laon said, with a solid conviction that chilled Ruadh. The prince propped himself up on a shoulder, stretched, and yawned. Then he said, "Are you ready for breakfast?"

Swan's Braid
Tanya Huff

Horses. Terizan cocked her head to one side and sifted the sounds of the city. A lot of horses. And no one rode in Old Oreen, although in the newer areas the laws had been changed. The sound of horses, therefore, could mean only one thing.

"Swan's back! The Wing has returned!"

Terizan grinned. Obviously, she wasn't the only one who realized what the sound meant.

Buzzing like a hive of excited bees, the crowd began to push back against the shops and stalls, treading both on merchandise too slowly snatched to safety and on one another. Terizan saw a number of small children being lifted to better viewpoints and decided the idea had merit.

Slipping sideways into a narrow alley, she leaped for a cistern pipe, touched toes to window ledge and awning pole, and swung up onto the sandal maker's flat roof. Settling down beside a large clay pot of hot peppers as if she belonged there, Terizan lifted a hand to block the late-afternoon sun just as Swan's Wing rode into view.

The crowd didn't so much cheer as scream its appreciation.

Helmless, her short hair glinting like a cap of mountain gold, Swan rode in front, flanked a half-length back by her second, the man they called Slice, and her standard-bearer, a girl no older than Terizan who bore a bloody bandage around one eye as proudly as she bore the banner. There were a lot of bloody bandages, Terizan noticed. It seemed that Hyrantaz's bandits had not been defeated without cost.

33

But, in spite of the popular belief that it couldn't be done, they *had* been defeated. Slice carried Hyrantaz's head on a pike, the jaw bobbing up and down to the rhythm of his horse's gait.

They'll be going to the Crescent, Terizan thought, eyes locked on Swan as she passed, the red-gold of her life-braid lying like a narrow line of fire against the dusty gray of her backplate. Terizan's heart pounded harder and faster than usual. *If I hurry, I can be there first.*

It seemed that half the city was already in the Crescent when Terizan arrived. She saw a number of people she knew, ignored most of them, and pushed her way in beside a friend in the front row. He turned languidly, and when he saw who it was, his heavenly kohled eyes widened in mock horror. "You're sweating."

Breathing a little heavily, Terizan wiped her forehead on her sleeve. "I beg your pardon, Poli. I forgot that you don't."

Poli smiled and patted her cheek. "Not without cash up front." His smile was his greatest asset; he had a way of using it that convinced the recipient that no other living being had ever been smiled at in such a way. Terizan wasn't at all surprised that he'd been able to make his way through the crowd to a place beside the Congress's steps where he could not only see but hear all.

The distant cheering grew louder and then spilled over into the surrounding crowd. Terizan wanted to leap up and down on the spot as others around them were doing, trying for their first look at the Wing, but she took her cue from Poli and somehow managed to stay calm.

"Swan! Swan! Swan!" The chant became a roar as Swan reached the Congress's steps and reined in her horse. The Wing spread out behind her.

Terizan counted, then counted again. There were only a dozen riders and two pack horses, plus the standard-bearer, Slice, and Swan herself. The twelve had seemed like a horde in the close confines of the old city, but here, in a single line, they were frighteningly few. "They *can't* be all who survived."

"The rest are camped outside the city boundary," Poli said calmly, not so much to her as to the air. "Not in the same place they were camped when they made their kind offer to rid the trade road of Hyrantaz's pack of hyenas, but close enough."

"How do you know?"

Poli raised an elegant brow. "Do you honestly think I wouldn't know where a great many mercenaries who have just returned from a dangerous campaign and will no doubt wish to celebrate their survival and are soon to have a great deal of money are camping?"

"Sorry." She wondered briefly how he'd managed the entire statement in one breath, then lost all further interest in Poli, the crowd, and the rest of the Wing as Swan raised a gauntleted hand.

"You're drooling," Poli murmured, his voice amused.

"Am not." But she wiped her mouth anyway. Just in case.

When the noise of the crowd finally faded in answer to Swan's command, the huge double doors of the Congress building swung open, and the council that ran the city-state of Oreen stepped out. All seven were present and all in full robes of state. *But then, they'd had plenty of warning,* Terizan reflected, for the runner who brought the news of Hyrantaz's defeat had arrived at dawn, his shouted news jerking the city out of sleep.

"We have done what we were hired to do," Swan declared before any of the councillors could speak. Terizan shivered as the other woman's clear voice lifted the hair on the back of her neck. "We have come for payment."

Reluctantly dragging her gaze from Swan, Terizan could see how agitated some of the councillors were—constant small and jerky movements betrayed them. *They didn't think she'd win; the idiots.*

Councillor Saladaz, who'd recently been appointed to his sixth straight cycle as head of the Congress, stepped forward and cleared his throat. "There was the matter of proof," he said.

At a gesture from Swan the two pack horses were led forward and the bulky oilskin bundles heaved off to lie at the councillor's feet. "It was…inconvenient to bring the bodies," the mercenary captain told him dryly as ropes were untied. "These will have to do instead."

Saladaz leaped backward as the battered heads rolled out onto the Congress steps, and the crowd roared with laughter. Out of the corner of one eye, Terizan saw Poli raise a scented cloth to his nose, even though the smell was no worse than a great many parts of the city in high summer.

"They will have to be identified," Saladaz declared, at his most pompous, struggling to regain his dignity.

"I'm sure there are those about who would be happy to help." From all around the Crescent came cries of agreement. Caravans that surrendered without a fight, Hyrantaz had stripped bare of everything save lives—it amused him to see a line of naked, helpless people stagger off toward the city, not all of them surviving to reach safety. "I'll take a third of what we're owed now and the rest at the end of the week."

Councillor Aleezan, who most considered to be the best brain in the Congress, stepped forward, laid a slender hand on Saladaz's shoulder, and murmured something in his ear. Too far away to hear what was said, Terizan saw Saladaz nod. He didn't look happy.

"It will take a moment to count the coin," he said, tucking his hands into the heavy embroidered cuffs of his robe and scowling up at Swan. "If we can have it sent to you later today…"

"By noon," Swan suggested, in no way making it sound like the ultimatum everyone knew it was. "We'll be headquartering at the Lion."

"By noon," Saladaz agreed.

At a nod from his captain, Slice whipped his pike forward, and with a moist thud Hyrantaz's head joined the pile on the Congress steps.

Terizan felt her knees go weak as Swan smiled. "To complete the set," she said and pulled her horse's head around.

"Swan! Swan! Swan!" The cheers that followed the Wing from the Crescent echoed off the Congress, battering the councillors from two directions.

"She's so—"

"Barbaric?" Poli offered. That at least one of Swan's immediate ancestors was a Kerber—a loose confederacy of warring tribes that kept the west in constant turmoil—was obvious.

"Beautiful," Terizan snapped.

Poli laughed. "Well, you do know where she's staying. You could always wander in and—" he winked—"introduce yourself." He laughed again as she paled. "Never mind, dear. I suppose you're still young enough for unrequited lust to have a certain masochistic fascination." Gathering up her hand, he tucked it in the crook of his arm. "I'm sure that with your skills you'll be able to get close enough to watch her without her ever suspecting you're there."

"I can't." Terizan pulled her hand free, suddenly remembering what the Wing's return—what *Swan,* she corrected—had pushed out of her head. "I'm going to the guild today."

Poli looked at her for a long moment. When he spoke his voice was softer and less affected than she'd ever heard it. "That fall really spooked you, didn't it?"

She nodded, trying not to think about the carving crumbling under her foot, about the long drop, about the landing. "If I'd broken something…"

"But you didn't."

"I'm not fool enough to think it'll never happen again." She spread her hands. "The guild takes care of you. You know that, Poli." The whores had one of the first guilds in the city.

"Granted. But somehow I just can't see you meekly accepting a guild's control over your life." His features fell into the nearest thing to a frown she'd ever seen him wear. "You don't even take advice well."

When she shrugged she could still feel the ache in bruised bone and the terror of lying in the darkness and wondering what would become of her if her strength and agility had been destroyed. "I've made up my mind, Poli."

He shook his head. "And you're not likely to change it, are you?" Sighing, he leaned forward and lightly kissed her cheek. "Be careful, sweetling." Then, just in case he should be accused of sentiment, he added archly, "Friends who don't expect freebies are rare."

The Thieves Guild believed that anyone who couldn't find them and gain access had no business applying for membership. The yellow stone building built into the inside curve of the old city wall showed no outward indication of what went on inside, but Terizan had heard the stories about it most of her life: "Getting into the house is just the beginning. You have to take a thief's path to the Sanctum, deep underground."

She didn't believe all the stories about the traps set along that path—wizards were too rare and far too expensive to use for such mundane purposes—but she believed enough to approach with caution. The roof would be guarded, likewise the windows that were even remotely accessible. Which left her with two choices: an inaccessible window or the front door.

While there was a certain in-your-face kind of charm to walking in through the front door, Terizan decided not to risk it, as that was very likely the kind of attitude the guild could do without. Besides, for a good thief no window was truly inaccessible.

A hair shorter and half a hair wider, she mused, squatting silently under the tiny window tucked into the eaves, *and I wouldn't have made it.* As it was, she'd very nearly had to dislocate a shoulder and slice the curve off both hips to get through. Strapping her pack to her chest—no point in carrying equipment if it couldn't be reached quickly—Terizan started looking for a path into the heart of the guild house.

Some considerable time later, she sat down on the floor of a gray-tiled hall and thought seriously about going out the way she'd come in. She'd dealt with all the locks, all the traps, and a dog—who'd been incredibly surprised to have a live and very angry rat tossed at him—but was no closer to finding the Sanctum than she'd been. Her stomach growled, and she sagged against the wall, about at the end of her resources, personal and otherwise. Her pack was almost empty, and the tiny lantern, now closed and dark at her side, was nearly out of oil.

And then she heard the voices.

Someone was making loud, angry accusations. Someone else was making equally loud, angry denials. Terizan sank lower and lower until her ear pressed against the floor. She still couldn't make out the words, but she didn't need to. Smiling in spite of her exhaustion, she traced the edge of the tile next to the one she was sitting on and felt a pair of hinges and a wire.

Movement of the wire would very likely ring bells or the equivalent to announce the imminent arrival of company. Resisting the urge to hum, she twisted it up so that the trapdoor no longer affected it and carefully applied pressure to the tile. Underneath was the traditional narrow chute. Bracing herself against the sides, she chimney-walked down, pausing only long enough to close the trap.

The voices were much louder.

"...pay for results!"

It was a man's voice, but it made her think of Swan dumping the heads in front the councillors and demanding payment. Hardly surprising, as lately everything made her think of the mercenary captain. Earlier the tiny beam of light from her lantern had made her think of Swan's life-braid gleaming against her armor. Sternly she told herself to get her mind back on the business at hand.

"...received exactly what you paid for. If the end result was not what you desired, that is not the fault of this guild."

Her fingertips touched the bottom trapdoor. She could see the thin lines of light around three sides and knew this had to be the end of the line. The voices were directly below her.

"You haven't heard the end of this." The growled warning carried more force than all the shouting. A door slammed.

Muscles straining against the stone, Terizan turned herself around and gently pushed the trapdoor open a crack. She could see the edge of a scarred wooden table, piled high with junk.

"Although we fulfilled the terms of the agreement, he could cause trouble later," a new voice muttered.

A third voice sighed and admitted, "He could."

"Don't be ridiculous. He has no desire to have his association with us made public. Still, although I hate to do it, I suppose it wouldn't hurt to make some small attempt to mollify him." A woman's hand with long, narrow, ringless fingers, reached into Terizan's limited field of vision and picked up a parchment scroll. It took her a moment to realize she was seeing it through a latticework of rope. A net. Obviously, she was intended to go flying into it, whereupon half the supports would break away, leaving her dangling helplessly in midair.

Her blood singing, she opened the door a little farther, grabbed the edges, and swung back with it. At the far end of the swing she let go. Momentum carried her curled body past the edge of the net. She uncurled just before she hit the floor, landing more heavily than she would've liked.

She could feel astonishment wash over her like a wave as she straightened.

Half a dozen lanterns banished all shadow from the small room. Two of the walls were covered floor to ceiling with racks of scrolls, one in a detailed map of the city; the fourth held a pair of doors. Spread out over the floor was a costly though stained carpet. A man, a woman, and a person who could have been either or both sat behind the table and stared at her openmouthed. No one knew their names, but they called themselves the Thieves Guild tribunal.

Terizan bowed, conscious only of how exhausted she was. "I'd like to apply to the guild," she said and stepped forward, pulling out the last two items in her pack. "I took this dagger from the captain of the City Guard—you may have heard it was missing—and this is Hyrantaz's earring—I took it this afternoon."

"From his head?" The man leaned toward her, his bulk suggesting he no longer actively indulged in the guild's business. "You took it from his head in the Crescent?"

Terizan shrugged. There'd been so many people crowding around, it had been embarrassingly easy—but if they didn't know that, she wasn't going to mention it.

As the fat man started to laugh, the woman looked speculatively up at the trapdoor.

"You brought the rat in with you," the third person said all at once, as though he or she had come to a sudden, illuminating realization. "It distracted the dog long enough for you to get away, then convinced the dog's handler that he was only after the rat. That's brilliant! But what would you have done if there'd been two dogs?"

Terizan shrugged again. "Gone looking for another rat?"

The fat man was now laughing so hard that tears were running down his cheeks. "Took it from his head," he kept repeating.

The woman sighed audibly and came around the table. "I think it's safe to assume the guild is interested in admitting you. Your arrival here was very...impressive."

"I thought I was *supposed* to make my way to the Sanctum."

The old woman nodded. "You were. But no one's ever done it before."

"No one?"

"We'd previously considered it a major accomplishment if someone got safely into the lower levels of the building." As Terizan glanced up at the trapdoor and the net, she added, "Of course, a good thief is prepared for every possibility."

Terizan heard the silent warning that she not get cocky about her accomplishment, so she merely said, "I agree," then had no idea of how to refer to any of the other three people in the room.

"You may call me Tribune One." The woman half turned, waving a hand at first the androgyne and then the fat man. "These are Two and Three. You realize you must still complete an assignment of our choosing?" At Terizan's nod she turned her toward the door on the left, opened it, and pushed her gently through. "Balzador, get our candidate here some nourishment."

The thieves playing cards in the antechamber looked up in astonishment, and Balzador leaped to his feet with such energy that a queen of destiny fell from his sleeve and fluttered to the table. "Candidate?" he squeaked.

The tribune smiled. "Yes. She's just dropped in, and as we'd like to discuss her...test, I leave her in your capable hands."

As the door to the Sanctum closed, Terizan heard Tribune One murmur, "You've got to admit, she's very clever." Then the latch clicked, and the iron-bound oak planks cut off Three's reply.

The card players continued to stare. "Just dropped in?" Balzador said at last.

"All things considered," One murmured over her steepled fingers, "there's really no need for you to prove yourself to us. However, formalities must be observed."

Terizan, who'd been fed and feted and had won six monkeys in a quick game of caravan, bowed slightly.

"We have, therefore," One continued, "decided to make your test showy but not especially difficult. You have five days to bring us Swan's braid."

It might have been only because of the blood roaring in her ears, but the acoustics in the room suddenly changed. "Swan's *what?*" Terizan managed to stammer.

"Braid. In five days bring us Swan's life-braid."

By thieves' standards, the Lion was not in what could be termed a profitable part of the city. Three-story sandstone tenements surrounded it, some with tiny shops on the first floor, the rest divided into small suites or single rooms. Almost all had external stairs; a few had roof gardens. Terizan lived in a nearly identical neighborhood—though closer to the center of Old Oreen—and knew exactly what the area had that would be worth stealing. Nothing much.

Except that Swan was at the Lion.

"In five days bring us Swan's life-braid."

She'd been too astounded to protest and had submitted without comment to being blindfolded and led by Balzador up to a concealed door in an alley near the guild house. "When you come back," he'd told her, "come here. Someone will meet you and guide you down."

When she came back. With Swan's braid.

She couldn't do it. Couldn't offer that kind of insult to the most beautiful, desirable woman she'd ever seen. *Face it, Terizan,* she sighed to herself as she watched the Lion from the shadows across the street, *if you got close enough to actually touch the braid, your heavy breathing would give you away.*

The large louvered panels in the inn's front wall had been folded back, and the celebration in the common room had spilled out onto the small terrace. A number of the celebrants wore the red swan on their tunics, but Swan herself remained inside.

Wondering just what exactly she thought she was doing, Terizan crossed the street and entered the inn. No one noticed her, but then, not being noticed was one of the things she did best. With a mug of ale in her hand, she became just another of the townsfolk who wanted to get close to the heroes of the day.

Swan, holding court in the center of the common room, had been drinking. Her eyes were bright—*Like jewels,* Terizan thought—and her cheeks were flushed. In one hand she cradled an immense flagon and in the other a slender young woman who, as Terizan watched, leaned forward so that ebony curls fell over her face and whispered something in the mercenary captain's ear.

"You think so?" The flagon emptied, Swan stood, kicked her chair back out of her way, and tightened her grip around the young woman's waist. Red-gold brows waggled suggestively. "Prove it."

"Here?"

The Wing roared with laughter at the matter-of-fact tone, and a couple began clearing bottles and tankards off the table.

Swan cuffed the nearest one on the back of the head and then turned the motion into a courtly gesture toward the stairs. "I think not," she declared. "This lot has a hard enough time keeping up with me without my setting yet another impossibly high standard."

As the two women made for the stairs amid renewed laughter and advice, Terizan slipped back into the shadows.

The next night she watched a nearly identical scene. Nearly identical in that while the young woman was again dark and slender, it was a different young woman. By the time Swan elbowed open the door to her room—both her hands being occupied—Terizan was on the tiny balcony of the building next door. By the time Swan began testing the strength of the bed, she was outside the window.

She'd spent the day thinking about the guild. Without intending to, she'd found herself outside the building she'd fallen from, picking a bit of plaster off the ground. It couldn't have fallen when she had, but it could easily have been from the same disintegrating carving. She'd turned it over and over and finally crushed it, wiping the gray powder off on the edge of someone else's tunic.

Dying didn't frighten her as much as an injury that would put her out on the street to starve.

The guild took care of their own.

When they were finished and the sweat-slicked bodies lay tangled and sleeping, Terizan measured the distance from the window to the bed, judged the risk, and decided it was twice as high as it needed to be. After all, Swan had a preference for slender, dark-haired women.

"A good thief is prepared for every possibility."

Including, it seemed, the possibility of stealing Swan's braid.

"Poli, I need you to make me noticeable."

One delicately plucked brow rose as Poli turned away from his mirror to face her. "I beg your pardon?"

"I've decided to take your advice."

"Which bit of advice, sweetling?"

Terizan felt her cheeks grow hot and wished he wouldn't look at her as if he was looking inside her. "Your advice about Swan," she growled.

"Did I give you advice about Swan?" He absently stroked cosmetics into his neck. "I don't remember. But then, you've never taken my advice before, so I admit I'm at a loss."

"You said that since I knew where she was staying, I should wander in and...and...." Unable to finish as memories of Swan and the dark-haired young woman got in the way of her voice, she waved her hands and assumed Poli would understand.

His smile seemed to indicate he did. "How noticeable?"

"Do I really look like this?" Staring into Poli's mirror, Terizan found it difficult to recognize the person staring back at her.

"No, dear, I created this out of whole cloth." When she went to brush a feathering of hair off her face, Poli gently caught her hand. "Don't touch. That's not for you to mess up." He twitched at the silk tunic he'd insisted she borrow and smiled proudly at her reflection. "I merely emphasized features you usually keep hidden," he told her, touching her temples lightly with scent. "And if we add my small contribution to your natural grace—try not to move quite so much like a cat on the hunt, sweetling—you should be impossible for our mercenary captain to resist."

Her heart beginning to race, Terizan managed a strangled "Thank you."

She felt Swan's eyes on her when she walked into the Lion, and only the thought of lying in that alley with broken bones kept her moving forward. Tossing her hair back out of her eyes—why Poli thought being half-blind was attractive, she had no idea—she hooked a stool out from under the end of a trestle table and sat down. When a server appeared, she ordered a flagon of the house white, mostly because she'd heard the landlord watered it. While she had to drink, she couldn't risk slowing her reflexes.

After a couple of long swallows, she looked up, met Swan's eyes, and allowed her lips to curve into the barest beginning of a smile. Then she looked down again and tried to stop her hands from shaking.

"Move."

"Ah, come on, Captain…"

"Zaydor, how would you like to stand fourth watch all the way to the coast?"

Terizan heard the man beside her laugh, obviously not taking the threat at all seriously. "Wouldn't like it at all, Captain."

Swan sighed. "How would you like me to buy you another pitcher of beer?"

"Like that a lot, Captain."

"How would you like to drink it on the other side of the room?"

Zaydor laughed again, and Terizan heard his stool scrape back. He murmured something as he stood, but all Terizan could hear was the sudden roar of her pulse in her ears. When Swan sat beside her, knee brushing hers under the table, she had to remind herself to breathe.

Although even Poli had long since given up trying to teach her to flirt, Terizan found her inability was no handicap, as the mercenary captain needed little encouragement. She listened, she nodded, and she let her completely besotted admiration show. That was more than enough.

"Shall we?"

It took a moment before she realized that Swan was standing and holding out her hand. *I don't have to decide about the braid now,* she thought, allowing the other woman to draw her to her feet. Desire weakened her knees, but she made it to the stairs. *I can wait until after.*

After.

Terizan stroked one finger down the narrow, red-gold braid lying across the pillow and tried to force herself to think. It wasn't easy, as during the past couple of heated hours her brains appeared to have melted and dribbled out her ears.

Swan sighed in her sleep and shifted slightly, brushing damp curls against Terizan's hip.

If I'm going to do it, I should do it now. Do it and get it before she wakes. As she tensed to slip from the bed, Terizan realized that she'd decided at some point to take the braid. It may have been when a particularly energetic bit of sex had pulled at a joint still bruised from the fall; she didn't know, and it didn't matter.

She dressed quickly, quietly, slipping her sandals under her borrowed sash—there'd be climbing when she left the inn. Picking up Swan's dagger, she bent over the bed and lifted the braid.

A hand slapped around her wrist like an iron shackle, and she found herself flat on her back, Swan crouched on her chest and Swan's dagger back in Swan's hand.

"And with my own dagger." Gone was the cheerful lechery of the common room, gone too the surprisingly considerate lover—this was the mercenary captain who'd delivered Hyrantaz's head to the council. "Were you planning on making it look like a suicide?"

Terizan swallowed and managed to squeak out, "Suicide?"

"Or perhaps," Swan continued, her thoughtful tones in direct and frightening contrast to her expression, "you'd planned on making it look like an accident. Was I to have become entangled with my blade at the height of passion? I doubt you could make that sound believable—but then, *I'd* be dead, so *I* wouldn't have to be convinced."

"*Dead?*" Incredulity gave her voice some force. "I had no intention of killing you!"

"Which is why I caught you with a knife at my throat?"

"It wasn't at your throat," Terizan snapped, temper beginning to overcome fear. "If you must know, I was going to steal your braid!"

"My braid?" Frowning, Swan sat back. Her weight continued to pin Terizan to the bed, but the dagger was no longer an immediate threat. One hand rose to stroke the narrow red-gold plait hanging forward over a bare shoulder. "Why?"

"To prove that I could."

Swan stared down at her in confusion. "That's all?"

"Of course."

"I suppose we should make an attempt to mollify him."

Her eyes widened as she suddenly realized whom the guild had decided to mollify. Councillor Saladaz had hired the guild and had not been entirely satisfied, and Councillor Saladaz was a powerful man who could be a powerful enemy. If Swan's braid was stolen, the mercenary captain would be humiliated, and apparently that would make the councillor happy. The thief sighed as deeply as she was able, considering that the larger woman still sat on her chest. The thought of Swan's humiliation didn't make her happy at all—though she supposed she should've thought of that before she tried to steal the braid.

Terizan stared up at the mercenary captain and weighed her loyalties.

Adding the knowledge that she was at Swan's mercy to the scale—and ignoring the spreading heat that realization brought—she came to a decision. "I'm pretty sure the Thieves Guild sent me to steal your braid in order to humiliate you."

"What?"

"They're sucking up to Councillor Saladaz. He wasn't entirely happy with something they had done for him."

Swan's eyes narrowed. "Why would Saladaz hire a thief?"

"To steal something?" Terizan bit her lip. *Oh, great. Now, on top of everything else, she'll think I'm an idiot.*

To her surprise, Swan repeated "To steal something" as though it were a brilliant observation. "Could a thief," she demanded, "be sent to *steal* through a mercenary troop and warn a bandit leader of an attack?"

"Someone warned Hyrantaz that the Wing was coming?"

"Someone, yes. One of my pickets said he thought he saw a slender, dark-haired woman slip through our lines. Moved like a thief in the night, he said. We found no trace of her, and we've had trouble with dryads before; but Hyrantaz was warned, and now you tell me that Councillor Saladaz—" the name came off her lips like a curse—"has been dealing with the Thieves Guild." She leaned forward and laid her blade back under Terizan's ear. "Could Saladaz have hired a thief to warn Hyrantaz?"

Terizan sifted through every commission that she'd ever heard the guild was willing to perform. "Yes. It's possible."

"It wasn't you, was it?"

Her mouth gone completely dry, Terizan had never heard so deadly a threat spoken so quietly. Mutely, she shook her head.

Swan nodded. "Good." Then in a movement almost too fast to follow, she was off the bed and reaching for her clothes.

Terizan drew her legs up under her, ready to spring for the window but unable to leave. "You've been waiting for the dark-haired woman, haven't you? That's why you've been—"

"Taking dark-haired women to bed?" Swan yanked the laces on her breeches tight. "I thought she might come back to finish the job, so I made myself available."

Terizan reflected ruefully, *I should've known that there'd be a reason, and I should've known the reason had nothing to do with me.* She tried to keep from sounding wistful. "Why do you believe me when I say I'm not the woman you're looking for?"

Swan twisted around, and, just for an instant, so quickly that Terizan couldn't be certain she actually saw it, her expression softened. "Maybe because I don't want you to be." Then she bent and scooped her sword belt off the floor.

"Where are you going now?"

"To separate Saladaz's head from his shoulders."

"You're just going to march into the Congress and slaughter a councillor?"

"Not slaughter, execute." Her lips drew back off her teeth. "I lost a lot of good people out there, and that asshole is going to pay."

"And then?"

Hands on her hips, Swan turned to face the bed. "And then what?"

"And then what happens?" Terizan slid her feet into her sandals and stood. "I'll tell you. You'll be arrested because you have no proof that Saladaz did anything, and then a lot more good people will get killed when the Wing tries to get you out of jail."

"So what do you suggest?"

Terizan ignored the sarcasm. "I suggest we get proof."

Both red-gold brows rose. "We?"

"Yeah, we. I, uh, I mean, I owe you for not killing me when you had the chance."

One corner of Swan's generous mouth quirked up in the beginning of a smile. "Not to mention for not turning you over to the city constables."

"Not to mention." Terizan spread her hands. "The most obvious reason for Saladaz to want to warn Hyrantaz is that he wanted to keep him in business, and he could only want to keep him in business if he was taking a percentage of the profits."

Swan nodded slowly. "That makes sense."

"The councillor has a reputation for admiring beautiful things—so just suppose some of his payment was not in plain coin but in the best of the merchandise taken from the caravans."

"Suppose it was."

"Well, if someone should go into his town house, they could likely find that merchandise."

"And how would this person know what merchandise to look for?"

"Easy; every fence and constable in Oreen has a list."

Swan looked surprised. "They can read?"

"Well, no, but scholars are cheap."

"All right." The mercenary captain folded her arms across her chest.

"What does this person do once she's found the merchandise in the councillor's house? It won't prove anything if you steal it."

"We could take it to one of the other councillors."

"We don't know that the other councillors weren't in on this deal as well."

Terizan smiled; if only for the moment, Swan had referred to them as "we." "Then we take it to the people."

"Are you sure you're good enough for this?" Swan hissed, scowling at the iron spikes set into the top of the wall surrounding Councillor Saladaz's town house.

"If you hadn't been expecting a dark-haired woman to try something, I'd have had your braid."

"You think." She shook her head. "I don't like this. It's too dangerous. I don't like sending someone into a danger I won't face myself."

Terizan flexed fingers and toes, preparing for the climb. "First of all, you're too good a captain not to delegate when you have to; and second, you're not sending me. It was my idea. I'm going on my own."

"Why?"

Because I'd cheerfully roll naked on a hill of fire ants for you. Something of the thought must have shown on her face, because Swan reached out for her. Terizan stepped back. That kind of distraction she didn't need right now. "We settled that already. Because I owe you for not killing me."

"So you're going to kill yourself?"

She wanted to say it was perfectly safe, but she didn't think she could make it sound believable. "Just make sure there's a constable or two ready when I come back over the wall. Are your people in place?"

"Everyone's ready."

"Good."

Terizan had spent the early part of the day investigating the councillor's security arrangements while Swan readied her Wing for the evening's work. If it was to be done at all, it had to be done before full dark. The wall wasn't much of a problem. That it hid nearly everything behind it was.

She'd heard dogs in the garden, so she planned to avoid the garden entirely. Saladaz probably thought that the jump from the top of the wall to the twisted wrought iron of a second-floor balcony was impossibly far. He was almost right. Two fingers on each hand hooked around the railing, and Terizan just barely got her feet forward in time to stop her body from slamming into the house.

The tall louvered shutters were closed but not locked, and before anyone could come to investigate the sound of her landing, she was moving silently down an upper hallway.

They won't be in the public rooms; they'll be someplace private, but not locked away. He'll want to enjoy them, gloat over them, or there'd be no point in taking the risk of owning them.

She passed a door that gave access to a room overlooking the inner courtyard, and all the hair on her body lifted. Unlike the Thieves Guild, the councillor had obviously considered it worth the expense of having a wizard magically lock at least one of his doors.

Terizan smiled and kept moving. *Might as well hang out a sign...*She had no intention of trying to get around the spell and pick the lock. Thieves who held exaggerated ideas of their skills quickly became decorations on the spikes of the Crescent, and a sensitivity to magic kept her safely away from things she couldn't handle.

At the next door she sped through a bedchamber—in use but, given the hour, empty—and went out the window and onto the inner wall. There were servants working in the courtyard, but her long-sleeved tunic and trousers were close to the same shade as the brick; the short, corn-colored wig she wore was only a bit lighter; and, as good thieves learned early in their careers, people seldom looked up.

Fingers and toes splayed into nearly invisible cracks, Terizan inched across the wall. For one heart-stopping moment she thought there was a spell on the window as well, but then she realized she was reacting to the distant feel of the door lock. The window had no lock—but then, why should it? The window looked over a private courtyard.

The room behind the window was a study. It held a massive table with a slanted writing surface, racks and racks of scrolls, a number of very expensive glass lamps—had she been on personal business, the lamps alone would've brought a tidy profit—and a cushioned lounge with a small round table drawn up beside it. There were beautiful ornaments on display all over the room. The three she recognized immediately, Terizan slipped into her pack. A quick search of the scrolls uncovered two sets of ebony handles chased with silver from the merchants' list of stolen goods. She took one and left the second. After all, something had to remain for the constables to discover. A malachite inkwell was far too heavy, so she contented herself with removing the set of matching brushes.

Even without the inkwell, the extra weight made the trip back along the

49

courtyard wall much more interesting than the initial journey had been. A handhold, barely half a finger's width, began to crumble. She shifted her weight and threw herself forward, stretching, stretching. Her toes clutched at safety, and she started breathing again.

Down below, the servants continued doing whatever it was servants did, oblivious to the drama being played out over their heads.

Bedchamber and halls were crossed without incident. Chewing the corner of her lip, Terizan measured the distance from the balcony back to the wall. Logic said it had to be the same distance going out as coming in, but logic didn't have to contend with a row of iron spikes and a weighted pack. *If I jump a little short, I can catch myself on the base of the spikes and listen for Swan. Once I hear her, I can pull myself up to the top.* She flexed her knees and tried not to think about what would happen if she jumped a little *too* short.

Then her hands were wrapped around the spikes. She bit back a curse as one knee slammed into the bricks, and she held her breath, listening for the dogs.

"I'm telling you, Constable, I saw someone climb over this wall."

They were directly opposite her. Gathering her strength, Terizan heaved herself up onto the top and began to run, bowlegged, for the far end, her heels touching down between every fourth spike.

"There! Up there! Stop, thief!"

Heart in her throat, Terizan threw herself up into a young sycamore tree and down onto the roof of a long, two-story building. She had to get to the center of the city. At the end of the building she danced along a narrow ledge, spun around a flagpole, then bounced up an awning and onto the top of another wall. Behind her, the hue and cry grew as more and more people took up the chase.

"There he is! Don't let him get away!"

She touched ground, raced through a tangle of back streets—peripherally aware of the occasional large body that delayed pursuit—crossed the High Street with what seemed like half of Oreen after her, darted between two buildings, and shrugged out of her pack. An ancient addition had crumbled, leaving a dangerous stairway to the rooftops. Terizan skimmed up it, hanging the pack on a projection near the bottom, and threw herself flat behind the lip of the roof just as the chase reached the alley.

"Look! There's his pack!"

Wincing a little as the thieves' stair crumbled under purposefully heavy footsteps, Terizan stripped off her trousers and turned them inside out to expose the striped fabric they'd been lined with. The sleeves came off the tunic and were stuffed into her breast band, significantly changing her silhouette. The wig she added to a pigeon's nest and couldn't see much difference between them.

With all the attention on the alley and her pack, it was an easy matter to flip over the far side of the building and into a window before anyone reached the roof by more conventional methods. It helped that two very large mercenaries were having a shoving match on the stairs.

By the time she reached the street, the mob had turned and was heading back to Councillor Saladaz's town house. Out in front were a pair of merchants who'd lost everything to Hyrantaz's bandits.

"Your left tit is lopsided."

Terizan slipped a hand inside her tunic and shoved at the crumpled sleeve. "Better?"

"Much." Swan grinned and stepped out of the shadow of the doorway. She linked her arm through the shorter woman's, and they began to walk back to the Lion. "Everything worked out just like you said it would. When the constable pulled the drawstring on the pack, everything in it fell out at his feet. He stared openmouthed, and a number of my louder officers stirred up the crowd, demanding to see each piece. When he held up the scroll ends, I thought the merchant they'd been taken from was going to spit fire. I've never seen anyone so angry. One of my people bellowed that the thief came out of the Councillor Saladaz's house, and that was all it took. The councillor is not a very popular man right now."

They could hear the roar of the crowd in the distance. If anything, it appeared to be growing both louder and angrier as it moved away from them.

"I left plenty for them to find," Terizan murmured. "And I expect when they're done with Saladaz it'll occur to someone that perhaps the other councillors ought to be checked out as well."

"You're quite the strategist."

Terizan's face flushed at the emphatic admiration in Swan's voice. She mumbled something noncommittal and kept her eyes on her feet.

"Given that what you do is illegal and the odds *have* to catch up to you sooner or later—which would be an incredible waste—have you ever considered taking up another profession?"

"Like what?"

"Oh…mercenary, perhaps."

Terizan stopped dead and turned to stare up at the taller woman. Although her night sight was very good, the shifting shadows of dusk made it difficult to read Swan's expression. "Do you mean—"

"Thanks to that son of a leprous baboon—" she cocked her head as the background sounds of the crowd rose momentarily to a foreground scream of victory—"who is even now being taken care of, I have a few openings."

"But I don't—I mean, I can't..." Terizan took a deep breath and tried again. "That is, I won't kill anyone."

Swan shrugged. "I can always get plenty of swords; brains are harder to come by. Besides," her voice softened and one hand rose to cup Terizan's face, "you're smart, you're beautiful, you're amazingly flexible; I think I'd like to get to know you better."

The thief felt her jaw drop, and the evening suddenly grew much warmer.

"There's no need to decide right away," Swan continued, her grin suggesting she could feel the heat of Terizan's reaction. "I'm not taking the Wing anywhere until we're paid, so we've got another two nights to see if we'll suit."

"Swan! Swan! Swan!"

The people of Oreen screamed their approval as Swan and twelve members of the Wing rode into the Crescent. Although all seven members of the council waited on the steps of the Congress, only four were actually standing. Councillor Saladaz and two others stared out at the crowd with sightless eyes, their heads having joined those of Hyrantaz and his bandits.

"So is it love?"

Eyes locked on Swan, Terizan shrugged. "I don't know."

Poli shook his head and sighed. "So are you going to accept her offer?"

"I don't know."

"Does she know that you're responsible for all this renewed adoration?"

"Don't be ridiculous."

"I am never ridiculous. But I do recall being asked to spread a rumor that Swan was behind the discovery of Saladaz and his little business arrangements." He smoothed down his tunic and smiled. "I guess he should have paid her right away and got her out of town."

Terizan grinned as Councillor Aleezan handed over the rest of the Wing's payment, and the crowd went wild. Then the grin faded. "Poli, what should I do?"

He had to place his mouth almost on her ear to be heard over the noise. "What do you want to do?"

What *did* she want to do? Swan was exciting, exotic, exhausting, and not an easy person to live with. The Wing would accept her initially for Swan's sake and in time for her own—but would she ever accept the Wing? They were as good at killing people as she was at stealing from them, and she'd never really approved of slaughter for a living.

His manicured nails digging into her shoulder, Poli shook her. "Terizan, you have to make a decision. What do you want to do?"

"I want..." She didn't want to worry about injury or sickness or age. She didn't want to leave the city. And as much as she desired her, adored her, maybe even loved her, she didn't want to spend the rest of her life trying to keep up with Swan. Not to mention that she strongly suspected she'd hate sleeping in a tent. "I want to join the Thieves Guild."

Poli released her and gracefully spread his hands, the gesture clearly asking, "So?"

"Swan! Swan! Swan!"

The life-braid gleamed like a line of fire down the back of Swan's armor. Terizan chewed on a corner of her lip and suddenly smiled.

Maybe not.

"Uh, Tribunes..." His eyes wide, Balzador peered into the Sanctum. "Uh, Terizan is back."

One looked up from a detailed plan of the Congress and frowned at his expression. "Did you forget to use the blindfold again?"

"N-no. I used the blindfold, but—"

"Good." Two cut him off. "Remember, she isn't a member of the guild until she fulfills our commission. Although," he added in an undertone, "all things considered, we no longer really need to mollify our late client."

"Y-yes, I know, but—"

Tribune Three sighed and turned from racking an armload of scrolls. "Well, if she's back, where is she?"

"Right here." Terizan pushed past the stammering Balzador and into the Sanctum.

One glanced up at the trapdoor in the ceiling, then smiled. "And did you bring us Swan's braid?"

"I did." Reaching behind her, Terizan pushed the door the rest of the way open.

Swan swept off her blindfold and bowed, eyes beaming.

The tribunal stared openmouthed, fully aware that if anything happened to their captain, the Wing would tear the city apart.

"What is the meaning of this?" One demanded at last.

Terizan echoed Swan's bow. "You never specified that I had to remove the braid from Swan."

"We—we—" Two sputtered; then Three began to laugh.

"We never did," he chuckled, slapping meaty thighs. "We never did. We said, 'Bring us Swan's braid,' and she most assuredly has done that."

Two's narrow lips began to twitch.

Finally, One sighed and spread her hands in surrender. "Welcome to the guild, Terizan." Almost in spite of herself, she smiled. "We'll remember to be more specific in the future."

"I'm almost relieved you didn't take me up on my offer." When Terizan looked hurt, Swan cupped her chin with one hand. "You'd steal the company out from under me in a month."

"I don't think so," Terizan began, but Swan cut her off.

"I do. I've seen you operate. Next time I'm back this way, you'll be running that guild."

Terizan frowned. There *were* a number of things she'd like to change. Most of them ran out her ears as Swan bent and kissed her good-bye, but she was sure she'd think of them again. Just as soon as she could start thinking again. She swayed a little as Swan released her.

Swan swung up into the saddle and flicked her braid back over her shoulder. "You've stolen my heart, you know."

"Come back and visit it."

"I will."

Terizan raised a hand in farewell as Swan rode out of the stable yard, then climbed to the top of the tallest building in the neighborhood to watch the Wing ride out of Oreen.

"Next time I'm back this way, you'll be running that guild."

She dropped onto a balcony railing and danced along it to a narrow ledge. The day was fading, and she had a lot to do. Plans to make. She grinned and touched her hip. Safe in the bottom of a deep pocket, sewn into a tiny silk pouch, was a long red-gold hair, rippled down its length from the weave of the braid.

Houston

Jewelle Gomez

Wind—soft, cool, and sweet—perceptible to only Gilda flowed through the shadowed grotto. She closed her eyes and sniffed the air, listening. In front of her was an empty corridor of stone, damp with the silence of underground. Behind the wind she heard the stealthy steps she'd noted earlier. The sound advanced purposefully, so it was not a random spelunker but a hunter. She stepped quickly into the bend, behind a shelf of rock. She was tired of being hunted and sought only to leave the cave, go into what was left of the city for her share of the blood. She was even more eager to then find a safe place to unroll her pallet and rest before dawn.

The almost silent tread brought the hunter closer as Gilda scanned the blackness, calculating how to move past him and out into the night. It was a ridiculous strategy but tried and true: she crouched down, and as the hunter stepped around the bend, she stuck out her foot. He fell, splashing into a fetid pool of water. As she reached down to render him unconscious Gilda almost smiled at the comic picture of her potential kidnapper sprawled on the ground. She decided to take her share of the blood and, in exchange, leave him with the thought of pursuing another profession.

But he shot her. It was as if he'd been expecting the fall. Without turning over he simply twisted his wrist and fired wildly. His narco dart grazed her shoulder, numbness immediately settled on her skin, and within a second her shoulder joint had turned to stone. Her fingers still worked, but she couldn't raise her right arm at all.

55

The hunter leaped up, astonished that he'd actually wounded her, but his eyes turned fearful as he saw that she did not collapse as she should. Gilda struck out with her left hand; it was equal in strength and speed to her right. She sent the hunter, a square, ruddy man, flying across the cave into the jagged wall. Even in the dark she could see the sheen of biphetamine in his eyes. The drug made him quick and merciless, ready only to make his capture and take his pay for her life. Gilda heard the hunter's breathing and pulse rates quicken in excitement; her own slowed to a steady pace as she poised to turn. The numbing stopped at her elbow, but she was not certain if the narcotic effect of the dart would allow her to move quickly enough to become invisible to the eye. The narrow passage of the cave was a trap, but it was her only recourse.

At the same moment her mind decided she should turn toward the darkness, she saw the dart gun move into position. *This time he has me,* she thought.

Then a soft breeze and a mild whistling sound rippled through the cave. The hunter crumpled into the type of heap that can only mean death is present. Her eyes flooded by shock, Gilda turned toward the breeze and saw a man in the shadows.

"He was going to kill you," the man said simply, as if he could hear her mind protesting death. He stepped forward. His thick, curly hair, tied back in a ponytail, revealed a broad face with sharp features and dark eyes.

"No, he would only have incapacitated me, then sold me."

"That's about the same as killing, I think," the man said, moving to the dead hunter.

"It is sometimes worse," Gilda said, thinking of the haunted look she'd sometimes seen on her mother's face, so many years ago, and in the eyes of many on the Mississippi plantation. A look she'd been afraid she'd see in the mirror one day. But she'd escaped. It was two centuries in the past, yet the fear of being hunted still coursed through her veins, imbedded in the life-giving blood that kept her young. She watched the man bend over the body, turn it, and from the wound pull a short sword—the wind Gilda had felt whistling past her. The sword's delicate silver handle gleamed even in the darkness of the cave.

"I don't like to leave him here," he said. "Sometimes children come out to explore, or—"

"Yes, let's bury him properly." Gilda said. Anger tinged the edge of her words, an anger she experienced when anyone, even a hunter, invited death foolishly. She moved to the man's side as he wiped the bloody blade on the dead man's pants leg.

"There's a clay deposit just farther in; we could dig a little, or maybe use rocks."

"Fine."

Gilda helped him hoist the body, using her good hand. They walked several kilometers into the cave, then found another alcove. There was a small depression the man's body fitted easily. They each labored in silence, piling rocks over it. Gilda was relieved to see that the man did not rifle through the dead man's pockets but worked solemnly as if this were a personal duty. She tried not to listen to his thoughts—they seemed too private right now—but she wondered what he did with the killing. Did he keep the man's face inside himself, as she'd been taught to do? She'd known few mortals who took such care any longer.

The silence echoed with their work. Rock and dirt fell with a dullness that sounded secret and ominous. Gilda sensed the man's eagerness to speak as well as his hesitation. She thought only of finishing the task and continuing on her way.

"My name's Houston," he said finally. "It's H-o-u-s-t-o-n, but like *house*. Houston."

He stuck out his right hand to shake, but Gilda's arm still hung leadenly, her right side pulled down by its weight. He switched smoothly to his other hand. When their hands clasped, Houston looked at Gilda fully for the first time. Her grip was granite-hard, but her dark skin was soft. As he gazed at her it became clear why the hunter had been after her. The steely strength of her arm was contained but unmistakable. Her dark eyes swirled with a liquid orange glow. Then Gilda felt his mind flood with confusion. Through her hand he felt her heart. It was calm, without malevolence or voraciousness. Nothing for him to fear. He was able to sense those things, just as all of those on his mother's side of the family could do. Yet he knew he stood holding the hand of a vampyre. In the hands of a vampyre.

"I am Gilda. You've nothing to fear from me. I would not take your life even if you had not just saved mine."

"You read my thought?"

"I can, when necessary. Whenever I'm in a dark cave with a man I don't know who carries a short sword, I try to read his thoughts."

They both laughed—Houston somewhat incredulous, but again, like those of his mother's family, he enjoyed a good wit.

"Why are you called Houston as *house* and not Houston as in the old city?"

"It's after a street in the place that was New York. It used to be a major thoroughfare."

"I've heard of it," she said softly.

"When my mother's family escaped from Poland, they opened a little restaurant—like a delicatessen?" He looked at Gilda, making sure she understood the old term.

"Yes, I remember New York City, and I remember delicatessens and boulangeries and *taquerías* and theaters and cafés and all the things that had wondrous names before the government mandated only English words could be used in public spaces," she said impatiently.

"Well, my mother's mother twice removed opened a place on Houston Street, and it was just called Eats. They served all the food her mother had taught her to cook, just like the old country. My mother used to hear the stories about it when she was young. There was this war, in Europe...." He trailed off and looked at Gilda as if she were from another planet, not familiar with the history. She nodded, remembering the war some had chosen to forget—or pretended never happened. She let him see the memories in her mind; the death and terror he'd only heard about were cold images deep inside her. He stood paralyzed by the magnitude of the small flash of the past that swept through his mind. Then he was himself again as Gilda loosened her influence over him.

"First it was mostly those from our country, Poland; then others. The restaurant never turned anyone away, whether they had money or not. Sometimes they'd eat a meal or sandwich and then wash dishes or hose down the sidewalk. Or they'd just eat, if that was all they could do. My mother used to tell me the stories, and she'd have tears in her eyes as if she'd been there. Full of pride, you know. She used to say, 'Take just enough and give as much as you can.' "

Gilda listened to the rhythm of Houston's voice and heard others she'd known before—Sorel, Anthony, Bird. Voices of those she called family, the ones she was searching for even now.

"I was her first. She named me Houston so the story would stay alive, I guess."

Gilda looked more directly at the man, her eyes somewhat incredulous.

"It's actually David Houston Klepfisz." He answered her look.

Gilda said nothing; her mind was full of pictures of New York as she'd last seen it, trying to imagine the teeming community of Polish immigrants, refugees from the horrors of war.

58

"I was lucky she didn't name me Eats, huh."

Their laughter rang off the walls of the cave again. Gilda was fascinated by this lighthearted man. It had been so many years since she'd been with her family, this one's stories made her ache. She rubbed her shoulder, trying to hurry the feeling back into it.

"And your generous mother? Where is she now?"

"She died ten years ago. I suppose she was lucky; she lived to be forty."

A sadness crossed Houston's face. The world had turned into a burial ground for the mortals. To Gilda he looked to be about thirty. He still had a healthy complexion, and she didn't hear any wheezing in his lungs. But the chances were he'd be dead, like most mortals, by forty or fifty at most.

"I have to ask you an open question," he said.

"Yes?"

"You don't kill? You take blood, but you don't kill someone who's hunting you, to sell you?"

"Killing is not my way. Not the way of my mother's family. When I take my share of the blood, the sharer does not die. And I do not kill when any other option is available."

"Then come with me. I know someone who can help with your arm."

"My arm will heal itself in time."

"I hear the government's been experimenting with even more toxic weapons. You can't be sure what damage has been done. My friend lives in the Jemenez Mountains just to the north. She's a witch and knows herbs."

A surprised laugh escaped Gilda. "I don't think I'll be needing a witch."

"Ah, a disbeliever. How'd you feel if she didn't believe in vampyres?" Houston said with a smile. "You must've heard of people with powers, healing, things like that."

Gilda thought of Marie LeVeau, the vodun priestess whom she'd only heard about as a young girl when she'd lived in Louisiana. And of those who'd given her life. Their lives were rich with powers, but she'd never call them witches.

"I know those who can speak without speaking," Gilda said cautiously.

"See. My friend Archelina can hear voices of people who aren't with us anymore. She was very famous among her people in Iowa. Too famous, so she moved into the mountains here."

Gilda's heart pounded. What voices from her past might she hear through the witch? But the hunger was rising in her. Her time had come a while ago; she could no longer ponder the past. She needed to reach the city and find the one she would share with before the night became much shorter.

"I can't make that journey now. I...I must go to share the blood soon." She was surprised to hear herself speaking the words aloud. "It's not good to wait too long. The hunger becomes a deep pain."

Houston watched, fascinated by the orange light swirling in her eyes, and saw the way she strained to compensate for the dead limb at her side.

"I can't meet your witch. I must go," Gilda said, sorry to leave Houston behind.

"What about me?" It was out of his mouth before he thought. He looked embarrassed as he sputtered, "I'm healthy, and your handshake says you don't lie about killing."

"I will not give you my blood." Gilda was suddenly wary. Was this open-faced young man a seeker, scheming for ways to prolong life in these unhealthy times, tricking her into the very trap he'd saved her from? She peered into his eyes and saw his thoughts—helping her. And something else: loneliness. He wanted company, someone to laugh with. Gilda had not thought of herself as a mirthful companion, but it was true, they'd made each other laugh.

Gilda pulled his consciousness into her mind, wound it slowly into a tiny ball, and put it to the side. She spread before him a green sea of grass so he felt comfortable as she laid him down on the rocky cave floor. As she leaned over him, his eyes closed peacefully. She sliced through the skin on his neck just below the line where his beard would be growing back in. The flesh was soft, the pulse was steady. The line of blood was deep red and familiar. She pressed her lips to the warm liquid before it could spill down to color Houston's gray shirt.

The ferrous scent filled her nostrils, sweet like sea air. She took it in and let the blood satisfy her need. *How odd,* she thought, *to take the blood from him—a stranger, yet not a stranger.* His dreams were not anonymous. Their pulses merged; his breathing slowed to meet hers. Gilda pulled back to listen to his thoughts and feelings, sifting through to see what hope or dream she might fulfill, as was her duty. In her probing she could feel he was a man of great principle and kindness. He was much like her friend Sorel. *Friend.* The word sprang from him into her mind. In saving her, his need for friendship was reawakened. But what could she do to give him a friend?

Gilda took no more blood. She rested his head gently on the ground and stood, preparing to leave. He would wake, find her gone, and go on with his life, she thought. But what of her part of the exchange? She'd left nothing

60

behind for him. Gilda listened to the distant sounds—slow drip of water, echoing wind—and thought of the dead hunter who'd tried to take her into captivity. He would have made a small fortune selling her to one of the rich ones seeking to escape the short life to which mortals had condemned themselves.

The limestone water in the puddles around her was now reflected in the tainted rivers and oceans around the world. Only in the caves was the air ever moist and cool. Since the turn of the century the millions of laborers, teachers, clerks, and others who lived from day to day had given up hope of health. That was reserved for the wealthy. The hunter would have retired on the money he'd receive after selling her, to be kept barely alive and transfused repeatedly until the buyer felt certain he too was immortal. Then death for her. Cleaving her head from her body. Or burning, like they used to do to witches.

Houston started to revive. The power of his blood shone in her eyes as Gilda looked down at him. Beside him his short sword gleamed with the care he so obviously lavished on it, yet violence did not lead his heart. *Friend* was the only word she heard echoing inside him. As the world had grown more desperate, the idea of friends had become more precious. Few had room for it in their hearts. Even those who'd suffered at the hands of the rich often sought only to become despots themselves.

"Come, my little delicatessen," Gilda said with a smile as she reached down with her good hand and helped him up. "Let's go visit your witch."

They traveled for several hours by hovercraft. Gilda thought and Houston talked. The highway they skimmed was overgrown and cracked; few people ventured this far outside the city. Yet Gilda sensed life in the brush. Some were encampments; occasionally she felt a lone figure on foot or motorcycle, but no others in hovercrafts. When they arrived at the Jemenez, Houston took them on foot through arroyos and along brambled paths until they were within sight of the mouth of a cave. Here they sat. As Houston explained, they must wait for Archelina to acknowledge their presence and invite them in. Gilda was still wrapped up in her thoughts of the past. And the future. This world she'd seen for so many years had become a festering sore. In all her almost two centuries of life she'd never held as much fear as now. Everywhere she turned there were fakirs and charlatans cloaked in numerous guises, promising the dying population salvation. Some wore spiritual robes, others wore the suits that signaled their sanctified prosperity; but no one asked the population to think about what was happening around them. In fact, their salvation was making the poverty, illness, and pollution invisible—or at least someone else's problem. One that could be ignored as the populace reached for some higher state of grace. And tricks had become an acceptable way of making their salvation possible. Digitalized broadcasts, slyly worded news stories, carefully crafted entertainments that created an alternate reality that few questioned or even noticed was a not-quite truth. As their world got smaller, their lives less content, people convinced themselves it was all happening somewhere else.

Gilda had struggled for years against despair, a by-product of the perspective afforded by her long life. She remembered the cities Houston spoke of so nostalgically; she remembered the beauty of the old people. In the late afternoon, before dusk frightened them inside, the elderly often walked through streets arm in arm as if surveying their long lives. Gilda would look into their finely crafted faces, smiling at the ones with light still shining in their eyes, knowing she would never wear the crown of silver or feel the soft folds of fleshy age draped around her. It had been many years since Gilda had seen anyone over fifty.

Gilda didn't know what she expected to happen when she met Archelina, so she was uncertain why she sat among the sparse grass and cactus waiting for a light to appear in the mouth of a cave several hundred yards above them. Except that she felt pulled by more than just Houston's enthusiasm and sense of humor. Having no desire to be surprised by another hunter, Gilda pushed her attentions outward in a circle that widened back down the mountainside. She scanned the surrounding area methodically to see what life was near. She was interrupted by Houston's shout.

"There she is!" Houston jumped to his feet eagerly.

"Yes, I know." Gilda peered through the darkness. The woman standing above them was broad, filling the space illuminated by the oil lantern she held aloft. Her skin was a dusky brown and her hair starkly white. It was in two long braids, which ended near her knees in bright red. At first it appeared to be fabric wrapped around their ends, but Gilda saw that the braids themselves had been dipped at the ends into a henna, making them red at the final half-foot. And her eyes were milky white, unseeing.

Houston had already started up the rocky path, so Gilda followed, quickly overtaking him.

"It's been a long time since I've seen her. But she always remembers. Even before I open my mouth."

In his excitement Gilda heard the child he'd once been and something that had been lost to this world. She did not lose patience with the pace Houston was setting—hurried for him, snaillike for her. Instead she simply settled inside the rhythm of the ten-minute climb, listening to the air around her as they ascended and the light from the cave grew larger.

When they finally arrived, they took the lantern Archelina had hung at the entrance and walked deep inside, uphill toward a chamber that lay even higher inside. They entered a large space draped with cloth and animal pelts; large cushions sat on ledges and the floor of the cave. At the center was a huge woodburning stove whose chimney seemed to feed directly, incongruously, into the stone above it. Archelina stood beside it, holding a loaf of bread and a knife. The fierceness of her face suggested, at first glance, that either might be a weapon. But then she smiled. "Houston. I wondered if you'd ever return."

"I told you, I'll come here to die. Nowhere else."

"The way you wield that short sword, you may have little choice about where you die."

"Are you saying I have no skill?" Houston's retort rode on laughter as he laid his gleaming weapon on a shelf of rock by the entrance.

"I'm saying you live too much with those who find your skill a challenge and who don't treasure life as you do." She turned her head as if she were peering at Gilda, but the blindness was complete.

"Gilda," she said, "good to finally get to meet you."

Shock coursed through Gilda. "You know of me?"

"Yes, and some of the others."

"They've been here?" Gilda said, barely containing the excitement in her voice. This witch might be able to assure her she was following the right path, reuniting her with her family and securing their escape from this dying world. Archelina walked to the large round wooden table that sat to one side of the room and started to slice the bread. "No. They passed on the other side of the mountains."

"May I ask how you know this?"

"I listen."

Archelina looked as if she were anywhere from sixty to a hundred years old. The skin of her face was full and healthy even where it was wrinkled. Her hands were large and strong as she sliced rapidly through a loaf of bread made from wheat and corn. Her broad frame was unbent, though Gilda could sense the delicacy of the bones. For the first time in her life, Gilda stood before a mortal with natural powers perhaps equal to her own. It made Gilda feel both comforted and afraid. And something else Gilda was unable to grasp: she could not read much from Archelina's thoughts. It was as if they only formed just as they left her mouth and entered the air.

"Whenever I find myself in a cave with a man with a short sword and a vampyre, I always shield my thoughts," Archelina said aloud.

Houston and Gilda both looked startled; then the three of them laughed, letting the ring of their sound bounce off the walls for much longer than the slight joke warranted. It was laughter of recognition and of bonding.

"Gilda took one of those narco darts. Just a graze, but will you examine it?"

"You don't really need my help," Archelina said as she held her hands stretched out in front of her, taking in the aura surrounding Gilda. "Not with your arm. That has already started to heal itself. Remarkable."

Heat suffused Gilda's face; she wasn't certain if it was a response to Archelina's uplifted hands or just to Archelina.

"Will you let me touch the place to feel the healing?"

Gilda walked closer and turned so that her numb shoulder was beneath Archelina's hands. They rested in the air just above her.

"Oh my, yes, how remarkable. That's how it's done, is it."

"I don't really know how it's done. Our bodies heal themselves; we don't grow old."

"The legend is true, then. I thought it might be, but the wealthy create so many fantasies."

"You know, there's a religion based on it now," Houston said. He sat back on one of the cushions as if he'd reclined there often. "Everlasting Life, Inc., or something like that," he went on. "People pay a lot of money, and some guy in red robes claims to be over a hundred years old and tells them about miracles he's done—always in some other part of the country."

"Not anymore," Gilda said.

"What do you mean?" asked Houston.

"I...communicated...with him recently. He now feels the need to work only at the bedsides of those with little time left."

"You took blood from him?" Houston's voice was full of impatience.

"And helped him remember his original impulse."

"You could change the world, you know that?" Houston said angrily, as if Gilda were playing with her powers.

"Only in small ways. Not everyone is so easily persuaded to return to their original path."

"She's already changed the world," Archelina said. "These small ways are what often mean the difference."

Gilda again felt the warmth, though Archelina had returned to sit at the table. She was wearing loose-fitting cotton pants, wrapped tightly at the calf and ankle. Gilda watched as Archelina crossed her leg and noticed her feet were much smaller than she'd have expected. Archelina leaned forward on her knee and turned anxiously toward Houston. "It's not like you to reach for quick fixes."

"There's nothing quick in this!"

Gilda saw for the first time the fierceness that lay inside Houston. Much of the laughter that flowed from him sprang from a well of hurt and anger.

"There's been no immune-booster medicine for generations. People gave up on fresh water before the turn of the century."

"And it will take generations to undo any part of it," Gilda said in a soft voice.

"And while you talk of generations, people we love die around us."

"The change must come from within, Houston. No one can impose the idea of justice, of caring."

Archelina held her hands clasped in her lap as she spoke tenderly. "We know these things. Houston sometimes forgets in his enthusiasm."

Gilda watched the exchange, fascinated by the interplay of emotions. The love between them, Houston's anger and fear, Archelina's concern both for him and for her own mortality. As they sat, Gilda felt her own body come alive with a desire she found startling. It rose from deep inside her and pressed against her center. She wanted to lie with this woman, feel her body close to her, smell her sleeping. She missed that simple pleasure more than she realized. Archelina raised her head as if she'd just caught Gilda's thought.

"I must go out," Gilda said.

"Why? Are you afraid?" Archelina asked.

Houston looked from one to the other, sensing the tension between them and understanding it immediately. Instead of his usual joke, he rose, spread jam on the slices Archelina had cut, and filled his mouth with bread.

"I don't know what you want from me," Gilda said to the old woman.

"To help, in a small way."

"What help do I need?"

"Do you truly wish to know that?"

It had been decades since she'd felt the need for anyone's help in any profound way. But now, what were the questions swirling inside her? It was more than simply what road to take. Where to find her family and make a new life would be revealed when the time was right, when everyone was in their appropriate place. What could she really need from this woman who stood before her like both a comforting grandmother and an irresistible siren? What was in those hands that drew her?

"To visit the past," Archelina said, with a hint of surprise in her voice.

"No!" Gilda almost shouted. "I don't need to revisit the horror of enslavement. Those who are dead remain so!" Gilda's uncertainty about her surroundings, and who might be following them, fueled her words. It wasn't safe to disappear into some kind of spirit trance, searching the past, with so much unknown right outside.

"I'll clear the table," said Houston as he removed the bread, jam, and knife with his now-familiar enthusiasm. Gilda watched as they prepared for a ritual that they had clearly performed more than once. Houston used a clean cloth to scrub the table, then went into a smaller chamber that lay behind the main room. He returned with four large branches. Gilda recognized scrub pine but not the names of the others, though they looked to be from local trees. He laid them on top of one another in the center of the table.

"Tell what you remember," Archelina said to him, as if intoning a prayer.

"I remember when water and the eyes of the people were almost clear. I remember soil full of life and the energy that healed from inside. I remember the idea of justice. I remember many mothers and fathers who remembered many mothers and fathers. My mother's touch and the words she sent to me after she died. And I remember when we gave each other shelter. Tell what you remember."

When Houston finished his recitation, he and Archelina drew close to the table and held out their hands to Gilda. She joined them, holding her palm upward as they stood around the thick brown circle of polished, rough wood.

Archelina spoke: "I remember when the sky, water, and eyes of the people were mostly clear. I remember fields reclaimed, and harvests. I remember the old and the young."

Gilda felt a frisson in her body, as if it were being divided in planes. Some parts were present; others were floating alongside, feeling the experience, not seeing it; and others rose above her and watched. She lifted her head and looked up to the ceiling of the cave, as if expecting to see herself there. Instead she saw the constellations painted in a soft white. Where the fire threw light, she recognized the stars of the fall sky. Small dots and fragments of clouds were painted in perspective off into the darkness. She looked back at Archelina and wondered how she accomplished such artistry, or if it were Houston's handiwork.

"And," Archelina continued, "I remember to provide shelter." As she spoke, her already erect body stretched and turned in the light flickering from the open grate of the stove. The room filled with shadows that seemed made of light itself. Houston's face glowed with joy, as if he were seeing or hearing something that was just for him. Archelina's brow furrowed in confusion. She rocked her head back and forth forcefully, her long braids falling first in front, than behind her. With each swing toward the table, her breath was expelled in a whisper. A knot of anxiety pulled across Gilda's chest. Archelina looked as if she were going to fall across the table. Then she stopped the distressing movement and turned toward Gilda.

"I don't remember any words," Archelina said, her voice croaking with effort. "It's much too far in the past for that. I remember feelings. Deep love. Sorrow. Profound exhaustion. Indignation. Anger at injuries done to others. Her love is still here. Tell what you remember."

Gilda picked up the memories, which were, in fact, her own: "I remember her muscled arms in fine velvet dresses. Rouged cheeks and sad eyes. I remember how it felt to be lifted to safety by her. I remember how she made family, how she loved us. She's gone. I remember. I remember to offer shelter." The last words were pulled from Gilda like an unexpected covenant. As she said them, she knew her path had been turned.

"I remember," said Houston.

"I remember," Archelina said as she drew her hands into her lap and held on to her braids.

"I remember," Gilda echoed. A burst of cool air filled the room, the rock releasing the energy that had bounded off its surfaces, working its way from the past into the present. Gilda looked around her, but nothing seemed changed, except that the fire in the stove had burned down quite low.

"Now we eat."

Houston brought the bread back to the table, along with some cheese and a plastic container of wine. Gilda and Archelina sat quietly while Houston went back into the chamber and returned with glasses glistening with colors.

"It's in his blood, you see. To serve food. He's inherited that from his mother's people as well," Archelina said.

As they sat around the table, Gilda sipped at the heavy red wine and watched them eat hungrily, as if the experience had sapped their strength.

"I love seeing my mother's face. She didn't speak this time," Houston said.

"Soon she'll be completely diffused, returned to the other energy."

"I know. But I have her voice inside me now," he said, smiling.

"And what of you?" Archelina asked.

The remembering was individual, private. Each of them had had their own visitation, which Archelina facilitated but did not recall.

"The one who made me has been gone for so many years, only the feelings were left to remember."

"That may be the most important part."

"They were so strong, so passionate. She cared so much for others, for me. In the end, the caring wore her down."

"Everyone has their allotted time. Years or centuries."

"Yes. That's a relief in so many ways."

"Why's that?" Houston asked, leaning forward across the table.

"A sense of time can make things more precious, more—" Gilda broke off, and Archelina held up her hand abruptly at the same moment. "Someone's in the cave."

Houston leaped to his feet and started toward his sword. Archelina stopped him with a slight movement of her hand. "No killing!"

"It's probably a hunter," he said to Gilda, "tracking us from the southern cave. Maybe they're working in pairs."

Gilda listened more deeply, then turned back toward the opening. "I'll see to it." Before he could protest, she added, "Stay here with Archelina."

"Your shoulder?" he asked, but Gilda had already disappeared through the opening into the darkness.

She moved quickly down the corridor of stone, listening as she went. This one had used more caution than the other. His movements were not steady but erratic, hard to track. He stalked her as if he had all the time in the world. Gilda steadied her attention on his sound and the silence surrounding him. Sound echoed around him, bouncing off, concealing rather than exposing his movements. Gilda then began to listen to the bouncing sound. When she focused around him—the dripping water, the wind, the rustle of animals—she could pinpoint him. Gilda took a position in the center of a corridor and probed his thoughts: calculation, sport, only the prey on his mind. She sensed the presence of some type of stimdrug, but not a biphetamine. This hunter counted on his prowess, not narcotics. Gilda fell back into the shadow and began to rattle things in his mind. She moved rocks and shuffled in his imagination so he followed a path almost directly to her. She pulled back even deeper until she felt the cool limestone through her tunic. As she did, she realized Archelina was by her side. Gilda almost gasped in shock but could not; her throat was locked in silence. Archelina spoke close to her ear. Her breath was warm, sweet with corn: "I will speak with him. No killing." Then Gilda was able to respond, except she was unsure what to say. There was no room for contradiction.

The footsteps of the hunter advanced as Gilda and Archelina stood motionless. Gilda saw Archelina raise her hands slowly and felt a warmth surround her. The hunter stepped around the corner, still in shadow, cautiously scanning his surroundings, attack-ready, making his way directly toward them. Gilda wanted to raise her hand and signal they back away, but it wouldn't move. Archelina turned her head, signaling *No,* and Gilda stood almost paralyzed as the hunter advanced. She then read Archelina's thought: *He can't see us, we're cloaked. Wait until he is just here, then you may touch him as Houston has told me you do.*

The hunter now stood less then two yards from them. He turned and should have been able to see them both, but his eyes brushed past as he continued down the path. Just as he was within arm's reach, Archelina dropped the cloaking that masked their presence. The hunter realized something was amiss, and Gilda kicked the narco gun from his hand. Archelina rendered him unconscious by simply raising her hand higher. Gilda stepped forward and caught him as he fell, laid him on the rock, and quickly removed his other weapons, throwing them into the enveloping darkness. Archelina stood beside them, unseeing yet knowing, her arms still outstretched. She'd turned her palms downward, her fingers spread almost as if she were playing the piano. Gilda knelt above the hunter, uncertain—she'd never taken blood with someone nearby, so cognizant. She could find no reason not to, so she leaned in and sliced the flesh at the hunter's neck. As the blood seeped out, Archelina's sharp intake of breath reverberated in the darkness. Gilda drew the warm red into her, relieved this hunter would not die. She touched his mind, his heart, seeking what it was that he sought beyond profit. Survival seemed to crowd everything else out of his mind. There were few aspirations for him beyond making the capture, making the money. Digging deeper, Gilda felt an ancient need—as a young man he'd enjoyed the respect of a young neighborhood friend after he'd saved him from a local gang. It was a pride he'd savored then almost as much as he reveled in the hunt now.

As she took her last share of the blood, Gilda reignited that impulse—to seek approval for a good deed—and then sealed the wound. She lifted him in her arms and carried him back out to the mouth of the cave. She left him in the brush as the sun began to round the horizon. When she turned back inside the corridors were empty, and she walked alone back to Archelina and Houston.

They sat silently at the round table, Houston's gleaming sword rested at its center. He looked up as she entered.

"He's gone?" he asked.

"Yes. On to a new career, I hope."

"Your gift is truly a wondrous one," Archelina said.

"I noticed you have a few tricks up your sleeve too," Gilda said. "I felt for a moment as if I was paralyzed."

"Like most things, it's only energy. Understood. Channeled."

"Who taught you these arts?"

"In Iowa, my mother's people were healers. They'd battled the colonialists for our land for many generations. But the one thing that could never be taken away was their energy. They were defeated often, but they always returned with new ways to survive. To gather enough energy to hide is no great skill. Gathering enough energy to stand in the open, to hold on to your spirit—these are difficult things."

"How old are you?" Gilda asked.

Archelina laughed as Houston answered for her, "Not nearly as old as you, I bet."

"But well-preserved, I hear," Archelina added.

Gilda flushed with embarrassment, as if Archelina had read her thoughts.

"I understand it's your custom to sleep during most of the day. Since it's almost dawn, I suggest we all retire for a while. Then you and Houston can set off refreshed."

Houston looked startled. Archelina continued, "You will be needing a guardian as you travel south to meet your family. Houston is a man to be trusted, to be valued. He can assist you."

"I have not settled on my direction or goal yet."

"The message will come soon, and it will take you south to the caves of the Land of Enchantment. Then farther south—to meet the voices not of the past but of the future."

Again there was no room for contradiction. Gilda looked at Houston, who appeared pleased with Archelina's prognostication, and asked, "What do you say to this?"

70

"Archelina has great faith in me. I'm honored by that. But I'd only travel with you if it's what you wished." Houston looked into Gilda's eyes as if searching out her answer, then turned his own toward his sword as he lifted it gently to return it to the shelf.

"I think our witch may be right."

Houston turned back to the table with a smile.

"I'd like to hear more of your stories, my friend. And maybe tell you some of my own. We'll start out at dusk."

Houston spread a blanket across the mat on a ledge below his sword. He sat up against the wall and wrapped the cover around him. Gilda followed Archelina into the inner chamber. She unrolled her pallet filled with her home soil onto the sleeping platform, which was built into the wall. She dropped her clothes beside it and lay down. Archelina unwrapped the leggings from her ankles carefully and folded them on the floor, followed by the rest of her clothes. Her body was muscular still, yet the skin had the looseness of age Gilda had so missed. Archelina folded Gilda into her arms under a feather cover and held her to her bosom, almost flat with the years. Gilda nestled against the witch as she might have against her own mother or a lover. The need felt undefinable. She only knew the desire to be held. They lay this way for the hours into dawn and afternoon. Gilda's breathing slowed to almost a stop, while Archelina's strong hands massaged Gilda's arms and back.

The darkness of the cave was complete, but both their bodies registered the changing day outside and the deliberate irregularity of Houston's breath as he sat watch in the outer chamber. Gilda was between sleeping and waking, her body in almost total stasis, yet she took in the thoughts and memories that wandered randomly through Archelina's mind. In them she found a sense of age. She already knew what it meant to have those she loved die around her as time seemed to simply brush past her. Even for the young, like Houston, this was a sorrowful pain to bear. But so many other things could only be taken in through experience that Gilda would never have. The ache that came from the inside of bones, the shadow of memory as faculties shed the needless details of the past, the sensation of nearing the end of your time. These were all things Archelina gave to Gilda as they lay in each other's arms. Their bodies were one being, listening to itself in profound silence. In these hours Gilda saw how much of the future lay in the past. And how much was embedded in the single moment of the present. In exchange she let Archelina experience the sense of being eternal—an open end of both familiarity and change. They lay together in wonder at each other's gifts and exchanged life in this way until dusk brought a new day, new roads, other magic.

Birthmarked
A. J. Potter

Keir was trying studiously, with limited success, to ignore the muttered and not-so-muttered complaints arising on either side of him. Keeping his horse on a tight rein, he hunched uncomfortably in his heavy dark clothing and light armor and stared straight ahead with a carefully constructed blasé expression. Sweat trickled down his sides as the warm dusk wandered into night. The horse itself seemed to be joining in the mutiny against him, veering first left, then right, and fighting him for control.

"Duncan Vaughn is not a man to play with, Keir."

Keir raised a single blond eyebrow.

"This is a stupid idea. What in the Depths can you possibly hope to gain by riding right into his camp? He's hardly going to turn tail and run because he sees the three of us coming."

Keir tilted his head slightly to the left as if considering the comment.

"*Is* he going to see the three of us coming, Keir? I mean, wouldn't a subtler approach be better? Huh? Sneak up, turn this into a surveillance mission. Get some information and go back home. Come back with an army. Huh, Keir? Don't you think?"

Keir finally deigned to comment. "Of course. Subtle. We'll leave the horses a few leagues off and go in on foot."

Armond's round, vacuous face twisted into a triumphant grin, which he shot over at Andianna behind Keir's back. "See, I knew he had a plan. Don't you, Keir?"

Andianna snorted. "Oh, he has a plan, all right. A plan to get skewered on his own bedamned arrogance."

Keir turned to her with the famous grin, almost visible in the gathering shadows. "Now, Andi. Is that any way to speak of His Highness, Your Brother, the Crown Prince of the Realm?"

Andi snickered at the oh-so-obviously capitalized "title," an old joke between the two of them. "No, that is how one speaks of the court fool. Take it or leave it, brother dear. This is an idiotic idea. I don't care what Vaughn was like when you and he were fostered together—and from what I hear, he was not any too trustworthy then. But all that aside, he is certainly a different person now. A different, dangerous person, who is sitting on Ervane's throne, such is it is. I repeat, this is an idiotic idea."

"Then why are you here?" Keir ducked his head and stared blindly into the forest ahead, urging the horse to continue at a steady pace.

"To try to keep the serrated edge of that arrogance from cutting out your tender little heart, brother mine."

Keir Alienor, crown prince of Rastoria, was an impressive figure on horseback. More so than on foot, really. Like all heroic princes destined for legends, Keir was visually ideal: blond, beautiful, perfect. Well, mostly. With the notable exception of the extremely crooked nose that sat between the huge, placid gray eyes. Noses that are broken more than once seldom return to perfect proportions. And there was also the matter of the highly unmanageable hair, and one leg that was rather shorter than the other from another old break that hadn't healed quite properly. The hair was truly a nuisance for formal court appearances. The leg didn't hinder him unduly, only producing a bit of a limp. From a ways off, when he stood with his hip canted and the wind was in his hair, he cut quite a dashing...impression. A sword in hand helped immeasurably. As did the extra long cloaks and capes he tended toward, which billowed about him nicely and lent a dramatic flair to his basically short stature.

He was a good person, though; in all that the banal phrase implies. Sweet disposition, kind, thoughtful, fair-minded. The arrogance could be forgiven, of course; he was, after all, nobility. A high self-opinion rather comes with the job description. But more importantly, no streaks of royal intrigue or malice trickled poisonously through those veins. Yes, a good person. As good, that is, as a human being can be expected to be. Which in actuality is not really very good at all, but Keir was one of the betters.

"Well, Crown Prince, do you want to pass along the truth to your pet toad, or shall I?" Andianna questioned archly. Keir remained noncommittal.

"What's she talking about, Keir? Huh? What's she mean?"

"Calm down, Armond. And if you're so concerned about being subtle, keep your voice down." Keir scanned the trees ahead and was relieved to recognize the markers he had noted a day earlier on his unannounced solo trek, which had been written off to all concerned as a headache that forced him to spend an entire afternoon in his quarters with the shades drawn. If Andi only knew he had come a-hunting Duncan Vaughn alone, she'd have skinned him herself.

He had originally planned to slither into the camp that day, but after evaluating the scene he'd realized that however high his own opinion of his abilities, he would be better off with someone watching his back. Duncan had gotten downright paranoid in his old age. Not that twenty-three was exactly ancient, but he was certainly carrying more guards these days. But then, Keir reasoned, Duncan had reason to be paranoid, with a very real threat of getting shot down by his own people. Keir sighed as he guided the horse to a nearby tree and dismounted less smoothly than intended. *Damn leg.* A light breeze lifted the thick tangle of blond hair at his neck and tickled the sweat on his back and sides into shivers.

"But what does she *mean,* Keir? What's she talking about?" Armond had lowered his whine to a whisper as he followed Keir's lead and jumped to the ground, securing his own reins to the lower branches.

"What I *mean* is that your hero here is still going to walk right into Duncan Vaughn's arms, whether he does it on horseback or on foot."

Keir smiled to himself at Andianna's sharp rasp as he finished lashing the reins. He could hear the tension that was twisting his sister's low tones into the strident syllables.

"B-b-but Keir...y-you, you...well, you *can't...*"

"Armond. *Calm.* And both of you, hush." Keir turned, lifting a hand as he spoke softly. Andianna's green eyes leveled him a withering stare that told him what she thought of being hushed. Keir's mouth curled slightly; it was hardly light enough to interpret her expression, but he had seen it enough times to be able to draw it on the most moonless of nights. "Now, I know you have reservations about this, but I'm confident about what I'm doing."

"Why, Keir? Duncan is a slimy bastard. He's pond scum. He is *not* reasonable! You can't predict what he's going to do. Why do you think he won't have you killed on sight? Why *wouldn't* his people kill you on sight?" Armond's voice was rising again in anxiety. Keir wished desperately he could have left him home, but Armond had long been a sort of self-designated bodyguard to the prince, and he wasn't easy to elude. Besides, despite his mothering tendencies, he could be damn useful to have around.

"They won't kill me on sight because I am rather recognizable. You don't shoot an arrow into the crown prince of the neighboring territory without checking with your master first. They won't be expecting me. I'll have the element of surprise, which despite being a hackneyed ploy is really quite useful. Now then—"

"You are not invincible, Crown Prince." Andianna's soft voice cut him off. She stood stiffly, arms crossed, staring directly at him. He lifted a hand to the brown curls lashed tight at her nape.

"I realize that."

"Do you, now? Do you also therefore realize that this is a slightly stupid idea?" She lifted her chin away from his caressing fingers.

"No, of course not." Keir lightened his voice and let his hand settle on the cool armor on her shoulder. "This is not a slightly stupid idea. This is an extremely stupid idea." With that he turned and slid into the shadows. Andianna rolled her eyes at Armond, and the two of them coasted after him.

Duncan Vaughn's Ervane forces had been encroaching on Rastoria territory for well over a week. As Duncan Vaughn himself was along for the ride, there was no question but an all-out offensive was somewhere in the making. The two territories sat close enough together for it to be noticed when the ruler of one took up residence on the moving campsites of the cavalry.

The Vaughn castle sat well back on the mountain that took up much of the Ervane territory. Rastoria was to the seaward side of the mountain's foothills; the other sides melted down into Ervane valleys. The current Ervane camp had traversed the border river and was established within Rastoria. The Rastorian outpost that had been watching the river crossing was no more. After all, it had not been armed for defense against a concentrated attack. Ervane had been quiet, and Vaughn had his own internal troubles. War had not been in the offing a mere fortnight previous.

* * *

The three pressed up against the trees, watching the armed sentries fondle their crossbows. Keir's hand brushed his sword hilt, his fingers dancing on the surface of the tooled scabbard. Andianna's breathing was to his left, as usual. Armond knelt at his right, peering out of the foliage.

"All right," Armond whispered hoarsely, "now, if we just take out one or two of the guards quietly and do our best not to draw attention, we can—"

"Mm-hmm." Keir's response was distracted; he was concentrating closely on the guard who was making the circuit closest to their trees. The sentry's hands were steady, and in the glare of the moon Keir could see she was not one of Duncan's greener recruits. *Not likely to be an itchy bow hand, then.* Of course, it was a guess, but so was most of life. As the guard crossed to the point where the trio would be most visible, Keir stepped out directly into her line of sight and lifted a hand. "Oh, guard..."

In the Noble Tent, Duncan Vaughn lounged against the wooden table, languidly studying the tentative battle plans to drive Rastoria straight into the sea. And drown Keir Alienor right along with it. Nothing was firmed up yet. This excursion over the river had been a test of the Rastorians' battle-readiness, with a full-scale retreat plan ready and waiting. Duncan was supremely confident that Rastoria would not have attempted an armed reprisal if their border forces had beaten him back originally; they were so given to diplomacy, those Rastorians. They would most likely have petitioned the Most High Royal House in Lustane and sent messengers to Ervane with documents questioning why he had violated their border. They probably would have even expected a response from him. Now, wouldn't it have been enjoyable if they'd sent a full-detail message brigade with Crown Prince Keir as the centerpiece? Duncan grinned darkly and drove his dagger into the sketched symbol of the Rastorian noble house.

As it turned out, none of that had happened, because none of it was necessary. The border forces had toppled with disgusting ease. Keir had grown soft in his old age. Rastoria had truly been taken by surprise, and the Ervane camp had established itself within the coastal territory's outlying lands. Rastoria had been oddly quiet, however. No hysterical responses, though a messenger had been dispatched to Lustane.

The High Court at Lustane would stay out of this if at all possible, Duncan was gambling. Two small territories with a touchy history would not draw much attention with "border squabbling." And that was the picture the

Ervane representative to the Lustane High Court had been instructed to por-
tray. The Most High Royal House made it a principle not to bind the nobility
too tightly—which accounted for why each of the territories maintained its
own royal lineage while being pledged to Lustane as allies and subjects. The
territorial nobility were regarded, and treated, as status equals by the Lustane
High Court. Little overt intervention was practiced on a governmental scale.
The collection of territories under Lustane "rule" was fairly loosely bound.
No, Duncan was not overly concerned with reprisal from Lustane.

But again, Rastoria had been rather too quiet. Duncan was not a man to
underestimate his rivals, and people called him paranoid with good reason.
His suspicious nature was asserting itself. He did not trust this situation, and
he was not convinced, as many of his captains were, that this heralded easy
victory. Keir, from appearances, may have grown soft, but he was still Keir.
The same Keir whose nose Duncan had broken—how many times?—during
their fostered teenage years together at the Lustane High Court. Twice? Or
was it three times? And he'd always come back for more. Keir was...Keir.
And he was not in the seat of power yet in Rastoria, as Duncan was in
Ervane. Keir's parents ruled still—which may have been a more accurate
reason for Rastoria's perceived softness. Duncan's own father was more than
a year dead, and the rumors of his poisoning the old man notwithstanding,
Duncan had assumed the throne. With a bit of help...

Ceylon materialized on the opposite side of the table, as if summoned by
the thought. "My lord." Somehow when Ceylon spoke there was little sub-
servience in his address to his superiors. "My lord" from Ceylon was rather
on the same level as "You insignificant speck." Duncan raised clear, cold
gray eyes to the sorcerer staring down at him. Duncan would have been quite
a gorgeous nobleman, with his angular, aristocratic face surrounded by
thick, straight, deep sienna hair and a truly magnificent body standing more
than six feet. Where Keir's illusionary perfection needed distance to uphold
the image, Duncan's presence withstood close inspection. No, it was more
the coldness that never quite left the elegant facial bones, holding them set
in detached disdain, that kept Duncan from being truly captivating. He simply was not a nice person, and the face and granite eyes displayed every facet
of his manipulative, calculating, vicious soul. The calm smile that slowly
molded Duncan's lips as he drilled Ceylon with his dead stare was more sinister than the dagger that his long-fingered hand now pried easily out of the
map parchment and the table beneath it.

"What do you want, Ceylon? I'm busy." The cool, clipped tones breathed from between sharp white teeth that clicked together in impatience. "The Rastorians are too quiet. Or are you too going to tell me all about how we have nothing to worry about?"

"Oh no, my lord." Ceylon curled his blue robes about him and stared implacably straight back into those large gray eyes; he was one of only three people who had ever mastered the art of meeting that gaze unflinchingly. One of the others was still at the High Court at Lustane, making her mark on the Most High Royal House. The third was...who knew where. Duncan's eyes wandered back to the dagger resting in his relaxed fingers. "No, not at all," Ceylon continued. "I believe quite the opposite and invite you to join my skepticism." His black brows lifted in perfect unison, his face smooth and neutral.

"Stop talking circles, Ceylon," Duncan gritted out between his teeth, longing to aim the dagger with one perfect arch into the wizard's chest. Fortunately, his self-preservation streak was just a bit too strong for that. "Get to the point." As he spoke the tent seemed fairly to vibrate with a sudden commotion outside. His head snapped up. "What is going on?"

"*That,* my lord, is the point you were so recently asking me to explicate."

Duncan looked back at Ceylon with a touch of confusion, covered immediately with icy arrogance. "What are you saying, Ceylon? You are incredibly tiresome when you play these intelligence games."

Ceylon's face twitched, and Duncan had a sudden suspicion he was keeping himself with an effort from laughing. Tense fury boiled in his throat. Before it could erupt, Ceylon clarified condescendingly: "That, my lord, is Keir Alienor."

Duncan's mouth dropped. He seemed to be choking. He could not camouflage his reaction, and he didn't even try. "Keir?"

"Yes. He just walked into the camp. He and two followers. Man and woman. They were apprehended on the eastern perimeter. Although I do believe 'apprehended' is giving the sentries a bit too much credit, as the three mostly just walked out of the forest with their hands up."

Duncan caught his breath, and an expression of ferocious glee lit his fine bones. "Keir Alienor just walked into my campsite?"

"I believe that is what I said, my lord." At this point Ceylon allowed himself a small smile. It *was* rather good fortune.

"Oh, how utterly perfect. How could the imbecile know just exactly what I wanted? Walking directly into my best-laid plan."

"I suggest caution, my lord, in this as in all else. He is not a fool."

"Oh, I know, Ceylon. I know. Better than you, I daresay. You just do your part." Duncan shot him a steely glare.

"Provoke his emotions to run as high as possible. I will then be in a position to…influence those emotions."

"I believe provocation is well within my abilities, Ceylon. Well, I must go greet my guest. Why don't you disappear yourself, hmm?" Duncan flicked a hand at the wizard as he uncoiled from his chair and stood to his full height. Ceylon was gone instantaneously, with the disconcerting habit he had of following orders exactly when least expected.

"I cannot believe you *waved down a guard.* By the Lady, you ill-begotten idiot, what were you *thinking?*" Andianna had been muttering to him out of the corner of her mouth since they had been escorted in from the perimeter. Keir hadn't bothered to answer. He could Sense Ceylon hovering somewhere nearby. Gita, Rastoria's sorcerer, had warded him against possible ensorcellment. The wards had better hold. If not…

He could see they were being guided, none too gently, toward the Noble Tent. Armond stumbled along on his other side in fuming silence. He still had not sufficiently recovered from Keir stepping from the trees right before his eyes and beckoning the guard over, like an ambitious tavern whore calling to a prospective customer.

They pulled to a stop in front of the Noble Tent, and as the front flaps wavered and retracted, Armond found his voice. "I told you this was a bad idea," he groaned softly. Andianna, on the other hand, had dropped to stone silence. The black-clad figure of Duncan Vaughn stepped into the light of the torches. The flickering shadows turned his face to a vicious mask, while the flickering lights turned Keir's hair to pure gold.

"Keir." The voice was a resonant purr.

"Duncan." The response was a cool neutral.

"It's been so long. And here you are come all this way to visit me. I'm touched and flattered."

"What are you doing here, Duncan? I didn't come 'all this way' to play the word games Ceylon's taught you." Keir's voice had a weary edge. This had to go just exactly right, or he could be dead. All three of them might already be for all intents and purposes dead.

Duncan threw back his head and laughed out loud, a full-throated expression of true amusement that turned no few heads in the camp, as soldiers of all ranks heard that particular sound from their leader for perhaps the first time. "Yes, his verbal exercises are a bit tiresome, aren't they? I was telling him that myself just this evening. But won't you step into the tent—all of you." Turning, Duncan led the three into the tent, followed closely by as many armed guards.

Once inside, Duncan whirled and grinned. "Now, who have we here?" He was looking at Andianna. "You," his hand lifted in Armond's direction dismissively, "I know. But you," the fingers turned to point directly over Keir's left shoulder, "I have not had the distinct honor of meeting." Andianna's blank green gaze slapped his face unwavering, and with some surprise he added a fourth name to the list he kept in his head. "Your sister, no doubt. Little Andi. You have changed some since last I'd seen or heard of you."

"And you," Andianna spoke precisely, without expression, "have changed little, as I hear. Still the vicious, traitorous tyrant who broke my brother's nose."

Duncan laughed again. "Why, Keir, she's delightful." He dropped his hands to his hips and turned back to the slight figure in the middle. Without warning the sword was suddenly in his hand, and his voice dropped all traces of conversational artifice. Flicking his eyes between Armond and Andi, he encompassed both of them with a gesture. "Now, both of you, get out."

Everyone jerked but Keir, who stood calmly with the black cloak draping over his previously emptied scabbard. Duncan addressed the startled guards. "I do not wish to repeat myself. Remove them and yourselves now."

"But my lord—" The sentry Keir had originally appraised spoke up. With one glance she fell silent.

"Give him his sword before you go." Duncan spoke directly to her.

She stared at him in astonishment. "My lord, I must object—"

Duncan cut her off with a sharp hand motion. "Now."

Keir was handed back his sword, which he kept in hand rather than resheathing. "Now, wait a minute," Andi was protesting loudly as she and Armond were dragged from the tent. Both of them kicked up an immediate struggle, and more guards were called in to assist in the removal. As the dust settled and the torches stopped their mad dancing, Keir and Duncan stood facing each other in the tent.

"I trust they will come to no harm." Keir's voice was soft and low.

Duncan's smile was pure malice. "You have an odd habit of misplacing your trust, Keir." The gray eyes so much like Duncan's own stared back at him without reaction—the gray eyes that reminded both of them that there was some common ancestry not so far back in the Alienor and Vaughn lineages. It was difficult to say if the reminder helped or hindered the present situation.

"I trust they will come to no harm." Keir repeated the sentence like an incantation or a geas. Duncan's eyes narrowed in reawakened suspicion.

"What *are* you doing here, Keir?" Duncan extended his sword and caught the edge of Keir's cloak. "And in those dreary colors. Why, aren't you playing my part? Skulking about at night wearing all black?"

"And isn't that my question, Duncan? What are *you* doing here? This is Rastoria—or was, the last time I checked."

Duncan laughed, a nasty sound unrelated to his initial burst of hilarity outside the tent. "Check again, Crown Prince. It is looking a bit Ervanian these days."

Keir sighed. "Well, then, you've answered your own question. That is what I am doing here. And yes, these are your colors." He gestured to the shadowy outfit he wore, a shabby mirror of Duncan's shimmering black leather and silk. "No offense intended. Just didn't want to...surprise your sharpshooters."

Duncan quirked an eyebrow and the corner of his mouth simultaneously. "And you accuse me of playing Ceylon's word games. Well, enough, enemy mine. Let's have at, shall we?" The conversational tone was back, and Keir didn't particularly like it. "Rather well-matched, aren't we? If I remember correctly." Duncan shrugged out of his own cape and lifted his sword arm in the en garde position.

Keir stared at him for a long moment. This was not a terrific sign. "Fine, Duncan. We'll play it your way." He unlatched his cloak and let it drop, discarded his scabbard, and set forward.

Back and forth over the dirt floor they sparred. Back against the table, toward the door flaps, guttering the torches as they went, the swords gleamed and flashed, ringing defiantly one against the other. Duncan had a size advantage; Keir had a hard-won and well-maintained skill. Closing, he battled Duncan back against one of the thick wooden tent supports. With a clash of steel the swords met and locked, with Keir in the stronger position, the sharp edges nearing Duncan's throat inch by inch. Duncan glared into that slightly lopsided face and felt the rising tides of conflicting emotions battering at his concentrated detachment. The lines dividing strong emotion are so fine, and his anger was acting as pure catalyst. This was what he was supposed to be provoking in Keir, not himself. The bonds he had poured years of bitterness into were snapping one by one. Just a little bit longer...

Sweat coursed down both faces, and breath came in labored gasps. "Yield, Duncan?" Keir pressed forward. Duncan's panting face was nose to crooked nose with him. And as the oh-so-similar gray eyes locked as firmly as the swords, Keir saw exactly what he had been counting on, gambling on, for this entire foolhardy "mission." A bit more surprising was the surge of response those eyes called up in himself....

Both swords released simultaneously and hit the floor in opposite directions. The two heaving figures pressed together in a grapple as close and intense as the one just broken. Lips met and fought for supremacy, tongues reenacting the fencing battle. Hands, fingers scrabbled on chain mail, and armor rasped on armor. Duncan forced Keir backward against the table, his legs pressing between Keir's thighs. Keir broke from his mouth. "Slow down before you lose a finger," he gasped, letting go of Duncan's neck and fumbling with both hands on the mail vest. Duncan gladly relinquished Keir's metal casings and began on his own. Armor clinked to the ground, scattering about the tent, and Duncan lunged again, lifting Keir to the table, hands stripping the leggings from the slim, uneven hips. Groaning and whispering, they dropped into a dance they'd learned by heart years earlier.

Neither noticed the vaporous presence of Ceylon's blue-shrouded figure just outside the tent, with arms lifted, conducting the music they moved to.

"What was Keir thinking? What possibly could have been in his mind?" Armond's whimpering sounded loud in the tiny pitch-black tent.

"Keir's motivation is hardly our most pressing concern." Andianna hissed fiercely. "Start concentrating on how to get us, and him, out of this marvelous spot he's gotten us into. Although it would serve the bastard right if we left him here."

"Andianna! You wouldn't...you *couldn't!*" Armond's appalled voice started to climb yet again.

Andi rolled her eyes in the gloom. He was the most overreactive, thin-nerved person she'd ever had the misfortune to deal with. "For Lady's sake, Armond, shut up. No, if I can help it, I'm not going to leave Keir here." She sighed. "Although we may not have much to say about any of it. Now, *will* you help me get my boot off? There's a blade there."

"I thought they took all your knives."

"No one ever gets all of my knives."

"But how—"

"It's a long story. Shut up and concentrate. I can't see a thing."

Duncan lay on his left side, staring intently down at the crumpled blond at his side. The piled silks and cushions at the very rear of the Noble Tent had eventually been a bit more inviting than the rough wooden table—although the table had certainly been entertaining. So much for the battle plans. Keir was curled, breathing heavily, his left arm thrown over his eyes. Duncan's eyes lingered on the woven betrothal ring on Keir's finger. The anger kindled, but he doused it with care. *Not yet, not yet.*

Duncan couldn't quite tell if Keir had slipped away into sleep yet. This would be the telling moment. Had Ceylon come through?

Keir stirred. The arm extended over his head, stretching, and the odd, somewhat bird-shaped purplish blotch on his inner left shoulder flexed. Absently Duncan's right fingers brushed over the similar mark on his own skin. The falcon in flight—or so the nobility liked to proclaim. Duncan had always thought he could better see a wilting rose. Ah, but Father had always accused him of being cynical. The white-tipped golden lashes fluttered, and the gray eyes that were almost too large for the face blinked open. Duncan's breath caught, and he carefully schooled his nonexpression.

Keir released a long breath, staring wordlessly up at the carved face, which told him absolutely nothing, as usual. His gaze zeroed in on Duncan's right eye. Lady bless. The old quirk as still there. The lid trembled almost imperceptibly, but Keir was an old hand at being at close enough quarters with Duncan to notice the telltale sign of his insecurity. How small a manifestation, how deep a well. The slight tic made Keir feel immensely better, however, and with renewed confidence he let his mouth relax into the Grin. Tenderly he lifted his fingers and brushed the very tips against Duncan's right ear, catching the bottom-most gold hoop on the down stroke. Duncan, visibly relaxing at the first indication of the smile, winced openly as the deft tug caught him unaware. At his sharp cry Keir laughed throatily.

"You," Duncan twisted Keir's fingers away from his adornments and forced his hands back to the pillow above his head, "you—" The wild edge of that smile was taking Duncan apart bit by bit. He groaned softly and lost the thread of his threat. "You gorgeous, beautiful thing, you." Duncan's gray eyes lit with a besotted glow.

Keir snorted. "Oh, sure. From about twenty feet away, that is. In the right light. In profile."

Duncan shook his head, releasing Keir's wrists and caressing his face with his knuckles. "No, no. You are lovely, you must know that." He stroked the hair back from Keir's temple, then traced the line of Keir's nose.

"Mmm-hmm." Keir's brows arched. "And of course we won't mention what you had to do with one of the reasons my face is quite as 'lovely' as it is."

Duncan winced again. "Never going to let me forget that one, are you, my sweet?" His eyes took on a shade of regret, and Keir marveled yet again at how beautiful Duncan's face became when there was a touch of expression in it. It was the dead look that chilled people to the bone. The utter remoteness. Keir knew intimately the pain and insecurity cloaked by that removed countenance. Duncan had learned long ago that removing himself from the world made it much easier to deal with. Keir thought back on the number of times he had wished for just the barest touch of that ability.

With an effort he pulled himself back to the conversation at hand, trailing his own fingers down Duncan's chest and thumbing his left nipple. "Hmm, never going to let you forget that *one*, Duncan? If I remember correctly, there were *three* times you were responsible for my seeing stars."

Duncan gasped lightly. Swallowing hard as the nimble fingers twisted gently, he tried to force some semblance of normalcy into his voice. "Oh, now, come come. By the third time you can hardly blame me. By that point your nose had just gotten so…breakable. I hardly did a thing."

"No-o-o. Of course not. Managed to win the competition, though, didn't you?" Keir smiled sweetly, his slightly crooked teeth flashing in the firelit interior of the tent. Becoming serious, he pushed Duncan away firmly and propped himself on one elbow. "But really, we do have a bit more important things to discuss than you breaking my nose at fifteen."

Duncan settled onto his back petulantly, annoyed at the sudden discontinuation of the thoroughly enjoyable, if torturous, foreplay. "Like what?"

"Duncan…"

"Oh, don't be a bore, Keir. Are you really going to tell me you didn't enjoy that?"

"Of course not. I'm just a little…confused, is all." Keir's brows drew together. "I didn't exactly plan for this to happen, you know."

Duncan shifted uncomfortably and evaded Keir's eyes. "Well, it did. Nature takes its course and all that. Apparently those old feelings were closer to the surface than either of us realized. I'm a bit startled by all this as well, you realize," Duncan added quickly. He paused a moment. "What are you doing wandering into my camp, by the way? Pushing your reputed luck just a bit, aren't you, my dear?"

Keir shrugged and smiled slyly. "Gambling as usual. I was wagering on you not stabbing me on sight—for old times' sake."

"Wagering with your life—fairly high stakes." Duncan was having a slight difficulty breathing.

"Yes," Keir responded simply. The guileless eyes stared with calm confidence. Duncan felt his chest constrict painfully at the realization that Keir still had a high enough opinion of him to trust him with his life. Trust *him*. The old fingers began to pluck the strings of Duncan's atrophied heart with the same precision and flexibility they had at fifteen. *Where in the Depths did that unshakable faith come from?* Keir had always seen more looking at Duncan than Duncan himself had ever seen in the mirror. Obviously, he still did. And, now, true to form, how had Duncan repaid that belief in the essential goodness of humanity...?

"Keir, I believe we have discussed your terrible penchant for misplacing your trust." Duncan's voice was a husky vibrato, a far cry from his usual frigid, controlled tones. Nobody could demolish his state of mind like this odd little blond. Maybe this really wasn't such a hot idea.

Keir smiled beatifically. "Oh, I know. Armond and Andi think I've gone completely round the bend. They knew I was planning on coming directly into your camp; they were both ready to send me for a long talk with a healing priestess!"

Duncan rolled his eyes expressively. "Oh, I'm quite certain. I know your pretty little feather-headed bodyguard has just the *highest* opinion of me."

"Oh, yes. I believe the words he used were 'slimy bastard' and 'pond scum.' " Keir was fighting his lips into a serious expression.

Duncan's eyes narrowed. "And your sister?" The words slid silkily across Keir's skin, raising the fine blond hairs on end.

"She just says you're dangerous."

"Perceptive girl, that. So you were counting on walking into camp and not getting strung up on the basis of your cute little ass. Correct? Now then, what did you have in mind for this little 'confrontation,' since you weren't expecting sweaty sex on my battle plans?"

"Well, I...hoped we might have a...discussion about what exactly you're doing invading Rastoria."

"Oh, so you *did* notice! Didn't know that you even gave me a thought these days." The sarcasm curled heavily about the words, the bitterness welling up despite Duncan's attempt to leash it.

"Duncan—"

"Keir—" Duncan mimicked Keir's exasperated tone.

"You know I didn't have anything to say about our getting separated. You didn't either. We're nobility, Duncan; our lives aren't our own, and they never have been."

Duncan sighed and made a wry face. Again his fingers coasted over the "flying falcon" that he preferred to think of as the dead rose. "Wonder if we could get these things removed," he mumbled reflexively.

"No. I've seen some attempts at it. It isn't pretty. Birthmarks aren't washable. Anyway, I came because I thought I would probably be the only person who might be able to talk to you. By all that's holy, the rest of the country is ready to grill you over an open flame and feed the remains to the sea gods. Why are you invading Rastoria?"

Duncan grinned evilly. "What makes them think the sea gods would have me?" He shifted suddenly and with a ripple of muscle brought himself up on his elbow, mirroring Keir's posture, face a breath from Keir's. "So tell me, my dear, since we're discussing familial duties: How is the Lady Mirette?"

Keir snapped away as if burned. His eyes kindled with a touch of the anger that was so slow to catch. "You always did know just how to ruin a mood, Duncan." Keir turned sharply, ignoring Duncan's rejoinder, "You wanted to discuss more serious matters." He swung his legs to the dirt floor, standing stiffly and searching the tent for his leggings. Finding them, he guided them over his feet and calves with jerky movements. "How the Depths should I know how Mirette is? I'm only supposed to *marry* the woman. We don't actually talk or anything. She seemed fine the last two times I saw her—over the course of eight months, that is." He paused in his caustic tirade, his voice dropping as he stood at a bit of a loss, shoulders sinking dejectedly, staring at the front of the tent. "And you know I didn't have anything to say about that either."

Duncan didn't move. He stared at Keir's back, the aforementioned lovely ass, molded by the skintight leggings, stirring Duncan's lust even as his emotions roiled. *You could have fought for us,* his mind screamed; *You always had some damn "noble" cause to fight for. Why not us? Weren't we worth it? Was I ever anything to you besides a broken toy to be fixed like everything else you ever touched in your life? The golden boy with the golden touch. And I must have been such a wonderfully hopeless project. Oh, yes,*

Keir, you fixed me just fine. Teach me how to feel so I can really feel *the agony when you walk away without a backward glance to fulfill your "noble" duties. Oh, you fixed me, Keir. You mended all the cracks. But somewhere along the way you got me addicted to the cure. Your parents would have listened to you. Like my father never listened to me. You had a chance. You had the only chance. And you didn't even bother. And now you're marrying that woman....*

His thoughts seared his mental pathways, leaving stinging welts. Nothing was coherent, and none of it would get past his frozen throat. His mind spun faster that his tongue could possibly follow, and he finally managed to spit out "You're marrying that woman, and you have the gall to *stand* there and ask me why I'm invading Rastoria?"

Slowly Keir's shoulders stiffened. With an effort Duncan unclenched his teeth and tried to focus his eyes past the red haze. He'd said something he hadn't quite meant to say. Now, what was it?

Keir was turning, slowly, ever so slowly. As he faced the makeshift camp bed, he stared at the shaking form still tensely stretched on the silks. "Are you telling me—" he stopped. Took a breath. Tried again. His mouth formed the words with an effort. "Are you telling me—are you saying—you invaded Rastoria because I'm *engaged?*"

Duncan fancied he could actually see steam rising from Keir's blond head. "Well, now, Keir love, I don't know if I would put it exactly that way...."

"That was easier than I thought, Andi."

"You know, Armond, I'm beginning to see why Keir says you are handy to have along." Andi shook her head in amazement, staring down at the four guards who had stood around their tent. After some hairy hours in the black of the tent trying to slice each other's ropes while sitting back-to-back, they had slid out to take on the guards. She was good. She had no questions about her own skill. But she had to admit that Armond had quite a flair for immediate dispatchment with minimum fuss. And for such a nervy little bastard. For all his wet nurse overprotectiveness, he had a smooth, calm presence in hand-to-hand, as the three dead guards would have attested to if they'd had the option. Andi's knife lay buried to the hilt in the fourth. She would have taken on another, but Armond had already snapped three necks with quiet precision. "Had a little assassin training, have we, then?"

Armond ducked his head shyly and shrugged. "Can we find Keir now?"

Andi smiled humorlessly. "I believe we won't have far to look." At Armond's puzzled expression, she sighed. Smooth, calm, deadly—and thick as a castle wall. "I think it's a guarantee that he's still back with Duncan. You know, I'm deciding Keir has a bit of explaining to do about why he was quite so calm about walking into this camp." Her brow furrowed as she remembered her brother's complacent expression in the Noble Tent when they had been ordered to leave. He'd known they wouldn't be hurt. How?

"Uh, Andi? How are we going to get to the Noble Tent? I mean, this is an enemy encampment."

Andi shrugged indifferently. "We walk through camp, and if anybody asks us where we're going, we tell them Duncan Vaughn sent for us. Since we aren't exactly being contradicted, they'll probably believe us. They know their master is a strange duck. But let's get rid of these bodies. Really, Armond, that was incredibly impressive. Could you show me that neck snap?"

Keir's dumbfounded expression would have been amusing if it were not for the fact that it was veritably sizzling around the edges. Duncan was expecting a lightning shower at any minute. "You *invaded my country* because I got *engaged?*" By now Keir had just about hit soprano.

"Keir dear, I believe you have quite a future in the bardic guild. I didn't know you could reach that note. Well, except for that one time we were— uh, swimming—together in the lake at Lustane. Mmm, water has such an …interesting effect. Remember? But that was before your voice had finished changing." Duncan's conversational tone was matched by his calm air as he levered himself up off the silks and moved toward Keir.

Keir's hands shot up, palms outward, holding him at bay. "Stop—right— there. Answer me. You actually brought an army across the border because I got betrothed?"

Duncan sighed expansively and dropped his fists to rest on his bony hips. "Keir, why do you insist on asking questions you really don't want answered? Hmm? You know you don't want to know the true answer. Part of you is positively dying to hear me say that yes, I brought an army over your border, attacked your homeland, started the makings of a war, all because you got engaged. I mean, honestly, that would just be the most incredible compliment. You're so excited by that thought, you're practically panting. And don't bother denying it." Duncan dropped his eyes pointedly to the thin material stretched over Keir's crotch, and Keir flushed darkly, shifting from foot to foot uselessly. "On the other hand, you are utterly repulsed by the very idea that I could actually make motions to start a war, kill soldiers of my own and soldiers of Rastoria, endanger uncounted other people, risk Lustanian wrath, for such a small, insignificant, *personal* thing as the fact that the man I loved is getting married to some…princess." He spat the word like venom sucked from a snakebite. "So why ask, Keir? Why? You don't really want to know." His eyes flashed silver, but the dead look was back on his face.

Keir swallowed hard. His voice was quiet and shook slightly when he spoke. "Answer me. Please."

Duncan stared hard at him. Walking slowly toward the still figure, who didn't ward him off this time, he lifted his arms and drew the cooled body against his naked form. He towered over Keir by a head. With one hand he gently tilted Keir's chin up to look directly into those mirror eyes. In a dead monotone he answered, "Yes, Keir. You see. I was right all those years ago. I truly was not made for this nobility thing. I haven't the self-discipline to put away my personal, emotional reactions and act in the best interests of my country and my 'people.' I'm not you, Keir. I'm selfish. Damned selfish. I've been looking for a reason to invade Rastoria since I took over the throne. Because of you. Dear Daddy was always too reticent. But dear Daddy is dead now. I'm on the throne, I wear the crown, I make the rules. And I got pissed off." Duncan's fingers, digging into Keir's chin, were shaking. His eyebrows arched as his eyes lit with an unholy fire. "I received the engagement announcement, Keir. All gilt-edged parchment and scroll and golden royal seals. And I got angry. So I attacked. It was the push I needed." Duncan let go of his chin, let go of him completely, and stepped back, his entire form trembling. "Satisfied?" His cool tone was belied by the physical tremors.

Keir felt as if he was fifteen again, with a broken, bloodied nose, staring at the breaker, looking at a shell of a person and seeing the core that everyone else seemed positive did not exist. That day he had reached out a hand almost blindly, instinctively, starting something that was now sending rippling effects outward, ever outward, and affecting two territories and scores of people. One thought echoed in his mind. *Here we go again.* But this time his eyes were open and seeing as he reached out the hand.

Duncan forced a hand through his hair. Focusing on the crumpled maps on the table before him, he started when he felt the hand stroke his shoulder and then move lingeringly down his back to rest on the curve of his ass. He turned his head to face Keir as Keir pressed against his side and nuzzled nose and lips into Duncan's throat, sinking his teeth lightly. Keir's other hand crept to the front of Duncan's thighs, stroking and seeking. With little effort he guided Duncan back the few steps to the silks and sank on top of him with dramatic effect.

Andianna and Armond reached the Noble Tent with adrenaline coursing and no small amount of giddiness. Andi couldn't believe the fearful idiocy of Duncan's people. "Well, here we go." With a quick glance at Armond, she pushed through the tent flap.

Duncan and Keir both whirled at the strangled noises from the doorway. Keir turned pure white.

"Oh, Keir! Please!" Andi was standing with a pained expression, one hand pressed to her forehead. "*Him?* Gods above, below, and in between, don't you have *any* taste, boy?"

Keir leaped to his feet. "Andi! This isn't what it looks like...." Andianna's brows reached her hairline, and Keir flushed. "Well, all right, it *is* what it looks like, but I can explain—"

The strangled noise was coming from Armond, and he was still gurgling. He was looking decidedly poleaxed. Duncan levered himself off the bed and swept up a drape of silk. "Won't you come in? Or rather, since you already are in, won't you sit down? Glass of wine, Armond?" His voice dripped coy sweetness. Armond was turning purple.

"Armond, "Keir begged, "listen, please."

Armond turned on him with a wounded face, then whirled. "I'll wait outside," he choked in Andi's direction and stormed out.

Andi glared at the two men. "Yezounds, Keir, you know Armond's never been my pick of the litter for you to be bedding down with, but when I was pestering you to find a new mate, I was really hoping for an *improvement*. This is disgusting!"

"Ah ha! I knew you were bedding that twit. Really, Keir—"

"Duncan, *quiet*. Andi, please. Just stop. Listen."

"I'm listening."

"So am I," Duncan chimed.

Dead silence permeated the tent. Duncan draped a second silk over Keir's shoulders and grinned evilly at Andianna from behind Keir's back.

Andi finally broke the silence. "Since I assume the frontal assault is called off for the night—well, at least the one that was going on outside—I rather think this is a discussion better held tomorrow. Maybe by then your tongue will have...recovered." Her eyes flayed her brother, who dropped his own to the dirt floor. "Vaughn, I'm sleeping in your barracks tents. On your orders. Good night." Turning, she strode back out into the night to collect Armond and find a reasonably comfortable place to lie down and forget this day ever happened. Her arm stung from a slice it had received during the blind rope-removal, and she belatedly realized she was oozing blood. Ah, well, a healer shouldn't be impossible to find. After all, this was an army encampment. Lady Bless.

"Keir love, I said it before, and I repeat myself. She is delightful." Guiding Keir back to the silks, Duncan leaned over and kissed his neck, nibbling at the jeweled earlobe. "Must run in the family." His murmured words were lost as his tongue delved into the hollow of Keir's ear.

"Oh, dear. This has gotten rather muddled." Keir pushed his hair out of his eyes. "I really need to think this out." Duncan's tongue was proving a potent distraction. "I came here to stop an invasion. To do some diplomatic maneuvering."

Duncan chuckled deep in his throat. "Why, Keir, I believe you have succeeded quite admirably. Your diplomatic maneuvering is some of the best I've seen. Or watched. Or felt. Or—"

Keir couldn't stop the laugh that bubbled up. "You've made your point. Oh, what am I doing?" He rubbed his eyes with the heels of his hands and sagged against Duncan.

Duncan rolled him onto his back. "You're spreading those sweet thighs and—"

"Duncan! Don't you ever get tired?"

"Well, it has been awhile. But maybe I am being overly ambitious here." He ruffled Keir's hair. "It's just so marvelous having you again. I think this time I'll keep you. You know, Keir, I love your hair." His fingers combed the locks in question.

"I hate my hair. I can't do a thing with it."

"No, no. I adore your hair. I can think of *plenty* of things to do with it."

"You are a sick man."

"But you already knew that."

"Duncan, what is it going to take for you to call off the army?"

"Do you really want to talk about that now?" Fingers wandering, Duncan pressed kisses to Keir's chin, sucking Keir's lower lip between his sharp teeth.

"Mmm-hmmph..."

Duncan pulled back. "What was that, beautiful boy?"

Keir caught his breath. "I said, yes, I want to talk about it now. It is what I came here for."

Duncan grinned fondly down at him. "Well, dear, I just told you." At Keir's puzzled look Duncan elaborated. "I do believe this time I shall keep you."

Keir raised his eyebrows and shot Duncan a Look. "Excuse me."

Duncan settled back, and a set expression glided over his features, though his hands continued the caresses. "Call off this sham wedding. Come back to Ervane with me. Be my royal consort."

"Duncan!"

"What? It's hardly unthinkable. I'm a king now. I need a consort."

"My marriage is a political marriage, in case you hadn't guessed. We're planning for a tighter alliance with Navvarone. The High Court has given its blessings." Keir was staring at Duncan in wide-eyed amazement, wondering even as he posed the arguments against it why the idea sounded so...possible.

"If your father thinks he needs to marry you off to Mirette to secure good relations with Navvarone, he is missing the obvious fact that good relations with Ervane are a more...pressing matter. At least at the moment. You are, after all, being invaded. And, of course, you do only have one chance to marry off a child. And I am a king. Mirette is a princess. I win by rank. I want you."

"I'm the crown prince! I'm due to take over the crown of Rastoria. I'm supposed to be king, not king's consort. What is my country supposed to do?" Keir's voice was spiraling hysterically.

"You are missing the obvious fact that there is an extremely capable, confident, and most likely eager and willing candidate to take over Rastorian royal duties." Duncan, by contrast, was growing infinitely calmer. This debate had been planned in advance, with Ceylon arguing Keir's point of view and answers being carefully constructed. Heart in his throat, Duncan mouthed his role.

Keir stopped short. "Andianna."

"Andianna."

"Oh, my. My parents are going to be thrilled."

"They don't have much choice. I'm asking for a handfasting to seal a peace treaty. No more nor less than any royal marriage is usually based on. It just so happens I adore you as well. Lucky you." The odd note in Duncan's voice on the last words caused Keir to glance at him quickly, but Duncan's face was stony. "Anyway, it is either that or war. Are the Rastorians ready for war, Keir?" Duncan tried not to betray that he was holding his breath. *Ah, now, who was the gambler?*

Keir thought slowly. He knew the answer was no. He had convinced his father to hold out on a full armed reprisal until Keir had had a chance to try his gambit, despite the vague explanations he had given of his plan. Like all good patriots, his parents were misguided about the strength of Rastoria by comparison to Ervane's. They were basing their judgments on old King Rasten. But as Duncan had so bluntly pointed out, Rasten was dead, and Duncan was on the throne. Keir knew how ruthless Duncan could be. And he could see from the calm, light tone Duncan was using that he had thought this out carefully.

And aside from all that, the idea was amazingly seductive. The fingers stroking here, there, and everywhere were no little part of that. Where had this resurgence of feelings for Duncan welled up from? He hadn't been expecting that. Keir was slightly frightened by the extent to which he had been able to hide the depth of his emotions from himself over the past seven years. Now that he had recognized it, could he walk away from Duncan a second time?

And again, what would the consequences be? Keir's head was spinning. The consequences for Rastoria—or the consequences for himself, personally? Where was the clear-headed noble, who by birthmark and birthright had always chosen based on what was right for his people? Keir was dizzy and felt himself slipping. All the arrows seemed to be pointing in the same direction.

"Yes."

"What?"

"Yes."

If Keir had thought Duncan beautiful with any expression touching those fine bones and reaching into the gray eyes, he was completely unprepared for the blinding brilliance created by one simple word.

"You're going to *what?*"

"Andi, please—"

"Have you lost all hold on what little intelligence you possess, you worthless, featherbrained, ill-begotten son of a hedgehog? Have you taken complete leave of your senses? You're—you're—you're *consorting with Duncan Vaughn?*"

"Andi—"

"How could you possibly—what in the name of the Depths—what has possessed you? This is lunatic. You're engaged—you're the crown prince—"

"*Andianna—*"

"You, you, you—" Sudden silence followed the sputtering. The light was dawning. "You're the crown prince." The repetition was slower.

"Yes. Exactly. The crown goes to you."

"Brother dear, I wish you the best with your chosen path. Lady light your way."

Keir burst into a laugh. "Andi, dear—"

"Yes, love?"

"Tell Dad and Mum, would you?"

Keir ducked as any and all loose objects at hand flew at his head.

"What did Armond say?"

"I'd rather not talk about that, Duncan."

"Keir, really—"

"What do you want to hear? That he was devastated? Crushed? Incredibly hurt? Extremely angry? Yes, yes, yes, and yes. And then he looked me straight in the eye and said, 'I'll be waiting.' "

"I'd rather not talk about this, Keir."

"Thank you."

Ceylon lifted his wineglass and stared at the liquid.

"Scrying wine now, Ceylon?" Gita's crackling voice snapped him to attention. He eyed the old woman speculatively.

"Now, how did you convince Master Keir that you were warding him against ensorcellment of any and all kinds? Doesn't he know that is entirely impossible?"

Gita's laugh rang in the small stone room. She glanced out the window of the tower and watched the two men ride into the castle square. The blond head reflected the sunlight, while the dark figure seemed to absorb all light within a three-foot circumference. "He happens to believe me to be infallible and omnipotent—a misconception I do my very best to encourage. So I waved my hands and mumbled the recipe for bread pudding in Ancient Navvaronian. Rather the same sort of sleight of hand you pulled that night in back of the tent when you were 'casting' Master Duncan's ensorcellment to make Keir fall madly in love with him once again." The old woman's eyes sparkled. "He was rather...occupied at the time. Was it even necessary to go through the motions?"

Ceylon shrugged implacably. "Just in case he happened to...look up. He has the oddest flashes of powerful Sight at times. And he would have expected to see me." He joined her at the window, watching as the dark man swung down from his horse and stepped over to assist the blond in gaining the ground. He maintained a supportive arm about him while the blond limped stiffly toward the main castle and the grooms took over the mounts. Ceylon shook his head slightly. "What have we done?"

"Or rather, what have we *not* done, dear." The laughter rang again. With her usual uncanny perception, Gita zeroed in on the statement behind the statement. "But as for your real question—have we done the right thing?— that is moot. We've prevented a war, yes?"

Ceylon nodded, allowing himself a slight smile. "But if those two survive three weeks with each other, I'll eat my last alchemy experiment. Or your bread pudding. Whichever's worse."

Gita held on to the stone wall to steady herself as she roared. "Oh, I give them at least six weeks," she gasped. "They may surprise you yet, boy. They've surprised each other."

"No doubt," Ceylon responded dryly. He turned his piercing gaze on Gita. "Do you really believe getting them back together was wise?"

"Humans aren't known for their wisdom, Ceylon. And one of the most common mistakes of sorcerers is the assumption that the very definition of being sorcerers somehow elevates them to a place of wisdom above mere mortals. No, more to the point: Do you ever think the mere mortals will realize the truths about us sorcerers?"

"Best hope not, old woman." Ceylon turned and offered Gita his arm to escort her down the back stairs and out of the castle before Duncan and Keir happened to cross paths with her. "Or we'll be out of a job. Although I suppose you could always sell Navvaronian bread pudding recipes."

The Tale of Small Sarg
Samuel R. Delany

And if, tomorrow, all the history on which it is based is
found to be defective, the clay tablets wrongly interpreted,
or the whole formed out of a mistaken identification of
several periods and places, our reading of it will not be
affected in the slightest, for the Stranger, the City, the sights,
smells and sounds, formed by the poet out of history and
human activity, are real now at another level of being.
— Noel Stock, *Reading the Cantos*

In that brutal and barbaric time he was a real barbarian prince—which meant that his mother's brother wore women's jewelry and was consulted about animals and sickness. It meant at fourteen his feet were rough from scurrying up rough-barked palms and his palms were hard from pulling off the little nodules of sap from the places where new shoots had broken away. Every three or four years the strangers came to trade colored stones and a few metal cutting tools for them; as a prince he was expected to have collected the most. It meant that his hair was matted and that hunger was a permanent condition relieved every two or three days when someone brought in a piece of arduously tracked and killed game or a new fruit tree was (so rarely) found: for his tribe did not have even the most primitive of agricultural knowledge.

Everyone said fruit and game were getting scarcer.

To be a barbarian prince meant that when his mother yelled and shrieked and threatened death or tribal expulsion, people did what she said with dispatch—which included stoning Crazy Nargit to death. Crazy Nargit, within the space of a moon's coming and going, had gotten into an argument with a woman called Blin and killed her. Everyone said that Blin had been in the wrong, but still. Then Nargit got into another fight with Kudyuk and broke the young towheaded hunter's leg so that Kudyuk would be unable to walk for a year and would limp for the rest of his life. Also Crazy Nargit had killed a black female rat (which was sacred) and for two days wandered around the village holding it by the tail and singing an obscene song about a tree spirit and a moth. The rat, Small Sarg's mother insisted, made it obvious that Nargit wished for death.

His uncle, shaking his blue stone strings of women's ear bangles, had suggested simply driving Nargit from the tribe.

Sarg's mother said her brother was almost as crazy as Nargit; the tribe wasn't strong enough to keep Nargit out if he really wanted to come in and just kill people—which is what, from time to time, with clenched teeth and sweating forehead, shivering like a man just pulled out of the stream after being tied there all night (which several times they had had to do with Nargit when he was much younger), Nargit hissed and hissed and hissed was *exactly* what he wanted above all things to do. Nargit, Sarg's mother explained, was bound to get worse.

So they did it.

Stoning someone to death, he discovered, takes a long time. For the first hour of it, Nargit merely clung to a tree and sang another obscene song. After two more hours, because Sarg was a barbarian prince (and because he was feeling rather ill), he went and found a large rock and came back to the tree at the foot of which Nargit was now curled up, bloody and gasping—two small stones hit Sarg's shoulder, and he barked back for the others to cease. Then he smashed Nargit's skull. To be a barbarian prince meant that if he wanted to, he could put on women's jewelry and go off in the woods for long fasting periods and come back and be consulted himself. But he preferred men's jewelry; there was more of it, it was more colorful, and (because he was a prince) he had a better collection of it than most. His older and radiant sister, who had very red, curly hair and whose reign, therefore, as barbarian queen was expected to be quite spectacular, was already practicing the imperious ways of his mother.

Small Sarg was left pretty much alone.

The stretch of woods that went from just beyond the fork of the little river and the big stream (where many weasels lived) up to the first fissure in the rocky shelves (two days' walk all told) he knew to practically every tree, to every man path and deer path, to almost every rock and nearly every pebble; indeed, most of the animals that lived there he could identify individually as well as he could recognize all the human members of the Seven Clans, which, together, formed his principality. Outside that boundary there was nothing: and nothing was part of darkness, night, sleep, and death, all of which were mysterious and powerful and rightly the province of terror—all outside his principality was unknown, ignored, and monstrous. The Seven Clans consisted of the Rabbit Clan, the Dog Clan, the Green Bird Clan, and the Crow Clan—the last of which was his.

It was only after the strangers came and took him away that it occurred to him that there really were just four to the Seven Clans and that therefore his tribe had probably once been much larger. Suddenly Small Sarg began to conceptualize something that fitted very closely to a particular idea of history—which, because we have never truly been without it, is ultimately incomprehensible to the likes of you and me—only one of the many ideas he had been learning in the rough, brutal, and inhuman place they called civilization. Once that had happened, of course, he could never be a true barbarian again.

Beneath the thatched canopy that covered half the square, the market of Ellamon was closing down for the evening. Light slanted across dust scaled, like some reptile, with myriad overlapping footprints, a spilled tomato basket, a pile of hay, trampled vegetable leaves....A man with a wicker hamper roped around his shoulders stopped shouting, took a deep breath, and turned to amble away from under the canopy, off down an alley. A woman with a broom trailed a swirling pattern as she backed across the dust, erasing her own bare footprints among a dozen others. Another man pulled a toppling, overturning, ever-growing pile of garbage across the ground with a rake.

In one corner, by a supporting post, a fat man stopped wiping sweat from his bald head to brush at a bushy mustache in which, despite his pulling and plucking, were still some bread flakes and a bit of apple skin; also something stuck the corner hairs together at the left. His dark belly lapped a broad belt set with studs. A ring with a modern and sophisticated key, a double forefinger's length, hung at the hip of his red, ragged skirt.

Beside him on the ground, chained in iron collars, sat an old man, knees, elbows, and vertebrae irregular knobs in parchment skin otherwise as wrinkled as vellum many times crushed and straightened; and a woman who might have just seen twenty in gray rags, a strip of cloth tied around her head, with an ugly scab showing from under the bandage. Her short hair above and below the dirty cloth was yellow-white as goat's butter, her eyes were narrow and blue. She sat and held her cracked feet and rocked a little. The third was a boy, his skin burned to a gold darker than his matted hair; there was a bruise on his arm and another on his bony hip. He squatted, holding his chain in one hand, intently rubbing the links in his rough fingers with a leaf.

A shadow moved across the dust to fall over the single heavy plank to which all their chains were peg-locked.

The slaver and the woman looked up. The old man, one shoulder against the support pole, slept.

The boy rubbed.

The man whose shadow it was was very tall; on the blocky muscles of arm, chest, and shin the veins sat high in thin, brown skin. He was thick-legged; his face bore a six-inch scar; his genitals were pouched in a leather web through which pushed hair and scrotal flesh. Rings of brass clinked each step about one wide ankle; his bare feet were broad, flat, and cracked on their hard edges. A fur bag hung on his hip from a thin chain that slanted across his waist; a fur knife-sheath hung from a second chain that slanted the other way. Around his upper arm was a brass bracelet, chased with strange designs, so tight it bit into the muscle. From his neck, on a thong, hung a bronze disk blurred with verdigris. His dusty hair had been braided to one side with another leather strip, but with the business of the day, braid and leather had come half unraveled. The leather dangled over the multiple heads of his ridged and rigid shoulder. He stopped before the plank, looked down at the chained three, and ground one foreknuckle around in his right nostril. (Black on one thumbnail told of a recent injury; the nails were thick, broad through heredity, short from labor, and scimitared at cuticle and crown with labor's more ineradicable grime.) His palms were almost as cracked and horny as his soles. He snuffled hugely, then spat.

Dust drew into his mucus, graying the edge.

"So. This is the lousy lot left from the morning?" The man's voice was naturally hoarse; bits of a grin scattered among general facial signs of contempt.

"The girl is sound and cooks in the western style, though she's strong enough for labor—or would be with some fattening. And she's comely." The slaver spread one hand on his belly as if to keep it from tearing away with its own dark, doughy weight; he squinted. "You were here this morning, and I was speaking to you about a price…?"

"I was here," the man said, "passing in the crowd. We didn't speak."

"Ah, just looking, then. Take the girl. She's pale, passionate, and pretty; knows how to keep herself clean. She's of a good temper—"

"You're a liar," the tall man said.

The slaver went on as though he had not been interrupted: "But you *are* interested in buying? In this high and loathsome hold, they seem to think slaves are too good for them. Believe me, it's not as if they were concerned with the fates of the wretches for sale. I want you to know I take care of my wares. I feed them once a day and put them through a bathhouse, wherever we happen to be, once every new moon. That's more than I can say for some. No—" He wiped again at his trickling forehead with a fleshy thumb. "No, they think here that such luxuries as I have out are namby-pamby and not suited for the austere mountain life."

A brown child with a near-bald head, breasts small as two handfuls of sand, and rags wrapped around her middle, ran up clutching something in leaves. "A dragon's egg!" she panted and, blinking, opened her hands. "A dragon's egg, fertile and ready to hatch, from the corrals of the flying beasts not two miles above in the rocks. Only a bit of silver. Only a—"

"Go on with you," said the slaver. "What do you think, I've never been in the high hold of fabled Ellamon before? Last time I was here, someone tried to sell me a whole tray full of these things; swore I could raise the beasts into a prime flock and make my fortune." He humphed, making to push the child, who merely turned to the tall man.

"A dragon's egg…?"

"A dragon's egg would be a good bargain at only a bit of silver." The man prodded the leathery thing in the leaves with a rough forefinger. "But this— I spent a week here once, picking these off the trees that grow down near the Faltha Falls. Dragonfruit they're called. Lay them in the sun for a week, turning them every day, and you have something that looks a pretty passable version of one of the winged wonders' seeds."

"Is *that* how they do it?" The slaver flapped both hands on his stomach.

"Only you forgot to pull the stem off this one," the tall man said. "Now, go away."

The girl, still blinking, ran off a few steps, looked back—not at the two men standing but at the towheaded woman, whose hair was as short as (if so much lighter than) her own, who was still sitting, still rocking, whispering something to herself now.

"So you know the lay of the rocks 'round Ellamon." The dark-armed slaver moved his hands up and down over his stomach, moving his stomach up and down. "What's your name?"

"Gorgik—unless I have need for another. When I do, I take another for a while. But I've stopped in many mountain holds over the years, fabled or unfabled, to spend a day or a week or a month. That makes Ellamon no different for me from any hundred other towns in the desert, among the peaks, or in the jungles." Gorgik inclined his scarred face toward the slaves, gesturing with his blunt, stubbled chin. "Where are they from?"

"The old man?" Who knows. He's the one I couldn't sell in the last lot— a bunch of house slaves and him. All the time asleep anyway. The boy's new-captured from some raid in the south. A barbarian from the jungles just below the Vygernangx—" one hand left the slaver's gut to prod at Gorgik's chest—"where your astrolabe comes from."

Gorgik raised a bushy eyebrow.

"The stars, set so on the rete, must be from a southern latitude. And the design around the edge—it's the same as one the boy had on a band around his ankle before we took it off him and sold it."

What's he doing?" Gorgik frowned. "Trying to wear his chains through by rubbing them with a leaf?"

The slaver frowned too. "I've kicked him a couple of times. But he won't stop. And he certainly won't rub it through in his lifetime!"

With his knee, Gorgik nudged the boy's shoulder. "What are you doing?"

The boy did not even look up but kept on rubbing the leaf against the link.

"He's simpleminded?" Gorgik asked.

"Now, the woman," said the slaver, not answering, "is from a little farming province in the west. Apparently, she was once captured by raiders from the desert. I guess she escaped, made it all the way to the port of Kolhari, where she was working as a prostitute on the waterfront, but without guild protection. Got taken by slavers again. Thus it goes. She's a fine piece—the pick of the lot as far as I can see. But no one wants to buy her."

The woman's eyes suddenly widened. She turned her head just a little, and a faint shivering took her. She spoke suddenly, in a sharp and shrill voice that seemed addressed not to Gorgik but to someone who might have stood six inches behind him and seven inches to the side: "Buy me, master! You will take me, please, away from him! We go to the desert tribes, and I'll be sold there again. Do you know what they do to women slaves in the desert? I was there before. I don't want to go back. Please, take me, master. Please—"

Gorgik asked, "How much for the boy?"

The woman stopped, her mouth still open around a word. Her eyes narrowed, she shivered again, and her eyes moved on to stare somewhere else. (The girl with the false egg, who had been standing fifteen feet off, turned now and ran.) Once more the woman began to rock.

"For him? Twenty bits of silver and your astrolabe there—I like the quality of its work."

"Five bits of silver, and I keep my astrolabe. You want to get rid of them before you have to waste more on their food—and bathhouses. The empress's slave tax falls due within the next full moon on all who would take slaves across province lines. If you're going with these to the desert—"

"Three imperial gold pieces, and you can have the lot of them. The boy's the best of the three, certainly. In Kolhari I could get three gold pieces stamped with the face of the empress for him alone."

"This isn't Kolhari. This is a mountain hold where they pay mountain prices. And I don't need three slaves. I'll give you ten iron pieces for the boy just to shut you up."

"Thirteen and your astrolabe there. You see, I couldn't take the thirteen by itself, because certain gods that I respect consider that a highly dangerous number—"

"I'll keep my astrolabe and give you twelve, which is twice six—which certain other gods regard as highly propitious. Now, stop this backcountry squabbling and—"

But the slaver was already squatting by the heavy plank, twisting one of his identical thick keys in the peg lock while sweat beaded the creases on his neck. "Well, get it out. Get your money out. Let's see it."

Gorgik fingered apart his fur sack and shook out a palmful of coins, pushing off some with his thumb to clink back in. "There's your money." He poured the palmful into the slaver's cupped hands, then took the proffered key and bent to grab up the loosened chain. "The iron coin is imperial money too, and supposed to be worth two and a half silver bits to the empress's tax collectors." Gorgik tugged the boy up by the shoulder, wound the chain high on the boy's arm, pulled it tight across the narrow back, and wound it high on the other arm; pigeoning the shoulders made running at any speed impossible.

"I know the imperial money. In five years' time you won't see any other sort—more's the pity." The slaver fingered through, translating the various coinage into imperials and adding them with silent tongue and moving lips. "And you know too, apparently, the way they bind slaves in the mines down at the Faltha's feet." (Gorgik finished tying the boy's wrist; the boy was still looking down at where his leaf had fallen.) "Were you once an overseer there? Or a gang foreman?"

"You have your money," Gorgik said, "let me be on my way. You be on yours." Gorgik pushed the boy forward and pulled the end of the chain tight. "Go on, and keep out to the very end." The boy started walking. Gorgik followed. "If you run," Gorgik said matter-of-factly, "in a single tug I can break both your arms. And if I have to do that, then I'll break your legs too and leave you in a ditch somewhere. Because you'll be no use to me at all."

From behind the slaver called, "Are you sure I can't buy your astrolabe? Two silver bits! It's a nice piece, and I have a yearning for it!"

Gorgik walked on.

As they passed from under the scraggly market awning, the boy twisted back to look at Gorgik with a serious frown.

He wasn't a good-looking boy. His shoulders were as tan as river mud. His hair, bleached in bronze streaks, was matted low on his forehead. His green eyes were bright, small, and set too close. His chin was wide and weak, his nose was sharp and arched—in short, he looked like any other dirty and unmannered barbarian (they had lived in their own filthy neighborhoods along Alley of Gulls at the north side of the Spur whenever any of them had ended up in Kolhari). The boy said, "You should have taken the woman. You get her work in the day, her body at night."

Gorgik tugged the chain. "You think I'll get any less from you?"

Gorgik ate heartily from a heavily laden table. He joined in an army song and beat a mug of rum on the boards in unison with the mugs of the soldiers; half his spilled over the horny knot of his fist. With the fifteen-year-old barmaid on his knee, he told a story to three soldiers that made the girl shriek and the soldiers roar. A very drunk man challenged him to dice; Gorgik lost three rounds and suspected that the dice were loaded by an old and fallible system; his next bet, which he won, confirmed it. But the man's drunkenness seemed real, for Gorgik had been watching him drink. In a long, long swallow Gorgik finished his mug and staggered away from the table looking far drunker than he was. Two women who had come to the mountains from the plains and, having eaten behind a screen, had come out to watch the game, laughed shrilly. The soldiers laughed gruffly. And at least the barmaid was gone. One of the soldiers wanted the older of the women to gamble with the drunken dice man.

Gorgik found the inn owner's wife in the kitchen. Outside, a few moments later, furs piled high as his chin, furs swinging against his ankles (as it was too warm for furs inside the house, she hadn't even charged him), Gorgik edged between the ox rail and the cistern wall and out of the light on the packed dirt behind the pantry window.

The inn—as was frequent in provincial middle-class cities—had once been a great house; the house had been closed up, ruined, parts of it pulled down, parts of it rebuilt. For more than a century only a third of it had stood at any one time; seldom for twenty years had it been the same third.

Gorgik carried the furs across what might once have been a great hall or perhaps an open court. He stepped over stones that had, centuries or decades ago, been a wall. He walked by a wall still standing and up a stand of rocks. Earlier, when he had asked the innkeeper's wife where to house his slave, she had told him to put the boy in one of the "outrooms."

Out of three, one had been filled with benches, branches, broken three-legged pots no one had gotten around to mending, and a cart with a shattered axle; the other two were fairly empty, but one had an unpleasant smell. The outrooms had probably once been quite as inside the house as the pantry in which the heavy, spotty-cheeked woman had paused, on her way from kitchen to common room with a basket of roots on her hip, to instruct Gorgik the way here to them. The rooms sat alone on a rag of granite that raveled away behind the inn itself, a single wall from one winding down (here and there fallen down) to join with the wall of the standing wing.

This was Gorgik's third trip to the outrooms.

The first trip, just before sunset, had been to chain up his young barbarian to the post that supported what was still left of the room's sagging ceiling (the straw was sticking out of the cracked daub): more than half the ceiling was down and most of two walls had fallen, so that the room was missing one corner.

The second trip, before his own dinner, had been to bring the barbarian his supper—a pan of the same roots the woman had been carrying, skinned and boiled with a little olive oil. In taste, texture, and color they were between sweet potatoes and turnips. Also in the pan were pieces of fried fat that, if still hot and served with salt and mustard, were fairly tasty. It was standard fare for a laboring slave, and substantially better than the boy would have gotten with his slaver. Gorgik had paid the extravagant price for salt and, in the smoky kitchen, stolen a handful of ground mustard and another of chopped green pepper from two crocks on the table, scattered them about the pan, and then, brushing his hands against his leg, ducked under the slant beam of the kitchen's transom with a yellow mustard flower on his thigh.

The third trip—this one—was to bring out the blankets—not that it was particularly chilly tonight. As he reached the room, a black cloud dropped its silvered edge from the moon (one of the rugs, up under his chin, tickling the side of his nose in the pulsing breeze, was white); as the leaf-rush up about the thick trunks stilled, Gorgik heard the sound that had begun before the end of his first visit, had continued all through his second, and was whispering on into this, his third.

Gorgik stepped over the broken wall.

The boy, squatting away from him so that only one knee was in direct moonlight, rubbed and rubbed his chain with a leaf.

The food in the pan was gone.

Gorgik dropped two of the furs on the rock floor and began to spread the third, black one.

The boy kept rubbing.

"I bought you—" Gorgik kicked a corner straight—"because I thought you were simple. You're not. You're crazy. Stop that. And tell me why you're doing it." He shook out the white fur, dropped it to overlap the black, and flung out the brown on top of both.

The barbarian stopped, then squat-walked around and squinted at his owner, dropping both forearms over his knees; the chain hung down from his neck (a length sagged between his two fists) to coil on the ground before snaking away to its pole back in the dark. The boy said, "I am dead, yes? So I do my death task."

"You're crazy is what you are. That scraping and rubbing, it gets on my nerves." Gorgik stepped onto the blanket edge and sat down. "Come over here."

The boy, without rising, squat-walked onto the white fur. (Behind him, the chain lifted an inch from the ground, swung.) "I am not crazy. I am dead. Nargit was crazy, but not—" The boy lowered his eyes, moving his thin upper lip around over his teeth—one of which, Gorgik had noticed by now, overlapped the tooth beside, giving all his barbaric expressions still another imperfection. "Crazy Nargit is dead too...now. Because I kill him....I wonder if I would meet him here."

Gorgik frowned, waited.

The mark of the truly civilized is their (truly baffling to the likes of you and me) patience with what truly baffles.

The boy said, "I have as many lifetimes as there are leaves on a catalpa tree three times the height of a man in which to go at my task. So I must get back to work." He brought leaf and link together; then he dropped his eyes again. "But already I am very tired of it."

Gorgik pursed his lips. "You look very much alive to me." He grunted. "Had I thought you were dead, I never would have purchased you. A dead slave is not much use."

"Oh, I am already dead, all right!" The boy looked up. "I figure it out, at the beginning. It is almost exactly like the tales of my uncle. I am chain in a place where there is no night and there is no day; and if I rub a single leaf against my chain for a length of time equal to as many lifetimes as there are leaves on a catalpa tree three times the height of a man, my chain will wear away, I shall be free, and I can go to the fork in the river where there will always be full fruit trees and easy game....But you know?" The barbarian cocked his head. "When they took me from the forest, they chain me right away. And right away I begin my task. But after a week, a whole *week* into this death of mine, when they gave me to the man from which you took me, they took away my old chain—and gave me a new one! And it wasn't fair. Because I had already work at my task for a week. Work hard. And do it faithfully every waking hour. A week, I know, is not so much out of a length of time equal to as many lifetimes as there are leaves on a catalpa tree three times the height of a man. Still, I *had* work hard. I had do my task. And it make me very discouraged. So discouraged I almost cry."

"Let me tell you something about being a slave," Gorgik said quietly. "Even if you work at your task a length of time equal to the number of lifetimes as there are leaves in an entire catalpa forest, as soon as your master sees that you are one leaf's thickness nearer freedom, he will promptly put you in another chain." There was a length of silence. Then Gorgik said, "If I take that chain off, will you run?"

The boy frowned. "I do not even know which way I should go to find the fork in the river from here. And I am very tired."

"How long have you been captured now?"

The barbarian shrugged. "A moon, a moon and a half...but it feel like a man's lifetime."

Gorgik fingered for the pouch dangling beside his buttock, took out the key, went forward on his knees, and reached for the boy's neck. The boy raised his chin sharply. The key went into the lock; the chain fell—soft on fur, aclink on rock.

Gorgik went back to sitting, rolling the key between his fingers.

The boy reached up and felt his neck. "Will you take the collar off too?"

"No," Gorgik said. "I won't take the collar off."

Slave and owner squatted and sat at opposite edges of the blanket, one frowning, fingering his collar, the other watching, turning his key.

Then the moonlight in the boy's matted hair darkened.

Both looked up.

"What are those?" the barbarian asked.

"The giant flying lizards which these mountains are fabled for. They raise them in the corrals farther up among the rock." Gorgik suddenly lay back on the fur. "They are the special wards of the child empress, groomed and trained with special riders. There—" Gorgik pointed up through the broken roof—"another one. And another."

The boy went forward on all fours and craned his head up to see. "I saw some out earlier. But not as many as now." Now the barbarian sat, crossing his legs. One knee bumped Gorgik's.

Dark wings interrupted the moonlight, and more wings, and more. Then the wings were away.

"Strange to see so many out," Gorgik said. "When I was last through Ellamon, I saw only one my whole stay—and that might have been a mountain vulture, off between the crags."

"No vulture has a tail—or a neck—like that."

Grunting his agreement, Gorgik stretched on the rug. His ankle hit the food pan; it scraped over rock. He drew his foot back from stone to fur. "There, the whole flock is coming back again. Move over here, and you can see."

"Why are they all over—no, they're turning." The barbarian moved nearer to Gorgik and leaned back on his elbows. "They have riders? What must it be to fly so high, even above the mountains?"

Gorgik grunted again. He put one hand under his head and stretched out the other—just as the barbarian lay down. The metal collar hit Gorgik's horny palm; the matted head started to lift, but Gorgik's horny fingers locked the nape. The barbarian looked over.

Gorgik, eyes on the careening shapes aloft, said, "Do you know what we are going to do together here?"

Suddenly the barbarian's frown changed again. "We are?" He pushed himself up on an elbow and looked at the scarred, stubbled face, the rough, dark hair. "But that's silly. You're a man. That is what boys do, away from the village huts, off in the forest. You become a man, you take a woman, and you do it in your house with her. You don't do it with boys in the woods anymore."

Gorgik gave a snort that may have had laughter in it. "I'm glad you have done it before, then. It is better that way." He glanced at the barbarian. "Yes...?"

The barbarian, still frowning, put his head back down on the fur. Gorgik's fingers relaxed.

Suddenly the slave sat up and looked down at his owner. "All right. We do it. But you take this off me." He hooked a finger under the collar. "You take this off...please. Because—" He shook his head. "Because if I wear this, I don't know if I can do anything."

"No," Gorgik said. "You keep it on." Looking up at the barbarian, he snorted again. "You see, if one of us does not wear it, *I* will not be able to...do anything." At the barbarian's puzzled look, Gorgik raised one bushy eyebrow and gave a small nod. "And right now, I do not feel like wearing it...at least tonight. Some other night I will take it off you and put in on myself. Then we will do it that way. But not now." Gorgik's eyes had again gone to the sky; what darkened the moon now were cloud wisps. He looked back at the boy. "Does it seem so strange to you, barbarian? You must understand; it is just part of the price one pays for civilization. Fire, slavery, cloth, coin, and stone—these are the basis of civilized life. Sometimes it happens that one or another of them gets hopelessly involved in the most basic appetites of a woman or a man. There are people I have met in my travels who cannot eat food unless it has been held long over fire; and there are others, like me, who cannot love without some mark of possession. Both, no doubt, seem equally strange and incomprehensible to you, eh, barbarian?"

The boy, his expression changed yet again, lowered himself to his elbow. "You people, here in the land of death, you really are crazy, yes?" He put his head down on the crook of Gorgik's arm. Gorgik's hand came up to close on the barbarian's shoulder. The barbarian added, "Every time I think I am wearing one chain, I only find that you have changed it for another." Gorgik's fingers on the barbarian's shoulder tightened.

Small Sarg woke smelling beasts too near. But his next breath told him the beasts were long dead. He turned his face on the fur, relaxed his fingers around the rug's edge (fur one side, leather the other). Beside him, Gorgik's great shoulder jerked in the darkness, and the rough voice mumbled, "Get away from me....Get away, you little one-eyed devil...." Gorgik flopped over on his back, one hand flinging up above his head. His eyes were closed, his mouth open. His breathing, irregular for three, then four, then five breaths, returned to its normal soundless rhythm. Stubbled overlip and wet underlip moved about some final, silent word; through none of it, Sarg saw, had sleep been broken.

The boy pushed up on his elbow to regard the man. The chain was coiled away on the rock. The collar, wide open, lay half on brown fur near Gorgik's cracked and horny foot.

Getting to his knees, Sarg reached down and picked it up. He drew his legs beneath him on the rug and held the half-circles in each fist, working the whispering hinge. He looked back at his owner. On that tree trunk of a neck, the collar—closed—would cut into the windpipe and pull in the flanking ligaments. On Sarg it had hung loosely, rubbing the knobs of his collarbone.

"Why would you wear this?" the barbarian asked the sleeping man. "It does not fit you. It does not fit me."

Gorgik rolled back on his side, and for a moment the barbarian wondered if the man were really sleeping.

A sound that might have been a leaf against a leaf came from somewhere. The barbarian noted it because that too had always been his way. With a disgusted grimace he put down the collar, rose to his feet in a motion, stepped to the rock, grabbed the broken wall, leaped (outside that sound again), and came down facing a moon shattered by a lace of leaves and four times as large as any moon should be, as it fell toward the obscured horizon.

He looked around at the fallen rocks, at the trees, at the walls of the inn, and at the flakes of light laid over them all. Then, because he was not only a barbarian but a barbarian prince as well—which meant that a number of his naturally barbaric talents had been refined by training even beyond the impressive level of your ordinary jungle dweller—he said to the little girl hiding behind the bushes in back of the fallen wall (she would have been completely invisible to the likes of you and me), "So, you have got rid of your false dragon's egg now." For he could detect such things on the night's breath. "Why are you crouching back there and watching us?"

What had been the sound of a leaf against a leaf became the sound of a foot moving on leaves. The girl pushed back the brush, stood up, climbed up on the wall, and jumped down. She was all over a dapple of moonlight, short hair, bare breasts and knees. From her breathing, which for the barbarian played through the sounds of night, Sarg could tell she was afraid.

The boy felt very superior to the girl and rather proud of his talent for detecting the unseeable. To show his pride, he squatted down without lifting his heels from the rock and folded his arms on his knees. He smiled.

The girl said, "You are not a slave anymore."

The barbarian, who had thought very little to date about what a slave exactly was (and therefore had thought even less about what it was not to be one), cocked his head, frowned, and grunted questioningly.

"You no longer wear the collar. So you are not a slave." Then she took a breath. "The woman is."

"What woman?" the barbarian asked.

"The woman you were bound with down at the market today. And the old man. I went down earlier tonight to the campsite where the slaver kept his cart. Then I came here where your new master had taken you. The woman still wears her collar."

"And who did you finally sell your egg to?" the boy asked.

"I threw it away—" In a welter of moon dapplings the girl squatted too, folding her arms on her own knees. (The barbarian heard the change in her breathing that told him she was both lying and no longer frightened.) She said, "Did you see the dragons earlier tonight, flying against the moon? I climbed up on the rocks to the corrals, to watch the riders go through their full-moon maneuvers. You know, the fabled flying dragons are cousins to the tiny night lizards that scurry about the rocks on spring evenings. There's a trainer there who showed me how the great flying beasts and the little night crawlers have the same pattern of scales in black and green on the undersides of their hind claws."

"And who is this trainer? Is he some aged local who has trained the great dragons and their riders to darken the moon in your parents' time and your parents' parents'?"

"Oh, no." She took a little breath. "She comes from far away, in the Western Crevasse. She has a two-pronged sword, and she is not a very old woman— she has no more years than your master. But she wears a mask and is the only dragon trainer who will take time off to talk to me or the other children who creep up to the corrals. The other trainers chase us away. For the other trainers, yes, are local women who have trained dragons and their riders all their lives. But she has only worked here since last winter. The other trainers only talk among themselves or to the riders—usually to curse them."

111

The barbarian cocked his head the other way. "So here in this mountain hold, the training of dragons is a woman's rite?"

"The riders are all girls," the girl explained. "That's because if the dragons are to fly, the riders must be small and light. But the girls who are impressed to be riders are all bad girls—ones who are caught stealing or fighting, or those who have babies out of wedlock and kill them or sell them, or those who are disrespectful to their fathers. To groom and ride the dragons is dangerous work. The riders ride bareback, with only a halter; and if a dragon turns sharply in the sky or mounts a glide current too suddenly, a girl can be thrown and fall down to the rocks a thousand feet below. And since the dragons can only glide a few hundred yards, if they come down in rough and unclimbable terrain and cannot take off again, then dragon and rider are left to die there. They say no girl has ever escaped...though sometimes I think they say that only to frighten the riders from trying."

"And would you ride dragons?" the barbarian asked.

"I am not a bad girl," the little girl said. "When I go home, if my cousin discovers I have been out, she will beat me. And she will call me the curse left on her from her own cousin's womb."

The barbarian snorted. "If I were to return to my home now, contaminated by this death I am living, my uncle would no doubt beat me too—to drive away the demons I would bring back with me. Though no one would call me a curse."

The girl snorted now (hearing it, the barbarian realized whom he had been imitating when he'd first made the sound. *Are these the ways that civilization passed on?* he wondered); the girl apparently did not think much of, or possibly understand, such demons. She said, "I would like to ride a dragon. I would like to mount the great humped and scaly back and grip the halter close in to my sides. I'd obey all the trainers' instructions and not be lazy or foolish like the riders who endanger their lives in their uncaring mischief and devilment....Do you know that the riders killed a man two months ago? He was a stranger who had heard of the fabled band of little girls kept up in the rocks and stole up there to see them. The girls caught him, tied him to a tree upside down by one ankle, then cut him to pieces. And the trainers just looked the other way. Because even though they are only the lowest mountain girls, from bad families every one, all of them criminals and thieves, they are wards of the child empress, whose reign is marvelous and miraculous. Oh, they are horribly bad girls! And I am not. You cannot fly, and I cannot fly. Because you are not a girl—and I am not bad."

"But you still try to sell strangers false dragon eggs," said the boy with gravity.

"The woman is still a slave," said the girl with equal gravity—though to the barbarian the connection seemed rather unclear. "And you are a slave no longer. I snuck down to the camp and watched the slaver feed the woman and the old man—only a handful of yellow mush, not even on a plate but just dumped on the board where they were chained. Then, when the moon was high, he roused them and drove them before him into the night. They will journey through the darkness, toward the desert. He wants to reach the desert soon and sell the woman before the empress's slave tax falls due. If the old man cannot travel fast enough, he will break both his legs and heave him over the side of the road. I heard him say it to a salt smuggler who had made camp on the other side of the same clearing." Then she added, "It was the salt smuggler to whom I sold my egg. I had to hide well so they would not see me....They will do terrible things to the woman in the desert. You may once have been a slave. But you are not a slave now."

The barbarian was puzzled by the girl's urgency, which, from her breathing, was moving again toward fear. Because he was a barbarian, the boy sought an explanation in religion: "Well, perhaps if she had done her tasks as faithfully as I had done mine, instead of calling to passersby to buy her, wailing and rocking like a madwoman, and getting herself beaten for her troubles, her scar showing her to have a nasty temper anyway, she too might have gotten a kind master who would have taken off her collar and her chain for the night."

The girl suddenly rose. "You are a fool, you dirty barbarian slave!" Then she was only a moon flicker, a leafy crash of feet.

The barbarian, who really knew very little about slavery but knew nevertheless that the moon was powerful magic, whether the branches of mountain catalpas or the wings of soaring dragons shattered its light, shivered slightly. He rose, turned, and climbed back over the outroom's wall.

Seated again on the blanket, he looked at sleeping Gorgik for a while; the broad back was toward him. The tight bronze band high on the arm caught the moon's faint breath in its chased edge. After a while, the boy again picked up the hinged collar.

He started to put it around his own neck, then returned it to his lap, frowning. He looked again at his sleeping owner. The barbarian moved up the blanket. *If I try to close it, he will wake up; though if I only place it around his neck*—Again on his knees, he laid the collar on the thick neck—and was settling back down when the great chest heaved, heaved again; Gorgik rolled over. His eyes opened in his scarred, sleep-laden face. Gorgik shoved himself up on one elbow; his free hand swept across his chest to his chin. The collar flew (landing, Small Sarg could not help noticing despite his startlement, near the foot of the blanket only inches away from where he had first picked it up by Gorgik's foot); for a drawn-out breath, owner and property looked at each other, at the collar, and at each other again.

True wakefulness came to Gorgik's eyes; the eyes narrowed. A certain handsomeness that, by day, overrode the scar, the heavy features, the reddened eyes, and the unshaven jaw had vanished in the shadow. Though it did not upset Sarg the way it might have someone less barbaric, the boy saw a combination of strength, violence, and ugliness in Gorgik's face that, till now, had not struck him.

"What is it...?" Gorgik asked. "What is it, barbarian?"

"That," the boy said, who only in the instant that he actually spoke saw what he now pointed to. "The man who sold me to you said that come from the south—from the part of the country which is my home. Do you know my home country...I mean, have you ever go there?"

Gorgik dropped his chin to stare down at the astrolabe hanging against his chest. He snorted. "I don't know your home, boy, and I don't want to know it. Now, lie down and go to sleep, or the collar goes back on. We have to move early tomorrow when we quit this mountain sump hole for Kolhari." Gorgik lay down again and twisted around on the blanket, pulling a corner over his shoulder that immediately fell off, kicking at a fur fold that seemed to have worked its way permanently beneath his shin. His eyes were closed.

The barbarian lay beside him, very still. After a few minutes Gorgik's heavy, brown, braceleted arm fell over Sarg's paler shoulder. The barbarian, feeling more or less awake yet drifting off to sleep far more often than he realized, and Gorgik, wide awake but lying perfectly still with his eyes closed and hoping to be thought sleeping, lay together till sunrise, for by now it was only an hour or two till morning.

Healer

Carrie Richerson

The market in Strennside was larger and busier than Tara had expected; it seemed she had arrived in town on a trade day, when all the Rift Valley communities brought goods to barter. Brightly colored awnings seduced with the promise of mysterious wares and shade from the summer's heat. People and animals hurried from one place to another, raising clouds of red dust that set hawkers to swearing cheerfully. In the space of a few paces Tara was solicited to buy dried fish, brass bells for Feather's saddle, and fresh plums and figs that set her mouth to watering—and was solicited for a sexual encounter. She kept one hand wrapped tightly around her purse and the other attached with equal firmness to Feather's bridle until she had emerged from the bazaar's prosperous chaos. A merchant stopped crying his baskets of fine doves long enough to point her the way to the smithy.

The lane wound close to the Strenn, and Tara, shaking dust from her long blond hair and wiping sweat from her sunburned face, looked longingly at the clear, rushing water. The three-day descent from Raven Pass through the Glasstop Mountains into the Rift had been hot and miserable. She was hungry, and Feather needed to be watered and fed—but first, the small matter of a horseshoe.

The smithy sat at the end of the lane: an open-fronted shed filled with benches, anvils, tubs of chain, barrels of horseshoes, racks of pig iron, and bins of coal. In the midst of the ordered confusion, a short, muscular woman beat a plowshare next to a glowing forge. Flakes of incandescent metal showered from each hammer blow. Tara stopped several paces from the front of the shed, but she could feel the heat even there. After a few more strokes, the smith shoved the piece into the coals, wiped her hands on her leather apron, pulled off her leather cap, and came forward.

Tara's attention was caught by the woman's limp. There was something misshapen about the smith's right hip; that leg dragged behind the left as she walked. But the woman moved with the quickness of one long used to her infirmity. She stuck out a large, callused hand, and Tara noticed the dozens of fresh and half-healed burns that dotted her arms all the way up to the military-style tattoo of a stooping bird of prey on her shoulder.

"I'm Margrete—Mar—and I'll bet you're here because your mare threw a shoe."

Tara glanced over her shoulder and saw that Feather was obligingly standing with her near hind hoof off the ground. She grinned and took the proffered hand. The palm felt as hard as metal against her own. "I'm Tara. You're correct. I have the shoe here in my saddlebag. Can you replace it?"

The smith had Feather's saddle and pack bags off in a moment, then cradled the hind foot between her knees. She pulled a curved knife from her apron and ran it around the inside of the hoof wall, then scraped at the sole and the frog. She replaced the foot on the ground; Feather promptly raised it again. The smith inspected each hoof in turn and felt down each leg from rump to fetlock. Then she took Feather's reins from Tara and walked the mare around the yard, studying her gait. As soon as she stopped, Feather raised the hoof off the ground again.

Margrete handed the reins back to Tara. "She's a bit footsore from walking out of balance without that shoe, and the front one on the same side wasn't fitted right. The hoof there is about to crack. Are you staying in town or just passing through?"

"I'll be staying for a few weeks. I'm a healer, on my practicum," Tara said.

The smith raised an eyebrow but didn't comment on Tara's profession. "Then I recommend we remove all the shoes and put your mare on pasture while you're here."

Tara smoothed the indigo-dyed hawk's feather braided into the mare's mane. "Would you like that, girl? Want to run barefoot in the grass for a few weeks?" Feather blew out a hay-scented breath and stamped.

"I think that is a 'yes.' Do you happen to know someone who will rent me pasturage while I'm here?"

Mar ran sooty fingers through her short, gray hair and left sweat spikes sticking out in all directions. "It just so happens," she said, her brown eyes meeting Tara's gray ones innocently, "that I've such a pasture. I'm already boarding two cart horses for my neighbor Dirk. I'll give you a good price: two pence per week. The ironmonger comes next month, and I'm short of cash."

Feather gave Tara no time think it over. She whinnied, stamped, and shook hard enough to send mane and tail flying. Tara pulled her head down and looked her in the eye. "Behave, now. You can stay."

Margrete went for pincers, chisel, and hammer. "Who's in charge here, you or that horse?"

The pasture was a large meadow bounded by a sturdy split-log fence. Tara was pleased to see it contained a pond, scattered trees for shade, and a small barn for shelter during bad weather. A roan gelding and two swaybacked drays clopped over to investigate. Feather nosed her new acquaintances, then treated herself to a good roll in the grass.

"I can see Feather will be comfortable here," Tara said. "Now, since I wish to be just as comfortable during my stay, who can you recommend for lodging?"

"Well, there's Dorris's Inn...." Mar frowned. "But he's expensive for such a long stay. What do you usually do?"

"Most times I stay with a family, usually someone who wants to trade lodging for a healing."

"And how do your other customers pay you?"

"Those who can, in cash. Others trade food, clothing, whatever they have. My services are as affordable as I can make them—and I never turn anyone away for inability to pay. That would be against the oath I swore to Aelis."

Margrete seemed to come to a decision. "Stay with me, healer. I have room, though you'll find the accommodations are not luxurious. You can pay me in part of the food your patients give you—and in cash, as you have it."

"For the ironmonger again?"

Margrete shrugged. "What is a smith without metal to forge and temper?"

Tara thought, *And what is a healer without damage to heal?* "It is a bargain," she said, and the two women clasped hands on it.

Margrete's holdings included, oh luxury of luxuries, a bathhouse. Tara immersed herself in a basin of sun-warmed water and scrubbed away trail grime while Margrete finished up in the smithy and fed the horses their evening grain. Tara was just donning her last clean tunic when the efficient Mar returned.

Margrete stripped unself-consciously and lowered herself into the soapy water. Tara sat on a stone bench to comb out and dry her hair before rebraiding it. She noted other tattoos on Margrete's body—including some she recognized as military marks of rank—and silently inventoried the thin, white lines of scars over the ropy muscles of Margrete's arms, shoulders, chest, and thighs—and the mass of scar lines over the twisted hip.

"This bathhouse is a marvel. Did you learn plumbing and masonry during your military service as well as smithing?"

"None of 'em," Margrete grunted, scrubbing vigorously with a dried yarrell cone. "I was a foot soldier, a squad leader. Served in Duke Brandt's company, the Screaming Eagles. I inherited this place from my partner, whose father had been a smith. I needed a trade when I retired from the army, so I apprenticed myself to the smith in Sweetmere until I could reopen the forge here." She raised a wicked eyebrow. "Boarding horses and the occasional healer is just a sideline."

Margrete stood and poured a pail of clean water over herself to rinse, then stepped out of the basin. Tara handed her a drying cloth. As their fingers met, Tara let a trickle of her healing power flow through the connection. Two scabbed burns on Margrete's right forearm healed instantly; a fresh, raw area on her left hand puckered dry and scabbed.

Margrete jerked back as though stung by a particularly hot spark, and her face closed. "Don't."

"I'm sorry," Tara said. "I should have asked. I just assumed you'd like those—"

Margrete frowned. "My past dealings with healers have not been very pleasant. Or productive."

Tara bowed formally. "I ask pardon. Do you wish me to leave?"

"No, a bargain is a bargain. Just respect my wishes." Margrete smiled hesitantly, as if to take some of the sting out of her words. "And besides, I still need the money."

After setting Tara's filthy clothing to soak in the bath, the women retired to Margrete's cottage for dinner. The stone house was small and sparely furnished: a common room with cook hearth, flagstone floor, and a few scattered storage chests and rugs for sitting. Two sleeping cubicles opened off it, separated from it only by curtains. The walls were almost bare of ornamentation, but above the mantlepiece a long sword hung on wooden pegs. Tara stepped closer to admire the chased scabbard by the light of the oil lamp. A hunting scene, complete with stag and hounds, was delicately traced in the metal.

"Your work?" she asked the smith.

Margrete lifted the sword off its pegs, drew it from the scabbard, and rested the blade on her sleeve for Tara to examine. The tapered blade was more than twice as long as her forearm, with a single fuller running down each side. The bronze hilt was formed as a pair of entwined serpents: the tails curved downward slightly to form the quillons, and the oval heads, fused jaw-to-jaw, formed the pommel. The blade was as bright and rust-free as if it had just been polished. The double edges looked sharp enough to cleave a thought in twain.

"No, I can't claim credit for this. There's no need for swordcraft here; the Rift's been peaceful for a hundred years under the rule of Rhys and the queens in Oester. It belonged to…a friend. It's Gorkan, from one of the famous armories down south. See the wave pattern in the edge of the blade? It's as individual as a signature. If I asked around I could identify the smith from that alone."

Tara watched the light ripple down the edge like water. "It's beautiful."

Margrete slid the blade into its sheath with a fluid motion and hung it back in its place of honor.

Dinner was a simple stew of lentils and vegetables, accompanied by flatbread baked in the coals and washed down with water. After days of dried meat and fruit and hard biscuits, it tasted like a feast to Tara. After the dishes were cleaned, Margrete dug in a chest and brought out a dusty bottle of wine.

"Company is an occasion for a celebration. Tell me your news of the road, if you're not too tired."

Tara smiled and settled onto a sheepskin by the fire. She took the mug Margrete handed her and breathed in the aroma of southern sun and ripe fruit. "Where shall I start?"

"Start with your reason for this traveling. You're a bit old to be on your practicum, aren't you? I thought healers generally came into their powers when their courses started."

"Ah, you know something of our craft, then. Yes, usually within a year of their first blood moon. For men, a little later. But some are slow, as I was. I was all ready to settle down to life as a weaver, had even picked out the young man I intended to marry, when my powers came upon me. And it seems the later one's powers mature, the harder they are to learn to control. I studied at Guildhall in Oester for years before I achieved mastery and could know that when I tried to mend a broken arm I wouldn't cause a hemorrhage instead."

Margrete made a face. "I assume, since you are here, that your teachers have confidence enough to loose you on a trusting public," she said. She examined Tara shrewdly. "Was it worth it, then—all those years of study?"

"Oh, yes," Tara replied and smiled at some cherished memory. Margrete waited, but her guest did not elaborate.

Mar added a piece of wood to the fire, then settled onto her rug again. "I have heard tell," she said as she refilled the cups, "that some healers do not even need to touch their patients to effect the healing. That they have the power to heal, or even kill, from a distance."

A shadow passed over Tara's face. "I know of no healer now alive with such power, but there is a story, of Aelis herself, long ago....

"It is said that the great Aelis's powers of healing were to other healers' as an ordinary healer's power is to the untalented. The consumptive on his deathbed, the unlucky fellow who had been crushed under a grain cart, the woman who had hemorrhaged herself white in labor, even the leper—she could bring all back to health. Her efforts on behalf of the people were unceasing; she accepted pay for her work only from the rich, the poor she healed for free. Seven days each week she sat in front of Guildhall in Oester and healed young and old, male and female, master and servant. If word was brought that someone was too sick to come to her, she went immediately to where that person lay and did not rest until the healing was done. Some said she could raise the dead, but assuredly that was not the case. No, she merely caught the leavetaker at death's lintel and coaxed him or her back.

"One day, the story goes, she was making her way to Guildhall and passed in front of the Court of Justice. A brigand had just been sentenced to death and was being taken out in chains to the place of execution. Suddenly he lunged away from the guards and snatched an infant from the arms of a mother standing nearby. In a rage he threatened to dash out the infant's brains against the steps of the court if he were not immediately unshackled and set free.

"The officer of the patrol was duty-bound to refuse, despite the brigand's ravings and the mother's pleadings. The condemned, mad with fear and hatred, swung the baby up to smash its life away. And Aelis, twenty paces away in the crowd, reached out and stopped his heart.

"A soldier caught the baby as the brigand dropped dead. Aelis melted away in the throng, and all thought the prisoner had burst a vessel or overstrained his heart in his fit. It was the punishment of the God, they all said.

"Aelis was sick at heart. That same day she left Oester and vanished into the Windfairn Mountains. For three years the occasional rumor reached Oester that she lived as a hermit in a cave in the mountains, teaching herbal lore and simple skills like bonesetting to support herself, but never healing.

"Finally, the guild magister himself, the great healer Tarn Smylson, journeyed into the mountains and sought her out. He begged her to return. He wrung her heart with accounts of women who had died in childbirth, lepers who had had to leave their families and wander the countryside as beggars, those who had fallen sick and died because the healers left in Oester could not match Aelis's power. After three days of persuasion, she agreed to return.

"Tarn retired to his sleeping roll outside Aelis's cave that night a happy man. In the morning he packed his gear and prepared to load his cart with Aelis's few belongings. When he entered the cave, he found Aelis sitting at her table. On the board in front of her were the drying jellies of her eyes, which she had ripped from their sockets. She said, 'Now I can heal by touch, but I can never again kill with a look.' "

Margrete stirred. "Could she not have healed herself?"

"Perhaps. Perhaps her powers were even that great. But she never chose to try, and she never let any other healer try. She said she could see more truly when she was blind than she ever could with her eyesight.

"This story was told to me by Elder Healer Samra, who claimed to have heard it from Tarn himself when he was at the end of his life. It is told to every healer candidate in Guildhall at some point in his or her studies, to teach humility. And a proper respect for life."

"But did it really happen like that?"

"Ah, that I cannot tell you." Tara stretched and grinned. "But if it didn't, it *should* have."

The next dawn Tara woke to the clang of hammer on iron—a reminder that she was a slugabed while Margrete was already hard at work. After a simple breakfast she visited for a moment with Feather, waved good-bye to the smith, and returned to the marketplace. It was much quieter than the day before. Most of the visiting traders seemed to have left for their homes. Tara found a shady tree to sit under, hung the small red-and-white-striped banner of her profession from a branch, and pulled the silver medallion with its likeness of her patron Aelis out of her tunic so that it could be seen.

Very quickly she had her first patient: a girl child with a harelip and cleft palate, brought by her anxious mother. A small crowd of the curious gathered while Tara placed her hands over the error nature had made and visualized its repair. When she was finished, while the wide-eyed girl examined her face in a mirror, Tara accepted the payment of a single chicken for her skill. The grateful mother, knowing now her daughter could hope to make a marriage someday, wanted to pay more, but Tara insisted the price was fair.

Word spread quickly through Strennside that a healer was in the village. Tara cured a merchant of a dark growth on his face (and searched out and destroyed the seeds it was spreading throughout his body), examined a lump a young woman had found in her breast and assured her it was not harmful, and cleared the milky scales from a grand-crone's eyes. She returned to Margrete's cottage just before sunset with two chickens, a sack of root vegetables, and a gold regal the merchant had paid her.

She placed the gold coin in Margrete's hand; the smith held it up to the light and looked at it wonderingly.

"Healer, I think you have just paid for you and your mare for six months of lodging."

Tara laughed tiredly. "We won't be staying *that* long."

After dinner the women sat before the fire again and talked. Margrete was eager for news of the world outside the Rift, especially the doings in Oester and the gossip of the court. Tara related the latest juicy scandals, told of affairs begun and broken off, made note of marriages, deaths, and alliances.

Margrete stirred. "Prince Dann will wed the daughter of Count Corliss? Rhys will be allied with Edain, then. I have heard that Powys is making noises again."

Tara shrugged. "Hallan is good at making noises. It's about all he's good for."

"And if they aren't just noises? If he invades...?"

Tara was silent for a long moment. "Then we will need that alliance with Edain. Rhys is prosperous, but the royal coffers are not deep. Queen Ellyn doesn't believe in taxing her people to death the way Hallan does. He can afford to hire mercenaries; Ellyn can't. And he hates her for spurning him—as she was right to do. He is a brutal man and cares nothing for the rule of law."

"Brandt defeated him soundly at Duncton Ford. It has kept the peace for a ten-year."

"Hallan has a short memory. And great ambition." Tara swirled the wine in her cup, adding, "Were you with Brandt's forces at Duncton?"

Margrete's eyes took on a haunted look, but her voice was even as she said, "No, that was after I had left service. Some of my comrades fought there. Some died there."

Tara reached out and took Mar's hand. "I'm sorry."

For a moment Tara thought Margrete would shake off her hand. Then she smiled sadly. "Old times. Old memories, some not so pleasant. Best left buried."

There was plenty to keep Tara busy each day in Strennside, from small healings like straightening a hand crooked by joint pain to rooting out diseases such as bloody lung and the pox. The village had a resident midwife who also knew something of herbal lore. Tara had no wish to appear as a competitor; when villagers came to her with minor ailments that did not require her skills of mind and spirit, she referred them to the midwife—and thus made an ally out of a potential rival. Several times Mistress Jan invited Tara to attend a birthing, in case there should be difficulties; and she cheerfully sent patients too ill for her simple skills to Tara. Tara in turn shared with the herbalist the store of leaves, roots, powders, tisanes, and tinctures she had brought from Oester.

Late one afternoon a boy of twelve or thirteen ran up to Tara's tree. "Please come—quickly—my father—" The youth doubled over, sobbing for breath.

The cottager was still alive when Tara arrived at the farm on the north side of the village. He had fallen from the roof beam of his house while replacing slates; the broken back and legs Tara could have healed, but the head, crushed by the slates that had fallen after him, was beyond her help. And the grieving wife was beyond hearing what Tara had to say. In the end, it fell to the boy who had summoned her to make the decision.

"It is not one I can make for you," Tara explained.

The young man knelt at his father's head and lifted the ruin into his lap. Then he nodded at Tara. She placed a hand on the farmer's chest. She could feel the life there, thrashing like a frightened animal trying to escape its cage. She opened the door. After a moment the man sighed, and the bubbling in his throat stopped. Before she took her leave, Tara helped the boy carry the body indoors and lay it out for washing by the neighbors.

Night had fallen. Tara hugged her tunic around her and plodded sightlessly through the village. At the cottage Margrete looked up to see Tara's tear-streaked face at the door. She pulled the healer inside, sat her by the fire, and pressed a cup of wine into her hand. "Drink."

Tara drank. "You heard, then."

"It's all over the village. Dirk told me."

Tara tossed back the rest of the wine and sat turning the empty cup around in her hands. "There was nothing I could do. Nothing! Except kill him. How is *that* for honoring my oath!" She hurled the cup against the wall, then stared in dismay at the broken pieces. "I'm sorry. That doesn't help anything."

"Doesn't matter." Margrete gathered the shards and threw them in the slops bucket. She came back and sat beside the healer, put her arm around the thin, young shoulders.

Tara bowed her head into her hands. "Aelis, I *hate* losing a patient."

For days afterward, a subdued Tara went to the market at first light and came home drained after dark. Margrete saw how the healer pushed herself to make up for her failure by eradicating every trace of ill-health from the village, saw her grow thinner and paler, and knew she could not keep up the pace.

One night, a week after the death, when dinner was finished and the cleaning was done, Margrete sat down beside Tara and took her hand. "This has to stop. You are punishing yourself for something that could not be helped. Do they teach you so little at this Guildhall of yours that they do not teach you how to accept death?"

Tara was silent for so long that Margrete feared she would not answer at all. But finally she said, "They try. But it is a hard lesson to learn, and I have not had much experience with it." She took Margrete's hand in both of hers and seemed to study it. "Mar, I *feel* the life in your hand. I can feel your heart pump and your blood rush joyously through your body—and I can feel the pain in your hip." She looked into Margrete's face, saw the shadow that passed over it, but the smith didn't pull away. "And I *felt* the life go out of that cottager and death come in. It was so cold...."

She sighed. "I know I've been pushing myself too hard. It was my way of dealing with something too large to take in all at once. My way of healing. I can accept what happened now. But there is one thing I would like to do. I would like you to let me examine your hip. I may not be able to straighten it completely, but I'm sure I can do something about the pain you live with all the time."

Margrete pulled her hand back from Tara's, started to say something, then clamped her jaw shut and shook her head. Abruptly she stood and walked out of the cottage. Tara frowned at the fire. After a few minutes she said,

"Oh, damn," and followed Margrete out the door.

She found the smith by the pasture, leaning on the fence. A full moon silvered the summer-dry grass, and a light breezed caressed Tara's neck and teased at the loose hairs that had escaped from her braid. In the trees that lined the back of the pasture, cicadas ratcheted; and the night air, soft after the heat of the day, was rich with the smells of meat smoking at the sausagemaker's, ripening fruit, new-cut hay, and horse manure. Tara leaned on the fence beside Margrete; Feather ambled over and nuzzled her hands in search of an apple or carrot.

The smith began to speak in a low voice, without looking at Tara. "My lover Megan and I served together under Brandt during the campaigns in Argonne. One day, four months into the siege of Gorka, our cohort was ambushed by a relieving force of cavalry from Arvia. They crashed into our rear and cut it to ribbons before we knew what was happening.

"My squad was in the back half of the cohort; our unit pivoted in good order, but by the time we were in position, we were the front line—the ranks behind us had already been overrun. I looked up to see a huge black gelding bearing straight down on me. Its rider carried only a long sword and a small, round cavalry shield. It's odd—what struck me most in that moment was the look on her face, focused intentness without anger or fear. I recognized it: it was the look I knew I got on my face in the midst of battle.

"I was a fifteen-year veteran, well-trained by the duke's best war masters. I remember how calm I was. Everything seemed to slow down; there was plenty of time to get ready. I shifted my grip on my shield, prepared to throw it at the horse's feet. If you're lucky, you can even break a horse's leg that way." Tara shivered at the thought and pressed her hand against Feather's neck. "And I braced myself to jump to the right at the last moment. I could feel Megan behind me, settling herself the same way. It was as if there were one thought between us.

"Unfortunately, the rider was just as well-trained as I was. She knew which way I had to jump. At the last second she twitched her mount left; my shield throw went wide, and I ran right into the horse. I was under its hooves before I even had a chance to scream."

She paused. Tara could feel a fine trembling, like that of a frightened horse, in the body beside her. She placed a hand over Margrete's on the fence. The smith gave no sign that she felt it.

"I didn't know how badly I'd been hurt. I rolled over, tried to get up before the pain slammed me back down. I saw everything that happened next. Megan did what I should have done: She slammed her shield straight into the horse's face and cut at the rider's leg. But the rider parried and rode past. I think Megan thought she was safe then. She turned her head, just a little, trying to see what had become of me. Behind her I saw the rider make this long, backhanded swing...."

Margrete's words came thickly, as though dragged from her throat through a glue of old tears. "I screamed then, but it was too late. Megan's body went one way, and her head the other. The rider didn't even bother to finish me. She looked at me for just a second, then rode off to find another target.

"I don't remember anything of the next few days. When I woke from wound delirium, Megan had already been burned with the rest of the fallen. The surgeons and healers had saved my leg and my life, and they said that I would even walk again, after a fashion, with patience and hard work.

"The Arvid cavalry had done a lot of damage to us, but they didn't succeed in lifting the siege. In fact, they shortened it. When they retreated into the city, it was just that many more mouths for the Gorkans to feed. I heard before the city surrendered they were eating the horses." Margrete turned to face her, and in the bright moonlight Tara saw an icy fury in Mar's eyes. "The thought of that rider having to eat her own mount is my only consolation." The fury faded, and Mar closed her eyes in exhaustion. "And it sickens me too.

"By the time the city threw open the gates, I was walking on a crutch. I hobbled everywhere, asked everyone I could find. I didn't have a name, but one prisoner recognized my description and identified the rider. Annis. She died on the battlements three days before the city surrendered."

"And you've loved her all this time," Tara said quietly.

Margrete's fingers clenched on the rail, then suddenly opened and twined with Tara's. "I *hated* her! She took *everything* from me. And then she died too—and left me nothing.

"And I loved her. I think I knew the moment I saw her bearing down on me. She was the most terribly beautiful thing I have ever seen. And I know— I think I know—that last look I saw on her face—she knew she could have loved me too."

Margrete turned to Tara again, this time her eyes blind with unshed tears. "That doesn't mean I didn't love Megan, does it?"

Tara put an arm around the broad shoulders, felt the thrumming grief that was the only thing keeping them upright. "It doesn't mean you didn't love her. And she knows that."

Margrete wept a long time against Tara's shoulder. When she was all cried out, Tara took her inside and tucked her into bed like a little child. She felt her own grief had been burned away in the smith's release.

"Sleep now, Margrete. We'll both feel better in the morning."

A few days later Tara announced she would not be going to the market the next morning but instead would head for the forest to search out herbs and roots.

"I've used up almost all of my stock of boneset and feverfew, and I want to find some more foxglove and apple mint. Would you like to come with me?"

"You mean, would I like to spend a day in the cool forest instead of hunched over a broiling forge? When do we leave?"

Before the sun had burned off the next morning's dew, Tara and Margrete were riding through the wooded hills south of Strennside. They followed a streamlet to a pocket meadow, hobbled the horses, and began to search for the plants Tara needed. She taught the smith how to recognize lemon clover and pig's ear, sweet nettle and ginseng. How to take small strips of the underbark from yew trees without killing the tree; how to harvest the most mature leaves of apple mint and leave the rest of the plant to grow more. She needed the root of boneset daisy, the fruit of the ground plum, seed pods of morning glory. Margrete learned quicky, and soon the women were able to split up and cover more territory.

In just two hours Tara filled her collecting baskets. She was working her way back to the horses when she heard Mar calling her. She found the smith calf-deep in a fernbrake, peering at something on a rocky bank.

"Look," Margrete breathed, pressing aside a sheltering frond. In a hollow in the rocks a wild strawberry had taken root. Dozens of small, ripe berries nestled under the leaves like fat rubies.

Tara and Margrete looked at each other. "Dessert," they said together.

After dinner that night, the women settled by the fire with their treasure. Tara peered into the heaped bowl. "I'm almost afraid to try them. What if they're sour?"

"Nonsense." Mar smiled and balanced a crimson berry on the tips of her fingers, then put it to Tara's lips. "How can you doubt?"

Tara closed her eyes and breathed sunlight, sweet dirt, freshening rain. She opened her mouth and let the fruit rest upon her tongue like a cooling drop of dew, then crushed it against her palate. Juice as sweet as love exploded across her tongue; she tilted her head back and let it trickle down her throat.

Margrete's fingers were still at her lips, caressing them lightly. Tara touched the tip of her tongue to a finger, then pulled it into her mouth and sucked the juice from it. The smith's breath grew short; Tara did not need her healing sense to feel the pulse trembling through Mar's hand. She opened her eyes and locked her gaze with Margrete's. Heat prickled between them like a fever, and Margrete's brown eyes went wide with desire.

Tara picked up a berry and fed it to Margrete. She traced the movement of the older woman's jaw, trailed her fingers down the hollow of Mar's throat as she swallowed, then slid her hand behind the smith's head and brushed her lips against Mar's. She pulled back, found assent in Mar's eyes, and kissed her again. The smith moaned deep in her throat; her lips opened, and her tongue tasted Tara's.

After a few sweet minutes, Margrete broke the kiss and took Tara's face between her hands. "It has been a very long time," she said ruefully. "I wonder if I remember how to make love to a woman."

"Let's find out," Tara said, standing and pulling Mar to her feet. She scooped up the bowl of strawberries and led the smith to bed.

Tara rested her cheek against the inside of Margrete's thigh and kissed the damp curls of dark hair. Above her head she could hear Mar's breath slowing, feel her heart easing from its pounding rhythm. She kissed the soft mound again. "By Aelis, I had almost forgotten how good a woman can taste."

Mar laughed, a sound more relaxed and happy than Tara had heard from her before, and ran her fingers through Tara's fine hair. "Has it been a long time for you too, then?"

"Long enough. Longer than enough."

Mar's hand curled around the back of Tara's head and urged it gently downward. "Then taste again, healer. You would not want to be mistaken about something so important."

As the sky began to lighten to gray outside the window, Tara pulled Mar's fingers from her moist depths, kissed them, and yawned. "Must sleep, sweet."

Margrete made a face. "Don't need sleep," she insisted in a petulant tone, then yawned hugely in turn.

Tara laughed and hugged the smith close. "Listen to you. You are like a child: you want all your sweets at once. Rest now."

"I'm not tired," Margrete protested. The last word trailed off into a soft snore.

Tara smiled with tender triumph at the unguarded face in her arms, then pillowed her head against the smith's breasts and fell immediately asleep.

Margrete drifted up from sleep and reached for Tara before she was fully awake. The healer was sitting up in bed contemplating the empty bowl. "We ate all the strawberries," she announced mournfully.

"And I remember every one," Mar said with a smile. She pulled the healer down on top of her. "You are all the food I need."

"Oh? So that deafening sound I hear isn't your stomach grumbling? Must be mine. Wait here, don't move." Tara slipped out of bed and stepped into the common room. Mar defied her instructions and rolled up onto an elbow to admire the fluid lines of the healer's body. She smiled at an intimate memory of that body.

Tara returned with bread, milk, and figs. She showed Mar how to open a fig at its eye and spread its pink, meaty flesh open like a woman's sex. They fed each other bread dipped in milk, exclaimed over the crumbs that fell in the bed, and wrestled each other down into laughing embraces.

When desire had been sated again, Tara placed a hand on Margrete's hip. Mar bowed her head. "All right," she whispered.

Tara let her awareness sink into the flesh. It opened out before her mind's eye like the Rift from one of the Glasstop peaks. Yes, here was the problem. And here. Splintered, mangled bone and muscle, hastily and imperfectly reassembled, like a puzzle not solved but forced into a semblance of fit. And after so long a time, muscles adapted to this deformity, muscles that ached each night with the day's exertions but would protest painfully any attempt to change the existing alignment.

She separated her consciousness from the flesh. Margrete wore a grim and nervous expression. "I can fix this," Tara said. "It won't be quick or easy. It will probably hurt. Do you want me to try?"

Margrete bit her lip, stared out the window. Tara waited, hardly daring to breathe. Tears gathered in the corners of Mar's eyes, but she did not shed

them. Finally, she turned back to Tara. "Yes. Yes, I do," she said.
"Good. We'll start tonight."

For four nights, when chores and dinner were done, Tara laid Margrete on her bed and focused her mind through her hands. Mar felt first a prickling warmth, then a maddening itch, then a hive of frenzied hornets loose inside her hip. Tara blocked as much of the pain as she could, but the nerves had been damaged as well as the bone and muscle, and Mar suffered through Tara's ministrations.

When the smith grew fidgety with the pain, when Tara could feel the rigid body trying to hold back the tears, she would stop and soothe her patient with kisses and caresses. Margrete complained that she couldn't decide whether to hate or love the cursed bed.

The changes Tara was making in the hip joint and musculature left Mar scarcely able to hobble to the forge. On the fifth morning she tried to get out of bed and fell back. She swore, a soldier's oath that made Tara's eyebrows rise. "I cannot continue like this. Finish it now."

Tara thought over how much she had left to do. "All right." She touched Mar's forehead. "Sleep." The smith slumped back into the blankets, and her eyes rolled up white.

Periodically Tara checked Mar's breathing and pulse. It was dangerous to keep her so deeply asleep, but Tara's work could not be hurried. By noon, though, she knew she had done as much good as was within her power. The arch and wing of the bone were normally shaped again, the head of the thighbone fitted smoothly into the hip socket, and the tendrils of muscle were attached in the correct alignments. Mar would have to do the rest.

The smith was frustrated to discover that the pain in her joints and stiffness in her gait did not disappear at once. "Impatient child," Tara scolded. "It will take you as long to learn to walk without a limp as it did to learn to walk with one." But Margrete's progress surprised even Tara. Within the week she moved smoothly and pain-free about the cottage and the smithy.

Tara rose one morning to find Margrete in front of the hearth, shadow-fencing with the sword. Tara let her eyes roam over the muscular body, savoring every feature she had come to know and love: the gray-streaked, curly hair; the compact, rosy-nippled breasts; the tattooed snake coiled around the left ankle; the large feet. She felt pride in the squareness of Margrete's stance and regret for the necessity of what she was about to do.

"I will be leaving soon. By week's end, I think."

Margrete lowered the sword and turned to her with a look of dismay. "I had hoped you would stay. Strennside is large enough to need a healer full-time."

"Yes, and when I return to Oester I will recommend that someone be sought for this posting. But I have accomplished about as much as I can here, and there are more towns to visit on my circuit before I return to Oester for the winter. I'm due in Meetwell before the haying, and Dortmund and Faircroft after that."

She moved to stand beside the smith and looked at the sword in her hands. "And what will you do? Will you rejoin the army, now that you can? Any company would be happy to have your experience, and we may be at war with Powys soon."

Margrete returned the sword to its scabbard. "No. That is long behind me. I am a blacksmith now."

"If that is true, why have you held on to that sword for all these years? You need the metal—come, let us go to the forge right now. I will crank the blower for you, and you can melt down this useless sword and make it into pothooks—or a plowshare."

Mar hugged the sword to her breast. "No!" she cried, shocked and horrified.

Tara put a gentle hand on the smith's arm. "The long sword isn't an infantry weapon. That's Annis's sword, isn't it?"

The older woman nodded without speaking and brushed her fingers over the chased designs like a caress.

Tara smiled sadly. "I came to Strennside looking for a smith, but I think I will be leaving a warrior behind. That was the part of your life that made you feel most alive. Perhaps I should regret making it possible for you to take it up again."

Margrete hung the sword back on its pegs and took Tara in her arms. "No, do not regret. I thank you for it—and much more. I will miss you."

"Then come and visit me in Oester. In the spring, for Festival."

Margrete smiled. "I would like that."

The sky was cloudless and the air dry, but for the first time that summer the morning held a faint tang of the turn of the season, a promise of cooler weather to come. Feather pranced sideways on her new shoes. Tara reined her in and leaned down to give Margrete a long kiss. "Spring Festival in

Oester—ask for me at the Hall of Healing. Promise me you'll come."

"I promise," Mar said, smiling over their clasped hands. Then Tara nudged Feather with her heel and turned the horse's head in to the lane. She rode twisted backward in the saddle; at the first bend she blew the smith a kiss. Margrete waved back, and then she was out of sight.

At noon Tara pulled Feather to a halt on a ridge high above the Strenn. She unsaddled and unbridled the mare, pulled her water bottle from the saddle-bag, and sat on a large rock from which she could just see the village below. She fancied she could hear the faint ring of hammer on steel—but perhaps it was only her imagination.

Behind her iron clinked clearly on iron, and a voice said, "By Aelis, it's good to stand upright again."

"Do you think she'll come?" Tara asked without looking around.

A brown arm snaked around her shoulders and grabbed for the water bottle. "Oh, she'll come. She'll be in Oester for the Spring Festival, when Powys invades through the Wasau steppes. She'll answer Queen Ellyn's call for volunteers, and old Brandt, knowing her experience, will put her in command of an entire brigade. And so she comes to Bernin, where the fate of Rhys is decided." The water bottle gurgled.

"Will she bring the sword?" Still Tara did not turn around.

"Yes, she will bring the sword to Oester. She won't know why, but some impulse will move her to take it with her, maybe for protection on the road. Now, do I get a kiss, or aren't you glad to see me?"

Tara laughed, turned around, and embraced her beloved. "Of course I'm glad to see you, but you've hardly been out of my sight for the past month!" She stroked the long brown hair and smoothed the blue feather.

Feather dropped four new horseshoes into her hand and grinned. "I wish I'd been farther out of hearing. I had to listen to you making love to that woman, and there I was, stuck with a bunch of geldings! Very unjust, my love."

"I'll make it up to you tonight," Tara promised.

Feather waggled her eyebrows. "How about right now? That patch of grass looks inviting."

Tara sighed and looked down at Strennside again. "Not yet, love. Let me put this a bit farther behind me. You and Ellyn asked me to heal her, but it feels more like a betrayal—of someone I've come to love." She was silent for a moment. "She falls at Bernin, doesn't she?"

132

The chief sorcerer to the court of Rhys sat down beside Tara and put an arm around her. "She falls, and Prince Dann takes up her sword and slays Hallan with it. That sword saves Rhys, beloved."

"All this, just to get one particular sword to the prince at a particular moment of a particular battle. Couldn't we just have *asked* her for the sword?"

Feather shrugged helplessly. "I don't make the future, Tara. People like Margrete—and Dann and you—do. I just foresee what will happen: victory for Rhys if this sequence of events is followed; otherwise, defeat by Powys, torture, enslavement, slaughter, Oester put to the torch, and the ground salted....Do you want me to go on?"

Tara shuddered. "No." She bit her lip. "Does Margrete live?"

"The auguries are not clear on that point," Feather murmured.

Tara caught the plump woman's chin in her hand and forced the green eyes to meet hers. "Don't lie to me. After all these years together, I can spot it a league off."

Feather sighed. "The wound is mortal. It would take a healer of extraordinary skill to save her."

Tara took a deep breath and smiled grimly. "Then I will be at Bernin, to save her if I can."

"If anyone can, you will," Feather said to the magister of the Guild of Healers in Oester, the great-great-granddaughter of Aelis the Good. "And I will be there, too—but *not* as a horse!"

O u n c e s
(a n   e x c e r p t)

D o r o t h y   A l l i s o n

Some of the small stones at the wall's edge were loose. Meh picked at them idly with her nails while watching the people below. It was getting late, so late that more people were moving away from the market than were headed toward it. Some of the city guards in their big-shouldered tunics watched her for a moment but apparently decided that she couldn't be up there if it weren't all right with the estate guards. Even so, they scowled darkly before turning back to scanning the market crowd for cutpurses and beggars. *What were the estate guards thinking of, letting her sit up there?* Even if she were a daughter of the house, it was unwise to let anyone sit on the wall's edge. It might give ideas to thieves.

Meh turned her head slowly, checking the towers at the street's corner and then the others back toward the flags that marked the entrance to the market. From where she sat both were clearly visible; from below so was she, but from the towers themselves nothing of her could be seen—a fact that would have greatly surprised the guards, city and estate.

"A thief's best allies," Tesla had always told her, "are the casual assumptions people make. It's always best to fit yourself into the expected, the natural, the everyday facts everybody is so sure of." Like the fact that hands in plain sight cannot possibly be doing anything unseen or that people are always what they look like. So a quick-handed, sharp-tongued gutter rat like Meh, sitting on the one blind spot on an estate wall dressed in an expensive gown and carelessly yawning from time to time, became magically what passersby assumed she had to be—a spoiled daughter of the house waiting for dinnertime.

Meh yawned and turned her head again so that her dark braid threaded with yellow blossoms swung loose. Her pale blue shift and embroidered sleeves caught the fading light. Shifting slightly, she raised her right ankle and hugged it to her left thigh. The silly little shoes she was wearing were awkward, the heels too fragile for jumping and too high for running, but they were the kind of thing rich girls were imagined to wear and therefore vital to her illusion. It was odd how much the reality of expensive clothing varied from the idea of it. Meh had gone home with enough wealthy people to know that expensive garments were neither fragile nor uncomfortable. The pale blue gown, for example, had been the castoff of a woman who had them made up for herself in lots. The fabric was sheer enough to suggest the curves beneath it, soft enough to smooth her skin, and made to cling graciously and drop in folds. It never failed to make the woman who wore it beautiful, and to Meh's delight it easily hid the tight black underbelt in which she kept her favorite blade and what tools she would need.

Meh tugged her sleeves down carefully and risked another glance behind her into the garden. The servants were finally clearing away the clippings from the baniaee hedges. Another few minutes and it would be safe for her to make her try down the inside of the wall. With any luck she wouldn't break an ankle in these shoes.

"She a bitch, that one," Quant had told her, "the great bitch TaTael of the House of Ha'om, but one of the richer ones and careful with her own safety. Her personal guards are the finest in the city. Have to be too, that close to the market. You used to work the market, didn't you, girl?"

"Not lately."

"No, of course not, you like the Rim, don't you. Your type would."

"My type's buying your whiskey."

"Oh, don't take it hard. I've been a Rim runner most of my life. Get crazy if I'm away from it too long, just like all of us. Nowhere else smells quite right, you know."

"Not enough spice in the air."

"And never any smell of whisky, never any little black-eyed girls to buy you glasses and ask you questions. Huh?"

"You haven't told me much yet."

"I told you 'bout the wall, and that's enough. If you're as good as

135

you're supposed to be—and I suspect you are." He rubbed the layered ridges above his eyes and winked at her.

"What's your stuff about TaTael?"

"She's just a bitch. Nasty and known for it. Ask anyone. Anyone will tell you about her."

"But you—what'd she do to you?"

"Well..." He looked around uneasily. His hands on the glass shook slightly. "I did some business with her. Me and my partner brought in some goods for her. It was a hard run, and she wanted only the best, the most precious...commodities."

"Drugs or slaves?"

"Never mind what it was. I ain't in the business anymore, but people don't like to hear that you talk about what you once did, you know." He glared at her. "You know that."

"Yeah."

"Well, it was business, and we were good at it. She paid the best prices, and we provided the best product; but it was a hard run, took longer than we'd planned, and her rate was set. We thought to bargain a little, sweeten the deal, but her man was a bastard about it. Wouldn't give a bit. So we took it out of the merchandise."

Involuntarily Meh shook her head. "Dangerous."

"It shouldn't have been. We didn't short her, you understand. We were businessmen, couldn't afford to do that. But there had been some leeway in the bargaining. We'd done awfully well, much better than she could have expected, so we just took that extra bit. She shouldn't have even known it was there to lose."

"But she did."

"She did."

"And?"

"Those guards of hers brought us back to her. Dragged us in like night cats, chained us down in her dining hall. Set up a scale and weighed out just what we'd taken." He stopped, finished the whiskey in the glass, and sat quietly.

"Then?"

" 'Value for value,' she said. Bitch. 'To the decimal,' she said. She weighed it out of us—from each of us. My partner—" He stopped, looked longingly at Meh's glass. Uneasy, she pushed it to him.

"O-o-oh, good." He wiped his wrinkled forehead.

"What was the weight?"

"Ounces, nothing. Almost nothing." He shuddered. "But she took it back from us. From *us,* you understand. She talked about justice, standing there with that bitch whelp of hers loving every minute of it, those creatures all around her, that little faggot whore laughing. We couldn't do a thing. She had her guards take it out of us, a few ounces from each of us. From my partner, they took it from right between his eyes."

Meh forcibly stopped her own shudder. Amazing how clearly she could visualize such a scene. Hadn't she read some story like that once? She shook her head. It was probably a lie after all, a story. The punch line would be when he told her just where they had got his few ounces. She waited, but he said nothing, just stared ahead into the crowd around them, the expression on his face a cold, dispassionate rage.

"Take my advice. Don't get caught." He stood up carefully and left her. Nothing else could have so completely convinced her that he was telling the truth.

"Cut-Butt!" A stone slapped the wall beside her. On the street below, an urchin dressed in mud and rags drew back to throw another. "She-shit!" Meh grinned and dodged the rock. Delicately, she arched her fist and slapped her elbow. "You," she giggled and swung her legs back inside the wall.

Nice. It gave her a good exit pose. Behind her the garden lay quiet and empty. She held her grin and started carefully down the inside wall. The sandy rock flaked easily. Later they'd be able to find just how she got in. They'd check and then fix that spot on the wall, build it up so no one would ever try this trick again. She used the sharp points of her heels to brace herself and dug in with her nails. Fortunately, she had always had strong hands.

"Training can't give you what you don't have to do with," Tesla had told her—an expression that both did and didn't make sense. At least Meh knew what Tesla meant by it: If you didn't have something to start with, no amount of sweat and struggle would make something of nothing. Meh wasn't so sure about that. Some things she was sure she had acquired through sweat and struggle alone. There had been too many times when all she'd had was a sheen of mud and rags and outrage.

Meh dropped heavily to the top terrace of flowered ivy. The gardeners were gone, and so was most of the light. This wasn't the best time for this kind of attempt. All her instincts told her she should hide out and wait for those precious hours just before dawn when all good thieves could relax and go about their business. But once off the wall she was committed. If she was going to get out safely, her only chance lay in doing her job quickly and getting back out just as fast. On the other side of the wall a few nondescript pebbles were maintaining the current that generally flowed along the sides of the estate wall. Without those pebbles she would never have made it to the top of the wall in the first place, and certainly not down the inside. She was betting her life on those pebbles remaining undisturbed when she tried to get out again—something she would only trust for a few hours at most.

"You love the gamble," Tesla had teased her the last time they had made love. "You like to push your chances just as far as you can. But one of these days you're gonna push it too far and then, Little Fish, I'm going to lose you."

"Never happen," Meh had told her; but she knew that was a lover's lie. One of these days it would happen. One of these days, but with any luck not tonight.

"Twwirr, twwirr!" A wide-tailed bird creature strutted out from between two baniaee hedges. Meh froze and cursed her own eagerness. "Twwirr?" the bird stared at her appraisingly, while Meh held herself motionless. *Go away, bird,* she thought, *nothing here but another artifact to decorate the garden.* The bird turned its head elaborately, beak going up and down and side to side as it approached Meh's still figure.

"Twwirr."

Nothing here. Nothing here but hedges and flowers and statuary. The bird pecked near the toe of her left shoe and then drew back.

"Twwirr, Twwirr," it crooned and wandered off.

Meh watched quietly. *I promise you, soul of my grandmother, with what I take from this I will buy you a bird like that and dedicate it in the temple at RimLight.*

Easy. Easy. Wait. Meh held herself still and let the light fade completely, the bird make its way across the garden. In the hedges little pinpoints of light began to come alive. Meh checked her earring with sweaty fingers and then swung her head back and forth. The sensor picked up insects, gentle currents along the wall, far-off voices, water dripping, the bird's steady pace, but no strutting guards and nothing of the market's din.

Oh! The protected gardens of the rich.

Meh took a deep, slow breath and let it out just as slowly. Concentrating. Concentrating. Her weight shifted down and her knees bent slightly while she pictured to herself a film of oil spreading steadily across hot metal. A skim of light that moved without flaw, without fault, perfectly a part of the metal itself, the life of the metal. Like that. She would move like that.

Around her the garden loomed, shadows and light and the hedges, the deceptive quiet of the high walls and the soft rustle of a sweet warm breeze. TaTael had to have arranged that, put blowers in some archway perhaps and flavored the wind to her taste. The moment stretched, and Meh turned her head again, putting great care into all the details, the placement of the hedges, spice and flower beds. If a guard had come on her then, she would have remained unseen, a smoke creature, a part of the bed she stood on. Meh lowered herself, straightened, stripped sleeves from her arms, and in one motion shed that gauzy gown. Rolled up, the gown went into a satchel slung under her left arm. In the dim light Meh was naked except for her dull black belt, satchel, and shoes. Now the magic was complete. When she moved toward the house, no one could have seen her at all.

"So easy, eh? Just bribe them, you say, kill the troublesome ones, and make the deal. Ahh! Why did I ever bring you into this house, anyway?"

"You don't really want to talk about that again. Do you?"

"One day I will grow tired of your arrogance."

"But not yet, huh, Lady, not yet?"

TaTael pushed her unruly red hair back angrily, though they both knew it was mostly an act. For all that people believed, she did not anger easily. She merely let everyone think she did. It made them more cautious, careful of her, and it gave her a pose that could shield what she was really feeling, really thinking. She loved feints within feints, the dance that does not reveal its choreography. Even when she did become angry, she did not make her decisions out of that anger. She calculated like a good businesswoman, the mistress of one of the great houses. Now she smiled as Bascon pushed open the garden doors. He was a fascinating boy, and she wasn't really displeased with him. She had just decided that she wasn't going to keep him much longer.

She had realized the problem more than a year ago. The pretty boy she had chosen for his intelligence and viciousness had begun to believe he actually was what she had bought him to play at being. He had not kept that edge of insight which had first attracted her, or he would have realized the danger in beginning to assume any safety in his role. He was the one she dangled for her enemies. Just by being there he deflected interest and danger from the two daughters she had sent off to the Ansharan. That he had proved fascinating had been a bonus but not the point. His role was his role. Only *he* confused things.

TaTael never confused anything.

"They trimmed the hedges today. You can smell the resin from the cuttings."

"Will you have wine?"

She liked it when he was ingratiating. "Of course, but open all the portals first. It's so beautiful tonight. I want the feel of the outdoors without having everything moved."

"They could move everything out easily enough." Bascon carefully swung the glazed windows open, folding them back into their arched recesses. "What else are they for?" He frowned as the two pets brought in the first trays of new fruit. They were naked except for their long blond hair, their jewelry, and the yellow ribbons TaTael liked them to wear around their loins. Diminutive, mild-featured boys with whispery voices and almost prehensile little cocks—Bascon despised them. In his opinion TaTael collected entirely too many of them. Another pair brought in the ices and liquors. *Entirely too many,* Bascon thought, reaching for the Pinou bottle. TaTael didn't like sweet wines until later.

"They are for me, of course." TaTael grinned at Bascon's petulant expression. She liked him this way, more boylike and less serious. She wondered how he would do under surgery. He wasn't that old yet—twice the age of most of her acquisitions, of course, but still young—and her surgeons had worked miracles before.

"If you want furniture moved, Bascon, you know to call the guards. My pets are aesthetic, not athletic." Her laughter was a fluttery tinkle that always annoyed Bascon.

He sighed and brought her the glass. "And you know they are not to my taste."

"You prefer the athletic, I have heard." TaTael sipped and watched his expression.

"In all things." He slapped his own well-muscled thigh and dropped into one of the carved seats near the garden steps. Instantly one of the boys brought him a glass of Dewbeer. All of them knew his taste and were careful to cater to it. His dislike for them made him dangerous.

TaTael nodded and looked out over her garden while sipping her wine. Well, maybe she'd try it. It would be very interesting to see what kind of pet he'd make, though even if it could be done, he was likely to kill himself at the first chance. She shrugged. Something to think about. One of the pets brought her a chair while another provided a pillow for her feet. Smiling, she tugged at the ribbons of the one closest.

"Wimsy?"

"Ma'am."

Probably his name wasn't Wimsy, but he would say it was now. They were very obliging, her pets. She ran her fingers down his soft skin to cup his little cock. The delicate rings at each side of the head twinkled. She'd like to thread a ribbon through them, let the ribbons hang down and sway. Under her hands the boy was still, almost not breathing, waiting. TaTael sighed with pleasure. It had been a very long day. Too much business, and too many hard-eyed women. The soft boy flesh under her fingers was a satisfying antidote.

"Are you waiting dinner?" Poised in the doorway, Smaka sounded both irritable and hungry. The pets quickly brought her a glass of Dewbeer and a little plate of spiced mushrooms.

"No, you're early." TaTael held her cheek still for her daughter's brusque kiss. The boy almost lost his balance when she did not let go of him but steadied at her glance. Smaka took a long drink of the Dewbeer and watched her mother fondle the child, wondering if in time she wouldn't develop a taste for that kind of thing. She'd tried them once or twice, but they were too obliging, too eager to please—not her kind of pleasure at all. The only good thing about them was how much Bascon disliked them. Made him feel like a pervert, probably, an idea he violently resisted. Silly, of course; they were all perverts, really. What was it the Ansharan had taught her? "A degenerate people in a degenerate civilization." Certainly Bascon was degenerate, a fool who didn't know enough to realize his own fate. Smaka scooped up a few mushrooms and gave Bascon a cordial nod. It would be delicious when Mama killed him. Delicious. She went over and sat on the garden steps, hiding her smile by looking out into the hedges. Maybe she could get Mama to give him to her. She could make a long session of him. He was strong, stubborn, proud, and curiously ignorant about his own mortality. He wouldn't be as good as a woman, of course, but it would be a pleasure to teach him the literal truth of his own fragility.

Smaka stretched slightly, and one of the pets ran over to begin rubbing her back. *Lovely,* Smaka thought, *maybe I should have a few prepared for me—little girls with strong hands and just a little more cerebrum than TaTael had left in her boys. How much cerebrum did it take to feel humiliation? To fear pain?* Smiling, she glanced over at her mother. *Degenerate indeed.*

"I think I can get you that lot from the Weavers Guild by season's close." TaTael continued to stroke her pet but turned her head slightly. "Think?" Smaka grinned. "I'll get it. Conny is handling shipments for the House of Kirdle now, and she's nowhere as careful as she thinks she is. It's still delicate, but even if they find out what I've arranged, she won't be able to stop me this season. It would be next season before she could get a new supply of dyers."

TaTael let go of her pet. "What do you think of Conny's chances of taking the baton? Once she loses her weavers, will she lose her place in the house?"

Smaka turned back around, a perplexed expression on her face. "I really don't think she will. Half a dozen of the house daughters have told me she's all but confirmed, and that's after the past few years of losing contracts and shrinking her share of the market. I don't understand it. If I were the tai', I'd have had her throat cut last year."

Yes, you would, TaTael thought and purred with pleasure. *I did right to send you to the Ansharan. Everything else aside, they have given me back a daughter I can trust with my house—assuming you don't become too ambitious.*

"Some of the houses are not so meticulous as we are."

"But to keep an obvious failure in a position of authority?"

"Look at it from the point of view of Tai' Kirdle. Conny is her last living daughter. Her hopes are with the grandchildren and keeping her losses manageable until one of them can inherit." Smaka went on frowning but nodded. *No, you don't understand,* TaTael thought. *That's the only flaw in the Ansharan: no real sense of family—not flesh and blood, anyway.* For a moment she thought of Smatham, her oldest girl. The Ansharan still hadn't sent her back, maybe never would—which did not necessarily mean she was dead. *Someday I might meet my daughter ruling one of their houses. That's what comes of a lack of family feeling.*

"She could adopt."

"What?"

"Tai' Kirdle. The House of Kirdle could take in an out-daughter." Bascon waved his hand, and one of the pets refilled his glass. "Or a son. That would change the politics of it all. You know the prestige a male heir would give the house. Think about the House of Sa'ban."

Mother and daughter held each other's glance for a long moment. The House of Sa'ban. Yes, there was a male heir there. Six wives in as many seasons, four daughters alive. Pride of place in every trading session, bowing and scraping and ritual respect during the ceremonies that opened each meeting. But then? Then silence and cutthroat trading; no woman in her right mind would make a binding contract with the House of Sa'ban. The house itself was being leached away. If one of those daughters did not turn out to be a raider of enormous talent, the house itself would fail in a generation. TaTael reached for her pet again.

"I think I'm not up to a long dinner tonight. Smaka, tell the cook to serve us only a plaka meal. No liquors after, either."

Smaka nodded and headed for the hall. Bascon hadn't very much longer at all.

Meh watched the young one, Smaka. She knew that one, a lesser daughter, supposedly, but that was probably one of those strategic lies. She didn't move like a lesser anything. She moved like a carne warrior, one of those trained dancer-fighters Tesla loved to bring home now and again. Dangerous.

Quietly Meh pulled back and wiggled closer to the hedge-scarred wall. Right along here should be the gap her source had promised, visible only when the hedges were freshly trimmed. But there certainly didn't seem to be anything. She ran her hands along the stone until she felt an irregularity, then adjusted her earring again. There was a satisfying pulse of recognition.

Good.

Her hands moved in careful, complicated patterns. The pulse in her ear followed her motions. *Good. Good.* The stone shifted, grated, opened. Meh stood rigid. The pulse in her ear did not stop. There were guards coming up the far side of the hedge.

Oh, gods great and small, grandmothers and ghosts, I will buy two birds for the RimLight temple.

Tall, lean, and muscled, muscles made with fighting rather than Bascon's careful work to create mass, the guards were sexless in oiled tunics, boots, and face guards. The face guards hid sensors as well as features. Meh tried not to breathe.

Concentrate. Concentrate. I am stone. I am air and stone and hedge newly cut. I am stone, stone, stone.

The pulse stopped. The guards paused, looking up to the brightly lit terrace and back to the shadowy grounds. If Meh had been farther away from the terrace, her own body heat would probably have betrayed her, no matter how hard she imagined herself cold stone. There was a bustle at the edge of the terrace, and one of the pets ran down to scoop up a stray baniaee cutting.

"Oh, I love that scent," TaTael told Bascon, while Meh felt sweat running down her back.

Stone does not sweat.

The guards moved slowly on, not wanting to catch the lady's eye. TaTael knew the necessity but didn't like to be reminded that she was constantly patrolled. Meh went on imagining dead stone until the pulse in her ear faded.

Two birds.

The great houses are all alike. Born in treachery, sustained by trade war, bastions of secrets and plots, none can afford to be less than mysterious and multilayered. Just so their architecture; enormous buttressed monstrosities with hidden courts, underground supply caches, and tangled skeins of secret corridors. Every room has to have a known and an unknown entrance, and yet a third for the private use of the mistress of the house. Since the houses grew in bursts in seasons of successful trade, all faced the problems of careful ground structure and mapping the secret corridors. Some abandoned secrecy and rendered one blueprint of all the passages, but most kept two or three; such blueprints were like those known and unknown entrances, always with that third and most secret map for the mistress's eyes alone. Maps like that were beyond price. Maps like that occasionally fell into the wrong hands and made someone's fortune. In this case, Meh's hands and Quant's fortune.

"It cost me everything I had," he'd laughed. "But it's worth it. Anything that strikes a blow against her. Anything."

"How many copies did you make?"

"Enough to cover my trouble, make back my costs, and guarantee her years of losses she can't prepare for...but what I sell you is the first one." He'd drunk heavily, and now sweat kept rolling down into his eyes. "Take your girlfriend, why don't you? The two of you together against her; I like the idea of that. I like it a lot."

Meh had laughed and agreed, lying with practiced ease. *Take Tesla into one of the great houses? Tesla with her pride and easy rages? No, too much risk—but Quant didn't have to know that.*

It was a damn good map, worth every cent of what she had paid. But there was no way to know when it had been prepared, what had been changed since it was drawn. As it was, there were all too many passages that ended in cul-de-sacs or opened into public hallways. It was obvious TaTael loved to change things, whether moving her personal rooms or building a sunken bath where once there had been a crossway to the dungeons.

For the first few moments in the dark passage, Meh found it difficult to keep her confidence up. The darkness was too intense, and the wherelight she had tucked in her belt didn't give her much illumination. Carefully she started marking the walls with glow streaks. "Get in, get out, but get what you came for"—a thief's ambitions were simply expressed. Quietly she began to hum under her breath as she crept forward:

> *"Eight lengths down and forty lengths over*
> *by the dark water where the gold rushes lay*
> *I came for my darling, I came for my lover...*
> *Oh, don't tell my secrets and I'll not give you away."*

"The high houses—they're the truly great thieves." Tesla had been both angry and disgusted. Her oldest friend, Mathia, had disappeared after doing one of those nasty little jobs the great houses loved to hire out. After two weeks Tesla and Meh had argued about starting an inquiry, an argument that had quickly become moot. At sunrise, Mathia's gutted and drained body had washed ashore near the RimLight temple, and even the onslaughts of the quadsharks hadn't quite erased the obvious marks of what had been done to her.

"Ahh, Mathia," Tesla had moaned when she had seen her, then fallen stubbornly silent. Even the rite of swearing herself a True-Friend, an act that was traditionally done with poetry and praise song, Tesla had performed almost mutely, as if she wanted nothing and no one to witness it. It was a surprise then when she had asked Meh to go with her to the temple to prepare Mathia for ritual burning. The Thieves Guild was putting up the bounty, and Tesla was standing surety for any debts put against Mathia's family.

"Not that she'll have any debts listed." Meh had stubbornly kept talking all the time Tesla had held Mathia's body for cleaning. "This kind of thing no one wants to be connected to in any way. Who knows how far their nets will fly, huh?"

For a moment she thought Tesla was going to hit her—which would have been all right. Anything that would penetrate the frozen silence would have been worth it. Instead Tesla merely spat in contempt and turned her face away. Not until the body had been rinsed three times of the gummy river mud did Tesla's face finally crumple and the tears begin to leak. Carefully Meh kept her own head down and let Tesla cry. She could count on one hand the number of times she had seen Tesla's tears, and this was the first time she had ever been glad to see them.

"O-o-oh, see what they took from her." Tesla kept gripping Mathia's ribs while Meh carefully washed her down. The bleached and swollen flesh told Meh nothing but shocked Tesla deeply.

"Someone had a long night of it, looks like to me." *Was it better,* Meh wondered, *to go on being callous or to let Tesla see her own grief?* Mathia had not really been a friend to her; Meh had barely known her. Still, her hands shook on Mathia's cheek while she kept her voice neutral. "A barbed whip, it looks like, to leave those welts..."

"Oh, a whip—" Tesla kept on gripping and shaking the bruised, torn ribs—"but not here. Here they used a fish knife. See that pattern?" The flesh was raked and scraped raw. "Like taking scales off, see? They did that while she watched, you know it. They made her watch it. Skinning her like that; the bastards."

Meh stopped her own hands, unsure of what she should do. "My love, I don't understand."

"Her tattoos. They took her tattoos. Someone knew enough to rob her of the one thing she treasured above all else. Mathia was Kartian. The ship people." Tesla stopped to wipe her eyes. "They're not much on material things, the Kartians. Mathia always said it was a joke of her gods that she'd become a thief. Kartians value family, spirit, flesh—in that order. Flesh is skin, skin shows rank, family—spiritual growth. The tattoos mark every trial, every success, everything. Temple made and very costly, Little Fish. Mathia was famous for her family, her rank, her spiritual progress, and all of it was visible to any Kartian she bathed or slept with."

Tesla sighed. "Naked, she was an advertisement for herself and proud of it. They took her tattoos to break her pride. Then they killed her."

Meh looked closely. Yes, perhaps once there had been color in that skin, tattoos. Now it was only raw and pale from too long in the water.

"I'm sorry, my love."

"So am I...so am I."

Meh had cleaned the body. Tesla had held it. Together they had carried it out to the priests and the fire pit.

"Flesh is flesh. Fire is fire. Be flesh. Be fire. The many ways of god."
Meh did not believe in male priests, but she stood still and respectful for Tesla's friend. She remembered Mathia buying whiskey for everyone in the Cat's Wing a few weeks earlier, proud of the contract she had taken and the money she would be paid. "Only the best for the House of Ha'om," Mathia had boasted, smoothing the fabric down over her new high-silk robe. Meh wondered if Tesla remembered that. It was the only clue she had to Mathia's employer and murderer.

"The weavers' crown," Tesla had whispered, squatting on her heels while they waited for the ceremony to be completed. "That was what she went after—the jewels in the crown they keep in the weavers' guildhall."

"Do you think *they* caught her?" The weavers had a bad reputation for keeping to their own law, their own justice. It was possible they might have skinned a thief instead of turning her over to the guards.

"No, she got away with it. Word's been on the street since she disappeared. Without their crown, things will get very messy for the guild at close of season; can't hold the pageant very well when your goddess has lost her crown. They've offered high coin for its return—it or the jewels in it." Tesla rocked back and forth and laced and unlaced her long fingers.

"Whoever hired her probably still has it, for whatever use they planned for it or waiting for the price to go high enough. But they had no reason to kill her—none that I can see, anyway."

"It could have been one of the great houses."

"As sure as god has teats."

"If it was, you can be sure, love, they're damn sure they can get away with it."

"And we think ourselves dangerous." Tesla laughed harshly, drawing a frown from a passing priest. Meh shot him a cold glance, and he kept walking.

"Remember what you're always telling me. We're not dangerous because we steal and kill; we're dangerous because of the care we take in doing it. Mathia, may the grandmothers comfort her, must have stinted on caution."

"Or trusted the wrong person."

"Yes."

"Don't worry, Little Fish. I won't do that." But for the first time,

Meh *had* begun to worry, understanding finally that Tesla wouldn't leave her friend unavenged.

"Shit," she had whispered to herself. "Now what do I do?" But it had not been so hard. She had found Quant.

Meh had never taken much interest in jewels, with the single exception of those stones suitable to crown a dagger's hilt. But even so, she was shocked when she saw the weavers' stones lying spread across the hearth of Smaka's private room. The size of serpent eggs and just as gaudy, the jewels had been removed from the crown with rough care. One or two still had an uneven layer of jeweler's paste staining them. Of the crown itself there was no sign. Maybe Smaka was having it fitted with fake jewels or lesser-quality stones. These were superb.

Meh lifted them one at a time to the glow of the wherelight. Beautiful, deep, hypnotic, and worth more to the Weavers Guild than to a jeweler. Meh sucked her lip and considered. Her plan had been simple enough: to return them for the promised bounty while pretending to be Smaka's agent. Done clumsily enough, such an arrangement would assure Mathia's revenge on her murderess. The guild would spend more than she or Tesla could ever have arranged to punish the House of Ha'om suitably. They might even lay one of those plots poets make epics of—to destroy the house and all associated with it. It would not be too hard to make it an affair of honor, arrange some slighting reference to their goddess and get TaTael and Smaka hanged naked from the harvest altar.

But the stones stopped her. Meh had never seen anything like them, each more beautiful than the last. If she got them out of here, why the hell should she have to give them up? Give up one or two perhaps; buy a revenge and keep the rest. It could be done. She pictured for herself Tesla in a woven collar of these stones, the belt she could get made for herself, the hilt of her favorite dagger. Oh, my.

"Soul of my grandmothers," Meh breathed and began to tuck the jewels into her belt. Why had Smaka left them lying out like this? Was the woman crazy? Even a private room wasn't totally private, not in a house like this.

"Who is she?" TaTael leaned forward and frowned. She did not want Smaka to know how upset it made her to imagine that anyone could so easily enter her home, especially not some little thief obviously just out of the market stalls. Deliberately, she pushed herself back and turned away from the view screen. "Do you know her?"

"She's familiar, but I can't remember yet from where. Maybe she's with one of the other houses, and I've seen her there." Smaka shrugged indifferently. "Or maybe not. I'll remember sooner or later, Maman. The question is, how did she get in, and what do we do with her?" *Don't say it,* Smaka told herself. *Don't say you want her, then maybe you'll get her.* She looked back at the crouching figure in her chamber. Oh! She wanted her. She wanted her badly. She was getting wet just thinking about it.

TaTael hawked in her throat and spat before Wimsy could run over. Smaka repressed a shudder, hating it when her mother did such things. TaTael stood still, hugging herself and frowning. "A thief," she whispered, "but a thief with a map. I want to know where she got it. I want to know what she came in here for—everything, Smaka. Don't come back to me with meaningless drivel. I want to know everything about her; who sent her, where that map came from, who knows she's here. Everything."

Smaka's face seemed to take on a glow. Carefully, TaTael pretended not to see. That kind of lust was a weakness, something she would have to do something about someday. Was that why the Ansharan had sent Smaka back to her? Was that why they had kept the cooler and more disciplined Smathan? *Weakness,* TaTael thought and closed her eyes wearily. She was getting old—too old—to allow herself any weakness at all. She took a deep breath and turned brusquely to her daughter.

"I give her to you. And the responsibility for her, I give you that too, Daughter." She wrapped her arms more tightly around her body and glared at her younger daughter. "See that you do not disappoint me."

"No, Maman." Smaka felt an almost liquid heat slip up from her thighs. "No-o-o."

Very rarely, Meh indulged her most dangerous passion. Though sexual, the act itself had nothing to do with sex as most people conceive of it. Other than special times with Tesla, sex for Meh was an exhilarating sport, played best in the lower quarters of the Rim with the few whose tastes matched hers in ferocity. But rarely, perhaps two or three times a year, Meh would get what she called her "wild bent."

Then she put on her earrings.

Delicate bells and hoops and chains in gold, silver, and trefoil, Meh's earrings had been given to her by Modeste'—the woman who had also given her her favorite dagger. "See what you catch with this, darling," Modeste' had giggled, knowing exactly what the ornate and precious baubles would tempt Meh to do.

The earrings chimed and tinkled and glittered, reflecting whatever breeze or patch of light Meh passed through. To match the eccentricity of such tokens in the Rim district, Meh chose a silky tunic with a wide belt or a one-piece loincloth-body wrap that barely covered her breasts. With this, she always wore her flat-soled boots and both her dagger and the even more deadly triple-edged ko knife, the latter tucked in her left boot.

"Such a bitch stitching up the hole that fucker makes," Tesla always joked. "Better to stick 'em a few more times and save the surgeon the trouble."

"Oh, I don't leave no trouble lying around," Meh always joked back. Always. She knew well enough that Tesla did not approve of this particular foolishness of hers, as well as she knew that Tesla would never tell her to stop it. You don't stop a shark who's got a taste of blood; you don't mess with a woman who gets the same taste now and then; and when Meh dressed herself in her earrings and knives that's just what she was out to get—the blood of any thief foolish enough to try to take those rings off her ears.

In the corridors of the House of Ha'om, Meh heard a tinkle in a slight breeze, heard a chink of metal striking against itself, thought briefly of her earrings, and more immediately smelled the scent of blood. Her own blood sweet in her mouth. She had seconds then, seconds to stretch her arms out in the blackness, seconds to turn and run, to plot desperately, to do the one little thing she could do. Then she thought of Tesla.

With a wild and terrible grief, she ran the corridors in the darkness, bitterly swallowing the shout she dared not let go. *Soul of my grandmothers,* she prayed, *do not, do not—by all I am—do not leave it to Tesla to lay me on the temple fires.*

Cats with cocklebugs, weasels with greensnakes, small children with frogs or turtles—all love the game of life and death, but none so much as those bred and trained to it. The guards of the House of Ha'om were drawn from the Me'than ranks of the Warriors Guild, not generals or strategists but the fastest and deadliest of the knife masters and bodyguards. Cloned from warriors who died defending their contract holders, most were also the products of crèches notorious for their brutality. The result was predictably a troupe that longed for just the opportunity Meh provided—and none so much as Kayman, groundsmistress and night marshal.

"Some little market rat wiggled her way over the wall," Bascon had told her. "But be careful. Smaka's got her tongue out and wants it alive."

"When am I less than careful?" Kayman ran her fingertips along her belt and grinned at Bascon's angry confusion. Pity he had no taste for women; she'd always liked the way he looked—a kind of full-bodied softness that contrasted nicely with the stringy muscles of the guards she generally fucked. She even liked to imagine him with TaTael. He probably screwed her like a puppy dog—all long-dicked eagerness and drooling submission. But then, in a place like this they were all puppy dogs of one breed or another.

TaTael awarded rank and cash on the basis of one's actions, which meant one did whatever one could to catch her eye—and nothing attracted her attention faster than protecting her property or her person. If Kayman was ever to achieve the status of day marshal, she needed a thief or an assassin, some threat she could render harmless while displaying her devotion and skill. She could not help but wonder which this market rat would be. An assassin would make the greatest impression, of course, but a thief might be even better. TaTael prized things much more than people, and it would be worth her life to drag in the thief and lay whatever trinkets were involved at TaTael's feet. And then to throw the thief before Smaka like a tidbit before a glutton. Oh, yes! This could make her very successful indeed.

The lower corridors were wet, slimy, and mossy where the dungeons had flooded during the big storms three seasons ago. The stones were slippery, and Meh was tired. Even her desperation couldn't keep her from falling every few yards. She had scraped her knees and opened a cut along the side of her left hand right up to the edge of her wrist. "Damn," she cursed, sucked at the cut, and kept moving.

"Give it up, rat." The voice was close, but in the darkness she couldn't tell how close. Meh stopped and tried to listen. They wouldn't risk killing her before they had the stones, and that gave her an edge. While they were being careful, she'd try her best to gut anything that came near her.

The knife in her hand was slippery, the hand itself shaky. Meh tried to control her breathing, to pull in energy from the deeper reaches of her own will. All her life she had been able to pull up that strength, but all her life she had also believed in her own survival. This time she was not so sure she'd get herself out—not sure at all—and that uncertainty was slowing her as much as her exhaustion. She prayed again Tesla never learned how badly this had gone.

"Pss, pss, here, rat." It was a different voice, coming from the darkness ahead of her. Meh held herself still and reached up, hoping for an outcrop of rock, something to grip, someplace to hide herself. Nothing. The rock was slimy but smooth. She turned, trying to use the sensor to locate the one behind her. Nothing. They must be using a disk shield to scramble the vibrations. *Shit.*

"Come on, rat, we've got a nice kennel waiting. Just your size."

"Just your smell."

That one was behind her. *Oh, grandmothers and great ones!* Meh forced herself to breathe slowly, quietly, to feel her way carefully forward. If she could just spot the guards before they were on her. If she could just...

The mass that slammed into her stomach was solid, unyielding, and stank of the dripping moss that coated the tunnel walls. *Someone's boot,* Meh thought and scrambled desperately, trying to draw breath and roll away at the same time. She got her feet under her, but she couldn't get enough air.

"Huhh, huhh," she heard herself wheezing, struggling to breathe. She slipped again, and the boot that had been moving toward her shoulder grazed the side of her face. They could see her clearly, she realized, falling again, this time to her knees.

"Lay her out," someone giggled.

"Care, take care." Some other voice; some fool moving close, carelessly.

Meh swung her left hand, the blade out and singing. The scream that followed was satisfying, the catch and tear as the point caught on yielding flesh.

"Damned bitch!"

"Watch it."

This time the boot landed heel first, the side of her head resounding with the blow. Meh crumpled and barely felt the pain as another boot stomped down on her left hand. She felt the loss of the knife, though, as if her heart had broken and lost her the one hope of doing them any damage at all. She spat, still trying to draw a clean breath while someone took hold of her hair and dragged her upright.

"Alive! They said they want her alive."

The light flared, blinding her before she could see more than five indistinct figures. Two of them got a good grip on her while the slightest one, a skull-shaven, near-naked creature with mottled skin, struggled to hold the tallest one back.

"Kayman, you know you don't want to make Smaka mad."...

152

Breakheart
Mel Keegan

Even the wolves were starving that winter. The north wind cut with a knife's edge, and only desperate men made the journey to Breakheart. For the first time in the memory of even the oldest at Brennan's rath, the River Cador was a ribbon of black ice. Serpentlike, it wound down from Spelling High Water in the cleft of the Osrand Mountains, and the ice did not begin to break up until it reached the city of Moorkind, which was once my home. In spring the lowlands would surely flood—one did not need to be a member of the Scryers Guild to know that.

I had been at Brennan's rath—Breakheart, as all who lived there soon came to know it—for a month under two years, and I would be there five years more. That time stretched before me like a field of desolation, and I had begun to feel the weight of the fetters that bound me. Not physical fetters, but shackles nonetheless. I was bound to Breakheart as surely as if I were chained like a bear. Only fools tried to leave alone, and no one would take me out.

The afternoon sky was a pall of gray as I turned back toward the rath. I let my horse pick her own way, since the trail was fetlock deep in snow and strewn with stones. On either side the mountains reared, forbidding as fortress walls, and the trees, dense thickets of owl pines, were like the hackles of a great animal slumbering in the earth.

As I reached the old stone circle on the shoulder of the hill above the rath, I heard the wolves, and I touched my heels to the mare's sides. There was no game left in the woods, and if those wolves were hunting, they were about to set upon a traveler. Over my shoulder I carried a short bow and a quiver of barb-tipped arrows. I was the lowest form of life at Breakheart, yet even I was not permitted to ride out unarmed on an errand.

The sky was black as a funeral shroud, but a shaft of sunlight somehow probed through the overcast and picked out the standing stones, the Nine Sisters, like a finger of gold. The wolves were beyond, marching a perimeter, intent on their quarry. I reined back, nocked an arrow, and swore quietly as I saw what they were after.

Crouched against one of the stones was the figure of a man. He was cloaked and hooded against the striking cold, and across his knees was a naked sword. The blade was already red, and two of the wolves were limping. I had no chance to wonder how he came to be on foot or what kind of man would tempt fate in these mountains at midwinter. The wolves were coming in again, and at a glance I knew the man was exhausted and hurt.

He was halfway to his feet, and I raised my voice over the rush of the wind. "Get down!" His head turned; he saw me and bobbed back behind the stone. I released that arrow and several more. I was always impressed by the intelligence of wolves. I never knew if it was an animal cunning or cleverness to rival man's, but these creatures needed only one warning. They were slinking back into the woods as I took my horse into the circle and slid to the ground.

The traveler stood, cleaned his sword with a handful of snow, and sheathed it. He leaned heavily on the stone and studied me from beneath the cowl of his cloak. His garments were sapphire-blue, embroidered in silver and trimmed in white fox. Perhaps I should have realized then that he was no common traveler, but I was cold and tired, and—if I am honest—I was so dazzled by the beauty I saw as he shook back his hood that my thoughts were muddled.

He was as dark as the Patai, that tribe from West Sakand, but his eyes were so blue they seemed luminous. The last of his summer brown made his skin the same pale tan as my horse, and though he was smudged with weariness, I was beguiled. He held out one gauntleted hand, and without thinking I took it.

"Is Brennan's rath near here?" he asked, in the accent of Moorkind. He was born there—or had lived there long enough to pick up their way of speaking. "Do you know the way, boy?"

"I should," I said bitterly. "I work at Breakheart. Let me help you; you're hurt. What happened to your horse?"

He gestured eastward toward Vilhaven. "Bandits, last evening. I was lucky to escape with my life. They took the horse and everything I had, save one or two things they missed. Since then I've walked. But you're right—" he slapped his leg—"I fell heavily, and I'm half frozen. Is there a healer at the rath?"

"There's a farrier," I said dubiously as I gave him my shoulder to lean on. "You'd fare better if I treated you myself!"

"You know the healing arts?" His face was pinched as he looked down at me. He was much taller than I, and broader, and the weight across my shoulders was heavy. Close to him, I smelled fur and leathers, sandalwood and the musky scent that was his own. "If you've the healing touch," he said, "you can care for this leg. I've no desire to trust myself to the farrier!"

My horse was standing with her head down and her nostrils flared as she scented the wind. No doubt she could smell the wolves, probably also the snow that was threatening. Animals sense a storm's approach, and even I had seen the soft yellow woolliness of the sky. I caught the reins and tugged her toward me.

"You'd better ride. The rath isn't far, but if you try to walk it'll be dark before we're there. The wolves will shadow us, and it'll snow again soon." I could have added that I would be fortunate to escape a whipping, since I had been sent on a morning's errand and had taken all day. Brennan's temper was notorious; I often felt the sting of the strap. "Let me help you."

I cupped my gloved hands for his boot, and he hauled himself into the saddle with a grimace, a grunt of discomfort. I took the mare's bridle and gave her a tug, out of the stone circle and southward, along the bank of the stream.

From spring to autumn the foothills of the Osrand Mountains can be beautiful, but in winter they are just dangerous. The passes are narrow, the trails confusing. It is easy even for one who knows the way well to miss a turn. The wind picked up, blowing a plume of snow off the crown of Mount Idris, and I hurried the mare as my feet began to freeze. The trail led down steeply from the Nine Sisters, curled around a granite outcropping, ducked through the trees, and approached the rath from the rear. I smelled smoke and heard the dogs barking before we left the woods, and I frowned at the stranger.

"Do you have money?" I asked dubiously. "Brennan won't extend his hospitality if you can't pay."

His brows arched. "I'd be tossed out into the snow?"

"No. But you'd work for your supper," I warned. "Brennan isn't a generous man. The bandits stole your purse?"

"Yes, but not these." He pulled off his left gauntlet and turned his hand to show me several rings. "The stones are fine, the gold thick and heavy. Will he trade?"

I grinned. "He'd be glad to. In spring the merchants pass through on their way to Valdenheim. One of those rings would fill Brennan's pantry—and his wine cellar—till summer."

We had reached the rear wall of the rath, and old Elbrin opened the postern gate for us. Breakheart is a town held captive by a stockade. The wall is three times the height of a man, made of whole trees. Brennan liked to say it was built by his grandfather—and perhaps it was—but to me it looked much older. The thatched roofs were heavy with snow, but in spring they would be repaired with fresh heather, and the banners of the Epidai would flutter at the gate.

A boy called Jedda, bonded like myself, ran from the stable to take my horse as I helped the stranger dismount. He leaned on me again, and I turned him toward the nearest of the three taverns, the Wayfarer, which was Brennan's own. The chieftain's house stood to one side, his stable at the rear, and before the tavern were the forecourt and main gate. It was all gray and white, slush and snow, but I heard music and laughter from the tavern and urged my companion inside.

Eyes turned toward us as the door closed. Weighted deerskins swept into place to hold out the drafts, and the minstrels paused. The traveler took his weight on both feet and pushed back his hood. I had not realized how tall he was until then, or that his hair was uncut and smooth as silk. It was like a cape on his shoulders, and as he stood straight in the yellow lamplight I saw the glitter of silver on his breast. He wore the hawk's-head emblem, and I was taken aback.

Brennan saw all this as he left the hearth. Although he challenged most strangers who limped into the rath, he inclined his head before this one. Brennan was past his youth, big-bellied and bearded but still strong, still commanding. He dressed like a chieftain in velvets and fur, tunic and leggings, but his manners would never have passed muster in Moorkind. He dismissed me without a glance, hooked his hands into the broad leather belt at his massive waist, and cocked his head at my companion.

"Well met," he offered. "You came to grief on the road? Bandits or wolves?"

"Both." Blue eyes flickered to me. "If this lad hadn't found me, I'd have been done for." He offered his hand, and Brennan had the grace to take it. "I am Richard Leon...and I need lodgings, a meal, a horse."

For a time Brennan studied him, thoughtful or suspicious, which was his way, and then all at once he gave me a rough shove, a kick in the backside. "You heard what he said—a meal, a room! Why are you standing there?"

I was used to the treatment and merely hurried to obey. My cloak, boots, and gauntlets I dumped by the door, out of the way. I heaped a platter with bread and cheese, filled a bowl with broth from the cauldron over the fire and a mug with mead, mulled with a hot iron. Richard Leon stood in the warmth of the hearth, watching curiously until I ushered him into the shadow, away from the light and noise.

He sank gratefully into an enormous chair. I set the laden wood tray on his lap and sat at his feet. I was tired, cold, and hungry, but as long as he wanted me I would be comfortable for the night. If he was warm, so was I; and for a change I would enjoy the best bed in the house. My eyes were on his food, and I licked my lips, wondering when he would favor me. I had set out far more than he could eat—my own meal as well as his—but he was new here, and, I realized belatedly, he might not know our ways. I could not prompt him; if Brennan heard me, I'd be whipped to within an inch of my hide.

Richard had been eating for some time when he asked, "Are you not hungry, boy?"

"Famished," I confessed, and wondered if he heard my belly rumble.

"Get something to eat." He gestured at the hearth.

My face flushed. "My lord, I can't." *Why was I still ashamed?* Two years, and shame still prickled me with heat. "I'm a bondsman."

For a moment his face was blank; then his brows rose. "They don't feed you—you earn your meal?"

"Yes." I looked longingly at his plate. "If you want me for the night, I belong to you. 'Tis you who feeds me."

"And if I don't want you?" he asked; but he laid one fingertip on my nose, which stripped the anxiousness from me.

I nodded at the other men by the hearth. Most were trapliners, miners, passing through and imprisoned here by the weather. Others were risking the mountains on their way to Moorkind on business. "Then one of them," I said softly, "though I'd be happiest with you." That was no lie. No exaggeration. I had served all kinds of men and had learned the truth of the saying that all cats are gray in the dark. But Richard Leon was the kind I dreamed about, and gods knew when I would taste another like him.

His hand cupped my cheek. "What are you doing in this place, boy?"

"As I said, I'm a bondsman," I said with that old flush of shame.

"But why?" He split a piece of bread, filled it with mutton and barley from his dish, and thrust it at me. "Eat!"

That command I was pleased to obey. Through a mouthful of food I said, "If you get hungry enough, you steal. If you steal often enough, you get caught."

"And for your sins they sent you here," he concluded, looking around the dim, smoky tavern. "What do you do?"

"What I'm told." I licked my fingers and looked at his cup and the cheese. "Mornings I work in the stable. Afternoons, in the kitchen. Evenings, here in the tavern until a man chooses me. Then he'll take me to bed." My belly shivered. It was a long time since I had seen a man and wanted him for myself. Coupling, mating, was just something that happened, a duty I performed to earn my bed and breakfast.

"Poor tyke," he murmured and held his cup to my lips. "You're from Moorkind."

I drank, and he gave me a piece of cheese. "I can go back when my time is done."

"What's your name, boy?" He stroked my cheek as I ate, and I turned my face to his hand.

"At home I was Fendel. Here, I've no name." I rubbed my face over his wrist, loving its strength. I'll see to your leg, unless you want the farrier."

He snorted at the suggestion and shared the mead with me. "Show me to the rooms, let me get out of these damned leathers. I don't have much time, Fendel. Have you eaten enough?"

I was still hungry, but I had learned long ago that when that question was asked, my own needs must be set aside. I threw the debris of his meal into the fire and gave him my shoulder again to help him up the narrow, creaking stairs.

The best bedchambers were at the front. Brennan saved them for wealthy merchants from Valdenheim or priests on their way to the shrines in the river land, across the mountains. Seldom did we see a man in Breakheart who had the right to wear the silver hawk's head on his breast.

The hearth was already bright. Every night fires were lit in each room, even if they were unoccupied, else they became damp and moldy. I bolted the door against thieves, lit the lamps, and turned my attention to Richard Leon and the bed.

He swung off his cloak, hung it over a chair, and sat on the bedside to heel off his boots. His swords were on the chair, and I noticed he never allowed them out of reach. I knelt to help with his boots and saw how scuffed they were, as if he had not been attended by a servant for far too long. In the light of four lamps I saw how his tunic was frayed at the cuffs, threadbare at the collar; but it was not my place to speak. The silver hawk was the emblem of the House of Ragnarson, and if Richard Leon still wore it, he was in Ragnarson's pay. If he was frayed and threadbare, he had been on the road a long time and would likely be cherished as a long-lost son when he returned.

He groaned as I unbuckled his harness, unlaced the leathers. I lifted them off and stripped him to the skin, but when I removed his linen shirt I forgot my place and murmured aloud. On his left breast, over his heart, was a tattoo I had heard described but never seen. His skin was smooth, the color of honey; his body was leanly muscled, like a man who had been running hard for months or years, and the tattoo was striking. It was an eye, with the areola of his nipple as the pupil. The symbol was very ancient; the tattoo itself was years old. I recoiled, then laid the pad of my finger on his nipple and whispered, as if afraid to speak, "You're a seer."

He cupped his hand over his chest, holding my own hand against him. "I was. And if the gods permit, I shall be again. It frightens you?"

"No," I began, but it was too obviously a lie.

He tousled my hair. "It does, a little. And why not? It still frightens me, and I was trained for it when I was much younger than you! Earn your bed and breakfast then, Fendel. I'm aching, the leg is twisted. It needs rubbing, and even so I'll be stiff as a plank tomorrow."

His face darkened as he spoke. As I pushed him down on the bed, I asked, "What troubles you about the morning? 'Tis a day, like any other."

Naked, he tugged a sheepskin pillow under his head and sprawled back, open to me but not flaunting himself. He was well made, head to foot, with long legs, wide shoulders, and the round muscles of youth. He was hairless, save for the dark flares beneath his arms and below his belly, where his genitals were heavy and inviting. But as I oiled my hands with the salve intended for my own comfort when he mounted me, I could not overlook his scars.

I counted six. The newest was still livid, though the skin was closed. All were sword nicks—anyone who has shared a bed with warriors recognizes them. But a seer is not a warrior; he is too precious to be risked in battle. What had Ragnarson's seer been doing, fighting and growing threadbare on the road?

Questions taunted me as I rubbed him, and I almost found the temerity to ask. I explored his right leg, high up at the hip, and discovered the bruise where he had fallen. He had wrenched the joint, if I was any judge, but the injury was slight. He would limp for a few days, but from this misadventure at least there would be no new scar.

As I worked he began to make small pleasured sounds, and I watched him rise and thicken, ready for another kind of massage. I leaned over, kissed the crown of him, petted his balls, and anointed him with the salve. He wore a bemused expression as I dropped my clothes at the bedside and lifted myself astride him.

"You were a thief before you came here?" he asked breathlessly as I settled on him. "Not a man's favorite bed boy?"

"I was hungry, so I stole," I said against his mouth, gasping because he was so big in me. Pain lanced me, peaked, and dwindled into pleasure that made me groan.

"How old are you?" He stroked me, discovered the rough skin on my back and buttocks left from so many healed welts. But he knew the plight of bondsmen and said nothing.

"Eighteen summers, eighteen winters," I said, losing my coherence as I began to work.

He rested his weary body and held me as I showed him what pleasures I knew. When we were lying quietly afterward, he turned me over and fingered my own scars. To my surprise I felt his lips on my back, moist and tickling, and I clutched his arms. I could scarcely make out his words and did not dare ask him to repeat them, but I could have sworn he said, "I would flog the man who abused my boy." Then he pulled up the quilted counterpane and swathed us both. "Lie against me. Keep me warm and go to sleep," he told me, rough-gentle.

That was easier said than done. Since I'd come to Breakheart I had known many men, but very few had I wanted for myself. Richard Leon would be gone soon, but I would dream about him for years. The memories of this one night would sweeten a thousand others. Sleeping, missing one moment, was the last thing on my mind. I wriggled closer and murmured in delight as he embraced me. Ragnarson's seer! I might have been in the arms of a Valdenheim princeling, a cardinal from the riverside shrines.

But I had been working since dawn, and I did sleep, so that his thrashing jerked me awake. By the water clock in the corner it was midnight, and at first I thought my bed mate was dreaming; but his eyes were wide open. He sat up, chest heaving, gazing into the distance as if he could see through the fabric of our world and into some other. Perhaps he could. Much is said of the Scryers Guild, some of it impossible, some magical. The Sorcerers Guild is closely associated with the seers. Some men are so gifted they belong to both, and every seer receives his scrying stone from the sorcerers—even I knew that much.

"My lord," I began, forcing myself awake.

He was not listening. "I see thee," he hissed, snakelike, dragging in great panted breaths, and I realized he was not awake, not asleep, but tranced. "I see thee through the veil of smoke," he gasped. "I see ashes...blood in the snow. Cruach! The snow eagle. I see thy talons, Koval Nah, I see thy thieving claws! Thou art here, and then, then—"

His hands clutched the air, making fists, and all at once he wrenched himself awake. The fire had burned down to glowing embers, the room was not especially warm, but sweat drenched him. I smelled its sharp tang, and when he turned toward me I caught him. I was frightened. Strange magic—any magic—has always frightened me. I was dry-mouthed as Ragnarson's seer lay trembling in my arms. I tangled my hands in his hair, pulling gently to fetch him back to the present.

"My lord, you were tranced," I stammered.

"I know." Even his voice shook. "What did I say? Did you hear?"

"A little." I helped him sit against the pillows. "Did you not hear yourself?"

His dark head shook, his eyes squeezed shut. "Cruach help me. Tell me what I said, boy. Tell me!"

"You're a seer!" I touched his breast, fingered his nipple.

He took my hand away, his fingers like an iron band around my wrist. "I am a seer without a scrying stone. Do you know what that means?"

"No." I winced as his fingers dug among the bones of my wrist, but he did not notice. "I know the priests watch children, looking for gifted ones, and such children are trained," I said, a rush of words as he hurt me without realizing it. "When your training is done, you're given the tattoo, you become a guildsman, you're given a scrying stone of your own."

He seemed to come back to himself and let go of my wrist. I rubbed it gratefully, and he slumped against the pillow and raked both hands through the glossy cape of his hair. "Not *a* scrying stone, boy. Not *any* stone. One stone, do you understand? One great crystal, a lens made especially, one stone for one seer. It's not the source of our gift, but it is the focus for it. Without it I don't command the gift, it commands me. I'm no more than a slave to forces that blaze through me." His face was bloodless. "Without the stone I cannot See, yet when I sleep the visions burn through my mind. They'll kill me, boy." His voice had fallen away to a hoarse whisper, and his shoulders slumped. He pressed his hand over his breast. "What did I say?"

I understood little more than before, but I was caught in the web with him. "You spoke of someone called Koval, a veil of smoke, ashes. Then you said, 'An eagle, blood in the snow.'" I licked my lips and looked into his face. His jaw was stubbled, his eyes fever-bright. "What does it mean?"

"That I'll fight." He gestured tiredly at his swords. "That the old woman was right, and Koval is coming...likely, that I'll die."

My belly churned with foreboding. "What old woman? My lord—"

"Don't call me that." He seized me and, with a sudden burst of strength that astonished and thrilled me, dumped me across his lap. I looked up at him wide-eyed. "I'm no one's lord," he rasped. "You may as well know the truth, since you'll bury me tomorrow. Then do me one service. Send to Ragnarson in Moorkind, tell him...." He looked away. "Tell him what became of me."

Ice water lapped through me. "I can't leave the rath. If I try to leave alone, the mountains or the winter will kill me. Even if I got through alive, I'd be flogged and gelded and sent back to finish my bond contract. You know I can't leave."

He blinked blindly at me. "Poor tyke. How long before you can go?"

"Five years, sire," I whispered.

"Use my name." He laid his mouth on mine, and for the first time I tasted his tongue.

No one had kissed me since I'd come to Breakheart. There had been so much mating, often I was sore and stiff in the hips; but no affection. I had not realized how much I was starved for it, and I drank thirstily, all he would give. At last he fended me off and regarded me with a little wry humor.

"What were you before you became a thief?"

"A man's son." I licked my bruised lips. "My father was a canal barge-man. I never knew my mother. My father died in the fevers four years ago, and I had a choice. Would I be a marketplace thief, or was it the whorehouse for me? At the time I chose the market—and see where I ended."

"Yes." He looked into the fire. "Can you write?" I shook my head and he tousled my hair. "No matter. I'll write a letter for Ragnarson tomorrow. Make sure it's delivered when the roads open in spring."

"Deliver it yourself," I urged.

"No." He looked hauntedly at me. "Blood in the snow, you said. That was my blood, boy. Koval will kill me. He was once a mercenary, and I…I took up the sword when I was damned for my sins, at the time they damned you to Breakheart for yours."

His web spun tighter around me. I pressed against his side. "What sins, my—Richard?" In two years I had never addressed a man by name.

He toyed with my hair, which was red-brown, roughly cut about my skull. "One seer, one stone, you know? When the gifted children are grown, the training finished, we're invited into the guild and granted the scrying stone. To us it's the ultimate prize, a tribute, given just once."

"But your stone," I faltered. "It was broken or lost?"

"Stolen." He mocked himself with a bitter half-smile. "I was a fool. I took Koval Nah into my affections and was duped. It was never me Koval wanted. He wanted a seer's stone."

I recoiled. "He's a guildsman?"

To my surprise Richard laughed, but the sound was humorless. "He has no gift! Like most idiots, he believes the power is in the stone, not in the man. To him it's a piece of crystal. In my hands—" He closed his eyes and shook his head slowly. "Koval knows by now he can't use it. It's just a jewel."

"Perhaps he no longer has it," I suggested. "If it's valuable, he would sell it. He stole it, so he clearly hasn't a scruple."

Richard angled a look at me. "You were a thief."

"I stole food, shoes, a coin for herbs when I was sick," I retorted. "My worst crime was to be a clumsy thief who got himself caught! Koval may not have your stone."

But he was sure. "He has it. This is what brings me to this forsaken place in midwinter. I begged a favor, and though I should by rights have been spurned, the old woman gave me what I needed. I said, 'Scry for me: tell me where he'll be; let me hunt him down and have it over, even if it's the death of me!' She did what I asked and sent me here." He glared at the room, its dim corners and oak ceiling beams, the stone hearth and shuttered window draped in tapestries till spring. "Merella was a great beauty in her youth. They said that even now she'll do favors for a handsome man."

"Favors? She might have sent you here to die!"

"I'll die anyway; rather sooner than later." He leaned against the pillows and pulled me across his lap. I pressed my face to his chest and breathed the scents of his body. "Without the stone, every time I sleep my mind is burned by visions I neither control nor remember. In the end, it'll kill me. That alone would have been punishment enough, but the guild excised me for the crime of stupidity, and even Ragnarson, who is my friend, held me responsible. He paid for my training: twenty years with the guild teachers! He could have flogged me or sold me as you were sold. Instead he put a sword into my hand. 'Find the man,' he charged me. 'Get back your stone, and if you return to Moorkind whole and healed, there's a place for you here.' He can make the guild reinstate me. He has the influence."

I digested this as I stroked him, but one question remained unanswered. We settled again, knowing we would not sleep. My hand was between his thighs, soothing and playing. If I could arouse him once more I would slip him into me for his comfort. "How did Koval steal it?" I said softly against his shoulder, half afraid to ask.

He sighed and pulled up the quilt. "He passed himself off as a Valdenheim merchant, said he loved me, and I believed him. In matters of the heart, even scryers are blind. When you see him, you'll understand. One night I took him to my apartment in Ragnarson's house. He wined me until I was insensible, bedded me for his own pleasure, and while I slept he took my stone and simply walked away. I should have *Seen* all this, should have known what he was about, but he dazzled me until I wanted to leave Ragnarson's house and—" He turned his head on the pillow, looked at me. "I don't know why I'm telling you."

"Because I share purgatory with you," I whispered, still stroking him. "Go to sleep."

"If I do, it'll happen again," he warned.

"And I'll be here." I kissed his mouth longingly, and he pulled the counterpane over our heads.

Snow fell thickly overnight, and the morning was hushed. Even Breakheart is pretty when it wears a pelt of fresh white under a brilliant blue sky, but I had hoped the sky would be storm-black over the mountains. Foul weather would have closed the roads, kept Koval Nah miles from Brennan's rath. The clear sky and gentle wind gave him the opportunity to travel, though the trail was difficult.

At midwinter the dawn was late. It was full daylight when I cracked open a shutter. Richard was half awake, half asleep as I rebuilt the fire. I scrambled into my tunic and leggings and ran down to the kitchen for his breakfast.

The kitchen was a dim, smoky cavern at the back. Three dogs lay panting before the cooking hearth, the ovens were baking bread, a pig was turning over the fire. A little boy, ten years younger than I, turned the spit while the women made broth and pickles.

I had loaded a tray when movement behind me alerted me to Brennan's presence, and I was not surprised when he caught a handful of my hair. I smelled ale on his breath as he leaned closer. "Who is he, boy?"

"The seer from Ragnarson's house, my lord." I winced. The day I was sold, this was how Brennan had fetched me down off the auction block. I was naked and cold; he took me by the hair and thrust me at his lieutenant, and I started work at once.

"What's he doing here?"

"Personal business, my lord. He came to meet a man." That at least was no lie. "He'll stay until the man arrives."

"You know this man's name?"

Now I lied. "I'm sorry, my lord, I don't." If Brennan knew the name of Koval Nah, the scene would be the end of Richard. Brennan would take Koval's part for a share in the price of the stone, and Richard would surely die.

"Hmm." He gave my hair a tug and let me go. "You pleased him last night? He mated you?" To him I was just a mare. He used me himself in the early days and knew what I was worth.

"I tried to please, and he coupled me." I picked up the tray and edged toward the door. "He's hungry." So was I. My own food was on the tray, but it would never be called mine. I ate off another man's plate, at his pleasure. I had grown so accustomed to this, I barely noticed any longer, yet that morning I felt a fresh pang of humiliation. Richard had treated me like a freeman. I had forgotten how that felt, and the prospect of the five years' bondage before me was a knife between my ribs.

"Find out his business," Brennan called as I made my escape. He liked to know everything about everyone under his roof.

I promised I would tell him all I learned, but it was another lie. The stairs creaked as I climbed back to the room, and when I bolted the door I discovered Richard wrapped in the counterpane, shaving with a lethal blade. The kettle sang on the hearth, but he was shaving with oil, as the highborn of Moorkind do. Beneath the quilt he was naked, and I glimpsed his body as he turned to me.

The tray clattered on the table by the bed, and I opened the shutter a little. "Blue sky, good traveling weather."

"Koval will be here." He sounded resigned, as if he was ready to die. He patted his face with a swatch of the sheet and inspected the food before he bothered to dress. I was laying out his clothes, absently noticing where they needed mending before he would be considered presentable in Moorkind or

Valdenheim, when he said to me, "Fendel, what are you worth?" The question took me unawares; I blinked stupidly. He smiled, leaned over the bed, and tongued my mouth. "The day you were sold on a bond contract, what was your price?"

"Three hundred shel," I said haltingly. "My contract would be worth less now, since I've served two years." I swallowed hard. I knew what I hoped. "Why do you ask?"

"I'm allowing myself to dream," he said self-mockingly. "If I live out this day—Cruach knows, it's late morning already!—and if it's Koval's blood in the snow, I can go home."

"To Ragnarson's house. Moorkind," I said hoarsely as memories of the city haunted me. I could smell the river, hear the cries of hawkers and tradesmen in the market, feel the heat of the sun on my face as it never warmed Breakheart. Tears stung my eyes, and I turned away before Richard saw the ridiculous emotion. Feeling was my enemy. If I let myself feel, I would never survive until my bondage was worked out. Brennan would sell my contract. I could end anywhere.

"Boy." Richard's arms closed about me from behind, and I felt his lips against my ear. "'Tis only a dream. But there's a ring on my hand that would buy you. Those rings are all I have left. Ragnarson gave them to me, though no one knew it. He didn't think I'd live this long. I'm no warrior, and without my scrying stone there's a fire in my mind that burns me to ashes."

I turned into his arms and hunted for his mouth. He was still naked, and I felt him come up hard as we kissed. I knelt at his feet and slipped him between my lips. His hands cradled my head, held me to the task, yet where others forced me, he was gentle. If he bought my contract, he would own me, body and soul. And I would not care.

We ate, and I rubbed his leg before I helped him dress. The shutters were wide to let in daylight and air, and we sat with a view of the gateway. His swords were across his knees, and he worked methodically with the whetstones, honing them to an edge of perfection.

Like any warrior of the Patai tribe, he had three swords. One was a two-handed weapon, worn in a baldric over his shoulder, to be drawn in a great arc overhead. I thought it would split a man in half. The second was shorter, one-handed and single-edged, its blade thick and slightly curved with a big, flared cross guard. The third was much shorter, a stabbing sword, double-edged. Their harness was scuffed and patched, and suspended from it was a small but heavy pack I had not noticed before.

Inside I found a light mail shirt, enough to turn aside a glancing blow. I held it in my hands and looked up at Richard as he finished with his swords. He cleaned his hands of oil, wrapped the whetstones, and nodded.

"It's noon," he said tersely. "The sun sets in four hours. Koval won't travel after dark, with the bandits and the wolves hunting. Help me dress."

I buckled and laced him into the leathers, harness, and mail and stood back to watch as he settled the weight of his swords. The two-handed blade was so heavy, I could lift it but could never have fought with it. He handled it as he handled a lover. Handled me. If he lived to see the night, it would be the tool of his survival.

"Can't you See?" My heart beat painfully. "You had the gift when you were a child, before you were trained. You must be able to See!"

He touched my face. "I can See a little. A jumble of images that confuse me. With the stone, it's often like looking through an open window. Without, I'm only guessing, and I do more harm than good. The stone is a kind of magic. Without it, all is chaos. You understand?"

"No," I confessed, "but I believe."

Blood in the snow, ashes, an eagle. I shivered and knelt by the hearth, following Richard with my eyes as he returned to the window to watch the gate.

It was an hour later when his whole body tensed, his hand clenched on the shutter until his knuckles were white. I hurried to him, leaned out, and below us were three horses, three cloaked figures coming under the gate lintel and heading for the stable.

A dappled gray horse, a big black beast with a white blaze on his face, and a brown-coated cob, so heavily muscled that his rider could hardly straddle him. "Koval?" I murmured as the nags pushed through the new snow.

"In the lead, mounted on the gray," Richard told me. "The others are Endoven Ron and a woman. Endoven's property, bonded like yourself. She is nothing, but Endoven is dangerous."

"A thief, like Koval?"

"A gambler, mercenary, assassin," Richard said grimly. "He and Koval are cousins."

So he was fighting not one but two. I touched his arm as he closed the shutter. "Richard—"

"Hush." He took my face between his hands. "On the table there, I've left a letter. See Ragnarson gets it. Promise me."

"My oath on it," I swore. "But there are two of them!"

He made some sound of bitter humor. "Koval never rides alone. He has my property. I can feel it, even from here."

"Let me steal it," I begged.

He reproached me with a look. "Last time you stole, you were caught and sold. What will Brennan do if you're caught stealing from his guests?"

I knew exactly what he would do. My face flushed, and my belly sickened. "I wouldn't be caught," I protested.

"You would, the moment Koval checked his pack and found the stone gone." Richard kissed my lips. "Stay out of the way." He drew one of his swords. "I was never a warrior before, but in two years I've learned a great deal. I've watched, practiced with fine swordsmen, and won several fights."

"I saw your scars," I said miserably.

"Trivial wounds, each one the price of a victory," he said sharply and fended me off. At the door he paused and turned back. "Thank you."

"For what?" I picked up the letter, turned it over and over, and wished I could read.

He smiled. "It doesn't matter. Just get that to Ragnarson. All will be as it must be. No doubt this is what the gods intend, and I was born to end my life here."

The door closed behind him, and I stared blindly at it for a full half-minute. Years of bondage will dull the wits of any man, but give him something to fight for and those wits sharpen in moments. Anger was an emotion so alien that I barely knew it when it began to seethe. But as it boiled up I dragged open that door and ran.

I could hear the commotion in the stable yard as the boys ran out for the horses: raised voices, the clipped, spat-out accent of Vilhaven spoken by a man who treated servants badly and abused bondsmen. Richard did not know the tavern well enough to be aware of the side door that led out by the shed where the ale barrels, firewood, and lamp oil were kept. He was on his way to the front door and would go around the whole building to reach the stable. If he was quick he would cut off Koval and Endoven before they could leave the yard—and this was to his advantage, though he did not know it yet.

My bow and quiver were with my cloak and leathers, by the door. In the deep winter Brennan hardly troubled to leave his fireside, and when messages must be delivered, I was most often sent. I was young, as worthless as any cheap bondsman, but I knew how to handle a bow and a horse. Those skills were my father's only legacy, and I blessed him again as I snatched up the weapon and ducked into the shed.

The door was snow-drifted, but Jedda and I had dug it out just days before, so I could get it open. The wind had dwindled; the sky was so blue it hurt my eyes. I wedged myself inside the door and nocked an arrow before I looked out. In the quiver were twenty more shafts, but I would never need so many.

Here was the absurdity of my predicament: I could have killed Brennan on any day of my captivity, his lieutenants and his seneschals. Often I swore I would, but when my welts had healed I would admit the truth. If a bondsman raised a hand, let alone a weapon, he could die. I was a prisoner until my contract was up or until someone bought it and took me out. The fear of who might buy me, where he might take me, was so dreadful that I had endured. Until now.

If Richard lived, he would take me away. If he died, part of me died with him. I had never felt love before. The madness came over me all at once, and it was like seeing a stranger in a crowd and knowing him like a brother.

I could be killed. For what I was doing, Brennan could beat me until I was dead. No one would stop him. My heart hammered, but I lifted the bow and looked into the sun glare.

Two men and a woman were waiting for Jedda to unstrap their baggage. The woman was small, so heavily cloaked that I could see neither her face nor her shape, to know if she was attractive. The men were tall, sparely built, dressed like highborn Vilhaveners. They wore the Sheal Clan colors, dusky red and creamy white. That clan had a reputation for treachery. My pulse beat harder. Which was Koval?

As Jedda lifted down the bags, the men turned toward me, and at a glance I knew which must be Koval. So this was the thief who had seduced Richard. His hair was yellow as wheat, his features fine and high-cheekboned, his lips full. It was a sensual face, but not a kind one. I saw foxlike cunning and was afraid.

"So, Koval. What brings you to Breakheart when the roads are almost closed?"

Richard's voice was deceptively pleasant. I leaned out to see him. He was in the arched gate that led out of the stable yard, standing foursquare, blocking the way. His cloak was thrown back, all his swords to hand, and the hilts of several knives poked from his boots and sheaths in his sleeves. The sun gleamed on his hair, his breath plumed in the sharp cold, and the smile on his face was a frozen mask. He was poised like a dancer, and though he swore he was no warrior, he had the look of one.

The thief spun, his eyes widened in the glare of sun on snow, and he spat a mouthful of Vilhaven crudity before he reined back his temper. "I heard you were outcast. I heard Ragnarson banished you, and the Scryers Guild stripped you of your rank."

"True." Richard's chin lifted. "But you should know me, Koh. Did you think I'd lie down and let you kick me?"

"Me?" Koval pretended surprise. "I don't understand what you mean. Step out of my way, Richard. It's cold out here."

But Richard stood firm. His voice was like broken glass. "Return my property and I'll let you leave Breakheart alive. I've a score to settle with you, but it can wait for another day, a better place." He held out his hand. "Give it to me."

"Your property?" Koval's blond head tossed as he laughed. "You're mistaken. The stone was mine from the moment I took it. That's Vilhaven law. He who holds, possesses."

A wolfish smile creased Richard's face. "Then by Vilhaven law, if I take it back, it's mine." He nodded thoughtfully. "That seems fair."

As he spoke he drew the heavy sword in a great arc over his head and grasped it in both hands. There is a way a swordsman stands—something about the sureness of his limbs—that proclaims his skill. Though I was breathless with dread, I saw all this about Richard, and my throat tightened. Two years he had been on the road, and he wore the scars of many victories. Where had he been? Who had taught him?

My eyes flicked to Koval, and I saw his surprise. When he had left Richard in Ragnarson's house, he had left a young man in disgrace, suffering the pain of many losses at once. Richard had lost his rank; Ragnarson had no choice but to discard him. His lover had betrayed him, and the Scryers Guild reviled him. Without the focusing power of his stone, his gift was uncontrollable, his sleep troubled, and his life would run out like a runaway grass fire. Koval must have believed Richard was dead already or that he must be sick, ruined. To see him here with a sword in his hand was the last thing the thief could have imagined.

Still, Koval recovered quickly. He stepped closer to his kinsman, and already Endoven had drawn his sword. After serving the mercenaries who passed constantly through Breakheart on their way between Moorkind and Valdenheim, I was a good judge of swords. Endoven's was a curved-bladed vash—a fine weapon, but not the match of Richard's.

With a serpentine slither, the sword was out of Koval's own scabbard, and he dropped into the familiar fighter's crouch. "What use is the stone to you?" he demanded of Richard. "The guilds won't take you back. Will you ply the seer's trade for money, like a common whore? Better to die honorably. Come onto my sword; I'll do the job for you."

The provocation heated my blood, but Richard seemed oblivious. His boots crunched through the snow as he stepped into the yard, and Jedda scurried to fetch Brennan or the lieutenants. They would be at the hearth and reluctant to leave, but if they did come, whom would they back? The Sheal Clan was notorious, while Ragnarson carried some weight even here. But Brennan had kinsmen in Vilhaven—his loyalties could lie anywhere.

"Jedda!" I shouted from the doorway. The boy broke stride, turned toward me. "Not yet, Jedda. See nothing for a few minutes!"

"But Fendel—" he began. Something about my face must have warned him, and he dived for the stables, where he could swear he was looking for the farrier or the groom.

Koval and Endoven were shoulder to shoulder, and steel chimed with a sound like bells, clear and ringing in the winter air. Richard was good. Perhaps he was not born to the warrior caste, but he had found good teachers, and his skills were sound. The heavy blade leaped like a bird in his hands; the sun cast a rainbow from its edge as he drove Koval back. If Richard had been pitted against Koval alone, it would have been easy, but no sooner did Koval falter than Endoven took his place.

Crows cawed from the eaves, and over the rath, hunting on outstretched wings, was a white eagle. The great bird dipped over Richard's head; its shadow raced over the snow, touching Endoven as it went. Of a sudden I recalled the superstition. Mountain folk have always said that if the shadow of a hunting eagle touches you, your time is short.

A flurry of cuts made Endoven retreat, and Koval launched himself again. Only I knew how tired Richard was. How poor were his chances against two. Endoven was resting while Koval wore down their rival, and I saw Richard begin to falter. He was exhausted; his hip was slowing him, as we had known it must. The torment of the past years haunted him. I marveled that he had survived so long and kept his strength. This match was so unequal, tears of rage stung my eyes, and the madness consumed me again.

My bow was already drawn, but the decision to aim and loose the arrow was instinctive. I had done it before I was aware of the action, and after running the gauntlet of the wolf pack I was a good shot. The shaft buried itself in the back of Endoven's thigh. He screamed and fell, clutching helplessly at his leg. Heart hammering, I dropped the bow, clambered over the drifted snow, and darted across the yard.

Down and writhing, Endoven barely saw me. I came up behind him, seized the arrow, and wrenched it out in one movement. The man screamed again as the barbs ripped through flesh and muscle. Then I was up, quick as a thief, and diving back toward the door with one thought in my mind. I might get away with this. Endoven was in no condition to know who had torn out the arrow.

But a shape whirled by me, a cloak billowed. I saw a gleam of sunlight on the blade of a knife, and before I could make it out of the yard I watched that steel plunge into the unprotected throat of Endoven as he lay cursing at my feet.

Blood gushed, hot as his insides, melting the snow into a thin, pink lake. Endoven's eyes bulged. He pawed at his gullet, but the finest healer in Moorkind could not have helped him. He fell, lax and dead, and I spun toward his executioner, fearing for my own life.

My fear was wasted. Koval's bondswoman had already turned the knife on herself. It was wedged beneath her ribs, its tip in her heart, and I watched her violet eyes glaze. I could only guess what she had suffered at his hands, how long she had waited for her chance to end it. Perhaps she had suffered no more than I, but she was no brat from the canals; how could she survive and keep her mind?

I threw the arrow into the shed and pulled the door shut with seconds to spare. Brennan's voice thundered from the gateway, but Richard and Koval ignored him. They were circling like prowling wolves, jabbing, attacking at any opportunity. Richard had thrown aside the heavy sword and was working with the lighter blade now. He could taste victory, and I saw the feral joy in his face as he felt revenge in his grasp. Koval had hurt him in so many ways. Many times Richard must have wished himself dead.

But it was Koval who fell as the sword's point gashed his belly, laid him open hip to hip. He went to his knees, pitched into the snow, and his mouth opened to scream though he made no sound.

Brennan was roaring, and for the first time Richard seemed to hear. He panted, his face was flushed with effort, and gestured for me to pick up his swords. "All right, Brennan, I hear you." He touched the silver hawk on his breast. "You know Ragnarson's device."

"I know it well enough," Brennan assured him.

"Then you know I'm Ragnarson's seer." Richard was getting his breath back rapidly. "This man—" he gave Koval's body a shove with one boot "—is a thief. Search his pack, you'll find a scrying stone. *My* scrying stone, without which I'm such useless baggage, the guilds wouldn't have me to sweep their floors! I'm here on Ragnarson's business. I came for my stone, and I'll take it now."

He could barely wait to get his hands on it. I felt his craving and guessed it must be as keen as lust or hunger. I dragged the saddlebags off Koval's horse and opened them at Richard's feet. His hands trembled and grasped as I rummaged, finding every trinket but what he wanted.

Then, there it was. A crystal that winked like an enormous diamond. A lens, a focus, the tool of the scryer's ancient art. With this in his hands, his gift was so precious that Ragnarson—or any man—would take Richard into his house and give him pride of place. Ragnarson would surely persuade the guild to reinstate him. I lifted the stone, gave it to him, and got to my feet.

He petted it like a kitten, held it to his breast where he wore the tattoo. For some time he seemed almost drunk, and then he blinked his eyes clear and looked at me. "Thank you. I saw what you did."

"You saw what?" Brennan rumbled.

Richard ignored him. "The boy's contract is for sale?"

This took Brennan by surprise. "You want him? You'll be returning to Moorkind. He's a thief. Take a thief into Ragnarson's house, and you'll rue it."

"Ragnarson's house has had its share of thieves," Richard said cryptically, with a glance at Koval. "I'll pay your price for the boy. Have his contract made over to me. And I'll take the horses belonging to these men." Turning to me, he added, "If we leave now, Fendel, we can be in Gaelgate by nightfall. In three days it'll snow so hard, the passes won't open till spring. There will be a fire here. That chimney is about to split. The thatch will blaze, because Brennan doesn't believe me and won't trouble to make repairs." He lifted the stone, let it catch the sun. "I have what is mine. And for that..." he held out his hand, and I clasped it. "I'm in your debt."

What Brennan made of this I never knew, but within the hour I was mounted on the dappled gray horse Koval had ridden, while Richard was on the black, leading the way south out of Breakheart. Behind us, funeral pyres were already smoking. The wind scattered ash across the forecourt, darkening the snow.

My contract was made over in Richard's name, safe in his jacket. According to Moorkind law, I belonged to him as I had belonged to Brennan. I would be his property for five years, to keep or to sell, and if he killed me, no real questions would be asked. But Moorkind law was wrong. I did not belong to Richard because of any bond contract, and I would be with him much longer than five years. I would be with him until he told me to go, long after my freedom was restored. Love is more binding than any bond contract.

The setting sun was bloated in a sky so crimson, it made me think of blood—of Koval, Endoven, and the woman whose name I never knew. I touched my heels to the gray's sides to bring him up alongside Richard, who had reined back on the shoulder of the hill. Below us were the roofs of Gaelgate. I could smell hearth smoke, and I was hungry.

Richard teased me with a smile. "I never owned a bondsman before. You'll eat from my plate, will you?"

"Tend your horses, sharpen your swords, clean your leathers," I added. "Then set your hearth, make your bed, and share it with you—if you'll have me."

"Oh, I'll have you," he said, a growl that made me shiver. "Five years until you're free, boy. I expect I'll have you a great many times!"

"And many more thereafter," I added. The wind gusted, and a flurry of snow brushed my face. "Let's get in before it starts."

He caught my hand and squeezed it tightly, a gesture of affection. Then he urged his horse down the sloping trail toward the town, and I was glad to follow.

Heart of Stone
Lawrence Schimel

At the sight of the farmhouse, Javi's heart began to pound within his chest, and in his excitement he tripped on a root and went sprawling to the ground. The lute he had cradled so carefully against his body went flying from his hands. Javi cried out, first in anguish as he flailed to grab hold of the falling instrument, then in pain as his knee scraped against a rock, which tore through cloth and skin alike. The lute banged to the ground and teetered forward and back on its curved belly. Javi scrambled to his feet, ignoring the twinge of pain in his knee as he put pressure on it, and picked the instrument up. *Aside from one broken string,* he thought as he examined it, *it looks fine.* He would just play everything but that string, he decided. He cradled the lute against his chest and turned toward the farmhouse again. At the sight of it all his troubles faded like mist before the morning sun, and his heart began to race once more.

The heir apparent to Kolofell was twelve years old and madly in love with Brun, the son of a farmer who lived just beyond the castle walls. His father, if he knew, would not approve, but Javi did not care. When he was two, his father had betrothed him to the daughter of a neighboring kingdom for a political alliance, and so long as he married the girl next year and produced an heir, his father did not have a say in whom Javi courted on the side. The gods knew, Javi had often enough stumbled upon his father in dalliance with one serving girl or another. Why should he begrudge his son the love of but one boy?

As he stared up at the still-dark square of Brun's window, imagining him lying abed, his dark yellow curls spread about his face like a halo upon his pillow, Javi forgot the words to the love song he had spent all night composing and then painstakingly memorizing, reciting it hundreds of times to his mirror by candlelight as he waited for the first ray of dawn. His mind was a blank.

Worried that they were forever lost, he looked down at the lute he cradled in his hands and tried anxiously to recall them. Something about his eyes, yes, and how for him Brun's words were music. He began to strum the lute softly, playing as if one string were not broken. Softly, so as to wake his love gently. Then, after giving him time to be awakened by the soothing music, Javi began to sing. He sang with feeling, loudly so that his words carried up to the window his bold proclamations of love. Oh, how his heart ached when there was a rustling at the curtains. Javi's voice cracked with his longing for Brun, who was come to the window to acknowledge him and say he would be his. Javi's voice rang with the overflowing emotion he felt, belting out the verses he had so painstakingly written.

The curtains trembled again, and Javi felt his knees tremble in sympathy. The love of his life's form filled the window for a brief moment. Even so early in the morning, Brun's aim was true; the boot struck Javi on the side of his head, ending his song with squelch of pain as he winced and dropped the lute again to clutch his boxed ear.

Staring at the boot, he realized he should have serenaded Brun in the evening instead of disturbing his rest. He was a farmer's son, who no doubt cherished his sleep after the full day of chores behind him and the one still to come. *Fool,* he berated himself as he bent to retrieve the token, *why didn't I think of that before?*

He placed the boot on the doorstep so Brun would not have to step barefoot in the dirt and sully his feet to retrieve it. And as if the boot were a crystal vase, he dropped two roses into its tall calf.

Whistling a phrase from his song, Javi turned to walk back to the castle and found Brun's father standing behind him. The farmer seemed tall as a tree as he loomed over Javi with a sour, pinched face. Javi hoped the man's displeasure was not because he had been serenading Brun; he imagined his own father's wrath if he had been the one to catch him just now.

"Good day, sir," Javi said, trying not to show his surprise or nervousness.

"It's not a good day," the farmer replied. Javi felt suddenly concerned for his safety and glanced casually about him. No one else was in sight. He wished he could hurry back to the castle, especially before his absence was noted, but he and the farmer stood at an impasse. *He seems a good, honest workingman,* Javi thought, trying to reassure himself. *Perhaps he is not so closed-minded as farmers are said to be.*

"It's not?" Javi asked meekly when the farmer ventured nothing further.

"Indeed not. My plow is blocked by a huge boulder in my field. I was despairing that I had no way to remove it when I heard you singing. *Another pair of hands,* I thought to myself. Come, it's not far."

Relieved that the man's displeasure was not caused by Javi's courting his son, Javi followed docilely behind the man, worrying how he could be of much help. This man dwarfed him in size and strength, and Javi's small addition of force would make no noticeable difference, he knew. But this man was Brun's father, and he wanted to make a good impression on him that he might plead Javi's case to his son.

To Javi's dismay, the boulder was as tall as Brun's father and twice his height in width. "What use am I to move such?" he pleaded as they approached the giant stone.

The farmer did not answer until they had reached the boulder. He set his hands upon it. "With the Stonesword it could be chopped into smaller pieces and thereby removed from my fields."

The Stonesword! Javi's mind raced with thoughts of his father's magical sword, which could slice through rock as if it were soft cheese. It was a powerful weapon, which Javi had touched only once. His father kept it well guarded in his armory, to keep it safe from all those who wished to steal it and misuse its powers. However, it wasn't being used for good at present, either—when its powers could be so useful to many of his father's people, in cases like the one at hand. He could ask his father, perhaps. But how would he explain his involvement with the farmer? He would have to explain as well about Brun, and…and Javi's father was as closed-minded as a farmer!

The farmer could see Javi wavering in his contemplation of the idea. "It would be a wonderful way to impress Brun," he said.

Javi blushed as his love for this man's son was so openly alluded to, yet he also realized how true the statement was. He would be like a hero to Brun, using a magic sword to help his father. So simply, he could use the Stonesword to cut through Brun's stony heart where he was concerned. He could borrow the sword from the armory and bring it back as soon as he was done. *It's like a quest with no danger,* Javi thought to himself as he told the farmer he'd be right back with the sword.

*   *   *

The castle was, as usual, abustle with activity. After being stopped twice on his way to the armory, Javi despaired of ever sneaking the sword out of the castle without interference. He headed for the kitchen to try to sneak some food from the pantry as breakfast; it would be easier for him to think of a plan on a full stomach. *And besides,* he thought, *it would be good practice for sneaking the sword out.*

Marge found him sitting in the preserves pantry with a loaf of bread. "And just what are you doing in here, child?"

"Looking for a bit of privacy," Javi replied, wondering briefly if he should try to cover up the food or if it was too late already.

"That'll be the day, when a stone pile this size gives you someplace to be private! I can tell you...well, you being the lord's son, I shouldn't say such things to you." She winked and turned to leave the preserves closet.

Javi stood up and grabbed her arm, having suddenly recalled that Marge's lover was the armory guard. "But that's just it, Marge. See, there's—" Javi opted for discretion as the best method of furthering his plan, "—someone I've a fancy for." He stared down at Marge, letting this information sink in and also marveling that in the past month he had grown taller than she was. "I was trying to think of a way we might have some privacy together. And I think I've just thought of one."

Marge stared at his smiling, smug young face for a moment, then demanded, "Well, what is it?"

"You're going to take me on a picnic," Javi declared.

Marge laughed. "You've a queer idea of privacy, child. And also of the things a working woman is free to do. Picnics aren't among them."

"But that's just it. You wouldn't actually go on the picnic with me. You'd just say that's where we were going. I'd cancel my classes, and that would mean no one would be using my classroom. You would be free to...have some privacy with Venn."

Javi could tell Marge was seriously interested by the way her face became suddenly skeptical when she noticed him watching her. "And what do you get out of it?" she asked.

Javi smiled, knowing she was hooked. "With no classes because of the picnic, I'm free to have some privacy myself." He puffed himself up to his full, if slender, height, trying to keep a sly, knowing expression on his face, and accidentally bumped into the shelf of preserves behind him. Jars came crashing to the floor, and Javi stared horrified at the spreading apricot puddle at his feet. "I'm—I'm so sorry," he stammered, while Marge began

178

laughing uncontrollably. "I'll help clean it up."

"Your face!" Marge giggled. "Your face!" Her body shook with laughter, and once the initial waves of mirth had passed she said, "Don't worry about these. I'll clean them up. You go cancel your classes and tell Venn to meet me in your classroom in half an hour. Then you and I will go on our picnic." She winked, then broke into another fit of mirth as she looked down at the puddle of apricots.

Javi pulled the sword from its sheath and admired its god-forged blade. *It all seems too easy,* he thought as he slid the weapon back into the scabbard and lifted it down from the wall. Venn had instantly run off to meet Marge as soon as Javi had mentioned the empty classroom. While Javi was grateful to be rid of him in order to sneak out with the sword, he was disappointed in his father's guard. *Of course,* Javi reflected as he wandered out into the hall, trying to walk as nonchalantly as he could while carrying the huge weapon, *it wasn't like anything was going to happen in the middle of the castle.* They hadn't been to war in years, which is why the sword had lain unused for so long. Javi's betrothal all those years ago had appeased Kolofell's last belligerent neighbor. But it was the principle of the matter; if anything, Javi's borrowing the sword might be an interesting prank to show how lax the guard had become.

So far the coast had been clear, but Javi heard footsteps around the next corner and the master-at-arms's voice. He'd never impress Brun if he got caught stealing from his own father! He ran back down the hall and dashed through the first door he could find. It was a storage room, filled with dusty crates. Javi had no idea what was in them, so to keep himself from worrying about the master-at-arms outside in the hallway he slowly poked around exploring his surroundings in the thin shaft of sunlight that entered the room through a high, iron-barred window. Staring up at the window, Javi suddenly had an idea for getting out of the castle without getting caught. He listened carefully for voices or footsteps outside in the hall, then pushed a crate under the window. He climbed atop it and stared at the gardens on the other side of the wall. They were empty. Javi smiled and drew the Stonesword from its scabbard. He might be growing, but he was still very thin and need only cut one or two of the bars from the surrounding stone to let himself wriggle through. *Will I ever grow to have a body like Brun's?* he wondered, envious despite the fact that his slight frame would be so useful in this situation.

Javi held the sword cautiously, regarding it in the dusty shaft of light, and wondered if he would feel a tingle of magic as it sliced through the stone. He inserted the blade between the bars and slowly lowered it until it touched the stone. A loud hammering rang out, the rumbling of stone against stone, and Javi dropped the sword in alarm. The hilt fell against his foot, and the sword clattered to the floor moments before he fell beside it on his backside with a heavy thud. "The gods take—" he began to curse, before remembering that he was supposed to keep quiet and sneak out of the castle without attracting attention. The gods alone knew how many people had already heard him when he fell, not to mention the hammering sounds the Stonesword made when it cut into the wall. Javi stood, rubbing his aches and wishing life were simpler. He dusted himself off, wishing Brun would simply open his arms to him and accept him without all this wooing and effort involved. Although the wooing itself wasn't so bad. It was even quite fun, and terribly romantic, which delighted Javi. It was just this particular quest that seemed to be going awry.

Javi climbed back atop the crate to inspect where the Stonesword had touched the rock. There was a thin, neat line carved a handspan into the stone— from just a touch! Javi smiled and climbed down again to retrieve the sword. There was no way for him to silence the hammering sound as the sword worked its magic, he knew, but he would work quickly and hope no one heard him.

As Javi hurried past the farmhouse toward the fields where Brun's father waited, he glanced up at Brun's window. His heart fluttered in his chest with pleasure. There, in his window, was a pickle jar that held his two roses! He couldn't refrain from singing his delight in a spontaneous serenade, extolling the virtues of Brun's beauty, his strength, and his loyalty. Javi's voice faltered momentarily as the curtains fluttered and he realized Brun was upstairs listening to him. But he sang on, ignoring the slight mishap. A moment later, the jar of roses was hurtling down at Javi. He ducked, lifting the sword to shield himself from the falling crockery. It shattered against the blade, drenching him in water and glass shards. Blinking in shock, Javi stared down at the broken vessel. The sword had sliced the stems of both roses in twain.

Attracted by the noise, Brun's father came walking toward him from the fields. Javi tried to dry his face on the back of his sleeve and make himself presentable before Brun's father came near. As he pulled his arm away, Javi stared aghast at his sleeve, now covered in splotches of blood, and realized that he had been sliced by the glass shards. He stared up at Brun's window, perplexed that Brun could hurt him so, and therefore never saw Brun's father raise his hoe in the air and knock Javi over the head.

Javi woke to see Brun's beautiful face bending over him. He smiled and puckered his lips to accept a kiss, trying to raise his arms to wrap them around those beautiful, broad shoulders. Javi would feel so safe protected by those shoulders, sheltered in them; they would go together so perfectly, Javi fitting snugly, comfortably inside them as they nestled together. Brun slapped him across the face, bringing him into stinging wakefulness. Javi tried to lift his hand to his cheek, cradle it against the pain, but his hands were bound. "Behave," Brun commanded as he fumbled with the ropes that bound Javi's hands behind his back. Suddenly Javi remembered bringing the Stonesword for Brun's father and the hoe coming down on his head and—

"The Stonesword!"

"Quiet," Brun commanded again, still working the ropes. Javi felt a searing sense of betrayal in the pit of his stomach. Here he had tried to impress what he thought was the love of his life, but Brun had been merely the bait to lure him with the Stonesword. Bile rose in Javi's throat, and he swallowed to try to push it back down, a dry, dusty swallow that was of little help. He licked his lips, which felt cracked, trying to moisten his mouth as he contemplated what to do next and what his feelings about Brun were.

"There," Brun said and stood, walking away from him.

Javi watched his retreating figure for a moment. He still wished to be held by those arms, betrayal or none, and cried out, "Wait!" Javi pushed himself up on one elbow and suddenly realized Brun had been setting him free, not trussing him up. His heart lifted once again; Brun had been true to him! And he had saved him.

Brun paused, then turned toward Javi again. "He's probably still outside the castle walls," he said coldly, "planning a way in." Brun turned away from Javi once more and disappeared inside the house.

Was Brun in cahoots with his father or not? Had he simply changed his mind? Javi couldn't tell. But at the moment it didn't make much difference. He stood and turned toward the castle. No one else had any idea that it was even under attack, let alone that a god-forged weapon was involved. Which meant that it was up to Javi to stop it. He would figure out Brun's involvement later on.

* * *

It was the hammering that drew Javi to him, a familiar sound he recognized as the magic of the sword and not mundane construction, as most people would assume. When was the last time any of them had heard the sword used? And who would suspect it would be used now? Against the castle itself, no less!

Brun's father was trying to break through the castle wall from the empty sculpture gardens. Javi had no idea what he was after. The treasury's gold? Or even Javi's father's life!

Forgive me, Brun! Javi thought, and he threw himself at Brun's father.

Javi was growing, but he still hadn't come into his full height and weight. Nonetheless, because the man wasn't suspecting anything, he fell to the ground, the sword flying from his grasp. Javi knew he was helpless against the farmer in a battle of strength, so his first instinct was to get up and go for the sword. He had nearly reached it when Brun's father grabbed his ankle and yanked him down to the ground. Javi continued struggling to grab the sword, although he wondered as he strained for it, his arm outstretched, if he could actually use it against flesh. He never got the chance to find out.

Brun's father dragged him backward, then picked up the sword. He advanced toward Javi, the sword upraised, and Javi knew deep inside that this man wasn't going to question whether he could kill someone with the sword. Javi scrambled to his feet and bolted into the sculpture garden, Brun's father fast on his heels in pursuit. Javi wove among the marble sculptures, hoping to lose his attacker, but to no avail. He was running out of breath and could feel himself slowing down. If he didn't think of something soon...

Javi tripped and fell to the ground with a heavy thud. *Good-bye, Brun,* he thought. *If only—*

But he couldn't give up that easily. Desperately, he crawled forward toward a cluster of sculptures, hoping to use them as a shield. Javi stood and peeked at Brun's father from under a marble arm. The farmer stood just on the other side of the sculpture, and Javi knew he was in desperate straits. Brun's father laughed and swung the sword. Javi saw the weapon coming toward his face and pulled back. The sword chopped effortlessly through the marble arm he had a moment ago been peeking from under. It fell to the ground. A hammering echoed in Javi's ears. In his distress, he had forgotten about the sword's magical powers! The sculptures would be of little use as a shield against the Stonesword.

In an effort to get away, Javi began circling back toward the castle, dashing from sculpture to sculpture. The Stonesword might be able to cut through the marble, but at least it slowed the sword down. Brun's father noticed where Javi was headed and blocked him off. They stood on either side of a tall, thin woman. The sculpture was too far away from the others; if Javi ran to either side he would surely be wounded. They were at an impasse.

The farmer laughed again, a cruel, deep laugh, and swung the sword at the sculpture's legs. Javi had jumped backward instinctively as the sword swung toward him, but in desperation he ran toward the sculpture again and pushed it forward. It toppled toward Brun's father, the heavy stone pinning him. Javi leaped over the fallen statue and grabbed the sword, running off a distance to catch his breath in safety. He turned to look at Brun's father, to make sure he hadn't managed to push the statue off himself and was again attacking. The man wasn't moving. Javi wondered if it was a ploy to lure him close only to grab him, but he couldn't help walking closer to look. A puddle of blood was pooling beneath Brun's father, and the white marble was splattered with red like berries against the snow.

Javi threw the sword away and fell to his knees. He had killed a man!

He was still retching when the guards found him.

Javi stared curiously at Brun, now on trial to determine his involvement in his father's plans. He wasn't sure how Brun felt about him for having killed his father, but Javi knew that he still loved Brun as desperately as he had before, if not more so. Javi had already given his side of the story and been duly reprimanded for taking the Stonesword. He would be working off his punishment for years, it seemed, and his body was already beginning to ache from the mere thought of the labors he had been assigned by his father. His killing of Brun's father had been in self-defense, it was determined, and in defense of the castle.

So far it seemed that Brun had had nothing to do with his father's plans, which heartened Javi. He didn't know how he would have dealt with his love had Brun been implicated. Javi's father was still asking questions, however, and Javi listened closely for Brun's responses.

"You seem very cold-hearted toward your father."

And me as well! Javi wanted to cry out. But he hadn't mentioned why he had been out at the farmer's house when he'd told his side of the story, so he kept quiet.

"And why should I be sorry to see him gone from the earth? I am glad to be free of him at last." Brun paused, looking around the circle of assembled men around him, meeting each of their eyes, but pointedly not Javi's, before continuing. "Since my mother died he would force me to lie with him."

Javi cried out, an inarticulate sound of frustration and outrage that rose above the surprise of everyone else. His father silenced the room and declared the trial over. Brun was not guilty and would inherit his father's lands and possessions.

The sun hovered just above the horizon, balanced as if it sat an orange globe upon the earth. Javi stared up at Brun's window and the soft light emanating from within. He brought the lute into position, its strings having been repaired in the long week since last he had seen Brun. Javi had felt that Brun needed some time to recover from the upheavals in his life and Javi's part in them, and though it tore his heart not to see his beloved, Javi had waited until now before resuming his courting.

Javi sang hesitantly, unsure of his reception. He had given much thought about whether and how to proceed after learning of Brun's having been abused by his father. He was so very much in love with Brun that the thought of dropping their courtship was an improbability in Javi's mind. But he would proceed slowly, winning Brun back from the negative experiences he had had with another man.

When nothing came hurtling out of the window, Javi gained more confidence. He began to sing louder, letting more of his feelings for Brun enter the music. He knew Brun was up there because candles were lit in the room, and Javi's heart swelled with happiness simply to know Brun was listening to his professions of love.

Javi was on the penultimate verse before Brun threw something.

His aim was still true; it hit Javi in the ear again. Javi stared down at this new token and broke into a smile. *It may take a while,* Javi thought, *but I'm slowly wearing him down, eroding my way into Brun's stony heart. And I'm willing to wait.*

Instead of his hard-heeled boot Brun had thrown a soft, embroidered slipper.

Rhezellah's Song
Nina Boal

T
his night. We were gathered in the armory, my sisters and I—sisters not by blood but through the thread of a common rejection of our slavery. Six months ago, Lord Julat ordered the flogging of our sister Linnet for a trivial offense. She died of her wounds.

After tonight. Our master would be put to death. Our vengeance for Linnet would be complete. The seven of us would celebrate a common freedom.

Our plan was simple. We had given our master no reason to doubt our loyalty; he did not think to guard against us. We would burst into his bedchamber, surround him. I, as our group's elected captain, would thrust a sword through his heart.

We were the *Anhillhin.* Lord Julat Kallia's female harem-guards, in a land where women were thought of as soulless creatures—fancied baubles or else wombs to bear sons. Ental, the god of heaven, had taught all his children the ways of our traditions—traditions that had ensured the survival of the Wadallhil people through the centuries.

Red-orange lights from the full fire moon poured through the armory's windows. She is the brightest of the three moons. Shal'lu. Goddess of flame, stealer of children and men's souls—or so it is said.

I reached into a pocket, grasping the small, round mirror all warriors carry, even *Anhillhin.* I gazed into it. I had been chosen to lead the revolt, to give directions to the others. Warrior mirrors were ancient, well-used devices. But this discussion, this calling ourselves sisters, was entirely new. We were accustomed to simply following Lord Julat's orders unquestioningly. As rebels, however, we had pledged ourselves to new ways of thought and action.

My own image gazed back at me. I wore the traditional *Anhillhin* garb, as did my collaborators—black boots, black cotton breeches and tunics, curved short swords thrust into sashes. I took in my braided jet-black hair, alabaster-white skin, blue eyes almost indigo in the torchlight. My sisters would likewise search inside themselves in their own mirrors. It was time to do the final purging in the mirror ritual before our battle.

Wadallhil warriors always perform the mirror ritual to Ental for protection from the fire goddess. Our ritual tonight would be different. Seven *Anhillhin*, Ental's daughters, would call on Ental's enemy—the ritual would be done in Shal'lu's name. Her rays flickered along my mirror's edge.

Let the Lord of Tarsia invoke Ental. My thoughts crackled with Shal'lu's fire. As one of the *Anhillhin* I had been initiated into the ways of Ental as a young girl. Virgin daughter of heaven, guardian of Ental's precious jewels, I had been given my sword on my tenth birthday. I had followed Ental's way; I had proved my loyalty well.

But my sword had sung a different song to me as I circled it, cutting the air in training sessions. Vainly, I had sought to block out its harsh melody. I had been told that women are content in their place, that it is the Wadallhil way. My blade had continued its quiet hum, ripping apart the shroud of my illusions, showing me the screams and cries of the unwilling.

My own fury swelled, flaring within. I had swallowed one lie after another, trained in my duties to uphold Ental's righteous rule. I had guarded the women, the "precious jewels"—and thus held them in their odious slavery. I thought of Linnet. My sword trembled in my hand as my heart pounded within me. My silent vows echoed my sisters'. *No more. No more. Not ever again.*

I peered again into the mirror. My mind gloated over an image of a *certain* woman, as I damnably knew it would. *Rhezellah.* I was virgin and celibate; the doctrine held that all *Anhillhin* women would be without sexual desire. I also knew this tenet to be grossly false. I felt the desires inside me, though I could not express them. I knew myself to be a lover of women.

I should have hated Rhezellah. The supple body, the flashing gray eyes, the silken blond hair that spilled to her waist. Most women I had seen served their masters because they were without choice in their situation. Rhezellah gave her entire self to Julat, willingly and without shame. I should have despised her kind.

186

Instead my dreams haunted me. She would lie in my arms, her hands caressing black hair, her lips trailing along my quivering skin until they would lap my ravenous cunt. Rhezellah had an almost magical voice that sang out ballads and airs, holding its listener captive. One night long ago, as I had paced to and fro during my guard duties, the thin, clear threads of melody had taken me as a helpless prisoner.

Some nights the dreams had assumed incredible, fantastic shapes. Rhezellah would walk, her body pressed next to mine, in a distant, foreign land where women dwelled free. Our love had journeyed far beyond my own desire. We had linked together in the bond of soul kin—the deepest joining two minds can make.

I stared at the still glass in front of me. *Hopeless,* my thought tore out of me. It could never be; I could not afford the foolish musings of these visions. Somehow I would have to purge myself. My face set itself firmly. *If Rhezellah lies by her master's side tonight...*She would be witness to our attack. She would have to die with him.

How was I to invoke Shal'lu? I had never done it before. I stared as my own image gazed back at me from the flame-flecked glass. Perhaps I imagined it—or perhaps the goddess whispered, summoning me. *Bedwin.* She called my name, a tendril within my mind. *Bedwin. You are your sisters' captain. Listen to me. Feel my rhythm rising within you.* I tore my eyes from the mirror and sought the face of the fire moon, which floated in the crystal-clear sky. I drank in her strength; my mind rested only on the coming battle. My purge was complete.

Presently the strands of the goddess's fire released me. I nodded and replaced my mirror in my pocket; my sisters did likewise. We gathered into our group, holding each other's hands. "Shal'lu give us strength tonight for Linnet's sake," I whispered a last prayer. "Or let us continue into our next lives as your sisters and daughters."

I heard a suppressed intake of breath from Dalisa, the youngest of our group, who stood next to me. Being born female was considered punishment for past sins in a previous life. No one had ever prayed to come back as a woman; it was unheard-of. Gray-haired Aleshah, standing on the other side of Dalisa, cradled the younger woman's hand in hers, reminding her of our previous discussions. "New prayers, new ways of thought. Remember?" Dalisa smiled at the group. Her laughter rippled.

We crept down the sconce-lit corridor—five of us toward our master's night quarters, two toward the stables; they would ready our horses for our getaway. My palms moistened as I clutched my sword.

Killing Julat would be the easy part. The difficult part would be the escape. Tolek, Julat's heir, would be honor-bound to capture and punish his father's murderers. His palace guards would pursue us as we traveled through the palace's secret passages. Dalisa had a map folded within her tunic; hers had been the task of researching our escape route through the winding, turning pathways.

There would be one other grim task. Julat would be entertaining himself with a "favorite." I swallowed hard. Perhaps it would it be Dacia, his wife, or Melith, his First Concubine. Then there was Gabriele, the beautiful boy he had just purchased recently. Cold shivers scuttled through my body. I knew it would be none of these. It would be Rhezellah.

I clenched my jaw, thrusting Rhezellah's image to the side. There was nothing more to it. Bedwin, captain of the *Anhillhin* rebels' force, could allow no obstacle to jeopardize our mission of vengeance and freedom. My eyes drifted toward a high corridor window. Shal'lu's fire-orange disk shimmered against the pristine sky. Her face gazed impassively upon us.

We crouched by the door to Julat's bedchamber. I peered in—and my worst nightmares had come true. Lord Julat lay sprawled upon twisted floral-print covers. A slender, almost feline figure curled over his bare chest. Blond tresses poured over thin shoulders while hands stroked the coarse brown hair of her master. Her tongue snaked out, licking the tangled beard.

My stomach roiled; I almost lost our mission by spewing out its sparse contents. Rhezellah was as breathtaking as ever, dressed in sheer tunic and billowing pantaloons of a pale emerald shade, trimmed in gold. Julat's hand trailed over her throat, fingering the gold filigree necklace, the matching earrings. She canted her head back, turning slitted, long-lashed eyes upward. Full, pink lips pursed, inviting her master's plunder.

My heart pounded. I no longer believed the doctrine of women's lack of substance—but Rhezellah truly showed herself a creature without soul. Voices clashed in my mind. Savage entreaties to kill fought with pleas of mercy. I strove to lift an arm, to signal our attack. It hung by my side, a thing made of lead.

And then Rhezellah opened her mouth—and sang. The lilting voice arched, curling toward the shadowy reaches of the ceiling. It flickered with the torchlight, then drew itself into a single strand of pure crystal.

Rhezellah sang. Time halted in its tracks—and her voice pried into the shell of my being. It burrowed itself, spiraling, a diamond tendril, fragile yet impenetrable. *Magic,* a harsh voice warned. A weapon, a spell from Ental or perhaps from his son, Bakan, who rules the underworld. My fingers wound tightly around my sword hilt.

And the voice ached inside me, ripping the surrounding silence apart. It sliced through barriers, piercing the throbbing heart inside. Tears erupted from my eyes. I fought against them. *Bedwin,* I cried to myself. *Battle against it. Invoke Shal'lu's strength.* Virgin I was—yet my own desire gravely threatened our mission. The rivulets of my craven weakness flowed down my cheeks. The voice wrapped a velvet cloak around me.

I lifted my face. The voice sang, twisting inside me again—a hollow, chill thread of solitude. Cloud-gray eyes seized my gaze. Storms raged inside round, glittering pools.

I glanced toward Julat, then toward the bedchamber's lone window. I sought Shal'lu's strength. The window faced the wrong direction—the fire moon was blocked from view. Julat lay still, stretched out on the flowered mattress. His body was frozen in place; blank brown eyes stared into a corner. He was as much a prisoner as I.

Rhezellah reached into a silk bag that hung on the bedpost. Something flashed in front of me. Rhezellah's slender fingers grasped a curved dagger. Pulses rippled through her song, while torch fires danced along her blade. Her chant swelled into a keening shriek. She plunged the knife into her master's throat.

Julat's body heaved upward. It flopped stiffly on the bed. His eyes no longer saw; his soul had already begun its journey into Bakan's realm. Rhezellah pulled a bloodstained knife from the corded neck, then wiped it on a blood-spattered sleeve. Her eyes bored through me. "Bedwin of the *Anhillhin* guard," a steel-steady voice said. "So you still intend to slay me?"

Tremors invaded my body as I stepped into the bedchamber. My four cohorts followed, forming a phalanx behind me. Rhezellah stood lance-straight by the bed, facing the invading army.

"You stare at me. You wonder how I would know of your revolt," she echoed my unvoiced query. Her eyes paced toward the room's ceiling. "I've planned my own revolt; I've waited many years—and I had a glimpse of Linnet's face right after her torture. Let's just say that the walls have ears."

My fists balled up. My thoughts hardened as questions streaked through them. The image of Rhezellah draped across her master, inviting his invasion, slammed into me. Did she plot treachery underneath her smooth replies? Was she allied to Tolek the heir; would she now seek his favor?

Storm eyes ripped into me. "You look at me," she stated, "as though I were the dirt underneath your feet." Her voice caught, laced by a single tear. "I am a soft, compliant creature, a soulless plaything who lives only to please her master. I allow his caresses; I beg for his hands to seize, his body to clamor on me and...and...." She could speak no longer. Storm eyes misted over. Her throat moved, swallowing down the threatened torrent. Uncontrolled shudders passed over her.

A wall in my mind crumbled. I had not seen it; the horrors of Rhezellah's life had been only a vague vision to me. It had seemed so easy to condemn, to revile her. Yes, I had lived in slavery, as any woman did in this Bakan-cursed land. But as *Anhillhin* we had been privileged. I reached my hands toward her. "Come with us, Rhezellah," I entreated. My sister *Anhillhin* drew around me in welcoming accord.

Rhezellah twisted away. Her fugitive gaze darted toward the door, then fell on the gauzy green shreds of silk that clung to her. "One such as I?" she whispered, a stark monotone.

Remorse stung my cheeks, burning deep inside me. I had been the traitor, not her—I had intended that she be cut down with her master. I cherished her. I longed more than ever to enfold her in my arms, protect her from all terrors. It could never be—how could I ever expect to gain, to deserve her love?

I could only whisper words of encouragement to her. "You are the brave one who rose up in revolt," I replied steadily. "Who destroyed the cruel tyrant that ruled over us."

Rhezellah peered at me. "Is it over?" she asked. "Is it ended? I truly am free of men's lusts. I will *never* have to return to him again, will I?" She pointed at me. "You and I—*Anhillhin* and...and a man's toy—we will escape together? We can live together in a new land?" A hesitant smile played over her lips.

The old dreams spun across my mind—incongruous visions of mind-joining. I shook my head against these dreams. Her lilting voice, the lack of condemnation, the music of her wonder would be enough, at least for now.

Rhezellah stepped toward Julat's closet, opening the oak door. "One cannot travel in this," she laughed, fingering her delicate clothes. Her hands searched through the hanging garments her master would no longer need. Presently she stood dressed in sashed tunic and trousers—so large on her slim body she almost swam in them.

She tilted up her head, thrusting the dagger into her sash. The storm lights shone once more in gray eyes. Silken blond hair rippled over her shoulders.

190

She nodded toward us. "Come," she spoke, her voice iron-firm once more. "Follow me, for I know a secret, safer passage. Serving as I have, I learn many things unknown to others." She took a torch down from a sconce, then opened another door, well-hidden in the wall. My fellow rebels and I lined up behind her. Together we stepped into the pitch darkness. My mind drifted to the fire moon, the goddess we had invoked. There were no windows in the passageway. Shal'lu could not show her face to us. But the torchlights flickered their skittering patterns on the tunnel's dank walls—as they had glittered on Rhezellah's blade descending toward Julat's throat. Shal'lu's lights could still guide us to our freedom. I could feel her smile inside me.

A crystal-clear spring bubbles, sending a ribbon of water down the sheer cliff of the peak that rises above. Khedai's Well, the hot, trickling source of the mighty Khedai River. In this precious land of liberty, women have searched out new ways of loving, with mind, with body—or with both.

Shal'lu rides full this night in the pristine summer sky, sending red blushes into cerulean surroundings. In a tiny cavern, carved out of the high peak's side, Rhezellah lies, her body nestled next to mine. I press my lips against hers. Her tongue seeks mine, questing, yearning.

Garments are quickly tossed to the side as a sea tide of desire rises, washing cool-hot waters over us. Rhezellah's tongue travels, swirling upon nipples, then trailing downward. My hands brush the silken-gold curtain of hair.

She will steal my virginity. I am a willing party to this theft as my body trembles, twisting to meet hers. The dampness of her tears splashes against me. Her tongue journeys onward, downward—savoring my thrusting cunt. Gladly I yield, bestowing myself on her—receiving a gift even more precious....

And the door of my mind opens. A stream of light flickers, then darts into the warm passageway. A space opens, and the stars above begin to spin. Shal'lu's round face flares against midnight expanses.

191

A Canopy of Green
Jim Provenzano

When I was a boy, I had a special friend for a while, and I thought he would be mine forever. It was Harvest, and on an agrarian world like Samaris, that's a big festival. Foods of all kinds are laid out, and singing and dancing goes on for days. Kids get to decorate mauvas, overgrown gourds that aren't much use for cooking. You stick small nuts on for eyes and paint a mouth or a nose and dress them up to sit outside your house with a big empty basket in their laps. The next morning the wood elves bring gifts—or so the tradition goes.

There was only one other boy my age in my village, and we fell together like skipping rocks once his family immigrated there. His father was from Samaris but had met a woman while stationed on Menudi. They declared and had a child, and he brought them back to his father's farm. That was when I met Han.

Our years together were like those of any two young boys in love. Our adventures sprawled over the farmlands of my home, and my tears hadn't abated months after his departure. His father, like mine, had joined the Rangers, only he took his family with him to Samaris's other side.

Long after I found out my parents were the ones putting the gifts in the basket and Han had become a mere memory, I still enjoyed the annual celebrations, even our little versions of Samarans like myself among the ranks. Even in the compound's formality, the songs and food warmed our hearts, in uniform or not.

It's one of the things that remain, that keep us rooted in our ways, despite the advances in travel and diplomacy that had been forced on us since the arrival of the Federates.

Certainly they were kind in their ways—allowing us to keep our planet, asking to create a few outposts for their docks—but once a new economy wormed its way into our lives, they took many a man away to get some of that new gold, including my father, who, despite having a star named after him, never came back after he joined the Rangers. The war on Eln between fuel importers and the Envo Party, having raged for half a cen, had taken him, among scores of others.

That alone should have been enough to keep me away, or even make me join the renegades who tried for a while to undermine the Feds. But as I grew, the talk of other worlds beckoned. I found myself joining the ranks as well and taking up a saber in the name of the Rangers and the worlds we serve.

It didn't help having that boyhood friend assigned as my partner.

Following tutorial ranks, many cadets were sent off to other parts of Glynnis, and new recruits joined us. I didn't even recognize him until the second day of our assignments, patrolling the outcropping of miako lizard mating grounds on Sunsi Beach. I guess it was some twist of a phrase or the glint of beach light on his face that made me remember.

But I didn't say a word.

See, I don't like to mix love and work. They don't go together. Not that I don't love my work. But declaring with your partner—and I knew I must someday, despite my withholding of our childhood bond—declaring leaves you pretty tightened in and not free. The closeness is great; but then, the potential loss of a partner from work tragedies is devastating. I speak from the experiences of my friend, Jorge. The widower. So I took it easy with Han, pretending that I had forgotten those boyhood promises and secrets, and I imagined he had.

Still, we had a bond like few others among the Rangers, both being from Samaris—at least he from half his kin.

That solstice Han and I, along with fourteen other Samarans among the ranks, all shipped out together for Harvest, our annual time off, and there was a lot of chumming about on the transport, what with old traditions to share. But with the shedding of military ways, we also parted company, each off to visit relatives and old homelands.

After time with my elders, I spent the remainder of my break with Jorge. We sat on the deck of his new, all-paid retire unit overlooking Crayneck Lake. That's where they send Rangers when they get injured or dismembered, or simply burned out. A few even get to grow old.

193

I don't know how it got the reputation of being mostly third gen, this tribe; well, we call it a tribe. It's actually the 45th Regiment of the Glynnis Environmental Security Unit, Corsair Federate Commission of Avek, but that's a mouthful. We prefer to call ourselves Glynnisides.

Sitting with Jorge, a cup of porte warming our bellies, the screech of the bala birds cooing over the lake, I tried to think up anything to chat about that wouldn't remind us of his lost one, Pietro. It wasn't easy.

"You like him?" Jorge asked. The conversation had led to me and my problem with Han.

"Sure." Sure, I liked him. How could I not like a man who'd stolen my heart as a child?

"The stars of Menudi shine in him."

"That's his mother's side," I explained. "Father's from Samaris, like me."

"But you like him."

"Oh, yes. When he speaks."

"And he's built."

"Isn't any well-trained Ranger?"

"Especially the women."

We laughed and grew silent, sipping our porte, enjoying the lake's shimmer. I thought about Jorge as if he were far away, even though he was at my side. I couldn't look at his handsome face too long, his beard the color of russet mange, his form so strong. But his spirit and eyes seemed somewhat lost. I didn't see how my love could repair that, or if he'd see it as anything more than filling in the blanks. I couldn't make up for the half-life he now had to finish out.

Not that the dom-part bonus doesn't attract its share of our kind on Glynnis. The commission prefers childless employees, and those who declare and pair up get a better choice of assignments. Sure, some declared couples do retire and have kids. That doesn't take any off-world skill. But most stay single, finding pleasure and companionship when they can. The Fed allows it—no, the Fed prefers it. Makes the pension payoff a little less tangled, what with whole clans from the other gen families sometimes descending on a small village, claiming grieving land rights. Oh, if those supervisors only knew what their decisions got the common folk into!

I stayed with Jorge a few more days before returning to work, but I couldn't keep my mind off Han, how he had so abruptly reentered my life after I'd spent so many years seeking a similar face or trust or feeling from off-world men, from pleasure givers, and from a few other Rangers. But none struck my soul.

They saw it in my eyes: the lack of desire for glory, the need to bond, the dream of retiring young with all limbs intact.

Not that there weren't joys to be had in the service of the Range. Take swirling.

Swirling is strictly forbidden. Ranger Rule Book, code 23: "There will be no reckless operation of a vehicle for amusement..." nla, nla, nla.

We call it swirling, for that's what it feels like.

On Samaris as a boy I had dreamed of flying on a small disk, having to keep my legs crossed—but it was nothing compared to riding the shell.

A pod looks a lot like a smoothed-out conch shell, and you fit into it like the warm mushy creatures they stole the pattern from. Powered on ion charges at the compound, these two-seaters were the only nonbio transport allowed on hab renewal areas, as they expel mere CO_2 fumes, a sort of sprit-zo for the countryside's hungry endangered trees.

Han and I were sent out to scan the surf side of Sunsi Beach for poachers, and I'd only been out a few times riding, but had gotten a true handle on the pod's full potential.

Driving the pod that unfortunate day, I coasted sideways along the beach's cliffs for sport. That was when Han lost it and started screaming. It wouldn't have been so bad if he hadn't grabbed my shoulders from behind. I was just trying out a new move. I'd heard that, given the right convection of oncoming winds, one could 360 without fail.

We failed.

I guess the winds were a bit too strong for my rookie hands. At least I had the skill to land us in the surf, but Han still fumed as we waited for help, sopping wet. We had to help drag the pod onto a carrier, which took all day, and do slag duty for days after that.

Han did all the talking at the scold session with our captain. I kept my eyes on the floor while he all but cursed my dead elders to the Outer Rings of Mar.

Nevertheless, the captain had refused to part us. He merely told us to go back to daily saber chambers, see to our minor bumps at Healer's, and await our next mission.

"Probably crop tilling after your little escapade," Han growled as we departed the captain's room.

"My escapade? If you hadn't turned chee bird and made me lose control—"

"Made you." Han said it short and angry. Those were our last words for several days.

Saber became a nonverbal, all-scen, nerve-racking chore. Twice I thought Han actually wanted to sever down through my practice pads and spill some, but he only got close.

I began to walk off-grounds on my free hours just to get away from Han's looming presence. I lay under bimmel trees and toyed with the wildflowers, wondering how my young life had become so ravaged. One morning I even took my uniform off and lay under Glynnis's suns, awaiting convergence, just to offer a prayer of alliance—anything to find Han's approval once again. I'd heard we had a mission and wanted to find clearance before flying out into the wilderness with this man I hardly knew.

It was late when I returned that eve, having slept too long. I should have known by the angle of the suns that I would be late, but fog covered the northern sky.

I would miss Late Saber.

Before I entered the compound, a heavy mist had begun. My cloak was a bit damp as I entered the compound, signed in, and went to my quarters. Han opened his door and stood in the hallway, as if having sensed my approach.

"You're late."

"I'm sorry."

"We've only got a half-par left in the chamber."

"Then we'll have to reschedule afterward."

"After what?"

"Our little journey tomorrow," I said with an air of mystery.

"For where?"

"North Woods. We have a mission."

"Well, then, I need the warm-up before we depart."

"Well, I need to eat," I said as I tried again to leave his company.

"Meet me outside. I hope your saber's charged."

It was, but I wasn't, what with sleeping outside and being half-starved. I followed him nevertheless.

By the time I redressed and got outside, Han was standing in the rain about twenty paces away, in dress greens. He looked stern and serious and handsome in the purplish night.

I approached to catch up, but he walked away without turning as he heard my footsteps and took off up a path into the nearby hills.

"Han! Han!"

He didn't wait. He walked fast, his big legs getting him anywhere he wanted. I hadn't taken the time to dress properly, and my boots were still unbuckled. I felt loose and unprepared.

By the time I got to the hill's crest, he had disappeared into a glen of bambus trees. The rain's insistence was deflected by their boughs. My footsteps fell on rotting leaves and soft moss.

"Han, please wait," I called out. "I want to talk to you."

A saber beam shot out only inches away from me and sliced off a low tree limb. I started back and jumped into fighting stance but relaxed slightly as I saw Han.

His eyes, however, were far from relaxed, and I became fearful again, as if I should have drawn.

"You failed me," he seethed. "Again. I give any man a second chance, but not thrice."

"What? Look, I'm sorry about the crash! I'm sorry I'm late! What do I have to do to make up for—"

"Not that! You're third gen."

I halted a moment, wondering what had upset him so. *Hadn't I told him at least that?* But then again, I realized, our silences had clouded any communication, even scen, except for training.

Perhaps he was just a spiteful single gen all along, and I never knew. It happened—country recruits had no contact with other gen like them. But it couldn't be that. He'd been so sweet when we were kids.

"Han please, let me explain."

"You never told me. You just avoided me and never told me."

"But I want to, please," I begged.

He stopped, awaiting an explanation.

"I didn't want to discuss it without...I didn't want you to feel I was...I wanted to wait, to see if you sought to...to..." I stuttered, almost saying it.

Han waited, but then his lips came together, tight and grim. He turned away.

Then it came out of me like those people with strokes who blurt things out. "Smashing mauvas!"

"What?"

"Harvest feast. We were just kids then, and we were smashing mauvas at night, on Samaris, running up the village, one house after another. And we almost got caught by the elders, and you wanted to turn us in, but I found a hiding place and saved us."

Han's face softened. He remembered. At least he wasn't walking away, and he'd lowered his saber. "So?"

"So, you still owe me."

"My parents wouldn't let me see you when they found out what we were doing."

"Just smashing mauvas? C'mon, you knew how I felt, and I still feel that way, and you couldn't handle it. You kept coming by every time I was home but never coming out and saying it. Then you're gone for years, and you come back from nowhere and you're in the Rangers and we're assigned together! And whose father is one of the higher-ranking captains of—"

"He only talked to a major in—"

"Not mine!"

Han shut his eyes, then brought his hands out, a sort of pleading. "Look, I'm sorry about your father."

"You never even asked about my father."

"True." We stood, sizing each other up for each of our glaring faults. Then my burned-away loss for my kin, my childhood, my all, brought me to take the offensive.

"What gen are you?" I asked him bluntly.

Han scowled and dropped his eyes. "That's a private matter."

"Private," I repeated, vainly trying to find the anger he'd hurled at me so often. But when I finally knew where it came from, I just felt sorry. "How far down the hole can you hide?"

"I'm not hiding from—"

"Save it, soldier," I said, now tired, disappointed in Han's misguided fury. "I'm the one let down. I wanted to declare with you since I was twelve." I turned away, then back, holding my arms out. "That's the advantage of declaring. I have the privilege of dramatic exits."

I dropped my arms and walked away, my saber heavy in my hand. As I left the boughs of the bambus trees, I let the rain tap me on the shoulder a hundred times. I heard footsteps. Then he fell on me.

Wet grass pressed against my back. We rolled. I grabbed him, not knowing if this was to be a serious fight.

He got me on my back. I flinched, waiting for a punch, but his eyes just drilled into me as he clutched my arms, hovering over me, a canopy of green dotted with the squares and stripes of his uniform. Han's panting breath warmed me as he lay atop me. His chest heaved against mine.

"I've got a root digging into my—" I struggled to rise.

Han gripped me and pushed me back down, his eyes riveted on mine. "Was that a proposal?"

I dropped my grip and snuck my hand up. A few alea buds clung to his beard, so I plucked them out. He didn't flinch.

"Partners get a hell of a great pension," I joked.

"Could you stand me for that long?"

I ran my fingers through his black hair. "Till this turns white."

I saw him measuring, considering, and I thought I was too. As he brought his stubbled face to mine, almost kissing, I hoped that at least one question would be answered.

Then he rolled off me and walked back to the compound.

Later that evening, after we'd cooled our tempers, I invited Han to my quarters. He promptly told me to meet him at *his* quarters.

I arrived—on time, just to surprise him—and offered a glim of Beluvian sumsquat bush, dried to perfection. Perhaps that would disarm him.

"I prefer the juice of the berry," Han said as he kicked up his heels on the wooden table and sipped. Han had requested the Runic Room for two years and, now that he had it, had no intention of giving it up.

I had the more pristine Enectran Room. All the quarters were done up in styles from other worlds and states in the hopes of increasing the comfort of diplomats, guests, and whatnot. Too bad so many of them were now on less-than-cordial terms, and the rooms were left vacant, then filled up by increasing numbers of us semisoldiers, the Rangers.

I took one of Han's ceramic cups from a showpiece shelf. Each item was worth a good twenty units, but Han never minded. He knew I'd pay if I broke the damn antiques. It wasn't the affront to his precious objects but more a symbol of trust after our confessions. Also, I liked smoking Beluvian the Beluvian way.

"So, what do you make of the assignment?" Han once again jumped back to business before I'd even caught a nice evening buzz or found the chance to prod him more about his gen. No wonder we hadn't swapped spit in all this time.

I tried to keep my mind on business, not even broach the topic of sex again, but he knew I wanted to, even if it was the night before a mission. He knew, and he guarded it, like a promise held back.

I maintained formal airs, eyeing him as he tried very hard to look relaxed.

"What were you told?"

"Nothing yet," I said, "but I found out a few things. I know that it's a distress signal from Glynnis 6 North Woods, in Phyrric general AmSlang, and it repeated twice before halting signal."

"Phyrric? Why that old language? Was that in the skid sheet?" He dropped his feet off the table to the console. The ceramic cup nearly spilled over.

"No, no," I tried to calm him. "You didn't miss any update. I heard it."

"From who?"

"A sub-cap."

"Friend on One Deck?"

"You might say so."

"Is he cute?"

"What?" I had no idea of his personal interests. He never talked of other men that way. Was he jealous?

"Just thought I'd ask." He grinned slyly, amused by my embarrassment. "I'm not the only one with friends in high places."

We'd reached a sort of truce with the issue, and being the night before a mission where we were supposed to prove ourselves competent after our previous blunders, the issue was put aside.

I went to my room and did some homework.

Glynnis used to be built up. But by third cen the rule of the Phyrrans had crumbled, and they departed for a similar world in the Mallen system, thanks to funds from the Federates. There was conflict, though, and many stayed, protesting the forced evacuation. Eventually the last of them died off, so the tomes say. The Envo Party took firm rule, and all construction halted to a glorious silence. Zero pop. Deletion of fuel imports. Total agrarian shift.

It became a touristy spot for a while, I read, but portion wars swept through and a bout of disorientation virus, making it risky. Now it was a mere reclaimed wildland grown over stone shrines to the Phyrrans' dead culture.

The planet's natural life was thriving, though, especially the continent of Glynnis with its numerous plants and creatures, all unique, all too close to extinction to suit the Rangers. I'd actually come to like the place once in a while and looked forward to the mission with a nervous pride.

At suns' dawn we ate while being recited our mission by a sub-cap. Find the source of the signal, report immigrants if any, and return, she said. Simple.

We had to drop down to Bay Deck and pick out a battered two-seater pod from the stock. Only two were running, and one had a grav spill problem, so we had to take the older model.

This time Han drove.

While his hand was steady, he certainly took his time. I decided to put away our fights and enjoy the ride. Wind whipped about our helmets, bambus limbs whizzing under as Han skirted the tops.

"We're going in," he said as his detec honed in on the signal. Han found a clearing and scooped down into the wood, slowing his pace.

A pod has features to seek out barriers. It can sort of take control, within limits. Scooping around limbs, under boughs, it made me wonder what could be in all this brush that we hadn't scoped.

We didn't see anything coming when it happened. Han had full control, it seemed. All of a sudden, though, we just banged against something in midair. The pod skidded out of control until we landed backwards and sideways.

After a moment of shock we both shook our heads, undid our belts, and checked each other for blood.

"What did we hit?" I asked as we climbed out and took off our helmets to check for head injury. We were bumped but not beaten.

"I don't know," Han gazed up and around in confusion. "The curvo should have seen all trees. I was only guiding in second pilot."

"A malfunk?"

"Well, it's sure malfunked up now," Han said as he looked behind him at a clump of wiring and split casing parts that now littered the underbrush.

"Why?"

Han didn't answer.

"We'll be fined if we don't get this cleaned up."

I stood to begin assembling the rubble but was yanked down by Han's swift grip.

"What the—?" I rolled over from my fall to look up at Han. He pointed.

A black line cut clean across the trunk of a bambus tree.

"Lasers?"

Han nodded.

"Who? Where are they?"

"Over there somewhere. Maybe what hit us."

"But nothing hit us. We were coasting and ran into nothing and then—"

Another shot cut the air above us. We scrambled to cover behind a large bambus.

We lay silent, catching our breath, once the laser stopped. The wild creatures that had fled from the crash resumed their chirping, and we had a moment to catch our breath in the shade. We could even hear a tree creaking in the breeze.

Until Han turned and noticed that the slight creaking sound came from the tree trunk in front of us. First the boughs wavered, then the bambus leaned with a soggy groan, and the massive tree fell before us with a hissing crash as it swiped shrubs and trees beside it.

Han and I hunched down farther, exposed. A yellow ooze of sap began to bleed from the rings of the tree.

"We move in now or die."

"Die trying," I added as we rushed out from either side, sabers drawn.

We shot out, but our lines of power went forward only a little distance and then disappeared at the same point, as if we'd shortened our beams. We crouched a few yards apart, silently looking at each other in confusion.

I peered up from behind a shrub and saw the reason for the beams' limits. A sort of wall, or an image of the trees beyond, began to slither away or melt down, revealing a tall triangular stone altar that had not been there before, or had at least been unseen. Carvings vined across the stone's surface, but the etchings were coated in moss and lichen at every groove.

A little man peered out from behind.

Well, he wasn't actually a man—more of a dwarf with a round head, no ears, and big rheumy eyes. Was he surrendering? Han and I each took aim.

The little man took one look at us, then closed his eyes.

Sudden shock waves of pain gripped our hands, until we fell to the ground, dropping our sabers. I'd never heard Han scream so, and despite the horrible pain that shot through my hands, I had to crawl to him. This torture: that little man was doing this somehow.

"Please, stop!" I yelled, begging. Han writhed about on the ground, and I fell to him, as if holding him might somehow halt my own pain.

Then it stopped. We rubbed our hands defensively, then sat up, looking warily at the little old knob of a creature. Our sabers lay on the ground.

He beckoned.

Han stood up, sniffed, and tried to recompose himself, but I saw a tear drop from his reddened eyes.

The little man gestured for us to bring our weapons, but somehow we knew that attempting to arm ourselves would be useless. We held them low, showing that we wouldn't.

As we approached the dwarflike man, I noticed small veins running about his skull. He was covered in a sort of sackcloth, with some shiny metal braidwork around the collar, what may once have been a regal frock.

We followed him to the back side of the small temple, which had a portal about five feet high. We had to duck to enter the dark entryway.

He never spoke as he led us down the mossed-over steps. Several times we slipped, but the little creature's surefooted pace was only slowed as he stopped to await us at each bending curve.

We halted as the little man held out a wrinkled palm before a large stone doorway. We stepped in.

Huddled around a glowing light, not a flame but something hovering, circular, was a small band of creatures similar to the little man. Some had bald heads, others strings of hair. All were pale, small, and wary of us, the looming intruders.

Nevertheless, the little man, obviously the elder of the clan, headed toward the circle, where, without words, the group shifted and made room for us.

Han and I awkwardly settled ourselves down, sitting with these strange people. Their glassy brown eyes stared piteously, yet we felt comforted.

The elder pointed toward the glowing ball that seemed to rest on air, but I was distracted by a movement in one creature's shabby clothes. It was a small baby, cuddling closer to its mother, who glanced up only once.

I looked at Han to see if he'd noticed, but his eyes were fixed on the light ball. I looked as well, wondering what its power held.

After only a few moments, it was revealed. Tingling warmth crept through me, and my mind clouded. A light ringing filled my ears, and swirling images began to fill the light—or my mind, I'm not sure which.

I cannot clearly explain what I saw or was led to see, but it was a sort of journey, a history, filled with these small people, their rise and development, their beliefs, their tragedies and downfall. I wasn't shown specific people or scenes yet felt as if the ball were feeding me, filling the open plains of my limited knowledge. I saw through the collective eyes of a dying culture, and among the many meetings and trials, what may have been a small fragment to them took me in and convinced me of their righteousness. I saw my vision deftly skulking from house to house of larger homes, not those of these people but larger, those like my boyhood home on Samaris. I saw little hands like the elder's delicately placing gifts in a basket of a stuffed man with a mauva for a head.

I felt a great surge of sympathy and knowing, and as the light seemed to take over again, I found myself once again sitting beside Han. My eyes flooded with tears. The stone floor seemed to push up under my crossed legs, as if I had perhaps been floating slightly all that time.

And it was a longer time than I realized. I found myself drained, hungry and thirsty yet complete, as if I had been tuned in to the desperation of these little creatures, all driven down into the underbelly of their culture, each fighting for the last bits of survival.

The elder was standing, and all the others were gone.

He waved for us to stand and led us down another corridor, where more doorways beckoned, each with another glowing lamp, each with another huddled circle of Phyrrans. The paths seemed to go on for much longer, but the elder seemed satisfied with his presentation and led us back.

Walking up in a daze, it seemed we had only a few minutes to travel before we saw the daylight of Glynnis beckoning at the top of the stone stairs. For a moment I was afraid to emerge, as if our parting would make the dozens, maybe hundreds, down under disappear forever.

The haze of our mind journey misted away. As we stood on mossy ground, the little man's eyes blinked under the bright puddles of light. We looked around. We were not where we had entered. No high portal stood behind us, only a small doorway in the side of a hill.

The little man held out his arms, our weapons in each hand. Han took both and handed me mine, hesitantly, as if he too were afraid of resuming what we came to do.

Then the creature turned and bent over, turning back with a small object. It looked like a booklet hundreds of years old, locked by a metal latch. It was a gift, a legacy of their race. He handed it to Han, and then took both our hands and laid them on the book's small cover. He smiled once, as if matching us, seeing the potential between us, and bonding it with this promise.

The little creature again gestured toward a path out into the woods, one we'd never seen, and Han and I awkwardly bowed. Then the man stepped back into the doorway. We turned a moment to divine the path before us, but as Han turned back a moment, he gripped my shoulder.

The doorway was gone, covered in years-old vines and leaves.

Evading a task.

That was what we were worried about, even miles from that doorway, the booklet hidden in Han's jacket. That was the concerned glint in Han's eye as we stood, afraid to part, shoulder to shoulder, relieving ourselves by a tree.

We heard the low burping of creatures and smelled the wild alea of the woods. I glanced up and down at the beauty of this world and the beauty of my partner.

"What are we going to do?" he said, our first words spoken aloud. My reverie broken, I too pondered our new situation. The secrets of Glynnis and the duties of rank weighed on our shoulders.

Withholding information, not carrying out a mission, or just plain sabotage—all were grounds for dismissal. No pension, no possible future could be had, except as a recon underling for a pirate ship. That or go back to farming on Samaris.

That understanding, and some other kinds that to this day escape my comprehension, have kept Han and me together; our pact, our secret.

But as we headed along the path, our minds cleared back to an illusion of clarity. We spoke aloud more of what had been unveiled to us.

"The man who led us down the passage—" I said.

"—wanted us to let them continue hiding." He finished my sentence, the first of many times for years after that day.

"We have to let them do it."

We'd made our report, listed the vehicle as wrecked, been cited our fines, and reported mission accomplished (sort of). We noted that the distress signal was a leftover time-lapse equipper, long abandoned. No life forms cited.

Less than a par after our report had been filed in the log, the captain called us in to his room.

A tapestry hung on one wall, a chart with the lands of Glynnis on the other. The captain stood with two chairs before him. We sat.

He didn't, of course. I almost cringed as he paced, calm though he was, expecting to hear at any moment those terrible words, "crop tilling."

"Gentlemen," he said, "I am not about to doubt your skill in this small matter. Han's skill and your—" he glanced at me—"enthusiasm, both more than suffice as trustworthiness."

"Thank you, sir," Han said, speaking for both of us.

"But can you explain why, when you said the pod crashed at this site—" he pointed to a spot on the regional chart—"you came to the station from the South Plain, the opposite direction from your assignment?"

Both Han and I did our very best to disguise our surprise. Had we been lost on that path? Where had that little man taken us? We glanced at each other in silence.

"Gentlemen, I'm waiting."

I spoke abruptly. "Uh, environmental disorientation because of atmospheric spores, sir."

"We have made a Healer appointment for this eve," Han added.

The long moment of hesitation before the captain's "Very well" told us more than we hoped. The captain knew something more had happened, but he didn't press.

After our Healer app, where we each feigned remnants of disorientation, we were both assigned to quarters for two days for recoup. Following orders, we spent them in bed.

Somewhere between the cuddling and the licking, the touching and the thrusting, we came upon the idea of retiring early. Neither considered the other's body worth sacrificing for Federate glory or conquest. Planets could be laid waste, but this union was a pact, a promise made to a little man with a bald head who lived in a cave.

"Do you think they'll be okay when the crew picks up the pod?" I asked as we lay in bed. Stretched at his side, I stroked Han's chest hairs with my hand. His arm wrapped around my neck, he occasionally toyed with my ear.

"Those half-wits?" he said of the crew coworkers, more out of relief for not having to do that labor this time. "It wouldn't take half their scen to make a shield to fool them. They'll be fine."

"I hope so," I whispered.

"We promised, didn't we?" The childlike look in Han's eyes—of wonderment, confusion, and trust—I still remember, and sometimes I see it on those quiet nights when we sit together around the fire at Crayneck Lake, trying and trying to talk about what happened to us.

I took his words for truth, the gleam in his eye showing scen. We almost fell into it, no words, but he broke it, rolling out of the covers to find a dram of water, I thought. Instead he dug in a drawer, bending over in a way that made me want to request another day of bed rest.

Han turned and stood, holding the little book in his hand. "Soon as I can, I'm going to take my paid leave, split up to Crayneck, lie naked with you by the lake, decipher this thing, and relax."

"Contraband," I said as I sat up. "You'll never get it by decompress."

"You watch. How do you think I got all my toys at home?"

"I wouldn't know," I said. "Never been."

"Is that all it takes with you? An invite?" He walked toward me.

"It's a start."

"So's this." He leaned close. Our lips met, and he tasted sweet and wet—his mouth, at least. His beard must have caught some alea buds, for it still smelled of that path.

To Steal Your Heart Away
Lauren Wright Douglas

L egend had it that the wizard of Lesser Clepping kept his heart in a crystal box, high within a tower in the center of an impenetrable thorn wood. Over the years the heart had lured quite a number of brash young adventurers to their deaths—youths determined to possess the heart, and its magical powers, for themselves. An ironic footnote to the legend maintained that the wizard tossed the hearts of these would-be thieves together into a large black vat in his tower aerie, where they marinated in one another's despair. The cries pleased him, the story said. Admittedly, no one knew this for a certainty, as no one had ever returned from wizard's tower.

Perrin intended to learn the truth of the legend. After all, every young cutpurse needs some truly great theft to establish a reputation. Perrin the Lightfingered—never one to dream small dreams—had resolved to steal the wizard's heart.

From a vantage point atop a dappled gray pony on a hill just outside the village of Lesser Clepping, Perrin gazed with shriveling confidence at the godforsaken collection of huts below. A mischievous, gusty rain stuck icy fingers into holes in socks and doublet, and the young thief sneezed. Perhaps this had been a mistake. Home—even though it was the attic of the faraway House of Hasty Pleasure—seemed particularly desirable. *Gods rot it! Why sit here on this midwinter hillside freezing hands and haunches when those same parts could be toasting in front of a cheery fire?—Ah, Perrin,* an interior voice said, *why so coy? You know full well the answer to that question, now, don't you?—Yes, yes,* the thief answered testily, sneezing again. *I know.*

It's power. Everyone knows that whoever controls a wizard's heart controls the wizard—that's why wizards hide their hearts. And although this wizard was at best only a third-rate mage, having a wizard in one's power was no mean accomplishment. It would make the perilous profession of cutpurse infinitely safer. It would provide an edge. And Perrin liked to have an edge.

"Go, horse," the thief said aloud. "We're not getting any richer sitting here in the rain." The gray roused itself sufficiently to manage a dispirited walk, and so it was that thief and horse approached the village of Lesser Clepping.

Perrin squinted through the rain, searching for the local public house. Even an inexperienced thief knows that a tavern collects gossip as a dung heap draws flies. And Perrin needed up-to-date gossip. The tales told of the wizard's heart in the town from which Perrin had come were sketchy at best. Perrin had a plan of sorts for the appropriation of the heart, but it lacked a certain depth. In fact, it was positively sketchy, the young cutpurse had to admit. Acquiring reliable information was, therefore, of paramount importance. Urging the gray horse to a reluctant trot, the thief hurried through the muddy streets.

Perrin had hardly settled down by the fire in the tavern—a frowsy establishment ambiguously named Heart's Leavetaking—when the first overture was made.

"Psst," a pretty young blond boy said, sliding up to Perrin and batting his eyes provocatively. "You're after the wizard's heart, aren't you?"

"Am I?" Perrin replied, taking another swallow of beer.

"Oh, yes," the boy said with assurance, looking the thief up and down. "Anyone can tell that. And I'm just the one to help you."

"Humph," Perrin said. "So what are you selling?"

The boy smiled. "Some...relaxation before your ordeal." He put one hand over Perrin's. "My sister and I have a room upstairs. Why don't you join us?"

Perrin finished the last of the beer and fastened disapproving eyes on the boy. "Because I can't afford you. Or your sister. Now, run along before I'm tempted to do what your mother should have done to you years ago."

The boy struck a pose of defiance, hands on hips. "Oh? What's that?"

"Turned you over her knee," Perrin growled. "Now, scat!"

Making a rude gesture with one finger, the boy flounced away. Perrin made a disgusted face.

The innkeeper deposited another beer, and Perrin had just wriggled out of sodden boots when the second overture came.

"Young sir," a bundle of rags said tremulously, scuttling up to the thief's bench. "Let me help you."

Perrin looked closely. It was an incredibly ancient little man, hoary with age, rheumy in one eye, and smelling of the stables. Perrin sighed and spread wet socks before the fire. "How, uncle?"

"I have a map—" the old man began, searching frantically among his clothing with gnarled fingers.

"Please," Perrin said, "don't trouble yourself. I don't need a map. The way to the wizard's tower is well known."

"No, no," the old man said. "This is a map *of* the tower. All the perils are marked."

"Oh?" Perrin said skeptically. "And who drew this map?"

The old man grinned, showing toothless gums. "Well now, that's for me to know, isn't it?"

"Sorry," Perrin said. "Not interested."

The old man began to weep.

"Oh, don't take it so hard," Perrin said, rescuing steaming socks from the andirons. "Some great gullible lout will soon be along to swell your purse." Tossing a copper penny in the air, the thief noted that the old man retrieved it with amazing dexterity for one so infirm. "Console yourself with a beer while you wait for someone more credulous," Perrin told him.

The old man scuttled away, clutching the coin.

"Neatly done," a voice said from the other side of the fire.

Perrin looked across the hearth, but the speaker was hidden in the shadows.

"Well, perhaps not so neatly, but done nonetheless," Perrin equivocated. It was best to appear humble in front of strangers, the thief had learned.

"Yet both the boy and the old man were right," the voice continued.

"Oh?" Perrin asked. This was a novel approach. Perhaps the hidden speaker had both hawkers in his employ.

"Yes. You need rest before your journey to the tower, and you definitely need to know about the perils."

Perrin laughed ruefully. "I'm not likely to get either one. I can't afford the price of a night in this inn, and I have real doubts that a map of the wizard's tower exists."

"It's wise to be cautious," the voice said. "But there comes a point when caution ends and stupidity begins. And you don't strike me as stupid, thief."

Perrin bristled. "Stupid I am not. But who calls me thief? Pray, show yourself."

A small figure dressed in brown wool pants tucked into high boots, a brown vest over a well-mended white linen shirt, and a very handsome silver short sword stepped out of the shadows. Hair the color of roan horses stood out from the stranger's head in a profusion of curls, and the eyes that were fastened on Perrin were deep green.

"Who am I? I am Sorrel, youngest child of the duke of Broadneath. My four elder brothers, may they rest in peace, now reside in the wizard's tower. At least, their hearts do."

Perrin grunted in surprise, remembering only at the last moment to acknowledge the introduction before asking questions. "I am Perrin the Light-fingered—thief, as you correctly surmised. But tell me: Why are you here and your brothers in the tower? Did you go and return safely? Or did you not go with them at all?"

The small stranger approached Perrin's bench and placed a slim hand on the silver sword. "I did not go. My brothers forbade me. It was my place to stay here, to watch the horses, and to wait, they said. Tasks fit for their little sister."

"Their sister? Then you are...a woman?" Perrin asked incredulously, looking Sorrel up and down.

"A woman," she acknowledged.

Perrin looked again and this time saw the truth of the matter—the delicate features, the soft skin, the slim hands. And those wonderful eyes. The thief's heart turned over. "But why are you still here?" Perrin asked. "In your place, I might have been gone long ago. Back to Broadneath perhaps."

Sorrel shook her head. "I can never go back to Broadneath. My half-brother, who has never been quite right in his head, rules there now. Since becoming duke, he has feared fratricide and thinks to forestall it by hunting down his siblings. He is quite irrational." Sorrel shrugged. "Last autumn, my brothers and I came here seeking the wizard's heart. We thought it would give us the power to set our brother's mind at ease and permit us all to dwell in Broadneath together."

"A pity," Perrin said. "I am sad for your loss. But what has kept you here for nearly a year? Surely there are villages more appealing than Lesser Clepping."

Sorrel grimaced and took a seat across the table from Perrin. "Traveling takes money. And I, alas, am suffering a temporary financial embarrassment."

"Ah," said Perrin. The condition was not an unfamiliar one.

"But quite apart from that, I wait."

"Wait? For what, pray?"

"For someone clever. For someone...special. Different. I think perhaps I have been waiting for you," Sorrel said.

"Me?" Perrin asked, trying not to be flattered. "What makes you think such a thing?"

Sorrel smiled. "You are the only one of the seekers who turned away the boy and the old man. Resisting both pleasure and knowledge in one afternoon proves you to be someone truly wise."

"Well, yes," Perrin agreed. The thief had already decided to humor this young woman. To cross her might be dangerous—that short sword looked frightfully businesslike. Besides, she was exceedingly good to look at. "Tell me something, young Sorrel."

"If I can."

"Tell me what you want with me."

Sorrel smiled. "Impatient, aren't you?"

Perrin sighed. "I have traveled a long way. I'm tired, and this beer is making my head swim. If I intend to get to the wizard's tower while there is still light, I'd best leave now."

"It's far too late to leave now," Sorrel said. "The tower is at least half a day's ride. You would only fall prey to the bandits who make the road to the tower their home. They wait for weary seekers the way vultures eye infirm cows. No, you will definitely have to wait here until morning."

"Gods rot it!" Perrin swore. Another night in yet another drafty stable, cuddled up to the gray horse, was less than appealing.

"On the other hand," Sorrel said, suddenly finding something worth examining on her fingernails, "I could be of assistance to you. I believe I have already mentioned that you might...suit my purposes very well."

"*Your* purposes?" Perrin said, raising an eyebrow. *Impertinent little snip!* "And just what might they be?"

"I want the wizard's heart," Sorrel said.

Perrin hooted. "Then go after it, little mouse."

Sorrel glared. "As I said, I want the heart. But I'm not...equipped to go after it. In a word, I lack the courage. Stealing it will take someone else. Someone like you." She thought for a moment. "I'm prepared to share it with you."

Perrin snorted. "You are, are you?" How generous of you, my dear. I don't see why I can't just walk in and get the heart myself. Why would I need you?"

Sorrel smiled thinly. "Because I—and only I—can tell you how to do it."
Unimpressed, Perrin began to put on socks and boots. "You'll have to do better than that. As I recall, that was the old man's offer."

"Well, here's a better one," Sorrel said. "Listen, thief. Once upon a time there were twins, a brother and sister named Sorrin and Sorrel. In times of trouble or danger, the voice of one would speak inside the other's head. Do you understand what I'm telling you, you hardheaded naysayer?"

Perrin straightened up, boots in hand, mouth agape. "Indeed I do. You and your twin brother Sorrin could read each other's mind."

"Yes," Sorrel said grimly. "And he went to the wizard's tower with our other three brothers. What he saw, he told me. Until the moment came when he saw no more."

Perrin said nothing, listening intently. *By the gods! If this were true...*

"I will tell you what Sorrin told me," Sorrel said. "With this information you will be able to get into the wizard's tower and out again unscathed. And you will have the heart."

Perrin swallowed, throat suddenly dry. It never occurred to the thief to doubt this earnest young woman. "And your price?"

She smiled grimly. "As I said, I want half the heart."

Perrin considered this. Well, it wasn't an insoluble problem. They could work out the logistics later. "Done."

"But there is one other thing," Sorrel said, eyes green as mossy stones in a brook. "You must come to bed with me. Tonight. Before you leave for the wizard's tower."

"What?" Perrin whispered.

"You heard me, thief." Sorrel looked Perrin up and down. "After you bathe, of course."

"If you insist," Perrin said with a shrug, trying to appear insouciant. However, under the table, the thief's palms had begun to sweat.

"I insist."

"Very well," Perrin said, and followed Sorrel upstairs.

"Well," Perrin said, tracing with one finger the line of Sorrel's jaw. The rain had stopped, and the moon shone through the clouds, casting silver and black shadows on Sorrel's face. "Was I the one you hoped for?"

Sorrel smiled ambiguously and moved one leg so it lay atop Perrin's. "Was I?" she asked Perrin.

"Oh, yes," Perrin breathed.

"Tell me that with more eloquence," Sorrel said, rolling over and straddling Perrin's hips.

"You were everything I hoped for," Perrin began, trying hard to concentrate on making a gallant speech. "In fact, you are far more than I could ever hope for," the thief said honestly.

Sorrel bent over and kissed the thief's lips. "Sshh. Not like that," she whispered. "Tell me like this." She opened Perrin's lips with her own.

So Perrin told her.

Perrin stood in the wizard's tower and looked out through the high window. The village of Lesser Clepping was just visible in the distance, across a pleasant meadow. There was no thorn wood. Just as there was no pit of vipers, three-headed dog, or paving stones that bubbled flesh-searing acid. It was all just as Sorrel had said—they were harmless illusions. All save one.

At the base of the tower, a small brown-cloaked figure on a gray horse waved. Perrin smiled and waved back. Then the thief turned to the business at hand. The wizard's heart, object of so much speculation, reposed in a crystal box on a high shelf. Just as the legend said. Perrin picked it up distastefully. It was a small, mean thing, hardly bigger than a bird's heart, and whimpered protestingly as Perrin handled it. The thief ignored the heart's pleas and transferred it to the small crystal vial Sorrel had provided. Once the stopper was in the vial, the heart's complaints were inaudible. Perrin sighed in relief and slipped the vial into a doublet pocket. One without a hole.

Perrin looked around the tower. Apart from the shelf that had once held the wizard's heart, the room was bare. Of the vat that reputedly contained the unsuccessful adventurers' hearts there was no trace. It had been merely a cruel and fanciful tale. But what of the bodies? The thief looked more closely. Against the opposite wall was an enormous spider's web. Perrin approached it cautiously. At intervals along the web were dozens of cocoons, each about as big as a thumb. The dried shells of some hapless insects, Perrin presumed. The thief raised a finger and touched one of the silk-shrouded forms. It moved just a little as the strands of web swung in a faint breeze, and Perrin jumped back in horror. The desiccated, cocooned husk had the shrunken face of a man. A dead man, to be sure, but a man. Perrin began to shake. Perhaps this wizard's power was no mean thing after all.

One hand on the pocket that contained the heart, Perrin descended the tower stairs two at a time and emerged into the sunlight, taking great gulps of fresh air.

Sorrel slid down from the gray's saddle and ran to the thief's side.

"Well?"

Perrin held up the vial. "Success."

"Ugh," Sorrel said. "It's very disagreeable-looking. And much smaller than Sorrin described." She looked up at Perrin quickly. "You didn't find—"

Perrin stroked her cheek. "No. There was nothing to indicate what he did with the hearts of those he trapped. Or with their bodies," the thief lied.

Sorrel nodded. "I never really expected to know. But still, I hoped."

Perrin swung up into the gray's saddle and held a hand out for Sorrel. The girl took Perrin's hand and vaulted up behind the thief.

"Tell me about the spell," Sorrel urged. "Sorrin said the heart was guarded by four beautiful maidens with breasts like alabaster, nipples like rosebuds, and lips like pomegranates." She was silent for a moment. "Were they really that beautiful?"

"Well, there was only one maiden," Perrin said. "I suspect the spell just multiplied the maidens according to the number of seekers. After all, each would-be thief had to be duly aroused."

"Yes, that's reasonable," Sorrel said, nodding. "And you weren't aroused?"

Perrin laughed. "If I had been, I wouldn't be here now, would I?"

"No. Of course not."

Perrin raised Sorrel's hand and kissed it. "Lust and desire are very powerful things. The wizard was clever to have thought to trap men that way. While they were busy lusting after an illusion, the wizard was busy immobilizing them." *In the web,* the thief thought, shuddering. "And had the wizard been a little more imaginative in setting the spell, I too might have succumbed. After all, I am an avowed admirer of lovely women." Perrin squeezed Sorrel's hand. "You know, it's just occurred to me that our wizard was never a fisherman."

"What?" Sorrel asked, laughing.

"Every fisherman knows that if you bait your hook for trout, you will catch only trout. But if you bait your hook in a rather more catholic fashion, you might catch a variety of things." The thief chuckled. "Fortunately for me, our wizard never considered that his hook should be baited with anything other than the standard voluptuous-maiden illusion. And that's where he erred. Oh, the illusion would certainly inflame the base carnal desires of some men—but by no means all."

215

"Oh?" Sorrel asked, amused.

"Certainly not," Perrin continued. "There are men who would have considered the illusion crude and blatant. They would have been offended, not aroused. My late master was one. He always preferred his women ethereal." Perrin shrugged. "And then there are those men who are not aroused by female pulchritude at all. The illusion would have been wasted on them too." The thief turned in the saddle. "My dear Sorrel, you weren't waiting for someone like that, now, were you?"

Sorrel laughed. "Certainly not. In fact, such an analysis had never occurred to me." She shook her head. "No, I was rather single-minded, I'm afraid, and perhaps as unimaginative as the wizard." She kissed the back of Perrin's neck. "As I said, I was waiting for you. Didn't we establish that last night?"

"Well, yes," Perrin admitted. "I thought so. But tell me: How did I give myself away? How did you ascertain that I was the person you sought?"

"I can't explain it," Sorrel said. "It's a certain way you have about you. But it called to me as surely as if you had spoken. And for another thing, you wear your thief's garb a little too rakishly. Anyone with half an eye can tell that you're a woman."

"Humph," said Perrin, miffed. "I really thought I was adequately disguised."

"Your clothes need just a little work," Sorrel said. She was quiet for a moment. "I have a confession to make," she told Perrin.

Perrin raised an eyebrow. "What, pray?"

Sorrel sighed. "My room at the inn was only paid for until this morning. I'm afraid there's no point in going back to Lesser Clepping."

Perrin burst out laughing. "Well," she said, "we will just have to put this third-rate mage to the test. Do you think he can conjure up a good meal for us? Or a room for the night? I hardly know what to expect from a man who thinks that desire wears only one face."

"Let's give it a try," Sorrel said. "We have to start practicing sometime. And besides, my stomach has been growling for hours."

"Quite right," Perrin agreed. "We'll put him through his paces. We need good food, decent accommodations, new clothes, and a horse for you. Then, after a suitable period of—ah, rest and relaxation—what would you say to a little trip to Broadneath?"

Sorrel sighed. "I'd like that."

Why the Moon Goes Away
and the Sun Only Sleeps
Stan Leventhal

T he first time I got to tell the story about the moon and the sun, and why everything turned out the way it did, was also when I changed from virgin-boy to ripe-man. So you can believe me when I tell you it's something I remember very well. This was when I was just a seedling who hadn't seen anything beyond the village territory.

The winds had been coming for many years, teaching us to behave, showing us the difference between right and wrong. According to legend, there was simply chaos before the winds came with their instructions and punishments.

His name, Turbo, sounded very strange to my ears, and the land he came from was stranger still. When I found out he'd never heard the story about the moon and the sun, I swore that I would be the one to tell him.

I'd broken one of my tribe's most sacred rules by venturing out beyond the confines of our village. All of my people were instructed as youngsters never to pass through the fence constructed of saplings interwoven with vines and tendrils; a living, growing wall that occasionally needed pruning. It had been planted a long time ago and had grown thick and dense enough to prevent the Others from entering. But with a little digging and cutting, you could escape if you chose. No one who'd left had ever returned. Mostly misfits who just couldn't seem to conform to our way of life. My reasons for leaving had nothing to do with the inability to fit in. Just the opposite, in fact. I'd come to know the inner workings of the village all too well. And when I became convinced that I wasn't being told the whole truth—well, being the kind of creature I am, I just had to leave to find out some answers for myself. You could say that I'd begun to mistrust the elders, all their stories, all their reasons why things were supposed to stay the same. I thought, *If I can find the knowledge to enable me to change their minds, they can certainly change a few rules and better our way of life.* But they would not change, could not change; and I decided that I wanted to find out what really lay beyond the living wall and whether it is possible for creatures to change the way they think, alter the pattern of their living.

The Quech-Wah and the Ling-Wah are my antecedents. Very set in their ways. I set out to find something different. If not the opposite of my ancestors' way of life, then people who are perhaps capable of some flexibility.

With my silver dagger, given to me at birth by the village Mother, I hacked away at the wall, close to the ground, digging as well as cutting, the sandy soil cleansing the sap and juice that flowed from the tightly entwined vines and leaves. It took a while for me to get to the other side of the wall, and then some more to attempt to replace what I'd removed and secure some getaway time. The dark of night helped, and I was as quiet as I could be. As the sun began to appear over the horizon, I was far enough away from the village to stop and rest for a time.

I found a shady glen, sat on a rock, and began to wonder what I'd do about food. I had a gourd of sweet water dangling from my belt and a small piece of dried meat in a pouch. As I began to unpack these things, suddenly—like a strong wind attacking me—I felt a powerful force, which I could not see, pushing me. I tightened my legs and tried to remain where I stood, and I found that I was able to if I leaned in the direction from which the invisible monster approached. Then the sound—like a thousand thunderclouds exploding all at once—hit my ears, and I became so frightened I froze for a moment, not knowing what to do or which way to turn. I couldn't see any danger, but all of my senses felt assaulted.

I stood there, leaning into the windforce, hoping that some idea would come to me, tell me what to do, when suddenly a man appeared wearing a large blue cape, carrying a long, sharp sword. He spoke to the weapon as though it had ears, and I thought he must be crazy, but ribbons of visible energy leaped from the glinting blade, and as they soared through the air the windforce seemed to diminish. Then the man cloaked himself and me in the large blue cape, and when the sound of the windforce had abated completely, he unwrapped us. We stood in the glaring sunlight with not even a gentle breeze stirring.

"My name is Turbo. What is yours?" he asked, but at the time I didn't speak English, so I didn't know what he was asking. He kept asking the same question in different languages until he finally came to Wah. Then I understood and answered him.

His skin was somewhat darker than my own, and his shiny black hair, the likes of which I'd never seen before, shone like raven's feathers in the sun. I told him my name, and then he asked where I was going. I had no particular goal or direction and told him so—just exploring, prepared to go wherever the winds might take me. I asked him about the windforce.

"You never heard about the sorcerer Venn? And his magic stone? And the furious winds he can unleash?" He looked at me as though I might be joking, unable to believe I had never encountered this information previously.

I explained that in Wah we've never heard of anyone called Venn, and nobody believes in sorcery, and the winds that we listen to come from the heavens, which are presided over by the sun and the moon. Everybody knows this, I said.

Turbo's face scowled in anger. "Apparently not *everybody*," he said. He looked me up and down, evaluating me. When he spotted my silver dagger he chortled, "What do you hope to accomplish with that puny thing?" I didn't know what to say. Then he asked if I would like to accompany him to the sorcerer's castle. He suggested that en route perhaps I could tell him about the sun and the moon, and he could tell me about Venn. I had never heard of the sorcerer's castle but told him that it did not matter, anyplace away from Wah was what I was seeking, and his destination would suit me fine. Also, it seemed prudent to stay with this person, as he had the cape and sword that had protected me once and just might do so again.

I told him to lead and that I would follow, and he laughed and said something to his sword, and the next thing I knew I was astride a huge winged beast, with my arms around Turbo's waist, looking down at the terrain upon which I'd been standing only moments before. The feathers and fur of the enormous avian reeked with foul odors, but as Turbo didn't seem to mind, I held my tongue, breathing through my mouth. The creature, whose coloring was a dull brown and a flat gray, issued screeching cries as its firm breast cleaved the oncoming air.

The first time I dared to look down, I grew dizzy and had to close my eyes and breathe very deeply. After a while I felt better, and when I next ventured a downward glance, I saw an amazing pattern of greens of differing shades and hues in assorted shapes and sizes. Walking through such fields one cannot know, cannot imagine, what the views look like from above. At first I was amazed. But eventually I told myself, *Of course.*

Throughout the airborne journey on the strange bird, I thought a great deal about this strange man called Turbo and prioritized a list of questions to slake my burning curiosity—which was further aroused by something curious that I seemed to notice at first but couldn't name. But I eventually realized that the colors of everything below—the trees, flowers, rivers, and rocks—seemed to be intensifying with the miles. As though layers of gauze were being peeled away and the deeper, richer hues of everything were slowly being revealed.

When the bird finally touched down and my feet could feel the solidity of good old familiar terra firma, I silently thanked the moon and the sun, and though I was grateful for having had the experience of flying—something I'd never even dreamed of—I was not especially eager to do it again very soon. But I did not want my new companion to think that I was cowardly, so I did not tell him this, hoping that the situation would not arise again anytime soon.

An enormous castle with turrets, gables, intricate carvings, flying buttresses, gargoyles, and barred windows seemed to emerge from the mist as we landed, and Turbo was able to open the huge gates with a simple command to his sword. He bade me enter, sweeping his cape back over his shoulders, and stepped aside, then gestured me to proceed. I did so with much caution and apprehension. Although I had come to trust Turbo somewhat, I had no idea what we'd encounter next. After the magic sword, the gigantic bird, my first flight, and this mysterious castle, it seemed that anything was possible.

The castle stood on an elevated plateau of sorts; the only way to gain access was a rocky, tree-shaded path that wound up the hillside like the spiral of a snail's shell. Beyond the massive doors, secured by large brass bolts, was a long hallway lit by torches in wall sconces. Flagstone paved the floor, and enormous tapestries in muted colors depicting violent battles adorned the walls. There was a kind of musty odor that I noticed immediately, which seemed to mingle with and then be supplanted by the aroma of some exotic incense.

Turbo's bootheels clicked on the stone beneath our feet, but my buckskin footwear made no sound as we strode down the hall and approached a double door with ornate carvings. Beyond the portals, beneath a high, domed ceiling, the throne room of the sorcerer stretched out long and broad, a repository of riches and finery. As Turbo spoke with an attendant stationed just inside the doors, I gazed at the chandeliers dripping with jewels, the intricate carvings like a ribbon around the base of the dome, stained-glass windows that admitted sunrays of innumerable hues. Gold statuary on slender pedestals and carvings of ebony, jade, and ivory on stout plinths stood before intricate tapestries, and rich folds of silk adorned the walls. There were animal pelts, like carpeting, on the floor, and I could hear the sound of a lone flute and a small drum playing a melancholy air. Where the musicians were hiding I could not ascertain, but the ruler of this castle and its occupants, the owner of all this wealth, sat on a large chair, elevated several feet off the ground. From where I stood, quite a distance away, I couldn't tell at first what he really looked like. But it was obvious that he was in charge, and everyone there seemed to give him their complete attention.

Turbo finished whispering to the attendant, who strode, in an exaggerated regal strut, to the potentate. They spoke softly and briefly; then the attendant returned to us and said that we could approach and speak. I followed Turbo toward the throne with a rising sense of anxiety. Each step closer to the sorcerer made me feel more uncertain. But of what, I could not have said.

He was large and somber, with skin lighter than mine, fat gathered in folds around his middle, white stringy hair framing a face that looked like it had never smiled. His eyes were dark and mysterious; there seemed to be no life behind them. But the way he moved when he breathed, his expansive torso rising and falling, and the angry look about his mouth told me that he lived as surely as did I and my companion. He wore a linty green robe trimmed with fur, and a large medallion, golden and jewel-encrusted, rested on his heaving chest.

Turbo waited for some indication that it was time to begin his speech. Eventually the sorcerer lifted his enormous hand and bade Turbo commence. They spoke in a language I could not identify, while I stood there, mute and expressionless, feeling like a complete idiot. I felt that I should pretend to be paying attention, but my lack of comprehension made this difficult. My mind began to wander. I started glancing at the sorcerer's courtiers and couldn't help comparing my simple buckskin attire with their costumes. Everyone, male and female alike, had all kinds of shells and beads dangling from their uniforms. And the cloth from which these chitons, robes, and skirts were cut had a metallic luster and smooth surfaces the likes of which I'd never seen before, certainly not obtainable from any creature or plant known to Wah.

The only thing I could tell about the dialogue between Turbo and the sorcerer is that they spoke quietly, in very brief sentences or phrases, and that the sound of the language was very lyrical, with lots of long vowels and little sibilance or guttural exertion.

It wasn't until after we'd landed somewhere far from the castle, after we'd departed from the court and completed another journey on the back of the huge avian creature that smelled like mole dung, that I found out what had transpired between Turbo and the sorcerer, Venn.

When we arrived at our destination and dismounted from the living conveyance, I expected Turbo to tell me everything. But instead, much to my surprise, he led me into a dark cave, hidden by rocks and brush. We'd landed on hilly terrain, adjacent to a thick forest that stretched beyond my vision. Within the cavern, which inexplicably smelled salty like seawater, there was a small chamber with a pallet on the ground, a natural shelf in the rock wall that held a few books and tiny figurines, and a small fire pit in the center. Turbo wasted no time throwing off his cloak, beneath which he wore only a well-filled undersling and a harness fashioned from strips of pelt.

By the light of a crackling fire I studied Turbo's body as the dancing flames cast shadows on his smooth, dark skin. His musculature was as well-developed as any I'd seen on a young male, and the proportions of his arms and chest, waist and thighs would please anyone with taste and sense.

Without preamble or ceremony, without warning or permission, Turbo began to disrobe me. I was so stunned that at first I didn't know what to say and stood there frozen, like a tree. He must have sensed my unease, so he paused, looked at me questioningly, and asked what was wrong. I explained to him, after recovering my senses, that in Wah when two men want to become physically intimate, they must first observe certain rituals. Turbo did not seem too eager to find out what these rituals were, and rather than get involved in a lengthy and pointless explanation, I just silently asked forgiveness of the moon and sun and allowed Turbo to continue with his probing, massaging, eventually kissing, and finally fucking. It felt good to my bones. Turbo's ways were rather aggressive and a bit rough compared to my previous experiences. But he was a man, not a boy, so since then I have become a man and am no longer a boy. It takes a full-grown man to change a young male from a virgin-boy to a ripe-man.

After he'd had his way with me, he laid himself down, ass end up, and indicated that I was to do to him what he'd just done to me. I hadn't had as much experience in this position as in the other, but I tried my best to satisfy Turbo the way that he had just satisfied me.

I couldn't believe how hungry I was when we were finished. And it was almost as if he was reading my mind when Turbo suggested that we eat something. I'd noticed by this time that he was a man who was not often moved to speak. In fact, I wondered how he felt about my sexual ability, as he'd said nothing when we were done, and I'm accustomed to many words of praise from my lovers after a satisfying union. But just as he did not offer any clues to where we were going or what would happen when we got there, neither did he make me privy to his thoughts regarding our sexual interlude.

Turbo creased his brow and stared at his sword, and there appeared before us a bountiful repast consisting largely of fruits and vegetables—I assumed they were fruits and vegetables—in colors and shapes that were new to my eyes, startling to my palate. We drank a sweet and cool liquid from a copper vessel that looked to me like a vase for flowers; then once more we mounted the big bird and flew off to I knew not where.

As we soared over the rugged terrain below, my earlier perception about the colors changing was confirmed. As we'd gotten closer to the sorcerer's castle, the greens of the leaves, the blues of the lakes and streams, the reds and browns of the earth and stones had seemed to intensify in color. More radiant, almost glowing, some of these bright hues looked highly unnatural, as though obtained from somewhere else besides the moon's and sun's painting box. And now, as we flew farther away from the strange edifice, the colors seemed to recede, lessen in their sharpness, and mellow into familiar, muted tones.

I confess to being completely surprised when Turbo directed the big bird to land, and we picked up another passenger. The smelly beast dug its claws into the earth as we skidded to a halt several yards from a small cottage nestled in a bower of greens, dotted with multicolored flowers and berries. The small shuttered doors opened, and a very tiny person, a pixie of a thing, emerged into the sunlight, blinking and rubbing its eyes. At first I could not discern the gender of this remarkable being, but as the distance between us closed and when I finally heard the voice, I was able to ascertain that she was quite female indeed. Her words seemed to fall on my ears like music, though there was no hummable melody, no instrumental accompaniment. But like a great singer shaping the sound, establishing a rhythm, inflecting with virtuosity, the charming creature spoke, and her voice captivated me like opium.

After Turbo made brief introductions, we boarded our avian conveyance and once again soared above the very earth. No longer frightened, I told myself that if I were to fly a million times I would still think it a grand thing

223

and never tire of it. On the way to wherever we were going, Mara, the pix-ieish woman, sang into my ear, explaining to me where we were going and what would happen once we got there. At the time I had no idea, but now I can state that every word she spoke proved to be as true as the orbits of the moon and the earth.

The realm we entered differed not one whit from the one we departed. I could see the same types of trees and hills, streams and fields. But the Realm of the Hidden One, as Mara had called it, had been appropriated by a mon-strous fiend—nemesis of the sorcerer, Venn—and it was the task of Turbo, Mara, and myself, apparently, to defeat the thing. Mara explained that this was a very dangerous undertaking, but we were to be grateful that the sor-cerer had bestowed this honor upon us. I asked her if it is an honor to be sent to one's death for no particular reason. And she told me that there was a very good reason, one that I'm not sure I understand. But at the time I could not think about their motivations, as my head was filled with dread and horror, imagining what terrors awaited us, attempting to summon the courage that would get me through this ordeal with my life, my health, my sanity, and maybe some dignity.

While Mara warmed up her voice, trilling scales that soared into the stratosphere, Turbo explained to me, in very different words, what Mara had whispered in my ear during our flight. We sat on the ground beneath a sprawling tree, the likes of which I'd never seen before. He cloaked me in his cape, the heat from our bodies warming up our little tent-for-two very quickly. The warmth felt delightful, but even more so when Turbo began to speak to me and make love to me at the same time. As his hands sculpted and molded my willing flesh, he informed me that he'd applied to the sor-cerer to fulfill this quest—and here is where it got very interesting and I finally began to understand—because the sorcerer was from a different world and had only come to earth because of an evil spell cast upon him. The only way to return home involved the defeating of the Hidden One and pre-senting proof, which would be like a passport. At the time I had no aware-ness of just how dangerous the Hidden One was, but Turbo's descriptions sounded scary. It's a good thing he held me while he told me all of this—not only because his presence helped to assuage my fear, but also the proximity of our bodies, his sweet caresses, told me that he was telling the truth. When a person of the Wah is in an intimate situation, falsity is very easy to detect. Subsequent events proved all of Turbo's words to be true.

And I finally learned the reason for the changes in color as we got nearer to or farther from the sorcerer's castle. The medallion worn round his neck was a sacred, enchanted talisman that provided the only entrance to and exit from the world of magic. The sorcerer had been banished from that world for transgressions that I was unable to understand. And the only way for him and his courtiers to return was to defeat the Hidden One. The medallion, a disk of copper with arcane markings, worked like a lighthouse beam, and anything that fell within the light was subject to the magical laws of the magical world. But the power emanating from this medallion had begun to ebb, shrinking the magical influence in our world. If someone did not defeat the Hidden One before the power was irretrievably gone, the sorcerer and his court would never be able to return.

When Mara declared that her voice had been sufficiently exercised, Turbo led us, very quietly, through a dense forest with tall trees that admitted no sunlight over a loamy, pungent floor of mulchy rotting leaves, which was slippery and difficult to walk on. After a medium-length hike through the stillness of the forest, we arrived at a clearing opposite a rocky hillside pock-marked with caves.

The concavities did not look like natural openings; they were too rounded and too uniform, as though they'd been drilled with a huge bit that left a charred and powdery substance around the opening, like a mouth with crumbs and gravy that has yet to be cleaned. My first thought was that these caves were the products of some asteroid cluster, charging into the atmosphere and burning up as they hit the side of the mountain. But I later learned that these unnatural caverns were created by the corrosive fluid that flows through the veins of the Hidden One.

Turbo stood behind a boulder at the edge of the clearing; Mara climbed up a tree with low-hanging branches and many knotholes and perched herself securely on the strongest of the uppermost limbs. I was instructed to walk to a spot midway between the forest and the hill.

It struck me suddenly that I was to be used as some kind of bait!

Had I known how dangerous this creature could be, I would have been more nervous and anxiety-ridden than I was. Still, I was very scared. Standing there waiting, I couldn't know what it was I would be facing. Now that I have been through the fire, I shudder, thinking back.

Mara began to sing in a very high register, a plaintive melody with words that to me were just abstract sounds. With each repetition of the verse, the tempo would increase and she would sing a little louder. By the fourth time around I could hear a rumbling, snorting sound. It seemed to come closer as each second passed, and then I noticed a peculiar odor, sort of pungent at first, then putrid as it seemed to overwhelm me. I began to gag and choke, but then my olfactories and their sensitivity were obscured by the sight before my eyes. As the creature emerged from one of the caves, I started to back away in abject fear.

The thing was unlike any living thing I'd ever seen in real life or my imagination. It was huge—as big as a yak but shapeless, a large hunk of mucousy bristles and mocking antennae with serpents' tongues obscenely licking the air all around. It moved in an amoebalike fashion except that the bottom part always stayed in contact with the ground, the upper part shifting to accommodate the lower, the movement seeming like a Möbius strip in motion. The thing moved closer, and I backed away. Mara was singing as fast and loud as she could. From some intermittently visible pore in the creature's upper half, a thin stream of some type of fluid arced from the beast and landed just a few inches from where I stood. It burned the scrub and charred the earth, creating a hole that widened so quickly I had to jump to avoid getting swallowed into it. The creature let loose another load of the corrosive fluid, this time in more of a spray than a jet. I simply could not take this lethal game of dodge, so, frightened out of my wits, I turned and ran straight for the protective cover of the dense forest. As soon as I felt safe, too far away for the creature to spit on me, I turned and watched, just in time to see Turbo advance toward the monster with his sword held aloft, his brow furrowed, his jaw set in determination.

It was later explained to me that the reason I was used as a diversion was that it took time for the Hidden One to work up another load of poison, and while it was preoccupied, Turbo was able to get close enough to strike with his sword. He pierced the creature in dozens of places, and viscous fluids ran all over the beast, down its sides and onto the ground, burning everything it touched, lethal vapors rising from the ground like a deadly mist.

Mara had stopped singing, I think, or maybe the beast's groaning and moaning had become so loud it masked any other sounds. The air filled with wretched shrieks as Turbo moved in closer and cut off one of the creature's antennae. As Turbo backed away from the creature, clutching the dripping stalk cut from his adversary, the moans of the dying beast began to subside, its color began to fade, and the dripping wounds ceased to flow.

At a word from Turbo, Mara descended from her tree, and the three of us tore through the forest as quickly as the undergrowth would permit.

It was during our return journey to the sorcerer's castle that we stopped for

226

the night to eat and rest, pitching a makeshift camp near the mouth of a large cave, far away from the Hidden One's lair—this cave bearing none of the traces of the ones we'd just fled. Turbo's magic sword produced a fire and provisions, and as we sat by the orange and yellow tongues of flame, we talked long into the night. Like magic, come the dawn, I could speak and understand English. And Turbo, who had been so quiet and reserved since the moment I'd met him, suddenly became quite loquacious and merry, telling me more about the magic world where the sorcerer and the Hidden One came from and how the magic was shrinking. About the wonderful future in store for himself and Mara who, in defeating the sorcerer's nemesis, had won the right to return to the realms of magic with the sorcerer when they got back to the castle, before the hole between our worlds closed forever.

Mara told me all about the intense and meticulous training she'd received once her remarkable vocal talents had been perceived. And of the odd race of pixieish creatures from which she was descended, one of many strange peoples living in the magic realms.

And I finally got to tell them all about the moon and the sun, the wind-force, and my little village. I started at the beginning, when the moon and the sun were lovers but found that they couldn't agree about many things. Instead of continuing to argue and struggle against each other, they decided to live apart. And the moon would only come out at night, increasing and decreasing in size and sometimes disappearing altogether as penance for its inability to stay with the sun. And for its punishment the sun was forced to stay bright and shining at all times, even when we turn away from it, which is the time to visit with the moon. There was much speculation among the Wah about what might happen if the moon and the sun ever mended the rift and got back together. But for millennia this has not happened, so the Wah just continue to go on as we always have.

Until now.

Because after I returned to the sorcerer's castle and witnessed the ritual in which Turbo and Mara presented the antenna from the Hidden One to the sorcerer—proof of its death—I returned to the people of Wah with many strange stories to tell. But first, my companions and I had to exchange our good-byes, which was very bittersweet. We laughed and cried and promised to remember one another. Mara stayed at the castle, there being no need for her to return to her cottage now that she would be going home with the sorcerer. Turbo and I flew on the big bird, up until the radius of magic began to fade. We had one more session with his cape, then he kissed me good-bye. As he headed back to the castle, I began the long walk home to my village.

At first the people of Wah did not believe me. The tales I had to tell were so strange to my people, they thought I was making everything up to amuse and entertain them. But eventually I was able to convince them of a few things, which ultimately changed our lives forever.

The Wah, my people, at a time long before I was born, came to worship and fear the wind—which they took to calling the windforce. And because they did not know any better, they came to think of the wind as a punishment for bad deeds. What must have happened sometime in the past was that somebody did something bad just before a turbulent windstorm appeared. Everyone became frightened and wondered what was happening, and the village elders finally decided that the terrible storm was divine retribution for the bad deeds done. Eventually, other things were attributed to the wind that were also just coincidental—like the time, for example, when a villager took two spouses. A furious windstorm developed the day after the double wedding, so for centuries my people believed that if someone takes two wives, two husbands, or one of each, the winds will come and destroy our property.

And now my people are not afraid of the world that lies beyond the walls of our village. Because I left and returned unharmed, others began to explore the far reaches of our world, returning with new knowledge, new friends, strange stories. I have achieved a measure of respect in my community—something that would not have happened had I not dared to venture forth. I was able to tell my people the things that Turbo and Mara had told me and eventually to convince them that the wind came randomly and had nothing to do with the actions or thoughts of our people. To prove this, I took two husbands and waited for the disaster. And to this day it still has not come.